COLD COMFORT

The snow had frozen Dion's hair, and the ice particles on her clothes weighed her down like stones. Beside her, Hishn and another wolf closed in, guiding her through the blinding flurries.

Cold, so cold, she sent without realizing. She fell. It was so comforting to rest.

Get up! Hishn shouted in her head. The wolf nipped Dion's nose, hard teeth piercing the numbness. The other wolf put his nose under her to shove her up, and Hishn tore at her jerkin, shaking her. *Keep going*, they commanded. *The den is just beyond those trees.*

WOLFWALKER

Tara K. Harper

A Del Rey Book

BALLANTINE BOOKS • NEW YORK

This book is dedicated to Sandy Keen, for whom I scrawled this note of friendship on her refrigerator one night:

> Down crumbling desert slopes
> and wind-wrought shapes of dusty stone;
> Where the sandy fur of the meer cat scrapes lightly through
>   the sod-cut tunnels;
> Into heights of wispy thoughts and layered twilights,
> Where red-eyed hawks lie flat on soft winds;
> Dreams, born and living,
> Have but one soul:
> Yours.

Table of Contents

plants, although they were comparatively few, had now

I

Ember Dione maMarin:

Dark Flight

Oh, moons of mercy, moons of light
Guide me in the darkest night
Keep me safe from evil spirit
Send your blessed light to sear it

Oh, moons of mercy, moons of might
If in shadow, dark, or night,
My body die with evil near it
Send your light to guide my spirit

It was dark, and she could not see. She could not hear for the roaring in her ears, and she could not move. *Oh, moons of mercy, moons of light* . . . She tried to spit out the panic but choked on grit and fur and dirty blood. *Guide me in the darkest night* . . . Struggling, she dragged a breath into her lungs, and then the fright that held her frozen burst and she screamed, the sound suffocating in the black death above her. *Keep me safe from evil spirit* . . . The body that pinned her to the ground was too heavy; she panicked and thrashed under it, straining back and forth to break free. Heat ate at her legs. She realized then that—oh, gods—the roaring in her ears was fire. *Send your blessed light to sear it* . . . And then the pain stabbed, rhythmically, with her pulse, throbbing, driving each second of terror deeper in her mind. Fire . . . A joint-ripping yank tore her free of the dead worlag, her ragged breathing punctuated by the fire's crackling, while sobs racked her body and the tumbling brands spread the flames and fed her panic.

The worlag's body shifted again, rolling toward her, and she jerked back in horror. Moons of mercy, were the dead rising to claim her? But the sudden movement sent a black wash of pain over her head, and she could barely see where the shadows of brush beckoned. With a silent scream against the agony, she slid into their sharp embrace like a broken doll, her teeth bared to bite back her shriek and her breath still caught in her chest from the frozen grip of fear. On the other side of the fire a worlag turned, its bulbous eyes searching. There was blood on the soil, blood on its claws. It hesitated, and then a waft of throat-choking smoke curled between them, hiding her where shadows of deep roots pressed against her back, steadying her as the burning forest swallowed her body and the blackening waves swallowed her mind. All she saw, all she heard, was the worlags tearing and snapping at the broken bodies and burning wagon, the flame-lit canvas and clothes.

Pain. Burning, crushing pain. She crawled, cringing under the brush, clinging to the gray shadow of the wolf that urged, carried, dragged her on. *This way . . . through here . . .* She could not focus her eyes, her mind anymore. *Wait . . . duck . . .* There was blood on her hands, her clothes, her face. *Hurry . . .* The roaring in her ears kept rhythm with the growls of bloated worlags feasting in the obscenely dancing light behind her, and the snap of human bones was the death drum in her ears—she did not have to look back to see the hairy forearms that dragged to their knees when they stood and the other, spindly middle arms that tore at the riding beasts like the cutters on a farmer's plow. Their beetle jaws dripped blood and tendons as they fought over a body. Ember Dione whimpered and dragged on. It was dark.

Night voices flickered in and out of her ears. But the gray shadow led her on when she cried out, and the rough tongue licked at the pain till she fell into the dark fire of her pulse, where the black heat blinded her. Blood, thin and warm, dribbled down her face and slid into her ear, and as the noise drowned, the dark again became complete.

It was dawn when she woke, her head throbbing dully, the air green with morning dusk. Her slender body was curled in the growth of a deadfall, her gashed leg stretched stiffly out to one side and her black hair tangled in the twigs. A sharp branch stuck into her cheek. Against her back, the gray wolf was warm, proof of the early chill that was seeping through the moss and the calm that greeted her wakening. No burned-out wagons met her eyes; no smoldering fires caught at her ears. Just the blood that stiffly soaked her clothes and the pain that killed her thoughts.

And she remembered . . . Her brother, Rhom, torn apart like a bird under the worlag's raging jaws. The slim woman bit back the sob, clenching her fists and closing her eyes. Oh, Rhom . . .

She forced her eyes to see again, forced her mind to admit she had seen him die. The worlags . . . She had seen him fall, slashing and cutting with his sword under the force of the beasts that tore him apart while Gray Hishn ripped at a monster's black carapace. And then the worlags closed in and the wolf jumped clear and her twin—he was gone. Just like that. Dead. Rhom, the merchant, the guards—everyone, she told herself harshly, everyone dead but her.

Her throat grew tight against the agony that racked her like a rising storm shaking a fragile house, and she pushed the thoughts away, curling closer into the wolf's thick fur. Was this the grief of death? she asked herself. The blinding ache? The Gray One's fur lay gritty against her tears, and she wondered if she was crying for the mangled bodies of those she once knew or the empty disbelief that her twin was dead. "Survive first," she whispered, gripping Gray Hishn's coat in her white-knuckled fist. "Then deal with the dead."

When she woke again, her mouth was parched into wrinkles and her tongue felt dried, stuck to the roof of her mouth. She pushed herself up on her side and rolled over, clenching her teeth against the jagged blast of pain that greeted her. Her leg felt crushed, and her head felt split. But it was the cluster of insects feeding off the filthy scabs that turned her stomach. Hurriedly she fought down the flash of nausea and scraped them off, brushing her hands on her pants while they skittered angrily back into the shelter of the moss.

Her movements awakened the wolf, whose ears had already begun to flick at her thoughts. Gray Hishn rose, and the woman felt the creature's hunger and thirst double her own. She fingered the few weapons left in her pouch, a bleak look on her face as she realized again her position. But the worlags must have been gone or Hishn would have long been alert. *Go eat,* she told the wolf, pushing a clump of long, black hair out of her eyes. *I'll be all right till you find dinner.*

Dinner for both of us, the Gray One promised, flashing her the double image of two wolves with furry rabbits hanging from their teeth. The haggard young woman managed a smile at the compliment, and the wolf melted into the woods, the gray hunter's impressions of the forest filling her head with soothing images: cool dirt under silent footpads, soft leaves brushing against fur. Muscles tensing and shifting as trees and downfalls shaded slitted yellow eyes from the evening sun; the tangy scent of a deer herd on shadowed grass . . .

The wolfwalker's head cleared further, and she remembered again the night, the death. Her throat went tight. Rhom! she thought with despair, raising her fist to her forehead and pressing as if she could drive away the memories or hold back the tears with the pressure of her hand.

But the snap of a brittle twig brought her abruptly back, and she froze, her breath pressed against her chest from the inside. She held it without moving while the leaves rustled—it was a mottled badgerbear, slinking by not ten meters away, its brainless head swinging from side to side as it searched for a place to set its trap. With its gaping maw hidden under its flattened stomach, it tasted the ground for the trail of a careless hare or young deer. Or a wounded human. The blood on the trail—surely it would be dried and tasteless already. Or would the badgerbear sense her fear from where it paused there on the game path, its sightless eyes swinging her way . . .

Abruptly she pulled herself together. Ember Dione, she taunted herself harshly, trying to control her shattered nerves. So eager to Journey with your brother. Well, you're here now and alone because of it. Get your act together and face the world you wanted or crawl back to the village where they said you belonged.

The Journey—the test of a young man's courage and skill. Rhom's sanction to see the world outside his home. Whether he came from a village or a city or a floating town like those of the southern sea people didn't matter. Only that he explore and return to tell his story to his father at the council fires, from then on to be counted as a strong voice in the circle of judgment. But Dion had not had to go with him. Women had their own Journey of sorts: the Internship, which let them test their own skills and prove their worth to the city of their choice. Dion had already taken her own Internship—but the elders had chosen her to go with her twin on his Journey, as well. And now, only Dion would return to tell their story to their father. Dion, the wolf-walker, she thought bitterly. Dion, the healer. Who could not even save her own brother.

She lay still for a long time after the badgerbear had passed. At last, when a half hour had withered away, she hooked her finger into the rough bark of the tree, then rolled onto her left knee.

"Moons have mercy," she gasped. Her breath strangled with the waves of speckled darkness that pounded her head. Seconds—minutes?—later it cleared to dim patches, and she pulled herself up against the tree and sagged, fresh blood spreading heat down the side of her face. It felt as if the only thing that held her pounding head together was the silver band that circled her brow. Blue and silver—that was for the heal-er's band—and gray, the color of wolves. She snorted and looked at her hands where the dirt blackened her nails and her strong, shapely fingers were trembling and marred with blood. Healer and wolfwalker, yes, but weak and sorry as a newborn pup. With her head resting listlessly against the rough trunk of the tree, the woman stared down at the bloody gash that had laid her leg open almost to her hip. It was a filthy wound. The dirt and blood had matted together to make a muddy scab that floated on the open slash. Where the wor-lag's claw had reached through her guard, it had torn into her skin like a knife splitting a ripe fruit, and she wondered vaguely if the gellbugs had started a nursery in the wound already. It would be too ironic if she, a full-fledged healer, died from gellbugs after surviving a worlag attack in which the guards and fighters had been killed.

She steeled herself to touch the jagged slash. She had treated too many ragged wounds to flinch from the gash in her leg, but this was the first time she'd had to treat herself, and she was not sure she had the guts to do it without screaming or the stamina to finish it without fainting. Now, as she tried to bare her thigh to see how bad the throbbing wound was, she stifled a groan. The leather of her leggings was stuck fast, glued by clotting blood and dirt, and the herb pouches she groped for were not to be found. She must have lost them in the fight the previous night. The fight . . . *The worlag tore at her leg and she screamed, and Rhom turned and went down*—"Oh, dear moons, help him," she whispered.

She shook her head, then wished she had not when the dizzy blackness drew its veil across her eyes again. But she could not escape the images that crossed her closed eyes. Rhom's sword as it cut through the worlag's casing. His face, eyes wide and flashing, as he went down under the monsters' claws. Dion took a ragged breath. What's done is done is done, she thought, the words echoing like rocks bouncing down a canyon's steep cliff. Empty words. *Rhom!* she cried out silently. *Hishn, I need you.*

The gray wolf answered like the touch of a leaf brushing against soft skin. It eased her anguish but left the breath of her twin behind, too. Did she deny his death so much that she could not let him go? What would she tell their father? She let her head tilt back against the tree, and the shaft of pain that lanced through it brought her back to reality as abruptly as it had sent her into a pain-racked swoon a moment earlier. How could she tell her father anything if she did not heal enough to survive the journey home? She opened her eyes. As she tightened her jaw, she drew on the stubborn strength that had sustained her through the long night and regarded the open gash one more time, then braced herself against the rough tree and pulled leather from the thickening scab. Only one gasp escaped her clenched teeth. When she got enough material to dig her broken fingernails into the claw-slashed pants, she gripped the slippery leather sternly and peeled the legging back. And fainted.

"Oh, gods . . ." she breathed unsteadily as she came to again. The fiery agony that shrieked in her leg was worse than she had imagined in her nightmares. Even with acupuncture, some of the pain gates were never completely closed, and with her needles scattered like the bones of the dead, she could not even think about closing her nerve gates before dealing with her wounds.

Rhom's wounds . . .

Desperately, Dion pushed the thoughts of her twin aside to deal with the pain of the present. Yet her eyes took in the empty forest first, and her heart almost stopped as his burly form jogged around the rise until she recognized the heavy biped bulk of a timin instead. She closed her eyes tightly and tugged at the leather on the other side of the gash.

It took another gasp and a half-sobbed groan to split the leather from the jagged flesh while the sweat broke out on her forehead.

It took almost all her nerve not to flinch each time the sledge-hammer crushed her veins with her heartbeat as she peeled the leggings back. But the pain stalled her grief, and the woman was grateful for the respite. Leaning back against the tree, she took a deep breath to calm the trembling in her hands, then shook her head to throw off the drop of sweat that clung to her nose. She was not yet ready to touch the raw gash that had split her leg so deeply—it had been all she could do to get her pants away from it, let alone start clearing the dirt and twigs that clogged it from her fear-fed flight. But the longer she waited, the more the drying blood from the reopened wound would add to the problem.

Blood. The color was red, bright red. How much blood had spilled from her brother? A deep sob climbed up in her throat and choked her, and this time she did not fight it down. "Oh, Rhom," she said, clenching her fist against the tears till her knuckles were white and bloodless.

The wolf, regarding her with eyes as yellow as the second moon, nudged her hand. *Be strong, Dion.*

It was Hishn who spoke but Rhom's voice she heard, as clear as if he were standing beside her. She squeezed her eyes shut and denied the agony again. That was what he had told her the first time she had run the Crush River with him and felt the white water from the uncertain seat of a kayak. It was what he had whispered when she had faced the weapons mas-ters for the Challenge and Test of Abis those two long years before. And it was what he had told her when they had clung to the Randonnen cliffs and dug their fingers into the rocks after the stone had broken off and she had fallen on that last tragic climb.

Be strong, Dion. Be strong.

"Damn you," she cried out to the ghost, pounding her fist on the soft earth. "Damn you for dying on me after everything we've been through. How could you?" She rubbed angrily at her face, drawing her hand away wet with tears and blood and welcoming the fresh rage of pain that swept her head.

Just nine days earlier—only one ninan—they had left home, eager for the Journey, impatient to test themselves against the world. Rhom had stood so tall and straight before the elders, their father ready to give his blessing to Journey, and Dion could still hear his words and feel the shock as the elders told him that she would be going with her twin.

"The sand and stones are cast three times, Kheldour, but the pattern is the same." One of the elders frowned at Kheldour, her father. "Rhom does not Journey alone." He had turned to her and nodded. "Healer Dione."

There had been a stunned silence in the crowd. Dion's heart leapt, but Kheldour was impassive. He did not look at her or Rhom. "It's not the custom," he said sternly to the elder. "The healer Dione is a woman, not a man. The Journey is a testing of manhood."

"The Journey is a testing of strength and courage," the elder corrected. "And the sand and stones don't lie."

Another elder spoke then. "Healer Dione," he said, nodding to the young woman, "hasn't had a customary upbringing. This isn't a criticism, Kheldour," he added quickly as her father's eyes flashed. "She's well prepared for a Journey, perhaps more so than most. You're one of our best woodsmen, and you've taught her well: Her feet are silent as the wolf in the woods. She also has skill in hunting and fighting—as many of our young men will testify," he added slyly. He spread his hands. "She has skill in the forest, in defense, in healing. And she is a wolf-walker. What more can she need when her brother—your son—is with her?"

"She's a healer," Kheldour insisted. "The village needs her here."

The elder looked at him soberly. "Your son may need her out there."

The third elder cleared his throat. "The moons gave you and your children a twin blessing, Kheldour," he said quietly. "Double strength, double courage, double skill. When would they need that blessing more than now?" The elder nodded to Rhom, then to Dion. "To split them now may hurt them more than letting them go."

Kheldour had looked at neither son nor daughter, but he had fumbled for Dion's fingers and she had squeezed his hand tightly as he nodded to the elders and accepted with the formal words. "It is cast. So shall it be done."

Dion dropped her fist from the dirty cloth she had pressed against the slowing flow of blood. That had been only one ninan before. Nine days. The words beat like a mortal bell. Nine days Journey to a death. *Oh, Rhom*, she cried. *Oh, gods, Hishn, what are we going to do* . . .

II

Aranur Bentar neDannon:

Raiders

A cry that knots your heartstrings
Is not easily untied

The peaks of Ariye rose sharply into the sky. Clear and cold, the mountain air warmed only thinly, but the three girls who raced across the meadow did not care. Lying low on the backs of their six-legged dnu, they called to the two youths chasing them, their hair whipping across their shoulders while their mounts covered the ground with the beat of drumming hooves.

Already tugging off her tunic, Shilia hauled her dnu to a halt and leapt down. "Last one in the water is a wet worlag!" she shouted at the boys who were pounding down the waterbank after the girls.

Her cousins laughed as they ran toward the lake, leaving their dnu to graze freely in the shore grass. They were younger than Shilia by only a few years. Slower and more timid away from the village, the other two had barely reached the water by the time the older girl was diving toward the center of the small lake, but then again, Shilia admitted, they were the daughters of the Lloroi of the Ramaj Ariye. They were not allowed out to swim or play the way she was, while she had to run and ride with the men to keep up with Aranur. Aranur, she thought with

10

a smile, arching into the water again like a dolphin. He was her only family. And all I want, she reminded herself.

When she finally surfaced, cool water spilling down her face and her loose hair dragging her back with its streaming weight, she watched the boys race her cousins to the water's edge.

"Is it cold?" Namina called, stopping suddenly at the edge and sticking her toes into the lake while the water lapped them like a pup.

"It's perfect," Shilia returned, ducking her mouth under and spitting like a fountain while she treaded water. "As if it was already summer." Her voice carried clearly over the new ripples, and, delighted with the patterns, she stuck her toes up and splashed them again. Namina laughed and waded out, followed by the others like a family of lake otters, unaware of the mounted figures that watched from the forest shadows.

In the shelter of the brush, a hundred meters or more above the lake, four black-clad men astride their war dnu watched and waited. The dark man in the center had a low gravelly voice, and the others listened silently as they cataloged his terse instructions. "We'll ride down when they're tired of swimming and not expecting company," the heavy raider said. "I'll take the eldest; Usami, the middle girl; Brid, the youngest. Gant, take care of the boys. We need at least three hours head start, and we don't want the brave young men—" He chuckled humorlessly. "—to sound the alarm before we're away. When we have the girls, stay behind at Pass Rock. Gant, you have enough arrows?"

The dusty raider studied the field, then the pass where he would lay his ambush. "I could use a few more. I lost a dozen in that last skirmish. Who would have thought these mountain folk as stubborn as bollusk?"

The raider captain twisted and unhooked one of his bristling quivers. "Take my extras. I have more waiting where we'll change mounts." His attention sharpened as the girls straggled out of the water one by one. He could almost hear what they were saying as the wind blew their faint voices toward the trees.

On the shore, Shilia dropped to the grass and pulled a small tuber from the ground, sticking it between her teeth and munching noisily on it like a dnu. "We should come here more often," she suggested as she pulled her sun-warmed tunic on over her wet swimsuit. "It's a beautiful place to swim."

"No sewing, no war games, no cooking or dust from the dnu." Ainna lay back and closed her eyes. "Close enough to keep Father happy and far enough away that the children don't bother us. It's a perfect place to get away."

Namina sighed. "This is the first day we've been allowed out this spring. Father's always too busy to take us, and Tyrel thinks he's too grown up to play guard for his sisters."

The oldest girl laughed. "Just tell them you'll go alone and see how fast you get an escort."

One of the boys who had flopped beside them gave Shilia a bold look. "Namina's not yet old enough to be Promised," he remarked obliquely.

"That's not fair," Shilia complained, blushing deeply in spite of her already sun-reddened cheeks.

"So that's how you do it," the youngest girl crowed, throwing her handful of tubers at her cousin. "You've got yourself a line of boyfriends two kilometers long just waiting for you to make a Promise and willing to do anything to get it, while we have to settle for our big-headed brother when and if he's willing to spend time with us."

"You probably have more escorts than days to be escorted on," the other girl teased. "I wonder if your brother, Aranur, knows this."

"Namina," Shilia warned, "you wouldn't tell—"

"He probably thinks you're out with Tyrel or Uncle Gamon—"

"Don't worry, Shilia," the taller youth interrupted, smiling lazily at the sky. "Your cousin can't tell. She's got eyes for Galway, and she's still two very long months from the Age of Promising."

"Mirik—" Ainna exclaimed, while the other girl flushed even redder than the cousin she was teasing.

"Truce?" a blushing Namina offered, trying to hide her discomfort and ignore Shilia's grin and the other boy's sly look.

The first youth hesitated, and Shilia tossed him a stern look. "Truce," he agreed. They relaxed on the banks, their dnu scattered in the grass and the spring sun warm on their bodies.

Silent and still beneath the shadowed trees, the raider captain waited as the young people's conversation fell apart and their eyes lulled in afternoon drowsiness. The shadows had crept a handspan across the grass from under their young bodies before the raider raised his hand and started out of the forest. Quietly the others followed, their deceptively heavy dnu stepping lightly in the grass-cushioned field. They were very close.

One of the boys stirred, rolled over lazily, and looked up. His eyes widened. "Shilia, run!" he cried, springing to his feet and lunging toward his sword as the raiders broke into a thundering gallop. The other boy sat up with a start and rolled, shoving the youngest girl away toward the dnu and grabbing for his own short blade. But the raiders were already moving at a dead run, and the soft clods of grass and dirt were flung away like bullets by the dnu's driving hooves as they leaned toward their prey.

Shilia took one look at the war dnu and scrambled for her beast. "Namina, mount up!" she shouted. Her cousin tripped, and the youngest girl shrieked for her to get up into the saddle before the dnu became scared and ran without her.

"Ride for the pass!" the older boy yelled.

"Mirik, Penek, come *on*!" Shilia screamed. She yanked on the reins and kicked at the dnu's midsection as she hauled its forelegs around and spurred it sharply to a gallop.

The boy bravely held his ground, his friend running to face the raiders with him, but the raiders loomed over them like a landslide. Hooves thundered, dust blinded and choked, and then they were crushed and brushed aside like twigs. The younger boy cried out as he went down, blood suddenly painting his chest and his small body convulsing and kicking on the ground, his ribs cutting through the spurts of blood. The older youth jumped at the raider who was sweeping by, cutting at the man's burly leg before falling to his knees, his shoulder bathed in a shocking red. His scream was thin and ignored.

On the banks, huge grimy hands grabbed the youngest girl and cut her shrieks off quickly as the raider jerked her struggling figure into his arms and smothered her against his dirty leather mail. Her sister turned in terror halfway into the saddle and tried to fling herself aside as another raider leaned across to sweep her up. He missed, threw his dnu back on its midhaunches, and leapt from his beast to grab her with ease, trapping her hands and throwing a rope quickly around them. He tossed her up into the saddle and vaulted back on, thundering away after the first man.

Shilia spared a frightened glance at the two boys staining the earth with their blood, then desperately spurred her mount into a breathless sprint. The raider captain grinned mirthlessly, cutting her off against the shoreline. She hauled her dnu around and tried to leap the other way, but the man smiled again, enjoying the chase as much as the thought of the gold he would get for the girl. Two of the Lloroi's daughters and his niece. He would have unmarked wares for Sidisport's slave blocks, and the gold he would get from these three alone would keep his raiders happy for two ninans. His reputation could use the recommendation, and his band could use the business when word got around.

He let the girl speed uphill for the forest, then ran her thoroughbred down with his bigger, heavier beast. Each time she twisted and turned, he was there, gaining meter by meter, till he finally hauled her out of the saddle as she tried to bring her whip to bear on him. She struggled awkwardly, and he saw her eyes flash before he felt the tiny knife stab viciously into his ribs. "Bitch!" he snarled, cuffing her brutally. She went limp.

The raider pulled the small knife from his side, grunting as the gait of the dnu jarred the blade in his hands. He spared a moment to pad the wound, then tied the girl's hands firmly to the pommel of the saddle and thundered toward the forest where the trail led to the mountain pass.

Behind the raiders, on the grass, only one of the boys stirred. Coughing and then gasping, the youth dragged himself toward one of the dnu that was still stamping in the field at the smell of blood.

"Come," the boy gasped. "Come here, girl."

The dnu gave the bloody figure a nervous look and shied away.

Leaving a swath of red-painted grass, the boy dragged himself close again, talking to the beast and finally getting a hand on the trailing reins. "Down, girl," he commanded weakly. "Sit down, now." He tapped weakly at the dnu's forelegs, and the beast obediently knelt, its knees hitting the ground with soft thuds though her eyes were wild from the blood scent. As its second set of knees dropped to the ground, the boy pushed himself up against the saddle and the dnu began to climb back to its six feet. He hung on grimly, pulling himself over into the leather seat with the lurching of the rising beast. The dnu, uncertain, took a few hesitant steps, then stopped, looking back at its rider. The boy gathered his last strength. He slapped the reins against the dnu's neck, and the beast began to trot, moving into the smooth six-legged gallop that would take it home, but not before the boy on its back collapsed against the pommel and lay with legs dangling nervelessly and mind closed against the pain.

It was an hour later when two herders noticed the dnu. On the outskirts of the village the lone animal still trotted down the road, but the sharp-eyed man who was watching the hills noticed its uncertain gait before he made out the shape of its burden.

"Joem, look that way," he said, squinting at the sun. "I can't make it out, but that beast rides strange."

"Runs like there's no rider," the other one answered, "but I see his shape on the back."

"Slumped like." Gunther gathered his dnu's reins and vaulted onto its back. "And that's Mirik's beast. I'd know its lopsided stride anywhere."

The other man looked alarmed and hurriedly wheeled his own mount down toward the road. "He was to be out with the Lloroi's girls today," he called over his shoulder. "Heard him bragging."

"Moons help him now if there's been trouble." The first man spurred his mount and thundered after Joem to the road. "The Lloroi lives for the light in his daughters' eyes."

"The moons help us all if it's Aranur who hears the news first. The weapons master's sister was with them, too."

"Shilia? Oh, gods . . ." Gunther pulled his head lower and pelted even faster across the field, passing the other man and reaching the boy first. He hauled his dnu up and leapt off. As he took the bleeding youth gently from the saddle, the other man reined in and jumped down, glancing up at the sky and pursing his lips as he judged the time.

"Dik-dropped raider spawn!" the thin man swore as he took in the boy's mangled shoulder where the bones and tendons gleamed white in the sluggish blood.

Joem tugged at his arms. "Give him to me and get going. You're faster than I, and it's ten minutes to the nearest horn."

"It's five minutes to the horn," Gunther returned grimly, easing the boy's mutilated body into the other man's arms and swinging back into the saddle, "or I didn't win the Rand title last spring."

Joem opened his mouth to retort, but the rider was already gone, the dirt torn from his dnu's hooves and marking his trail like a dust devil.

III

Ember Dione maMarin:

And More Raiders

Gray skies for gray memories;
Echoes follow where thoughts once rode strong.
The pounding of your heart
And the sighing of your lungs
Wound the time-driven dreams that were sung.

Light gray clouds hid the sky when Dion woke again. The gash in her leg was stretched from thigh to knee and throbbed angrily; the bandage she had made from her tunic was blood-soaked from her restless sleep. Even with the protection of the wolf, she had not been able to relax until she had covered her head so that the stingers would not bite her face off as she slept, and she looked like a ragged earth child now: no shirt, torn leggings, stained leather mail. At least there had been no dewfall or she would have woken up chilled, as well.

Brushing the leaves from her lap, the wolfwalker sat up and almost fainted again. The blaze of instant agony reminded her harshly that she was no longer at an advantage in the woods since her weakness and blood scent marked her as prey to even small-sized predators now. She shuddered at the thought of waking up to a worlag's hideous jaws.

At Dion's fear-tainted thoughts, Gray Hishn looked up and pulled her lips back from her gleaming teeth. *I killed two who threatened you before,* she snarled silently. *And I will hunt any others who stalk your scent.*

"Would that it were men and not beasts," Dion returned.

The Gray One licked her teeth, then ducked her head and nipped at a bug that was crawling on her thick-furred flank. *If there are men, we will scent them. If any of your pack survived, we will find them.* The wolf's image of Rhom was unmistakable.

Dion blanched. "Rhom is dead," she said harshly.

The Gray One merely panted, regarding the haggard woman with her yellow eyes and gray-white mask until her long tongue curled up and around her gleaming teeth again. *Do you want a rabbit?*

Taking one look at the thick, raw strand of muscle caught in the gray beast's claws where they still tore at the mammal's once-plump carcass, the wolfwalker shook her head. Maybe it was the throbbing pain in her leg and maybe not, but the thought of food made her queasy.

Experimenting, Dion found that she could almost stand on her left leg, resting her weight lightly on the other. The worlag's club had surely left dents in her body, she told herself raggedly, realizing once more how vulnerable she was in her weakness. She needed weapons, but she hesitated at the thought of going back and seeing where Rhom had—had died, she admitted again. The memory was too unreal in the calm, green dusk of the forest, and it was hard to bring herself to believe in his death. He was one of the best—and he died, just like the rest, torn to shreds like a bird between starved dogs. And as the insecurity hit her again, she realized that she was alone in Fenn Forest while somewhere around her was the band of worlags that had killed her brother, the merchant, and the guards she had been traveling with. How long did it take a worlag to get hungry again? And would they realize she had escaped their feast and was now alone?

You're not alone, Hishn reassured her instantly, nudging her with a cold, wet nose. *You have me. And Rhom is sly as a water cat. He may not be running with the moons yet. If he isn't, he'll be waiting for the dust to settle out of his nose before he comes looking for you.* The gray wolf's image of Rhom as half man, half beast almost made the woman smile.

That Rhom could still be alive . . . It was too improbable. How would he have escaped? "Useless hope," she muttered, brushing her tangled black hair back from her bruised face and wincing at the swelling across her cheek. But the thought lingered. If Rhom lived, where would he be—and what if he was wounded worse than she? How would he survive alone? Then again, she sobered herself, how eager was she to find his chewed-up corpse under a stack of decaying worlag casings?

You won't know until you go back.

"Maybe I don't want to know," she returned in a low voice.

You'll never find another fang like the one you dropped, either, the wolf prodded, reminding her of the sword she had lost when she had gone down.

Her father's blade, the one he had made to fit her hand with all the skill he had. She had dropped it when she had gone down under that last beast. Lost the sword her father had given her to wield when she gained the skill to do it well. Yes, she had skill, she admitted to herself bitterly, but not skill enough to turn the clubs of death.

She clenched her hand and relaxed it carefully. "The blade will be there," she answered steadily. "Worlags have no use for a sword." She stuffed her hair up under the cloth and gingerly bound the makeshift bandage over the wound. In fact, worlags could handle nothing more subtle than a club, either because they did not have the intelligence to figure out how to use a blade or because they just liked to crush instead of cut. The wolfwalker did not care which reason was right as long as the sword was still waiting for her to search it out. "If I go back," she said to herself.

Hishn snorted. *You could depend on your own claws,* she growled, *but as weapons, they're weaker than wilted grass.* The wolf extended a paw and bared claws thick and long as the woman's fingers. *Now these—* She grinned and tilted her head up at the woman. *These are weapons.*

"Hah," Dion retorted. "This," she said, tapping her forehead and trying not to wince, "this is a weapon."

The wolf merely gave the woman a quizzical look until her long, lupine tongue hung so far over her teeth that Dion gave in and laughed. The sound was strangely muffled in the woods.

Lean on me, the Gray One told her when she took a step, staggered, and clung to the tree that seemed to lunge suddenly into her outstretched hands. But Dion dragged her leg back under her and gritted her teeth. "Damn if I don't feel like an ancient," she said as she stepped again, ignoring the wolf's offer and letting her weight settle down on the leg until her face paled and she stifled the curse that leapt to her tongue.

Hishn nudged her with a broad shoulder so that she was forced to grab fur to keep her balance. *Lean on me or I'll carry you like a disobedient pup.*

"You're a strong mutt, Hishn, but you're not strong enough for me to ride you like a dnu."

You were easier to handle when you were out of your mind.

"I think I still am out of my mind to be letting you chastise me like a mother," Dion retorted. She lifted her leg over a branch and blanched at the repeated pain. Would she never get used to it? Hishn, sensing the blinding agony her wolfwalker was going through, froze until the woman could move again.

You need an extra set of legs like worlags, the gray beast offered when she rested again after only ten yards. *But there are no other Gray Ones near enough to call the pack for help.*

"I don't need more legs. I need crutches." She projected the image as clearly as possible, and the Gray One tilted her head to look at the woman curiously.

You would rather trust small trees you must drag along as you walk than use me to lean on?

"I know it's hard for you to believe, but it's a lot easier to hop along with something that doesn't move as I walk."

The wolf was silent a moment. *If you need this wood more than me, I will find it for you.*

Dion stopped her before she could trot off. "Gray One," she said quietly, "you honor me with my life. It's not that I don't need you—moonworms, you dumb dog, I need you more now than ever before. It's just that I'll walk better if I can just find a stout stick to lean on so that you can go on ahead and find an easier way for us through this brush."

Mollified, the great beast twisted its head to lick the woman's bare forearm, leaving a clean streak that scarred her dirty skin and made her smile wanly. "Too bad I can't just wave my hands and heal myself like the ancients could," Dion suggested. "We'd have been out of here like skitters from a fry pan."

Hishn sneezed and perked her ears to one side. *Stay here. There is a game trail a short run from here, but there may be a better way back to the road. I will try to find you a small tree while I'm gone.*

Nodding, the woman sank gratefully back onto the soft earth, brushing aside a pocket of bugs that burst angrily from the moss. It was broadmoss, she noticed, pulling a clump from the tangle and examining it more closely—it could come in handy when Hishn found her a cane and she needed some padding for her hands. So occupied, the black-haired healer wove the moss into tiny mats, building a pad that fit her hand and would cover a stick firmly at one end. She was just finishing when the wolf returned, projecting a smugness that Dion had to smile at.

"Find the road?"

And a small tree.

"So," she said, dragging herself up from the ground, "how far do I have to go to get my new leg?"

It's a small hunt, like the distance a deer runs when shot with a weak bolt.

Dion nodded. Hishn offered her a shoulder again, and the healer leaned on the wolf as if her life depended on it, although, in spite of the jags of pain that shot through her leg at every step, she swore it was getting easier to move. Half the stiffness must be coming from the bruises that covered her right side, she decided. Since the worlags' clubs had bashed her well enough that even breathing was painful, the woman's face was in a permanent grimace, and the only sounds she made for the first hundred meters were bit-back curses and the gasps that accompanied them like a soft percussion.

Don't worry so, Hishn protested, nudging her to continue when a broken twig froze her into a crouching stance that cost her much of her painfully gained stature. *I'll tell you if anything threatens. Then I'll kill whatever comes,* she added with savage pleasure.

Dion gave a shaky laugh. "Gray One, I wish I still had your confidence."

You do, the wolf returned calmly. The images sent by the beast became a sudden flood that swept her consciousness until she found herself on her knees again, her face buried in the Gray One's fur as the wolf remembered their bonding two years before: . . . *the blue eyes of a pup meeting the violet ones of the healer for the first time . . . a tenuous bond of love that thickened into a cord . . . the furry heat of the growing cub on her feet when she slept . . . hot breath, bad breath kissing her with a wet tongue . . . a cold nose on her neck at night . . . gray fur thickening under her fingers . . . water spilling over those blue eyes now green, terrified in the flash flood that had swept the camp the previous spring . . . a dive, a shock, a desperate swim through a canyon thick with debris, and the bond growing strong . . . racing through a meadow at night and wrestling with a growling wolf now grown to match her own size . . . resting her head on the warm stomach and falling asleep in security . . . tracking deer at dawn . . . the green eyes turning yellow with the growing age of a hunter . . .* The wolf's love washed through her mind and bolstered her sagging strength the way a wind lifted a slack sail and pushed it on.

Dion shook her head to clear it. "Silly mutt," she muttered shakily. But her hand remained in the thick fur, and when she stepped again, her weight rested more heavily on the broad shoulders of the wolf.

Hishn stayed by her side for a while, but after leading the woman to the wood from which she painstakingly chipped out a crutch with the dagger that was the only blade left to her, the wolf began scouting ahead, slinking silently away, then appearing again anxiously. The Gray One gave the wolfwalker directions with images, letting her read her natural thoughts so that the woman felt she was in two places at once. But at least Dion did not have to follow her own trail back to the clearing on the main trail. She had crawled through so many deadfalls and fallen off so many inclines in her delirium that though her trail was obvious with blood and broken branches, there was no way she would have been able to go back along the same path with her uncooperative leg. Hishn must have dragged her a long way that night.

It was a good two hours before she reached the burned wagon site, but the smell warned her long before she saw the burned brush that marked the perimeter of the fire. She had to swallow her bile when she saw what was making the stench. After only two days there were still plenty of uneaten, rotting remains to identify those they had traveled with. The six-legged dnu, most of which had been eaten down to the bones, could not be identified, just counted by their bloody skeletons. Eight worlags had died in the fight, several of them burning in the fire Dion had almost been trapped in. And their death smelled vile: urine and blood and wasted guts and the sick smells of melted wing casings and acidic insect fluids. And in the middle of it all the sweet, nose-retching smell of half-cooked and rotting human flesh. She swallowed, tried not to breathe, and kicked at the burnt weapons and torn leather packs. A boata bag had spilled its wine when it had been crushed under a foot, and the dirt pooled damply at its split seams while hundreds of small insects crawled in and out of the sack. The bales of cloth had been torn apart, soiled, and scorched by flame; the supplies had been crushed, eaten, smashed into the earth; the bones, though clearly picked at by scavengers, were crossed and piled like pickup sticks, and the skulls had been smashed so that jaws hung awry and loose teeth stuck in the ground as if the earth itself were trying to bite those who had brought their violence to that place.

Wolfwalker.

Hishn's soft call caught her attention. Depressed, she turned and scuffed at the ground before sighing and looking up.

Rhom is not here, the Gray One said abruptly. The wolf nosed the brush again, then trotted behind the low growth and snorted as she pushed the branches aside and sniffed the stained earth carefully. *His scent is not among the dead.*

"By the moons, Hishn, are you sure?" Dion took a step too fast and went to her knees, swearing at her weakness and loosing a sob before she regained her composure.

I am here, Hishn reassured her instantly.

The woman caught her breath as the searing pain faded to angry throbs. "I saw him fall there—to your left." She hauled herself back to her feet and hobbled slowly to the wolf, twisting her hand in the long gray hair while the beast sniffed from side to side and suffered Dion's slight weight on her back.

He fell here, but the bloods are not his.

The wolfwalker pushed the brush aside and studied the tracks carefully before stepping across the broken area and letting herself sink down where she could see the earth better. "The stains are too blue . . . the smell wrong . . ." She rubbed the dirt between her fingers, feeling the subtle graininess irritate her skin. "This is worlag fluid."

I smell little of Rhom here, the wolf said eagerly, her tongue hanging out as she panted.

"He got away," Dion said in wonder. "He's alive!"

But gone on. Sniff here. The wolf nosed farther along the ground. *He comes back to look at the clearing, then turns away again.*

"He must have seen me go down. He thinks I'm dead." Oh, Rhom . . . "Hishn, let me find my sword, then we'll catch up to him."

You'll be running like a hare with three broken legs, the gray beast snorted. She turned her yellow eyes on Dion. *You're weaker now than you were this morning. We can catch up later. You need to rest now and lick your wounds.*

"I'm fine," she protested. "And if we leave today—"

Tomorrow, the wolf insisted. *The tracks will still be fresh enough.*

"But—"

Tomorrow.

Dion sighed, resigning herself to the wait. Arguing with 120 kilograms of stubborn wolf was rarely productive. Besides, she had to admit that the Gray One was right: She had little enough strength to stand, let alone jog through the dark half of Fenn Forest.

She desultorily picked up four more knives, short ones, for throwing. There were others lying around, but their handles were too charred and brittle to use. Two of the good ones went in her belt, the other two in her boots, above the slits that held her safe money. With raiders, as well as worlags, known to be about, she could not be too careful.

The wagon gear had been torn apart, but she picked through the mess anyway and managed a light pack to travel with and another tunic to replace the one that had become a bandage. By the time she was ready to follow Rhom's trail, she was armed for war. She found and cleaned her sword; and since her bow had been smashed in the fray, she took the dead merchant's light hunting bow, which she could manage better than the guard's war bow. She had a bad moment when she lifted the merchant's gnawed arm away from the bow and his nearly severed head rolled away from his neck—the man's eyes opened suddenly and stared at her as if she were a grave robber—but after the initial shock, she steeled herself and pulled the bow from his slack grip anyway. At least there were enough arrows scattered in the clearing and surrounding brush to fill the barely charred quiver she picked from the fire's circle.

The last thing she did was drag the human bodies into a pile. In her weakened state, it was almost more than she could handle, especially since Hishn said a flat-out no to helping—the taste of a rotting human turned the wolf's stomach as much as the smell did Dion's. After four guards, the fat merchant, and his rail-thin son, the haggard woman was ready to collapse. She rolled the last body into the pile and thanked the moons again that she had stopped to gather some night-blooming herbs when the worlags had attacked—Hishn's howl was the only thing that had saved her. She looked down at the four mangled bodies and looked away again. She had no strength to bury them, and the smells of the worlags would keep other, more timid scavengers away for only a few days.

"Gray One," she pleaded, "I just can't do any more. I need your help with this."

The wolf growled low in her throat and turned her head.

"Please, Hishn, I've got no strength left to dig the grave."

The creature pulled her lips back from her teeth but finally slunk out of the shadows. She wrinkled her nose and glared at the wolfwalker, then tentatively put out a paw and scratched at the blood-darkened soil. She woofed in disgust.

"I know, but it doesn't have to be deep . . ."

Hishn snarled silently and started digging.

The shallow grave was enough to burn the bodies in, and Dion set pitch-dripping branches in the bottom of the pit before rolling the dead over the edge. She could not start the fire till she was ready to leave—it would broadcast her presence, and sticking around while the hunters gathered would be sheer stupidity. Even with a head start, she would be hard-pressed to keep them off her trail, and she suspected she would have to take to the water to discourage some of the more persistent predators.

While Hishn dug the ditch, the wolfwalker had found her warcap, and now she jammed it on her head, the leather-covered mesh bloodstained but still serviceable. Bending over and getting up and down with her head throbbing so badly made her nauseous, but it was really the gash in her leg that worried her most. No one ever bled to death from a head wound, but without some way to stitch the split in her leg closed, it would break open again and bleed out for days. She could not afford to lose more blood, and with the loss she had already suffered, she would find it hard to fight off infection.

Dion looked at her grimy hands and sighed, picking at the dirt under her nails. Every healer dreamed of rediscovering the secrets of Ovousibas, the healing art of the ancients. To hold her hands over patients and watch them heal before her very eyes . . . She stretched her hands out as if to grasp the mythical wisps of that healing, but all she felt was the constant throb of her leg. She clenched her hands against the pounding of the wound and picked at her flattened herb pouches again.

It took her a few moments to realize that her eyes had been vaguely focusing on a line of movement. A string of largon bugs had made a busy trail going from the woods to the clearing, where they were scavenging at the rotting bodies, slowly stripping away the meat, and Dion frowned. An idea flashed in her head as she watched them bite down on the flesh, but even for an open-minded healer, the idea was a bit farfetched.

"Not exactly sanitary," she told herself, considering the possibilities and trying to convince herself that she was not going to do what she was thinking of. "But I'm not going to heal myself with dreams of Ovousibas, either."

She studied the line of bugs again. Largons, the large-jawed crawlers with segmented bodies, looked like tiny worlags. They were about as long as her finger, but their heads made up a third of that length—and most of the head was a jagged row of teeth. The healer made her decision and loosened the blood-soaked bandages on her leg, taking out the glass beads she had gathered and put in to stimulate healing. At least she had not lost those, she thought, though most of her herbs were gone since her medicine pouches were as scattered as her weapons. She carefully cleaned the wound again, stopping twice to wipe the sweat from her face and calm the shaking of her hands.

Gray Hishn watched with interest as the healer grabbed a largon behind its head and brought it near her leg. When it smelled the blood, the bug went crazy, its legs scrabbling frantically in the air, massive jaws working away at nothing, just above the gash.

Even though she was expecting the sensation, Dion was still shocked when it bit into the raw edges of the wound, and the image of agony she unconsciously projected brought Hishn to her feet with a snarl. "Gods!" she gasped, barely pinching off the bug's head before it opened its mouth to take another bite. The muscles of its jaw held its head tightly on the gash, binding her leg as well as gut would have done. She wiped the tears from her eyes with a dirty sleeve and took a shaky breath that sounded more like a sob.

Do not do that again, the wolf growled.

She closed her eyes, tightened her jaw, and grabbed another

bug. "You do what you have to do, Gray One. You do what you have to do."

It took sixteen largons to seal the gash, and Dion was sobbing uncontrollably by the time she was done. All she could do was clench her fists and shake till the blinding pain settled back into what seemed like a gentle throb. Hishn, pacing and snarling while the wolfwalker tortured herself, finally howled and tore at the ground, unable to handle Dion's anguish. And all the while the largons hung in a hideous line, their black eyes rolled back to glare at each other while their bodiless heads bit gruesomely into her flesh.

At least they would hold as well as gut thread, the woman comforted herself. Long enough for the gash to heal shut. If so, a ninan from then she could break their jaws to remove them. She looked again at the now-closed wound and shook her head at her own audacity—the Healer's Association would have a field day with what she had done if they ever found out.

"Good thing I tried it on myself and not a patient," she muttered, dragging herself to her feet. The initial shock of the new, raw pain was fading into simple mind-crushing throbs, and the wolfwalker gathered her bow and sword. "All right, mutt, we can start any time now," she said, sliding the sword into her scabbard and shifting the quarrel of arrows to a comfortable spot across her shoulders. "I'm ready to run with the best of you gray ghosts."

You run like a pup with three lame legs, Hishn snorted, pulling her lips back in a snarl to show her pink and black gums. *You project pain, not brains, Healer. We'll run slowly, and I'll nip your tail if you don't behave.*

"Nip my tail? Hah! I'll step on your face so fast you won't know what hit you till you spit my boot out of your teeth." Dion wrapped a length of salvaged cloth around her leg, and bound it tightly with her last lengths of leather. "And you better keep up with me, too, or I'll leave you behind for Gray Tholan to find."

Hishn let her tongue loll around her mouth. *Gray Tholan smells like old rabbit poo. He rolls in it whenever he finds it, and I prefer the scent of deer.*

"Like Gray Yoshi? You just like your males a little younger," Dion teased. "I'll make sure Gray Tholan hears that."

And I'll make sure you miss Rhom's trail by a ninan, the wolf snapped, trotting to the edge of the clearing and sending the wolfwalker a haughty look.

Dion snorted. "You better not. When I light this fire, everyone in Fenn Forest will know we're here, and it'll be a race to find a safe place to spend the night. Besides your fangs, Rhom's sword is the only thing I want to see, come twilight."

She dipped a branch in pitch and lit it, turning her eyes from its fierce flame before dropping it on the ragged bodies. "May the moons bless your passage, give you guidance to the stars." The breath caught in her throat as the flames raced around and found the pitch-soaked clothes near the bottom of the gory pile. She took an involuntary step back from the sudden heat. "May your children find your death song and its melody lighten their hearts." The yellow tongues leapt up and licked at the confining air beneath the beckoning trees. "Mistress of the moons that guide us, make your passage short and sure."

She threw the torch at the bonfire and swung her meager pack onto her left shoulder. It was done. She did not look back as the torn faces of the merchant and his son boiled and melted under the pitch-fed fire. At the edge of the clearing, Gray Hishn led her back into the forest, and Dion was surprised to find herself shaking. It was not until the slight breeze chafed her cheeks that she realized she was crying.

It was some time before the thought that Rhom was only two days away steadied her. It would not be easy, she knew, but with the hope of seeing her twin, she forced herself to set aside the pain that racked her every step and quell the nightmare glimpse of melting bodies. That more worlags could be waiting for her mistakes was a reminder that danger was as much a painkiller as drugs, she realized with new insight.

With that threat to dampen the unwanted sensations of her beaten body and the weariness of a day's rough travel, Dion made it only five kilometers before twilight fell and she had to admit defeat. She barely glanced at the place Hishn had chosen, trusting the wolf and dropping into the mossy hollow asleep almost before the driving pain began to beat at her unconsciousness. But even her restless dreams kept her running in pain as the largons on her leg regenerated and grew into worlags that chased her through the forest by the dim light of the seventh moon.

When morning finally came, overcast and dull, Dion's violet

eyes were dark with sleeplessness and pain. The sorry shape she was in, there was no way she would catch up to her twin in two days—if she was lucky, it would be more than four, and unless he watched his back trail like a lepa on a hunt, he would miss her coming after him at all. She yanked her fingers through her hair and swore suddenly at the tangles as tears came to her eyes.

Hishn snorted, and Dion resisted the temptation to snap at the wolf, too.

Even with the Gray One, Dion felt as if she were walking in peril every step of the way. Hishn would protect her as best she could, but even a wolf had limitations, and Dion was weak; in her exhaustion she would make mistakes that could cost them both their lives. Moonworms, but traveling in a group was not safe even in populated areas these days; traveling alone, as she had to now, was asking for trouble. Even if she avoided the badgerbears and water cats, there were still the raiders to worry about, and even Hishn could not protect her from the gang fighters that roamed Randonnen with growing impunity. She shook her head at the thought of the raiders. A quick and dirty war in the east had merged two counties and added to the general unrest, which seemed to be growing inland from the coast. In many places people had withdrawn from their devastated homesteads and villages, leaving the abandoned farms as bases for the raiders to work from. And there were always the worlags. She swallowed convulsively and shivered as a small finger of fear crawled up her spine. The images of her first battle pushed their gory way in front of her eyes, and she could not help but think, What if another band of worlags found her before she found Rhom? The broken wagons, the bodies . . .

Wait, Hishn snapped suddenly, freezing into immobility as if the thought of worlags had brought danger down on them.

The woman was a statue. Her ears picked up only faintly the soft rustle that the wolf heard like thunder, but the bond between them included senses as well as thoughts. Feeling the threat move closer through the wolf, Dion silently strung the bow, brought out an arrow, and notched it, drawing the string back until her bowstring finger rested at the corner of her mouth and her eyes stared toward the brush where the Gray One slunk. The wolf's thoughts became unreal, focused into the hunt of a primitive animal, and the wolfwalker had to separate herself from the depth of rage that enveloped her . . . *tawny fur, yellow eyes*

*. . . a crouched shape on an overhung bough . . . the hunter
waiting, hunger calling like the worms that gnawed its gut . . .*

A glint of fur gave the tree cat away. It was close—too close.
Hishn was almost under it, trying to draw the creature down so
that she could kill it. But the cat wanted no part of the Gray
One. Rather, the scent of blood the human carried was more to
its liking, and the remembered taste of soft flesh was a goad that
held it to its perch until the woman came within range. With
narrowed eyes, Dion watched its crouch, judging the leap it
would take and aiming through the wide leaves that hid the bulk
of the cat. Its heart should be right there . . .

She loosed the bolt, and the quarrel struck true. With a yowl,
the forest cat fell in a tangle, its middle legs ripping at the arrow
while its hind legs and forelegs sought to catch its balance in the
air. Hishn lunged. By the time the cat hit the ground, the wolf's
teeth had already snapped on its neck, and Dion's second arrow
was unnecessary. The creature dangled from the gray wolf's
bloody mouth, a limp form sagging this way and that as its legs
dragged on the road.

"Enough, Hishn," Dion said quietly, calming the wolf from
its blood lust. "Give it up, now." She stepped closer and
snapped her fingers to catch the Gray One's attention when Hishn
made as if to slink away in the woods. "We can have it for
dinner."

. . . Blood. Hot, sweet blood, the wolf sent. *Sweet meat and
the stringy taste of fur . . .*

"For dinner, Gray One. We have to keep moving."

The wolf growled low in her throat, but she obeyed, allowing
the woman to take the dead cat from her mouth and lay it out
on the ground. Its fur was crawling with red lice, and Dion
carefully slit and peeled the creature's skin back to expose the
meat without letting the lice discover her own tender flesh. It
was a small cat, so she took both haunches and forelegs, making
a neat, quick bundle of the meat they could eat that night.
Thoughts growing more coherent, the Gray One sniffed at the
woman's task, her instant hunger driving her to tear the meat out
of Dion's hands, while the wolfwalker's control forced her to
wait.

It is a long run till dusk, she complained with a nudge at the
woman's hand.

"It isn't that long," Dion promised. "I won't last till sundown, anyway.'' As soon as she had placed the meat in a wallet, she told the wolf to take the carcass away from the path. It was too obvious that a knife had cut the meat away, and the fact that only half the flesh had been taken would be a dead giveaway to any raider that a lone hunter was around.

The weight of the meat was not much, but the thought of the extra pounds in her pack was as fatiguing as the thought of the eight kilometers they had run; by evening Dion was so tired that she simply stumbled down the path. The constant flood of pain had driven her thoughts back to oblivion, and even the faint growl of hunger sent up by her stomach failed to rouse her mind. When Hishn tugged her sleeve and gently guided her off the road to rest, she just fell into the soft humus and found herself curled against the wolf's warm stomach, suffering only to open the wallet and expose the parcel of meat to the hungry creature's claws. She knew nothing more till dawn broke across her eyes again.

Even then she woke grudgingly at the wolf's insistent nudge. From the damp heat of the Gray One's stomach, Dion raised her head and winced at the returning throb. *Two and a half days,* she sent, looking up at the green canopy. *That's a lot of distance to make up.*

The longer you sleep, the greater it grows, Hishn retorted. She twisted suddenly and bit at a bug that had crawled onto her tail, and Dion was left to sit up or fall back into the brush.

"Ow," the healer wailed. "You could have given me a warning." Her headache suddenly took on the proportions of a major hangover, and she pressed both hands into her temples to control the hammers that threatened to burst through her skull.

The wolf merely cocked her head. *You felt better yesterday after running a while,* she encouraged.

"All right, all right." Dion rolled out of the moss, groaning at her sore muscles. She dragged her fingers through her tangled black hair once, then followed with her fire-blackened comb, only to realize that without a bath, straightening out the knots in the once-glossy mass was impossible. With a sigh she stuffed it up and out of sight in her warcap. They should cross a stream that day and again the next, if she remembered the merchant's map correctly, and with luck she could then take the time to wash her hair before it matted up like a wild dnu's tail. Cup-plants, although they held enough water to live on, had nowhere near enough fluid to wash her face in, let alone her hair.

In the end it took wolf and woman five more days and 130 kilometers to near the plains where the river Phye flowed. Rhom's trail was fresher, but she was still a full day behind him—she had been too weak to hold a strong pace as well as she could have wished—but if the moons sent her a clear path, the next evening would see her at his night fire. At least she had found a couple of streams to wash in, she consoled herself as she dropped wearily into a shuffling run, though another day of jogging through Fenn Forest had ruined any cleanliness she had stolen from the sparkling water. The long shadows filtered into dusk with the dimming evening light, and the wolfwalker sighed, rubbed dirt from her face with an equally dirty sleeve, and told herself that she would find a hollow to sleep in after the next hill.

Hishn had been dropping back to run closer to Dion and now came up beside her. The Gray One was uneasy. The edge of fear she caught snapped the wolfwalker awake, but she was so tired that she was not up to much of a fight with whatever was disturbing her partner, and she barely noticed how the wolf's head turned slowly from side to side as the Gray One tried to catch scent or sight of the danger.

The wind is wrong for me, she told Dion with a puzzled mental tone. *But someone watches . . .* The Gray One's mind grew more chaotic as instincts and emotions took over her reasoning. *Danger!* She pulled her lips back in a snarl.

Dion froze, looking into the dark forest shadows with her eyes, her ears, her mind. But she saw nothing, heard nothing, felt nothing except the unease that grew till she wanted to scream at the unseen watcher. Was she walking into a trap, or had the jaws of one closed already? Hishn's senses colored her own till she felt as if it were herself, not the wolf, who was searching the woods, stretching for an identifying scent of man or beast. She strung her bow and stepped silently to the crest of the hill, crouching low to see over it before exposing herself. Hishn slunk to her right. Still Dion saw nothing. She drew back on the arrow and moved over the rise. Still nothing. She was too tired to keep the tension on the arrow of the heavy bow for so long, so she eased it back and held it lightly ready with two fingers. They edged down the small but steep slope, wagon ruts on each side, Hishn stalking the unseen. The wolf growled.

There! A sound, and an arrow whapped by her hip. Hishn lunged in front of her, and she leapt back and to the side, her leg collapsing and rolling her across the wagon tracks, just short of the safety of the forest. She bit back her cry and scrambled for the shadows as she shot back, but two more vicious bolts cut her off from the brush. There was more than one, then. There was always more than one, she reminded herself in despair. Raiders worked in groups of three or more.

"Halt or you die!" The harsh voice was as cold as the water she had splashed in that morning, and she shivered involuntarily. "Throw the bow away from you and drop the sword. If the wolf moves again, it dies at your feet."

"Hishn!" She whispered urgently. The Gray One crouched between the woman and the raiders, her teeth long and white in the dark. Two hulking forms stepped carefully out of the brush on either side of the road, but Dion knew there was at least one more still in the shadows with an arrow notched at her heart, and she could not afford another deep wound. One of them lit a torch and held it high over his head, its light casting a macabre shadow twice as big as the man it illuminated.

"Look what we have here," the other man growled. "A wanderer. He must be tired. We should take him home with us for sport, huh, Grost? Haw." He moved carefully, his bow still ready as he loomed across the trail. The one called Grost was only a few inches shorter but still about two meters tall. Their faces looked as if they had taken a beating recently. As they moved up, the third man stepped into view to keep a clear line of fire on the captive. Gray Hishn growled and backed against her, staying between her and the raiders who advanced across the darkening evening dust. The wolf's mind was primal, animal, the blood lust combining with her protective instincts to attack.

Hishn. Dion checked her again, though the controlled fear in her own mind did not help calm the wolf. She had never met raiders before, but as a healer she had seen the effects of their weapons on men and their sport on women. How long would they continue to think she was a man?

"Keep the wolf down," Grost said sharply, his sword out and gleaming under the torch as he edged closer.

"Just kill it," the first hulking raider suggested crudely.

"Don't be stupid, Kerr. There's a high market for trained wolves. Bolan, check on our other guest. This one's in no shape to give us trouble." The man in the woods grunted and turned, and a shadow shifted where he disappeared from the murk of the night. Dion stayed silent. She could not run with her leg, but she could not let them take Hishn, either. The wolf was her only chance—Hishn had to get away, find Rhom, and bring help if she could. Kerr got too close, and the wolf got set to leap, her mind sending the woman in one staccato burst the flashed images: *the attack, the throat slashed and spurting beneath white flashing teeth, the feel of flesh and bone in her jaw, the taste of hot blood, the incense of the scream . . .*

Hold! Dion ordered strongly. *Wait!*

Grost stayed to the side, letting Kerr advance, and Dion thought he did not care if the other man died under the wolf's fangs. Kerr's bow arm was ready, but he was not prepared for the direction the Gray One took when she did go. The wolf-walker flung her hand up suddenly, and Kerr's eyes followed. "Rhom!" she snapped sharply. Hishn would understand.

The wolf leapt, but not for the raider. The shadows reached out to take the gray wolf as one of their own, and Kerr's startled arrow skittered into the brush. There was a shocked moment's hesitation, and then Grost reached out almost negligently and slapped her jarringly hard across the cheek.

My voice, she thought dimly. It gave me away.

"Bitch," she heard as the familiar fuzzy patches swam in front of her eyes. She hardly noticed when they tied her hands in front of her, roughly, but with a foot of line between them, and pushed her to walk before them. Even with her hands spaced, she fell twice. The first time Kerr yanked her to her feet and muttered something about taking her there in the dust since she would not make it to the camp. She shuddered and felt very small, her body dizzy and weak.

The dirty raider laughed cruelly at her shudder. "Have to see what you look like by firelight. Might even be downright pretty." He reached over to feel her chest, and she shrank back against Grost, terror and fury in her eyes. They had taken the knives from her belt but had not looked for others, and with the two in her boots, she would send the man to the seventh hell if he so much as touched her.

Protect . . . Hishn's thought charged abruptly into Dion's dim thoughts . . . *one lunge, one snap, one scream* . . .

No! the wolfwalker commanded as sternly as she could. The Gray One was in the forest, pacing like a dark shadow of death, but Dion needed more than the fangs of the wolf to get clear of the raiders. *I'm too weak to run. Find Rhom, and hurry!*

"Leave her," Grost's voice was dark over her silent interchange as he snarled at Kerr. "Didn't you see the healer's band? She'll bring a poor price if you mark her before she sees the market block."

The other man muttered an obscenity under his breath. But the woman fell once more, dazed by the throbbing in her leg and head, and he grabbed her and swung her like a sack of potatoes over his shoulder, ignoring her awkward pack. The world faded into a red haze as she was jounced against his back by his stride. When they reached the raiders' camp, he dumped her roughly against another body that lay in the firelight, then re-bound her hands tightly while she lay limp, her senses coming back slowly as her hands grew throbbingly numb.

The man bound next to her shifted and groaned softly. His gray eyes opened, and the two prisoners looked at each other for a long moment. Surprise, then a frown, then pity showed on his beaten, weathered face as he realized that she was a woman and a healer—and in the raiders' hands. But he was not in a good position, either, she realized. When Dion was sold, at least she would be protected by the harem laws, but the older, graying man would be destined for any number of miserable deaths— raiders were not known as gentle sorts. Already blood trailed from the man's mouth and nose, and his left eye was swollen almost shut.

"I wish I could help you," she whispered involuntarily as she saw the mess of his face.

A bit of ironic humor glinted in his right eye, and he managed a twisted smile. "It's I who should help you, Healer," he whispered back. "Gamon Aikekkraya neBentar, weapons master of the Ramaj Ariye. Now weaponless but still at your service."

"Healer Ember Dione maMarin," she returned, then fell silent. Grost, having dropped his weapons at the other side of the fire, was coming over. As she struggled to sit up without wincing, Grost squatted in front of her, reached out, and gripped her chin in his hand to study her face as if he were checking a dnu's teeth for age. She yanked her head back, her face burning with instant fury, but he merely smiled and forced her forward again.

"Feisty, huh? The ones with spirit always bring a better price." His other hand pulled off the healer's headband and warcap, and her tangled hair tumbled free. "Definitely pretty. In fact, I'd say unusually so. With the healer status, we might be able to get forty, maybe forty-two pieces of gold in spite of this—" He gestured at her leg and head gash. "—and this. Maybe more from the right buyer." He laughed harshly and let her pull her burning face from his grasp. "Healer, I respect your trade, so I'll give you the choice of telling me where you keep your money or letting me dig through your herb pouches. What'll it be?"

Dion was shocked. No one ever touched a healer's herbs. But then, no one was supposed to harm a healer, either, she reminded herself warily. So she tempered her anger, though her eyes flashed. "Third pouch on the right," she answered mutinously.

He gave her a lazy smile. "Stay cooperative," he commented, untying the pouch and hefting it in his hands, "and you'll stay alive." The pouch contained only silver and copper, but it would be enough to appease the raider. The moons knew she was not dressed as if she had money. As he peered in the small bag and counted the coins roughly, Dion's left leg itched where the jewels and her few pieces of gold were small bumps in her boots against her skin, but, satisfied, Grost retied the pouch and tucked it in his jerkin. "Now, what happened to the rest of your party?" he asked, appraising the bloodstains and cuts on her leather mail.

"Worlags," she said shortly.

Grost gave her a speculative look. "And you alone escaped their claws? That wolf must be pretty handy in a scrape. We'll just have to set you out as bait till it comes back for you." In spite of herself, Dion's eyes flickered, and Grost smiled, knowing he had guessed right. His smile had humor like that of a hungry worlag.

As she glared at him and tried to read his face, the wolfwalker told herself that she had no reason to be shocked by the raider's tactics: She had listened to her father and her twin talk about their experiences, she had seen the wounds and tortured bodies the raiders left behind, she had studied under the best teachers in the martial art called Abis—if she let this raider scare her so that she forgot everything she had learned, then she had wasted more than half her life training in something she could not bring herself to use. He was a raider, yes, and a slaver as well, but he was only a man, after all.

And men can be killed as easily as hares, the Gray One whispered savagely from a shadow behind one of the raiders.

Hishn, get back—get away from the light. Leave me. Find Rhom. He's got to be close. Desperately, Dion forced herself not to look at the wolf.

But the raider's voice sharpened suddenly and went cold, breaking into her thoughts. "Who is Rhom?" he barked, as if reading her mind and trying to catch her off guard. "What is he to you and how far away?"

Next to her, Gamon stirred but stayed quiet, and in the sudden tension Dion felt her heart beat hard against her ribs. *The fear is real enough,* she told herself, *but use it, don't let it consume you.*

"No one you'd know," she returned steadily. "Rhom has better taste than that."

Grost did not even change expressions. "Try again, Healer."

She gave him a resigned sigh. "All right, the truth is that he's a pet worlag I picked up on the way. Looks kind of like you, in fact. Same beady eyes, same black and blue face—"

The raider's smile did not reach his eyes. "I can make things very unpleasant for you, you know." He reached over and fingered her chin again, chuckling when she shrank away from him. "Brave little girl," he mocked. "What would you do if I decided to buy you for myself?" His smile died suddenly, the fire's shadows darkening his face. "Who is Rhom?" he demanded.

Dion looked down, not answering, and the raider's slap almost caught her by surprise, rocking her head back. *Stay!* she shouted at Hishn, stopping the instinctive leap with her command as she licked blood from her lip. The blow had been emotionless and brutal, Grost merely using his hands to get the information he wanted, and she was shocked more by that than the act itself. She stifled her gasp and caught her breath, answering in a low, trembling voice. "My grandfather."

Grost leaned back and eyed her thoughtfully. "Grandfather, huh? How far from here is the old man?"

She hesitated, waited for him to raise his hand to threaten her again, and kept her voice high and hurried as if she were trying to get the words out before his hand fell. It was not difficult. "Two days, maybe less," she said as the words tumbled over each other, "if he goes quickly. He went to get help for the wagons before we were attacked." Her eyes flickered to the dark shadow behind Bolan, and she licked her torn lip again. *Wait, Gray One. Soon, soon we'll both fight.*

Grost thought for a minute, nodded to himself as if figuring distances, and asked, "Can you cook?"

Dion said nothing, hoping she had gained some leeway by letting him think her rebellion would be verbal and not physical but feeling honestly mutinous and insulted at the same time. By the moons, all healers could cook. Why learn only the bitter ways to use herbs?

The raider slapped her again, and the blood from her cut lip fed her fury. "Can you cook?" he repeated pleasantly. She could feel the heat in her face and the flash in her eyes, but she held her temper. *Movement means opportunities*, she told herself, tasting blood on her tongue. Hishn's own image of blood was as much a goad as the rage that smoldered deep inside. *Not yet*, she told herself as much as the wolf. *Just a little longer . . .*

Grost retied her hands a foot apart again, pulled her to her feet, and pointed at the fire and the pot hanging over it. "Do something with that," he said. She remained silent but clenched and unclenched her burning hands to get the blood moving in them again as she glanced toward the fire. She still had the boot knives—but the raider was watching her closely, so that she had no chance to slip a blade from her boot and leave it with Gamon. She sniffed at the pot and tried to stir the lump in the bottom. Whatever it was, it was not salvageable.

"Cook," Grost commanded pleasantly, though his voice was cold underneath.

The fear she felt was sour in her mouth, and she was angry. Even a raider has no right to treat a healer like this, she told herself, lifting her chin. These men were killers who cared nothing for her or each other except for the gold they would get by selling her. But hells, she told herself, if spirit was worth more to them, she would give them some spirit and a piece of her temper, as well. Right then, she did not have much to lose.

"I can't cook a mash of burned tubers or whatever it is you've wasted in the pot," she snapped, glaring at Grost and throwing a spoonful of scorched goop at the ground in disgust. "You want supper? Tell Bolan there, or what's his name, to dump this pot and dig some fresh roots."

Bolan's jaw dropped at her words. Kerr gawked. Grost stared at her for a long moment, and Dion thought she was going to die as the raider fingered his blade with a surprised frown still on his face. And then, incredibly, Grost laughed outright. "Bolan," he chuckled, "dump the pot. Then get out the supplies for our mistress healer." He turned away, still chuckling, and Bolan shook his head in disbelief.

With the fresh supplies, Dion made a strong stew, stumbling as she moved, tired and scared, though she knew that Hishn was still in the shadows. How the raiders were unable to sense the danger, she did not know; the hunting aura of the Gray One was strong enough to keep her on edge even in her exhaustion. And as if he knew something was wrong but could not put his finger on it, Grost kept Dion under his eye. She ignored him. The raiders ignored Gamon.

She wondered what they would do with the older man: Sell him in a slave market, too? If they asked her to treat their cuts and bruises, she might be able to put them to sleep with a slow-acting tranquilizer that would not be noticed as being different from normal sleepiness. But they had not asked, and she guessed it was because Grost could not trust her not to do what she was thinking of. She could not poison the stew because Gamon and she might have to eat it, too. But, she thought, she could use the tranquilizer in their grog. They would not waste a good brew on prisoners, and it might provide the edge necessary for Hishn to distract the raiders and she and Gamon to escape. With the smoke from the fire wandering about, Dion had a good excuse for not staying in one place, and so as the acrid fumes tracked her way again, she turned her back to the raiders and loosened the thong on her weapons pouch. The vial, meant for dipping the throwing stars and moons, was in her hand in an instant and then up her sleeve. *A little longer, Gray One,* she sent. *Just give them half an hour after they drink, and the moons will give us a clear path of vengeance.* Gamon, who was facing Dion as she sent the thought, casually looked away.

She served supper as politely as if the raiders were sitting at her father's table at home, though her hands shook when she poured the stew into their bowls. Bolan and Grost seemed to appreciate the irony of being served like gentlemen, though the other, grim-looking man just watched her when she had to come near to fill his plate. The old weapons master must have put the fear of all nine moons into Bolan, because after the raiders ate, Bolan untied Gamon's arms and retied his hands so that the weapons master had to eat awkwardly, spooning the stew past his torn lips. The burly raider sat barely a meter away, and his sword never wavered from the older man's heart.

"You have a name?"

She started, looking up from rinsing the pot. Grost was standing near her, his face pleasant as always, but Dion thought he would look that way even if he were tearing the guts from a mother and child. She gave him her mutinous look again and said nothing, so he dug his heavy fingers into her shoulders on the nerves and twisted her painfully so that she dropped the pot and faced him with a gasp. "When I ask you a question, Healer, answer," the raider said, slapping her again. "It'll save you some grief."

. . . white teeth sinking into a thick arm, tendons tearing and joints ripped apart . . . The instant and possessive rage of the wolf was hard to separate from Dion's own stressed emotions, and the woman knew she could not hold the wolf back much longer.

Wait, Gray one, she begged. *Three against one is certain death. They will just hold me hostage for you, then chain you so you will never run again.*

Grost ground his fingers into her nerves again as she hesitated, and she could not help writhing away from the pain. With her violet eyes flashing murder, she gasped, "Healer Dione."

"Ah." He nodded. "The Healer Dione. And what is your *maiden* name, Healer Dione?" His voice caressed her ear.

"That's none of your business," she started, angry enough to take any blows he would give and double them back to the rast-spawned raider, but she got hold of her temper just in time and let herself flinch back from his raised hand, two hot red spots burning in her pale cheeks. "Ember," she said furiously. Her shoulders throbbed where his iron fingers left bruises on her nerves.

"An odd name." He searched her with his eyes as if looking

for a threat he could not quite put his finger on. "But it adds to the attraction. Serve us the grog, Ember Dione."

The wolfwalker's hands still shook, but the movement covered the small splashes of potion that fell into the heating grog. But when she poured the mugs, Grost silently indicated two more. Dion's heart sank. *He's too clever,* she thought fearfully. *Hishn—get ready.*

. . . *crouching, waiting, hind feet dug into a root to lunge . . .*

Steady—no, wait. It had been a test. The raider picked up his mug when he sat that the woman did not hesitate to take hers or offer the other to Gamon, and she realized that he had watched her taste the stew before he touched his own, too.

"Drink but don't swallow," she whispered without moving her lips as she lifted the mug to Gamon's lips. Her position shielded him from the raiders' eyes as the older man let the grog dribble away down his face and soak his shirt and pants while he made loud gulping sounds. The silent threat of the wolf pounded in what should have been quiet. Then, in the deafening noise of the wolf's breathing, Dion slid a boot knife from her footgear and dropped it in the shadow cast by the older man's hip, not meeting his eyes as his gaze glinted suddenly with the steel of the unexpected blade. *Soon, Hishn. Then we'll both have a fight.* The older man shifted casually to hide the knife and work it back toward his hands. Across the fire, Kerr drained his mug quickly and got up to dip out more. Bolan had already taken several swigs, as well. Grost sipped slowly and seemed to turn his attention to other things, but Dion suspected that he was still watching the two prisoners.

"Drink your grog, Ember Dione," he commanded from the fire, proving her right.

"I don't like swine's ale," she snapped back. Bolan smothered a snigger as he dipped himself another mug from the pot. Would he return to the log he had sat on before? The wolf would be right behind him . . .

"Drink, Healer." Grost's voice was cold, the threat obvious. She took the mug she had poured for herself. *This is it, Gray One,* she sent. She hated grog. Even without the tranquilizer, she would have avoided drinking the bitter brew. *When I yell . . .*

. . . muscles tensed, eyes like slits, prey like sleeping pags . . .

Dion took a swig but wiped her mouth with the back of her hand, spitting the grog back out on her sleeve and letting it run down her arm, hot at first and then cold as the night air turned it to a chilling bath. Even though she spit it out, she could feel the tranquilizer working through the flesh of her mouth and tongue. Would it slow her too much?

. . . hard, black claws flexed, lips snarled back . . . The Gray One's projection was a blast of blood lust that blinded Dion for a moment until she dragged her thoughts back to her own mind and remembered she was human. *Almost, Gray One . . .* she whispered back.

"Healer," Grost's voice was like ice, and she almost bolted. Was there a touch of slurring in his voice? Bolan was relaxing more and more. Gods, couldn't he smell the danger? Kerr had settled against a tree and seemed to be watching the fire. Just five more minutes . . . But Grost got up, stalked over, and stared at the wolfwalker as if she were a rabbit herself, to be spitted and broiled. Dion held her breath as he took another lazy swig of grog but froze as he spit it out to the side.

Now, Hishn! she shouted.

She lunged for the dark brush and came up with a jerk facing the raider's fist as he caught her hair and yanked her around. The rope between her hands snagged her, but then she swayed in sudden shock as he viciously grabbed the gash in her leg instead. She screamed and fell to her knees. A red haze filled her eyes. A snarl reached her deafened ears dimly, and a man's scream choked the night. Where was Kerr? The ground was miles beyond her, and the sounds of mortal agony were thin beyond belief.

Grost's knife slashed, the glint cutting into her instincts so that she flung her hands up and took the blade on her bonds instead of her neck. Snarling, he dragged her down by her hair, yanking her head back so that she arched and fell beneath him. She kicked his knee viciously as she landed, his weight trapping her ankle and panicking her like a worlag on the kill. There was suddenly dirt in her fist, and she threw it at his face.

"Bitch of a lepa—" he snarled rubbing at his eyes as she scrambled back and scooped the hidden knife from her boot. Hishn streaked behind the fire, tearing at the other burly raider, who screamed again and dragged himself toward his sword with one hand while grabbing at the wolf's red-gleaming fangs with the other.

. . . blood . . . hot, sweet blood. Lunge and slash and tear and kill . . . Wolfwalker, I come for you . . . wrist open, blood spurting in the fur . . . hard bones snapping between my teeth . . .

Bolan lunged for his blade and tripped. Dion sliced up at Grost and slashed his arm; the raider cursed and cuffed at empty space. She rolled. He dived. She grabbed a brand from the fire and twisted, thrusting it at the man's face. Grost recoiled and slapped the brand aside, but Gamon kicked the raider in the kidneys as the dirty man forgot his other prisoner. Dion clutched the unexpected instant to loose the flaming branch at Bolan instead, as the other raider finally grabbed his sword and charged her wolf. She staggered up, and then Grost leapt after her, his face evil, his eyes death. She dodged around the fire and grabbed for the grog pot, which was still simmering on the coals, but the raider ducked the stream of scalding liquid. With frantic haste she grabbed the throwing stars in her pouch. She threw three, but he was very good; only one touched his skin deeply. He swore violently again, slapping at them, but they slowed him only a little. She ducked, kicked, punched his throat, and slid away, but even with the sleeping potion affecting him, Grost was a stronger, dirtier fighter than she. . . . *whirl and slash . . . tear . . .* If he hit her even once . . .

Desperately, she dodged another blow, twisting from the raider's grip as the knife sliced empty air. She struck again and again at his gut, his hard muscles like rocks to her fists as she cut the punches in under his own blows and stomped savagely on his foot, driving her knee up into his groin.

. . . bleed and die . . . soft neck in white teeth . . .

He thumped her on the ribs, then grasped her arm, but she panicked and caught his throat with her elbow before throwing him over against a log. Bolan screamed behind her. Grost only grunted as he hit the ground hard. Dion whirled. Gamon—his bonds—she slashed at them in an instant, freeing the older man's feet to run if nothing else. But the old man jammed them instead against the raider as Grost lunged across at Dion, the raider's knife cutting by her desperately twisting side. Grost pulled back the blade to throw its silver death at Dion. Hishn howled. Gamon shouted. The wolf appeared like a mortal shadow on the raider's back, and Dion threw her own knife. It sank into his eye like a hoe into soft mud.

Calm down, Gray One. It's over. Dion knelt by the wolf and gripped the animal's cheeks in her hands, staring into the slitted eyes and shouting into her mind. *No more. Bring it down, now.* She strained to hold the beast in her arms while Gamon knelt quickly by Bolan, who had no time even to beg for his life before the weapons master stooped and made the cut. Blood spurted, and the wolf jerked. Dion, lost in the Gray One's inner rage, did not even notice that the execution was real until the human image of the death throes brought her consciousness to the fore and put horror back on her face.

"Gamon—no . . ."

Gamon stood again and met her blanching gaze steadily. "There's no trial block handy, girl. They won't bother anyone else now."

She struggled against her growing weakness as the dark woods enveloped them and the overcast sky held the light of the moons from their camp. "I could have saved him," she whispered.

"What?" The weapons master looked at her in disbelief. "For what? So they could rape and kill again?" He rolled the body over till it lumped up against the limp form of Kerr. "Think it over, Healer. They weren't worth your time."

"By the moons, Gamon, I swore to save lives, not take them."

"Are you fighter or healer?"

The question stopped her cold. As a healer, she had sworn to protect life, and as a fighter, yes, she had sworn to strive for life, but how could she explain that this was the first time she had killed not a worlag or badgerbear or beast for food or survival but a man, a human being? And worse yet, how could she justify dragging the Gray One into the murder as well—a creature bound to humans, killing humans. What would it do to their bonding? What would it do to themselves? And Hishn trembled under her fingers, longing to roll in the piss of her kill and taste the blood again. Abis? Dion shuddered. All the years of training, the sweat and tears of frustration, the pride with each lesson mastered, the training, the discipline—it was all meaningless now that she was facing the raider's kicking, dying body and taking her own gore-dipped knife from his empty eye. Her stomach roiled.

"I—I've never killed a man before," she said in a low voice.

He shrugged, kicking dirt over the remnants of the raiders' fire.

"You had it to do, Ember Dione. And you did the job well enough."

"Oh, moons, you don't understand," she burst out, her violet eyes tortured with self-loathing. "I'm a healer and a wolf-walker—and I just killed three men. Oh, damn the gods," she choked out, "I should never have left Randonnen." She buried her face in the Gray One's fur.

Gamon was silent a moment, then he began gathering up the raiders' four dnu. He mounted one of the beasts easily in spite of his bruised shoulders and held out another set of reins to the woman. "You played a dangerous game, Wolfwalker," he said quietly. "And if you hadn't, I'd be dead by now, and others as well." She lifted her head and stared at him. "Save the self-pity for someone who thinks you deserve it," he continued. "As for me, I think you're strong enough for anyone to Journey with."

She stared, wide-eyed, searching his eyes for the lie. But he merely nodded at the bodies. "I do understand, Healer. But you can let it tear you apart, or you can deal with it. Like most men," he said, handing her the reins, "I learned to deal with it."

She got to her feet slowly, trying to hide her shudder as Hishn nudged her in the side. "I am not a man, Gamon."

The weapons master chuckled. Her silhouette in the firelight revealed a slender shape that was taut and toned, her legs long and shapely while her grace was like an echo of the wolf's. "That much you'll never be able to hide, Ember Dione." He pulled the other two dnu around to lead them as he rode. "But we live in a world that gives no second chance for those who roam the woods. To survive, sometimes we have to pick blades of steel, not grass."

Dion looked down at her feet, at her sword, and at her bloodstained hands, then set her jaw and mounted the six-legged dnu. She looked back at the carnage only once. Then she spurred the dnu into a trot and sent the wolf loping in front of her like a forethought. "My brother is ahead of us on the trail,'' she said suddenly over the drum of hooves that filled the night.

''I know.''

She sat suddenly still in the saddle. ''You know? How could you?''

Gamon shrugged. ''I was backtracking him. It's how I got into trouble in the first place.''

''So you knew he wasn't my grandfather all along?''

''Or a worlag you picked up along the way,'' he returned with a sudden glint of humor.

''So why were you trailing him?'' The words came out harshly in spite of herself.

''Oh, Ember.'' Gamon turned in the saddle and held out his hand. ''Trust me as I've trusted you. Your brother, or is it twin—you look enough alike to be the same fighter, though it is true that only the shadows could mistake you for a man—surprised us on the trail and decided to join us. We weren't sure that we could trust him, so I trailed him back a few kilometers to see if his story was true. Well, it was, but in the meantime I walked into a raider trap much like you did. Stupid of me, falling for a trick as old as the moons,'' he said ruefully, touching his tender nose. ''One of them pretended to be attacked by the other two, and I went to help. Then all three jumped me.'' He shrugged. ''They weren't prepared for some of my talents, but I'm a little too old for most of their tricks.'' The older man paused and looked at her across the saddle. ''Your brother's fine, Ember Dione. A bit worse for the wear but in better shape than you right now. He can't seem to believe you're dead but still had no hope that you're alive.''

''How far ahead are they?''

''They were in a hurry but couldn't chance missing the raiders' trail at night. I had about an hour of hard riding before I was jumped, and I'd guess it's about midnight now.'' Gamon tilted his head to figure the distance. ''If they leave at first light, they'll be about fifteen kilometers ahead by the time we hit the plains, and they're moving fast, trying to catch up to the slavers that kidnapped my nieces . . . I'd say we'd meet up with them around noon at the river Phye if we keep riding.'' He paused and gave Dion a sideways glance as if to judge what was left of her endurance. ''How long can you stay in the saddle?''

"All night, all day, and to the moons and back if it means I'll see Rhom that much sooner."

The weapons master laughed. "He's a lucky man, Ember Dione. If I were your brother, I think I'd ride to the moons and back for you, too. Would you consider taking me for a mate since I can't be your brother?"

A blush heated her face, but she laughed. "Gamon, you'd be tired of my stubborn ways in a ninan. Be glad that I'll cook your meals and keep my mouth shut till I see my twin."

"If that grog was any indication of your culinary skills," he teased, "I'd rather stay away from your cooking."

IV

Aranur Bentar neDannon:

In Pursuit

When the winds blow down the canyon of the Phye
And the summer waters shrink in the dry,
The birds pick fish from the shallow river rocks
And the river rocks reach to the sky, boys,
The black rocks reach to the sky.

Then the waters rush faster down the canyon of the Phye
And the wild boiling waves leap high.
The river tries to take whoever's passing through
But whoever passes through is a man, boys,
He who makes it through is a man.

It was midday when the four men reined in at the river. The raiders had beaten them to the Phye by hours, and Aranur stood on the banks, his anger growing cold and hard as steel within him: The raiders had had a boat waiting at high tide.

Damn them to the seventh hell, he swore, slapping irritably at a stingfly. An icy fury raged in his gut while he paced the bank like a trapped water cat and tried to figure a way to beat the raiders to the slave markets. They had been outmaneuvered twice, and it rankled; the branch he was holding broke with his hidden tension, the crack of its fiber like the sound of his fists on a raider's bones. Aranur did not need to remind himself that he had debts to pay. There was the boy buried the day they had left Ariye, another one crippled for life, and his own sister—and Tyrel's two sisters—headed for a harem and maybe already marked by those scum. He dropped the shards of wood, slapped the dust off his pants, and stood up. He owed the raiders, and they would pay.

48

"Tyrel, Bentol," he said sharply to his cousin and the trader who were still arguing by the dnu. "Cut it out or I'll cut the tongues out of both of you."

The boy said a last word under his breath that turned the trader's face an ugly red, but at another look from the lean, hard-muscled man whose sword hung so ready in its scabbard, the boy turned back to watch for their uncle.

"Worse than a saddle burr," Aranur muttered, running his hand through his black hair and striding to the shore's edge, where he squatted to study the prints embedded in the mud. He was a tall man, his shoulders broad enough that many mistook his height until they looked up into those cold gray eyes and fingered their swords with unease. His face was too strong to be handsome, but there was a look about it that arrested the eye and made another man look twice and a woman look long—a quality of tensile strength that was built into his bones and sup-ported by the well-used laugh lines that gathered around his eyes. The eyes themselves were quiet but quick, noticing each blade of grass bent down and each sound the bugs made near them and the way the other men stepped carefully around the mud to leave few prints. He was not a patient man, but he was careful. Even when pushed, he was careful. And he was feeling pushed now. He ignored Bentol's stomping as the trader checked the packs, angrily tightening straps and jerking at the dnu's sad-dles. But he was as aware of the merchant's mounting tension as he was of the boy's subtle prods. And as he considered how long a trail they still had to ride, he frowned. His cousin Tyrel was more like Gamon than the boy had any right to be, and Aranur had wished too often that the youth would take more wisdom from his father, the Lloroi, than wisecracks from his Uncle Gamon.

"Aranur." The fourth man caught his attention with a low voice, drawing the leader's sharp glance to the drying mud. As Aranur rose and moved over to the burly stranger, the younger man perched on the well-trod bank like a lepa, his violet eyes scanning the sludge as if his prey would break out of it any instant. "A woman's prints," he said shortly, pointing out the scant sign another would have overlooked.

The man had sharp eyes, Aranur acknowledged as he dropped down beside the young fighter. The prints were nearly obscured by those of the raiders, but they were there: two tracks dug into the mud. Shilia, he identified instantly. Her riding boots had always been distinctive. He nodded with approval. His sister had been struggling when she was dragged into the boat, making sure she dug her marks in deeply for her brother to follow.

The lean man stood up, slipped in the mud as the bank gave way beneath him, and nearly splashed a foot into the Phye before he recovered his balance like a cat. Rhom glanced at the man and remained silent, but he noticed the way Aranur's hand never strayed far from his hilt.

Aranur shook the water off his boot and scraped the slimy mud from the leather. "Moonworms in a lepa's den," he swore under his breath. He climbed farther up on the bank and stomped to test the integrity of the ground while he studied Rhom as closely as the other man studied the tracks.

Ignoring the subtle scrutiny, Rhom absently fingered a cut in his bloodstained leather mail, his dark eyes a haunted grayviolet while he examined the depressions left in the matted grass by the slavers' dnu. Rhom was a stranger, Aranur reminded himself, wondering how far to trust the black-haired fighter. Then too, Rhom's debts were to worlags, not raiders, and Aranur had no right to ask the man to draw his blade for another's revenge. But Rhom was running from something, he knew—the grief perhaps of whatever had happened behind him, for the man showed no fear, only an anguish he tried to hide and a fury that smoldered dark and hot in his heart—but even a fighting rage grown of grief would be welcome when they met the swords of the slavers. Aranur shook his head, considering his motley band. Of the three who rode with him, he trusted the stranger Rhom more than the others. Tyrel was too hotheaded to listen for the silent cut of the steel instead of the taunts a fighter could throw as well. And Bentol . . . Aranur sighed. The trader was good enough with a sword but better with a bow or knife; other than that, he kept his word, but one had to check one's wallet to make sure he did not walk off with it after he backed one in a fight. Aranur's trust was held completely only by his Uncle Gamon, but the old man had not returned from backtracking the stranger, and Aranur wondered if Rhom's trail had held more trouble than the old weapons master could handle.

He glanced across the river and judged the speed of the current. The water rolled fast, carrying the debris from the mountains down to meet the sea and breaking it on the way so that only twigs reached the inhospitable shore. "There'll be fighting in Sidisport if we can't catch the raiders on the river," he said grimly.

Rhom nodded absently. "There's no other boat at this crossing unless it's sunk."

With the rocks humping the water up so far, the Phye looked like a huge, flat serpent writhing through the muddy banks, catching the chill air and tossing it along like the clouds of gnats that bounced above the water. Aranur tightened his jerkin against the cold. The sun was not yet strong enough to break the water's hold on the shadowed banks, so the reeds and brush grew thick and strong, hiding the sticky stalks of catchplants that trapped unwary passers in their open mouths.

He used his foot to edge a stand of reeds aside while he peered upstream through the rising tide of green, but the low growth was undisturbed. No broken or wilting branches marked the passage of more raiders; no telltale strands of dnu hair told him where they had gone.

"Rhom, check the waters downstream. I'm going to circle out from the bank and see if they split up."

The stranger nodded, and Aranur felt another twinge at his conscience. He was used to using people—ordering life and death by the strategy of a battle—but what right did he have to do that with Rhom? The young blacksmith had joined them of his own free will, it was true, but still, the odds were that if he stayed with them to Sidisport, he would not live to see the autumn leaves turn. But neither would Tyrel or any of them, the gray-eyed leader reminded himself harshly. It was not his job to decide the fates—leave that to the moons and thank their light for the blessing of another sword. He would pay for his reckoning after he rescued his sister, not before.

Swatting at a grafbug that landed accidentally on his eyebrow, the lean man ducked under the brush. He held his breath as a clove bush released its sudden cloud of irritating mist—an acidic warning to animals to keep them from eating its tempting, purple-streaked leaves—and, while he waited for the mist to settle, ignoring the sweet scent of the bush, he studied the ground and surrounding growth carefully. After circling the entire bank and separating each dnu by its distinctive tracks, he knew that none of the raiders had split off. "Took to the water like rats," he muttered, spitting at the dark river that sucked noisily at the banks.

"Any sign of Gamon?" he called back to Tyrel. He could just see the top of the boy's head at the rise from where the youth watched the back trail.

Tyrel shook his head and hesitated before he called back softly. "We're being followed, but it can't be Gamon. The dnu are the wrong color, and there's two riders, not just one."

Scraping more mud off his boots, the tall man strode toward the crest and dropped to his stomach as he joined his cousin, parting grasses and squinting across the short expanse of plains to the place where their trail led back into the forest. He frowned. "Where did you see them?"

The boy motioned with his chin, careful to make no overt movement. "I caught a flash of movement about five kilometers back, then another a moment later. Now I can't see anything, but I think they went into the brush down on the banks."

Aranur grunted, squirmed back till he could sit on his heels, and thought a moment. Had he been so careless as to miss being followed? Where could two raiders have split off and circled around? Maybe back at the lava lake, although he should have seen the signs if that were true. Either they were better than he thought, he acknowledged, or these were a new pair riding to join the other party.

"More trouble," he said shortly to Rhom as he eased down the slope and took the reins of his dnu from the stranger.

"Raiders?"

"Looks like it, though there's only two—there should be more unless they're part of the group we're following."

"Out of the Fenn?"

"Maybe." Aranur gestured for the trader to mount up. "Get a move on, Bentol. We haven't time for you to repack every ounce the way you want."

"An easy pack makes an easy ride," the trader retorted, flicking an imaginary spot off one of the stiff leather packs but mounting as he had been directed. "Especially if we're riding hard."

"Well, we may be riding harder than you think. There are two raiders on our trail. Tyrel," he called quietly. "Come on down. You won't see them again if you haven't by now. They're down in the brush and not coming out till they find us."

"Raiders that close?" the trader broke in angrily. "How could you miss them coming?"

Aranur bit back his words. It would not do to irritate the merchant further—the paunchy man had put much of his own money in this, too. So he took a breath and found an overlooked fragment of the patience he had thought was lost. "What's done is done. They're close, and we need to move on before they reach us here. It's obvious we're following the main group of raiders, and they've left a trail so wide that even a bollusk could follow them—it'll be no great trick for the pair behind us to come up on us if we sit here like rabbits."

"If they're that close, they'll know I'm carrying gold." Bentol put his hand on his sword hilt.

"Maybe. We can't help that now." The heavy gait of Bentol's dnu would give away the weight of his saddlebags, but that was the least of Aranur's concerns.

"Look, I'm carrying enough money to chase the slavers all the way to Breinington and back if necessary. Letting a couple of raiders follow us like nightshades is stupidity itself. Even if Gamon were here—"

"But I am here," Aranur returned quietly. "Not Gamon. We pooled our savings with you because you offered—and only the moons know why you did that; your miserly ways are known all over the south coast. But you did offer, and we did accept. The money is ours now, not yours alone. With it, and with or without you, we will get our sisters back."

The trader said nothing, though he glowered at the tall, lean man who faced him in the saddle. Aranur's quiet assurance and calm readiness spoke of more ability even than the worn sword in his scabbard and the two knives that rode so easily in his belt. Even at rest, there was a tension about him—a taut patience, like the long second before a cat leaps or the instant in which a wolf waits to attack. Bentol shivered. There was in Aranur's eyes a flash of gray colder than a shade of death, an anger that merely blanketed the storm of violence he could unleash. And Bentol knew it well. The trader glanced down at his hands and clenched them in a futile fist—Aranur's hidden rage was more than enough to make him hesitate before he spoke again.

Aranur, seeing that the merchant would not go back on his word, nodded shortly. "We'll deal with the raiders when they catch up," he said as he slapped the reins across the dnu's neck. "Let's get going. This is a lousy place to defend."

Glancing back before he led the others through the thick brush, the gray-eyed leader allowed himself a moment of concern. Still no sign of his uncle, but the old man knew the sorts of tricks his nephew would pull on a few raiders and should have little trouble tracking Aranur into the brush. He wheeled the dnu around. "We'll look for a good position along the next half kilometer."

They galloped away from the river, Aranur's eyes searching the land for a good spot to set the raiders up for ambush. "Here." He raised his hand and brought them to a sudden halt in an unexpected hollow. "We'll wait for them to catch up. Rhom, go out on that side; I'll cover this one. We'll move out and flank them before they reach us or split up to surround us. Bentol, Tyrel, we'll be falling back to you as they come in. We want them alive, Rhom," he added as he dismounted and flung the reins at his cousin.

The boy swung down immediately, grabbing the leather straps and leading both dnu into the hollow. Aranur might accuse his young cousin of being too eager for action in the sport fighting ring, but he could not fault the boy's speed now. The lanky youth already had one dnu bedded down in the shadow of a rocktree and was working on pushing the other into as good a position on the other side of the thick bushes. Rhom disappeared almost silently into the brush, the black hair not hidden by his worn warcap in sharp contrast to the yellow grass he stepped through. Aranur looked after him for a moment, then shrugged. He had a feeling the quiet stranger could take care of himself.

Aranur faded into the brush away from the other man, his trail-hardened body shifting so that he blended nearly invisibly into the bushes. He could hear the stamping of the dnu as his cousin made the last beast lie down behind him, then they, too, were quiet. He moved on. The click bugs fell silent, then started up again almost immediately as he passed, so smoothly did he cross the ground.

He was guessing that the raiders would split up a kilometer out. It was a favorite tactic of theirs; also, they would have lost the men's trail in the tracks of the raiders being chased. But if the raiders had left a few men behind to waylay Aranur's group and prevent them from following, were there really only two?

The lone pursuers could have circled west from downriver and left others to wait for the group there. The tall man frowned, skirted a thornbush, and came eye to eye with a stickbeast. The stilted creature stared at the long, lean man for a minute, two of its lanky skeletal limbs holding a beetle to its mouth, then it stalked into a bush and melted into the wood of the growth, camouflaged almost perfectly.

As he climbed above the trail, the crest of a small hillock hid him behind its grasses. There was no tree with thick enough branches to support him, so he wriggled deeper into the earth, making a small depression for his narrow-hipped body as he wedged himself into the rise. The plains rolled on into the forest to his right, and he worried again about Gamon. But what trouble could his uncle run into that he could not handle? The old man had been an Ariye weapons master for twenty years already—he would see through any raider tricks in a hot second, especially since he was already looking for trouble backtracking the stranger Rhom. But there were always worlags, badgerbears, and other things. Aranur shook off his concern with a frown. He had no doubts about his uncle. Gamon was as woods-wise as the best of them, and still better in fighting than most of those. He would be catching up soon.

The ground rumbled slightly with pounding hooves. The vibrations grew stronger, but he waited, not daring to move to shift the pebble that was gouging his hip so sharply. He could hear the smooth drumming of a dnu's six legs hitting the earth: only one rider. The ghost vibrations he had felt must have been the second rider a ways off, closer to the river, over on Rhom's side. The raiders had split up, searching for the trail. He crouched, ready to spring as the man passed. There, he could almost smell the sweat of the running beast. He tensed and—

Leapt out and down. His timing was perfect. He hit the man full force and knocked him right out of the saddle. There was an instant's impression of tangled black hair and violet eyes wide with a sudden fear and fury before they crashed to the ground and Aranur rolled to pin the raider down. He drew his fist back to smash into the man's face, but there was no need. The man was—man?

Oh, moons of mercy, he thought with shock. He was looking into Rhom's face, except that it was that of a woman. The healer's band and warcap had fallen off into the dust, and black, silky hair tumbled out, but it was the high, fine cheekbones and slender body that the battle-stained clothes could not hide. Aranur rolled off and saw where her leg had been gashed open six, maybe seven days earlier. No wonder she had gone down so easily. Moons of light and blessing, he thought, thanking his gods that he had not reopened the long wound on her shapely thigh. I could have killed her.

And it hit him then as he stared at the pale face that was at once familiar and strange. It was Rhom's sister. The man must have thought her dead, he realized, his mind jumping to the two riders Tyrel had seen. She had been following them, and Gamon, too. His thoughts still had a stunned quality. Dnu hooves pounded the ground again: Rhom and Gamon. He gathered the woman into his arms. She was light enough, for all the mail and weapons she wore; he wondered briefly if she could use the things she carried so casually.

There was a crashing of hooves and brush, and he turned to greet the two men. But what burst from the growth was not a dnu or a man. White fangs, yellow eyes, red snarling mouth, and a gray body bigger than the powerful leader himself—the wolf lunged straight at him. Aranur froze for an instant, the woman in his arms and his sword hanging uselessly in its sheath. Then there was a shout, and he dived to the side, dropping her unceremoniously and grabbing his sword, and another dnu burst from the brush, and Gamon charged the wolf as the wolf charged Aranur and they hit. The wolf was flung off its legs and off the path, and Gamon's dnu flipped at the impact. The riding beast screamed, coming down on its side and breaking two of its six legs. The old man went flying. Rhom burst into the clearing. The Gray One twisted in midair and landed with legs thrusting, dirt thrown back from its claws as it slashed back like a spear at Aranur. Rhom yelled. He threw himself between Aranur and the wolf, and the man on the ground leapt forward and shouted for the stranger to get away—Rhom did not even have a blade, but the burly fighter flung himself on the wolf and managed to tumble it without it tearing him to pieces.

"Down!" Rhom shouted, his voice almost a scream. "Gray One! Down! Back!" The beast snarled horribly, teeth gleaming and snapping at his throat, grass flying as their limbs churned. Gamon was scrambling to his feet. Aranur did not dare strike. "Aranur," the younger man yelled. "Get back! Get away from her!'' The wolf almost got free of him again, the fighter grabbing its tail and hind leg and flipping it into the dust again.

Aranur stepped back, then back again. "Let go! I'll knock it out!''

"No!'' Rhom yelled. "Don't hurt her!'' He grunted, ducking his head away from the beast's fangs. "Hishn!'' he shouted again. "Down! Down!'' The wolf seemed to struggle less, snapping at the stranger's circling arms but not tearing his flesh. And then the man was laughing and crying out that name over and over. He let go suddenly and rolled away, and the wolf leapt again, but this time toward the woman. Aranur hesitated, his sword ready to protect her slender form from the wolf—he had never heard of a Gray One attacking humans without reason—but Rhom stopped him with another shout.

"I must have been in the sun too long,'' Aranur muttered in disbelief. The wolf was circling the woman's body, sniffing at her and snarling at the men, but he slowly realized that the circling and snarling were protective, not threatening. Except maybe to them. "Is it, uh, friendly?'' he said warily, still holding his sword.

Rhom got to his knees and shook off the dust and grass and fur from the struggle as Gamon limped to join them. "She runs with my twin,'' he said, carefully edging toward his sister and the wolf. "She won't attack me, but she may not let me near Dion just yet.'' The wolf growled low in its throat, but the younger man just edged nearer, talking softly all the time. "What did you do to her?'' he demanded over his shoulder, still watching the wolf with the caution of a man who was about to put his hand in a downed worlag's jaw.

"I tackled her off the dnu. She went out like a match in a millpond when she hit the ground.'' He paused and looked bleakly at the downed dnu with the broken legs. "Rhom, I had no idea who she was.''

Gamon started laughing. "You should see the look on your face, Aranur. You look like you were sandbagged—like you've never seen a woman before.''

"You should see your own face,'' he retorted. His uncle was sporting a wild assortment of bruises. "And where've you been? You could have warned us you were coming in with a guest. We figured you were lost in the woods.''

The older man guffawed at that.

"With only the ale in your flask to keep you company," Aranur continued sourly, "we didn't think you'd make it through one night, let alone have enough to fortify yourself to find us again."

The two men grasped arms, and Aranur thumped his uncle's back. He did not realize how much of a beating Gamon had been through till the old man grunted and told him to control himself before he sent his uncle to an early grave with his bone-breaking hugs. So he contented himself with admiring the weapons master's black and blue face.

"It's not enough that you send me to single-handedly take care of all the raiders in Fenn Forest." The older man grinned. "You try to break my bones when I return."

Aranur grinned back. "I was worried."

"You should know by now that the moons take care of their own." Gamon gestured at the girl, who was coming around. She opened her eyes, and they went wide for an instant, and then her arms were around Rhom's neck and he just held her. Aranur felt a strange wrench in his heart. My own sister, Shilia . . . He turned back to the dnu at his feet, swallowing against the rush of feeling that almost blinded him.

The dnu was finished. They did not take shocks well, and with two broken legs, that one was as good as gone already. Ignoring Rhom's reunion with his twin, Aranur leaned down and compressed the arteries that ran beside the creature's eyes. In twenty seconds it was dead, its limp body lying like a day-old carcass in the sun, its ribs holding up its sagging hide like weight-strained poles in a too-big tent.

Rhom helped his sister up and turned to Aranur. The grief he had been carrying had dropped from his shoulders like a heavy pack, and Aranur could see the lightness in the younger man's eyes and hear it in his voice as he introduced his twin. "Aranur Bentar neDannon, nephew to Lloroi Volan, who is leader of the Ramaj Ariye. My twin, the healer Ember Dione maMarin," he said with pride.

She winced as she put weight on her leg, and the wolf growled deep in its throat, but the healer smiled. "I'm pleased to meet you," she said. Aranur was still staring. Her black hair was like molten glass in the light of her violet eyes, and the meeting with Rhom had brought color to her pale, gaunt face. The only sign of her status was the blue and silver healer's band circling her brow; she wore fighting clothes over a man's tunic, the leather mail as stained and cut as Rhom's, and her leggings were slit where the gash had split her leg from knee to thigh. He stared again as he realized that she had held the edges of the wound together with largon heads. The clean, stubborn line of her chin and the clear strength in her eyes told him of the nerve it had taken to withstand such treatment. But then Gamon coughed, reminding him of his responsibilities, so he swept his warcap from his head and bowed deeply, saying in a solemn, ceremonious tone, "Healer Dione, you have graced us with your presence."

"If you think you can find your wits, Aranur," the old man said sourly, "we can get going again."

The leader replaced his warcap, winked at Rhom, and returned glibly to his battered uncle. "Well, at least I have no competition in the impression you must have made with your own handsome face." He gestured for the wolfwalker to ride the one dnu left, then led the way back to the others. The Gray One, taking its place beside the woman's six-legged mount, trotted silently behind him, forcing the man to turn his head constantly to reassure himself that the wolf would not attack. It was those damned yellow eyes, he thought. Every time he looked into them, he swore the creature was laughing at him. As if a dog could laugh. And then every time he turned back to the trail, he could almost sense the Gray One's muscles tensing to spring. He shook his head, biting back an unpleasant thought that came to mind.

As they approached the hollow where Tyrel and Bentol were waiting, Aranur grinned slyly. The looks on the two men's faces as he jogged up with a woman healer and a Gray One would be worth seeing. Rhom's sister a wolfwalker—and the man had never said a word. Aranur shook his head again and stole a glance at the huge gray beast that loped alongside the dnu and cast its own baleful looks at him. What he would give for a painter to catch Tyrel's expression . . .

He hailed the hollow before riding over the small ridge, but his cousin was already up and over the top. "Gamon! What—" The boy faltered, seeing the healer. "—happened to you?"

The Gray One halted, poised, licked its teeth in a careless way as if considering how the boy would taste, then turned and circled the clearing. Unobtrusively, the woman watched its moves as carefully as a rabbit regarding the slal bird—the bird that gave warning of danger—Aranur noticed. Her eyes took in the hollow casually, but the tall man would have bet his bow that she had seen and cataloged everything that mattered. She was a lot like Rhom, and he nodded imperceptibly to himself in approval.

In the meantime Gamon slapped dust from his pants and grinned at the sandy-haired youth. "I fell for the oldest trick in the book. Thought someone needed help, and it turned out to be me. Had to be rescued by this moonmaid from the jaws of the second hell." He gestured at Rhom and his twin. "If it hadn't been for the healer Dione, I'd not have returned at all."

"That's not true, you old liar." The woman laughed, her eyes suddenly alive in her wan face. She handed Rhom the reins and slid gracefully off the beast to face the Tyrel and the trader. "You put the fear of all nine moons into the raiders before I did a thing."

Aranur looked from one to the other, then back at the wolf-walker. "What exactly did you do, Healer Dione?"

"Nothing, really," she said. "Outwitted three raiders while bound and helpless," Gamon said at the same time. They looked at each other and started laughing.

"Nothing really," she asserted again. "Hishn did all the real work." The Gray One, trotting back to Dion, grinned toothily and let its tongue curl up against its lip so that Aranur had the feeling the creature would as soon have them for supper as let them ride on. Then the wolf's yellow eyes met the man's straight on, and he felt a disturbing sense of disorientation for an instant, as if he were looking at himself through a distorted glass. "This is Gray Hishn," she introduced formally, and the tall man bowed. As he blinked, his eyes shifted and the tenuous contact was broken, and Aranur could not have explained the strange and unexpected sense of loss that pierced his guard.

"Wolfwalker?" Tyrel asked, eyes wide. Aranur understood his feelings. Generations earlier, the emotional bond that linked wolves and their empathic partners had not been unusual, but the Gray Ones were growing scarce—their litters were smaller, and fewer of them ran in the hills each decade. Only four people in Ramaj Ariye currently ran with with the wolves, and of those four, three stayed deep in the mountains most of the time.

Rhom stroked the huge and well-fanged head, and the creature nudged his hand like a dog. "Gray Hishn has run with my twin for two years now," he explained.

"And she obeys you?" Aranur asked Dion, respectfully inclining his head toward the wolf.

The Gray One's mouth snapped shut, and it glared at him with its yellow eyes sharp and clear. Aranur had the feeling he had said the wrong thing, but Dion shrugged and dug her fingers into the creature's thick fur, tugging at it until the powerful beast relaxed. "She's not a pet, Aranur, she's like another person."

"She obeys Dion because she wants to," Rhom explained further. "She doesn't really have a bond with me except through my twin, so it's hard for me to pick up what she means, but for Dion, she'll do almost anything."

"And you can actually talk to her?"

The yellow eyes narrowed again, but the woman continued scratching, and the wolf leaned its head against her side and forced her to take a wider stance to keep her balance. "If you're a sensitive, you can pick up their impressions. You have to get used to it, though. Wolves see things differently than we do." She scratched the Gray One's ears when the animal nudged her hand with a wet nose. "When you talk to them, you pick up what they see and smell and hear, too, and it makes the images confusing."

"I noticed," the tall man murmured, and the woman gave him a sharp look.

"If you can pick up what she sends, she can pick up your thoughts also," she warned with a smile that almost hid her blush. It did not occur to Aranur until later that if the wolf could sense what he was thinking, then so, through her, could Dion.

Clearing his throat, Bentol presented himself before Rhom and his sister, and the blacksmith obligingly turned to him. "Trade Master Bentol, and Tyrel Tyronnen ne Volan, son to Lloroi Volan and nephew to Gamon, weapons master. My twin, the healer Ember Dione maMarin."

She smiled. "You can call me Dion if you prefer."

"Dion seems a manly name for so lovely a lady," Bentol remarked as he took her hand.

"It's habit," she explained, blushing more deeply. "When I trained with the men, they were uncomfortable calling me Lady this and Healer that, so when they found out that Rhom always called me Dion, they did, too. And then, when I was chosen to

Journey with my brother, we thought it'd be better for me to dress as a man to avoid trouble.''

Aranur could understand. On Rhom, the coloring was handsome. On Dion, the black hair and violet eyes made her a harem prize worth fighting for. If a slave owner in Sidisport saw Dion and guessed that she was a woman, she would have a hard time staying out of chains. But one of Rhom's words caught his attention, and Aranur frowned. "Journey?"

Rhom nodded. "We were Journeying together, but—" His voice broke off, and his jaw tightened before he could speak again. His twin touched his arm, and he finished. "Worlags."

Aranur felt some shock at his statement. How could Rhom let a woman—especially his sister—go with him on Journey? Women had Internships—they did not have the training, the skills, or the stamina to go on Journey. What if they got hurt? And Dion had gotten hurt, he reminded himself, looking at the burly stranger with a frown. Maybe he had misjudged the man— taking a woman on Journey was not a light decision, although he had to admit she looked tough enough. Then again, Randonnen was a different county with different customs, and it was not supposed to be half as war-torn as Celilo or Bilocctar.

"But how can you Journey together?" Tyrel asked bluntly, echoing Aranur's thoughts with little tact. "Dion's a woman."

The healer's eyes flashed, but she held her tongue, letting Rhom speak with less heat than she might have.

"Dion's no fool," her twin said quietly. "And she's trained as I am. She knows weapons and Abis, she's a wolfwalker and full-status healer, and she has, well, almost as much skill in the woods as I." He ducked the look she threw him at that comment but could not avoid a shove from the wolf that staggered him. The man grinned and shared a silent joke with his sister, and Aranur felt suddenly jealous.

But Gamon nodded, too, surprising the gray-eyed leader. "She knows what she's doing, Aranur."

"We're in a hurry," Aranur said flatly, thinking of the time already lost.

Rhom did not hesitate. "We Journey together. If we're a burden . . ."

"Think about it, Aranur," Gamon suggested smoothly. "It would be lucky to have a wolfwalker and healer along, especially one that can fight."

Aranur hesitated. He told himself that having a woman along would slow them down, but then he looked again at the way she had stitched herself together with largon heads. She was one tough woman. He opened his mouth, then heard himself offering the formal greeting as he had to Rhom. "You are welcome in our midst. You are welcome as a—a sister," he amended. "Ride and eat and fight with us, and your children will be as my own."

The wolfwalker met his look with her own steady gaze. Her hand dropped to the wolf's shoulders as she said, "We join you, and take your burdens as our own."

Gamon turned to the trader. "Bentol, I started to bring you two more dnu for pack beasts, but they heard how you put half a ton on a lepa once and told it to fly. They decided to go lame and avoid the whole situation." The trader turned slightly red as the others chuckled. "However, I did bring you some presents in the saddlebags, and we all know how willing I'd be to pack them for you, but . . ."

"The way you pack—" the merchant started angrily.

"I know, I know. Only a master trader such as you, honorable Bentol, can remedy the mess I'd make of the packs. So," the silver-haired fighter said, flourishing his warcap in the air, "I give you my leave to undo what I'd cheerfully have done."

The pudgy man snorted and stomped to the new packs Tyrel had set on the ground.

Dion, still pale, stood with Rhom's arm around her as if that were the only thing in the world that mattered. She had a haunting grace, Aranur noticed as she moved, though he kept his glances infrequent—he could not tell which would be the more possessive adversary: Rhom or the wolf. But as she slung her worn bow over her shoulder and settled her well-used sword in its scabbard, he reconsidered her weakness. She may look frail, he thought, but that's a lady that can ride the mountain trail. Maybe. They were not riding to a county fair, he reminded himself, and they did not have time to coddle a wounded woman. Mounted, the raiders had stayed just ahead of the group during the chase. They had traveled by day, as did the men from Ariye, neither daring even in their haste to risk stirring up a tribe of worlags.

"We can't all ride," Bentol said as he readjusted the packs, reminding them that they were one dnu short. "If two of us run, we can use one dnu as a pack beast and make better speed."

"I'll run," Rhom volunteered instantly.

"And I," Tyrel said.

"We'll trade off. Tyrel will ride first," Aranur decided. "Gamon also." Dion would not be running for a while yet. Her color was still pale, the fatigue obvious in her drawn face, and Aranur still felt guilt that he had hit her so hard. He could almost sense the pain he had renewed in her wounds as the yellow eyes of the wolf followed him around the camp. He wondered if it was his imagination, but between the unnerving stare of the wolf and the striking beauty of the woman, he found his thoughts scattered and his tongue tied like a shoe. His initial enthusiasm at Dion's arrival had quickly dimmed.

Luckily, the trader cleared his throat and brought his mind back into focus on their problems. "I've been thinking," the pudgy man said slowly.

"And a novel thing that is for you to do," Gamon cut in with a sly grin.

"Gamon!" Aranur broke in. His uncle had a way of irritating the stodgy trader till they were almost fighting among themselves. Bentol's face was already dark with suppressed anger. "Do you have an idea, Bentol?"

Gamon opened his mouth for another comment, but Dion leaned toward him quickly as if to ask a question and took his attention away from the trader. Aranur was grateful for the respite.

The trader snorted and gestured at the sun. "It's obvious that we won't be able to catch the raiders now. But it might be better that we let them reach Sidisport ahead of us." He held up his hand against Tyrel's automatic protest. "Right now our problem is not quantity of money to buy the girls but quantity of swords to keep them once we get them back. Instead of trying to take on the whole shipload of raiders, we have the option of simply presenting ourselves as foreign traders in the slaver square. As traders who've heard of the luxuries of Sidisport, this would give us a good opportunity to find some pretty slaves for our master's pleasures." He grinned slyly.

Tyrel tensed for a minute at the unexpected accusation of his father, then relaxed, catching on to the game. "Bentol, you're a genius. We walk in, buy our sisters in public like we were strangers, and take off again like the wind."

Bentol beamed. "You're going to make a fine Lloroi someday, my lad. A light disguise for a crowded public place, a handful of gold that no one in their right mind questions, and no one will be the wiser that we've come and gone. And if we're looking for a few slaves of our own, where better to look than the world-renowned markets of Sidisport?''

"Sure, but when we get the girls to a safe place, we go back for blood," the youth said darkly, mounting his dnu for the next leg of the chase. He flexed his shoulders and hefted his sword as if testing its weight. "I have a score to settle with them."

"Brains, not just brawn, make a good Lloroi," Bentol said sharply. "One man doesn't take on a shipload of slavers for revenge unless he's making of himself an offering to the moons."

Tyrel set his jaw but said nothing.

"Gamon." Aranur caught his uncle's attention with a low voice and indicated Dion with his chin. "Is she strong enough to keep up with us? We're several hours behind already, and we'll be losing ground with every step."

"I explained the situation to her. She's a strong woman, Aranur. She'll keep up, if only to stay with her brother."

Aranur nodded, reassured. He and Rhom ran first, the dnu stringing out behind them where the yellowing plains stretched long and grassy beside the river. Spring flooding kept the trees from attaining deep footholds along the banks, and the thick brush tore at their clothes even after the dnu pushed ahead. Wiping the dust from his face where it made an irritating mud with his sweat, Aranur spit and settled into the dull breathing rhythms of running. Breathe, thud, thud, thud, breathe, thud, thud, thud. The sounds of his feet hitting the earth kept time with his hungry lungs, and the sky blued, then paled into noon as his concentration narrowed to the ground around him.

Sweat soaked Aranur's collar, chafing at his neck. As his legs pounded the hardening dirt, his shadow stretched and shrank with each step so that the beads that glistened on his shoulders flung themselves away to spatter first in dark, then in light soil. The salt of the perspiration was beginning to rub him raw. With that irritation on top of the heat of the day, the narrow-hipped man stripped to his undertunic, leaving his muscular arms bare and sweating in the sun. He caught Dion stealing a glance. She blushed and turned her head, but Aranur smiled smugly to himself before catching a sharp glance from the woman's watchful brother.

Tyrel and Bentol ran then, the pudgy trader setting a good pace for all the excess weight he wore at his middle, and Rhom and Aranur settled back into the rhythm of riding. Even with the river current helping the slavers, the men of Ariye might be able to reach Sidisport soon after the slavers hit the city. The fleeing boat would have to stop each night or risk going aground on the sand and mud bars that all but plugged the river in spots. For the group that rode, unmindful of the passage of time except that it moved too fast for the distance they traveled, the sky turned slowly whitish-blue, the bloodless sun rising higher and brighter until it cleared the washed-out sky of color. Then Rhom and Aranur took their turn again, stripping down to their shorts for comfort in the hot afternoon. The soft pounding of their feet made a smooth rhythm as they led the dnu in an easy canter, and packs creaked and swayed slightly with their beasts' motions while soft but firm commands held the dnu to the trail. The afternoon drew on.

They did not travel quietly, accepting the pounding feet as the price of speed, and the wildlife was vocal. Snowy white birds coiled their long snaky undernecks into springs to strike at their prey in the river's shallows. They screamed as the humans passed, and small brown- and yellow-haired beasts flattened to the ground when the pounding mounts cut them off from their burrows. A water cat growled and twitched his tail when they spoiled his dinner with their noise.

By evening Aranur's legs had gotten used to riding again as Bentol and Tyrel again took their turn running. They had stopped twice for water and a brief rest, then continued. They would go till it was too dark for even Bentol, who had traveled this path many times, to lead.

Tyrel rode ahead after a while, finding a good place to take a short break, and so they settled in the small depression and checked the packs. Dion was looking much better for having ridden all day.

"Want to stretch your legs, Ember Dione?" Gamon turned to the healer, who was tightening the laces on her boots and checking her belt pouches to make sure the knots were holding well.

The Gray One's eyes flickered. Dion, scratching vigorously on the stomach of the wolf with her free hand, laughed. "Hishn says if I run, can she ride?"

"That mutt?" the older man snorted. "Hells, I'd give two silvers just to see her try."

Dion chuckled and tugged on the wolf's ears. "Hear that? He says he'll pay for your dinner if you get up on the dnu."

Aranur watched with interest as the massive beast got leisurely to its feet and stretched, rolling its tongue around its teeth. Its yellow eyes met his for the briefest instant. "Damn," he whispered, unnerved by the gray wisp of thought that touched his brain, "but I think she'll do it just for the dare."

Dion shot him a sharp look as Hishn trotted calmly over to the dnu. "Gamon," she said over her shoulder, "Hishn says to make it a brace of pelan and you're on."

"Sure, and I'll make it three birds to be fair." The older man turned to Aranur with a sly grin. "That dnu knows me," he said in a low voice. "It won't let that gray mutt near it."

"You may want to reconsider," the tall man returned softly with a glance toward the wolf.

"You ever see what a wolf that size does to a dnu? That bat-eared dog won't be able to sniff its hindquarters, let alone get up in the saddle."

Aranur just shook his head. The Gray One paused in front of the dnu, the riding beast's eyes wild and rolling; the wolf's yellow eyes were like slits of new fire, and then something happened. The dnu stamped its feet once and snorted. As if it were greeting one of its own kind, it lowered its head to that of the gray wolf, who stretched her nose to the other creature. Hishn raised up on her legs like a man and set her massive paws on either side of the riding beast's face, and Aranur reeled. Moon-worms, but the intensity of the wolf's command was like a fist in his stomach. He shook his head. As his eyes cleared of the close-faced view of the dnu that suddenly sprang to mind, the wolf calmly trotted to the side of the beast and leapt into the saddle, perching precariously on the smooth leather as the six-legged creature took an uncertain step and then stood still.

Rhom chuckled behind him, and Tyrel breathed. "I don't believe it."

Aranur, looking at the wolf in wonder, started to laugh. "Looks like you've got a brace of pelan to bring down, Uncle." He gestured at the Gray One, who regarded them from her now-calm yellow eyes. "And you'd better do it quickly, or the Gray One might ride you instead of the dnu."

Gamon, after one incredulous look, glowered at the wolf and shook his fist. "Get down off that dnu, you long-eared mutt." He swore under his breath as Dion gestured imperceptibly and the Gray One leapt down as easily as she had gone up. "Probably left gouges in the saddle," he muttered. He yanked his quiver over his shoulder and checked the sights on his bow.

"Uh, Gamon," Tyrel broke in nervously.

"What," the old man snapped grumpily. "It'll take me half an hour to get those birds. I'll catch up to you later."

"Gamon—"

"What is it, boy?" The old man turned and found himself facing the wolf as it had faced the dnu a moment earlier. Dion was hiding a smile behind her hand, but her eyes sparkled with mirth she could not conceal. Hishn, turning her yellow eyes on Gamon, froze the man in his glare, raised up halfway on her hind legs, and, opening her mouth so that the old man had as good a look at her fangs as he could ever want, panted twice and then licked the weathered face with a wolfish grin.

"Aagh!" Gamon stumbled back and slapped at his face. "It licked me. The gods-damned dog licked me. Blech!" He wiped the slobber off his nose and swore. "Dion," he roared, "get that moonwormed mutt out of my face." He staggered back as the wolf leaned up again and licked his chin under his hands. "Dion!"

But Dion was laughing so hard that she started to cry. "Hishn . . ." she gasped between giggles. "Hishn says since you've taken your . . . licking so well, you don't have to hunt her dinner."

The old weapons master choked and spit to clear his mouth of the taste. "Dog breath," he muttered. "I'm paying for a bet with dog breath."

Bentol, holding his belly as if it could somehow contain his laughter, opened his mouth to say something, but the old man spun on his heel and glared at him so violently that the pudgy man closed his mouth with a snap and almost choked on his own glee.

"All right," Gamon snapped. "We've had our fun. Let's get going."

Dion tossed her pack to her brother, who lashed it behind the saddle on his dnu. "Still want to race, Gamon? Or do you have the breath for it?" she teased.

He swore, glared at her, opened his mouth, shut it again, and finally gave in to his own humor. "Okay, Healer." He chuckled. "You're on. You won't be able to keep up with an old warmonger like me, but you can try."

"You'd be surprised." She smiled with a sideways glance at the wolf.

"I'd rather not," he returned.

Dion laughed. She left her tunic on but wore shorts and moccasins to run in, and Aranur's eyes followed her legs as she flashed in the sun ahead of him. Tyrel looked, too, until they caught the warning look from her brother. Rhom gave the two a hard stare.

Aranur cleared his throat and offered, "She paces Gamon well."

"She's my sister," Rhom said flatly.

The air was cooler, and the dnu was more placid after running all day; long shadows cast crests of light across the water and trail. "Bentol," Aranur called across to the trader, "you've been this way before. Have you ever tried to ride the river through the canyon? If we took to the water instead of riding around it on the portage route, we could gain back almost all the time we've already lost."

Bentol shook his head at the suggestion. "Only fools ride those rapids, Aranur. The rocks reach to the sky, and the water throws up the boats so they splinter like glass when they come back down on the stones."

"But there are people who know the route—the Clan Celilo. They run the rapids for fun in slivers of boats, then port back up. I've heard that they sing in the canyon at sunset, too."

"Yes, but they're crazies who treat the Phye like a child's game. The stories don't explain why they sing to the canyon, do they? Well, I'll tell you. They sing the Moonsongs to guide the spirits of the dead down the river, out of the rapids." The trader shivered. "They lose people every season. They believe that the Phye's waters try to hold the dead under so that the spirits will call others to them. The dead want the living to show them the way out of the white water and up to the moons. So they call that stretch of the river the Spirit Walk."

"Do they take passengers?" Tyrel asked, listening in from the right.

"If you pay for your death song beforehand," the merchant said shortly.

It was a sobering thought, but Aranur said slowly, "I think I'd like to see the route."

"There's no reason to go out of our way, Aranur," the other man insisted. "You can bet that the slavers ported around that stretch of water. This is late spring; the river is still wild with the mountain runoff. I know you've run some white water in your hills, but this stretch of the Phye is death to any who haven't got all nine moons riding their wings. And so far, I don't think we've been so blessed."

Tyrel's eyes flashed at the dour talk. "My life is worth nothing if I let my sisters die in shame in a slaver's harem"—he spit the word—"just because I was too cowardly to take the chance to catch up to them by river. What is a quick death by water to me when my sisters will die slowly each day they are owned and"— his face tightened—"tortured by a stranger!"

"Tyrel, Bentol, you're both right," Rhom said. "But I have to say that if it was my sister," he continued, gesturing toward Gamon and the woman running in the trail ahead of them, "in the hands of the slavers, I'd shoot the rapids in a tin cup if it meant saving her from that kind of shame."

Bentol turned away sharply, his sour movement indicating that he would not argue with Aranur's decision further. When they stopped next to water the dnu and switch runners, the dark-haired leader brought it up to Gamon and Dion. "There's a chance that we could cut half a day from our ride," he mentioned, watching the woman's face closely. "It's dangerous, though."

"The Spirit Walk?" Gamon looked up sharply.

Aranur nodded. "We could leave the dnu at Celilo and hire guides to take us through. We'd gain enough time over the raiders to make it to Sidisport almost as soon they do."

Dion frowned. "Why is it so dangerous?"

"Because the river is wild at that point. You see how wide it is here, almost a kilometer, with silt and mud bars. You could walk across it in half a dozen places except for the sand suckers. In about five kilometers, where these hills rise into mesas, the Phye channels into a narrow canyon. All this water runs through a space no wider than the length of a barn, and it runs fast."

"We run rapids in our mountains," she said slowly. "And

Rhom is very good with a kayak. We can both swim, too. If the river is the way to go, we wouldn't slow you down."

"Swimming is not a consideration when all the water in the world is thundering about your head," Aranur warned, though he was relieved that she was not afraid of going through. He turned to Gamon, pretty sure he knew the older man's answer. His uncle was always game for a little more action. "What do you think, Uncle? Could your ancient body stand a few more aches and pains?"

"This ancient body has been swallowing white water since before you were born, boy. Hand me a paddle and a rope to tie myself in, and I'm off."

"Why do they call it a Spirit Walk if it's so dangerous?" Dion asked as they walked back to the group.

"Because the spirits of the dead walk that stretch of the river looking for the way to the sky," the old man answered with a grim smile. "When you run those rapids, you walk with the dead."

"Bentol says it takes over an hour to go through," Aranur said, "so we'll have to hurry if we want to get guides and try it tonight." He gestured to the trader, who had a strange expression of fear on his face.

"Bentol," Dion said suddenly. "You've run this river before."

The merchant started. "Yes, I have," he admitted slowly. "And I'd not be more terrified of it if I were to ride death itself down the run."

"Well, at least we know it can be done," Gamon said. "How long before we reach Celilo?"

"That 'we' won't be including me," the trader said flatly. "I'll meet you at Portage or beyond, whenever I catch up."

"Bentol," Aranur said sternly. "You've been this way before. You know you can ride this river, so why worry so about trying it again?" He had never before seen the man so upset about something that had nothing to do with his trade. "We'll tie the gear in tight so there'll be no chance of losing any of it."

"It's not the trade goods," Bentol snapped.

"Ah, then it's the gold," Gamon said with a wink at the wolfwalker. They all knew the trader's miserly ways.

"It's not the gold," he snarled, "so leave it alone, Gamon."

Aranur looked at the pudgy man sharply. He had also never

heard the merchant admit that there was something more important than his money. The trader did not even have a woman that Aranur knew of. They had always teased him that it was because he did not want to share with anyone, even a mate. The tall, gray-eyed leader shook his head. "Get a grip on yourself, man. If it's not the goods or the gold, where's the problem?"

"Yeah," Gamon drawled, though his eyes were sharp in his weather-beaten face. "What is your problem, Bentol?"

"Gods dammit, leave me alone, Gamon!"

"Bentol," Aranur said sharply. "I'll need a hell of a good reason to split up the chase at this point, so you might as well tell us or take off and don't come back."

The trader stared at him, his eyes wide with barely controlled panic. "Damn you, Aranur, you wouldn't understand."

"Try me."

The red-faced man shouted suddenly, "I told you, you wouldn't understand. Just shut up about it, will you."

"The reason for the problem, Bentol," the leader said quietly, moving his dnu to trap the trader between himself and the old weapons master.

Bentol looked from one to the other in a rising rage. "You want to know what the problem is, you dnu-dropped bastards. All right, I'll tell you what the problem is." He spit, furious at having to admit his fear in front of everyone, especially the violet-eyed woman who sat quietly to the side. "My life is the problem," he said harshly. "I'm afraid, damn you. I'm friggin' scared out of my pants. I'd rather die in Zentsis's torture chambers than ride that river through the canyons and lose my soul, you moon-damned bastards." He turned away and clenched his hands on the saddle.

Gamon stared, coughed, choked, and started laughing while the trader's face blackened with enraged humiliation. The chubby man looked as if he were going to draw his sword and strike the old weapons master down in the saddle. "Bentol!" Aranur commanded sharply. Rhom moved quickly between the two men, and Aranur grabbed the trader's sword arm, forcing it down.

The old weapons master held up his hand to forestall the man's fury. "Bentol," he broke in, still chuckling, "you've fought raiders and worlags and thieves to get at a piece of worthless stone or protect a cold nugget of gold. You've risked your life against a nest of lepas to rescue your trade goods without thinking of the odds against coming out alive. And now you're off chasing a shipload of slavers just for the chance to get a better deal off the Lloroi next time you've got him in a bargain, and what do you confess you're afraid of? A little bit of water." Gamon guffawed. "A bitty little river that you've been around all your life. You've even ridden through its puny waves already, and you try to sit here and tell us that you're afraid of doing it again." He pointed his finger at the trader. "You're a fraud, Bentol. You've probably bested the entire village in trading and are afraid to go back just in case they're out to get you now."

"Gamon," the pudgy trader choked out, "if you weren't a weapons master—"

"Bentol," Aranur interrupted, "Gamon makes sense. You've done things, risked your life for cold rocks and poorly spun silk. Honestly, Bentol, what's a piece of stone worth compared to your life? This is important, Bentol. We're not talking rocks and cloth. We're talking about our sisters' lives. How, when this is so important, can you let your fear turn you around and chase you away? How could your fear matter more than Shilia's life?"

The trader looked down, clenching his hands.

Dion cleared her throat, and they all looked at her. "I think that Bentol feels this way *because* what he's doing does matter now," she said softly.

Bentol shot her an angry, miserable look.

"Men—people," she amended carefully, "do risky things when they don't care what happens to them." She looked at the trader, and he had to nod, admitting that she had spoken the truth. Aranur was silent, puzzled by her intuition and Bentol's acknowledgment. What had he missed about the man? And what secret did the trader share with her? he asked himself with a twinge of jealousy, but she went on. "Sometimes—" She hesitated. "—when things are important, when you do start to care—or when you have something to live for—it hits you then that the danger is real. And that you may not finish the job before the moons reach out to take you."

Aranur looked at the healer and then at Bentol. Were the Lloroi's daughters so important to the trader? Or his sister? Or was it something else? Bentol had never approached any of them—Shilia, Namina, or Ainna—in courting that Aranur could recall, no matter how hard he thought about it. Moonworms, the trader was more than twice the girls' ages. "Bentol," he said finally. "If you want to meet us below this stretch of the Phye, I understand. We can't wait for you, but you know where we're heading. On the north side of Sidisport, there's an inn—"

"I—" The man cleared his throat. "I'll ride with you."

Aranur looked at him and nodded curtly without belittling the trader's offer, but Gamon saluted him. "Good man," he said.

The trader ignored him and looked at the healer instead. He opened his mouth as if to say something, then closed it and turned away.

Aranur stared after him for a moment, baffled. "The trail forks just up ahead," he told the others finally. "Celilo village is another three kilometers beyond that. We'll see the edge houses first because they're up on pilings—the spring flooding gets pretty bad around here. The rest of the village is at the point where the river dives into the canyon." He paused. They had traveled about forty-five kilometers since Gamon and Dion had joined them, and they were all tired, but he cautioned them. "With raiders about, I don't know what kind of welcome we'll get. Be ready."

They warily approached the cleft in the rising rocks that marked the boundaries of Celilo and, at Aranur's signal, halted. The gray wolf melted into the thick brush. Behind them the path sloped gently back to the flatlands where long grasses faded into a lake of yellow-green growth. To one side the river Phye eased away from the mud banks and urged its current to greater speed; here the snags were treacherous in the run, their legacy of long, churning whitecaps a V of danger to any boat caught in their boil. The water was clear enough to see the boulders that stumped the river—spring rains had not fallen in days, and the fish that clung to the tiny holes of rare calm were well fed off the insects that hovered over the runs. Aranur glanced at the narrow pass the road led through but hesitated. The Gray One had gone down the banks, he knew—he could almost sense the conversation it had had with the wolfwalker—and in minutes it would be up on the other side of the rocks. If there were any men waiting for them, he would know as soon as the wolf sent the images. He frowned, wondering why he could almost see the slip of gray that touched his mind. It was like a soft hand brushing his face—a feather touch that was never quite real.

They waited. There was no movement yet from the pass, but

his instincts had never let him down before, and he let his quick eyes roam the rocks again. To the left, great boulders were strewn as they had fallen from the cliff. Behind them, where the wall of rock actually began, the granite was smooth and rounded, broken only by great cracks that edged along the gray stone and created holes where the birds nested messily. The gray wisp in his mind became a needle, and Dion stiffened beside him. Aranur's senses sharpened instantly. At his gesture, the group spread out on the wide trail, Dion dropping back and Rhom taking her place. Ahead of them, where the pass beckoned, three men stepped out of the late shadows with bows drawn and arrows notched. Aranur did not move.

"What do you want on this path?" Behind the three, five others stepped, and Aranur knew that there were others on the cliff where he could not see them.

His cool gray eyes took in their arms at a glance, noting how one of the men in the first group was as silent and dangerous as a sand sucker hiding in a calm pool. If it came to trouble, that one would have to die first. "We wish to see the Spirit Walk," he said quietly.

Two of the men murmured, but he could not hear what was said. "Raiders rode this path last night," the middle one stated. "Perhaps you ride to join them." His glance, when it rested on Aranur again after cataloging their stained mail and weapons, was cold.

"They have our sisters. We ride to get them back."

"Slavers have many guises."

"But none of honor."

The man in the middle regarded him steadily. "You are from Ariye?"

Aranur nodded.

"You are a weapons master?"

Aranur smiled slowly, though his eyes remained cold. "I am what I have to be."

One of the men in the back said something in a low voice, and the middle one nodded imperceptibly, but the arrows did not shift. Aranur's eyes narrowed. The men of Celilo were not known for their hospitality. And if they knew the group was carrying gold? Even honest men could step left when money was involved—moonworms, but a lot of men were honest simply because they had not yet been tested. Behind them a low growl sounded, and the men in the back whirled.

"No!" Dion cried out.

But the arrows were frozen as the Celilo fighters realized they were facing a wolf. The man in the center listened to the startled comments behind him without taking his eyes from Aranur. "Does the Gray One honor one of you, or have you bound it some other way?"

"Wolves do not run with raiders. The Gray One honors us."

"Perhaps. Perhaps it warns us of you." The stocky man paused. "You." He gestured at Dion. "You spoke for it. Go to it. Let us see if it knows you."

Dion shifted, but Gamon whispered to her out of the corner of his mouth, and she remained still. "The healer will remain here," Aranur said flatly. "Let the Gray One come to us. That'll prove what you want to know." His hand rested easily on the hilt of his sword, something none of them could fail to miss.

"You are the wolfwalker?"

"Does it matter? Let the Gray One pass."

"No. If it's raider spawn, it'll kill all in its path. We are not patient men. Prove your honor or die now."

Dion opened her mouth, but Gamon held her back. Aranur, looking down at the score of arrows that would skewer him and his band, smiled suddenly. One of the strangers shifted uneasily: The lean-hipped, broad-shouldered man before him was too confident. What if the Gray One was with him in honor, as he said? What if there were others? The blessing of the wolves was not a thing to trifle with, and two of the men in the back scowled as they looked at the Gray One's fangs. Hishn let her tongue lick her long teeth and then began a long, low snarl that hit each man's sternum like a deep drum vibration. Aranur looped the reins of his dnu around one of the saddle horns. "There's no need for violence," he said quietly. "Nor for a hostage." He dropped silently to the ground. "But I will honor your doubt as the Gray One has honored me."

The man in the center stepped to the side as Aranur strode between him and the others, but notched arrows led his steps on finger's edge. Aranur hoped the archers were not nervous.

"Gray Hishn," he said in a low voice, though loud enough for the Celilo men to hear, "we thank you for the warning." The wolf looked at him out of her yellow eyes, rimmed now with a faint line of black, and tilted her head until she could look directly at him and keep the archers in sight, as well. He had a momentary feeling that the wolf was tempted to growl at him, then it passed, and the Gray One nudged his hand instead.

The tension snapped. The Celilo fighters grinned suddenly and relaxed their bows. "You really are a wolfwalker," the stocky man in the center said. "Never let it be said that Celilo turned the Gray Ones away, nor any man with honor. Welcome." He stepped forward and gripped arms with the dusty man who stood on the path. "I'm Tramis."

"I am Aranur."

"Aranur of Ariye? I've heard of you, but not that you're a wolfwalker."

"It's not me who runs with the Gray Ones, but our healer."

Tramis whistled. "Luck rides your blade like a lepa on the hunt that you have a wolfwalker and healer in one."

"Luck will have to ride our swords," Aranur returned, suddenly grim. "What I said before was true. The raiders have our sisters, and if we don't catch them before they reach Sidisport, we will lose them to the harems."

By that time the others had filed through the narrow pass, greeting the Celilo men and following Tramis and Aranur as the stocky man swung up on his own mount and led the way. "But if you're man enough to ride the river, the Spirit Walk will take you there in half the time that the Portage route docs. How many of you wish to make the run?"

"We leave none behind. We'll need all our swords at the coast."

Tramis cast a sharp glance at him. "You have a woman there, an older man, and a boy whose temper even from here I can see. The Spirit Walk is no run for the uninitiated, weak, or careless."

"I will vouch for each of them," Aranur returned. "But you shouldn't worry. The woman is Healer Dione, the wolfwalker, and she's tougher than a wounded worlag. That 'old man' is Gamon Aikekkraya neBentar, and he has been a weapons master for over twenty years. He's also one who runs the mountain rivers for fun. And the boy, though he has a temper, is the son of a Lloroi. Whatever else he is, he is not careless."

The Celilo leader nodded doubtfully. "We'll see. I'll show you the Spirit Walk tonight, during the singing—we lost a man yesterday, and his death song is being offered tonight. You can make the final decision then.''

''You've not mentioned the cost of the run.''

''I've not,'' the other man agreed with a sly grin. ''But I see you have a trader in your group, and he'll be sure to try getting the better of any bargain I'd mention now. One thing, though,'' and the man gestured with his chin back at the wolf, who was loping alongside Dion's dnu. ''The Gray One will not sit a kayak. They don't, you know. Don't trust the water, and with reason.''

Aranur nodded. ''I'll tell the healer to send her overland tonight.''

When they reached the village, Bentol made the arrangements to take the group through, talking with gold as much as he did with his mouth. In the end he traded the five dnu and ten pieces of gold to pay for the group's death songs, their gear, and the two guides, but they could not get any of the guides to run the river till the next day. ''The river is stronger at night, and the shadows misleading,'' Bentol reported after trying to persuade the guides to lead them through that night. ''But we're to stay with Elunint and Tramis's families.'' He paused and gave Aranur a grim look. ''By the way, that death song they're singing tonight—it'll give you a good idea of what your path to the moons will be tomorrow.''

They left their dnu with Elunint, a tall, wiry man with a shock of white hair over his forehead. Tramis led the group to his house, and they settled down with weariness to go over the plans and pack for the morning.

The kayaks would each hold two people and two packs. Tramis and Bentol would make up one kayak. Since the rest of the group had about the same river experience, Tyrel and Aranur would make up another kayak, with Gamon and Rhom together. Elunint insisted that Dion—he could not believe that a woman not from his clan would know how to ride the white water—be in his kayak.

''But that's settled,'' he said. ''Right now I've got two daughters and a son in the singing, so I'll be heading up the cliffs. You're welcome to tag along or come up later with the others.''

Bentol declined quickly, but Gamon dragged his weary body off the floor cushions. ''What the hell,'' he grunted with a wink at Tyrel and a pointed look at the trader. ''It might be interesting to hear what I'll sound like on my way to the moons.''

Aranur despaired of ever keeping his uncle off the trader's back, but he had to admit to his own curiosity about the death songs. In the end it was only Bentol who stayed behind.

The roar of the water was an almost unnoticed sound in the background until Aranur, Dion, Rhom, and the others climbed along the trails to where the singers stood on the cliffs. As they neared the canyon, the sun dropped over the edge, and a cold wail moaned with the shadow that darkened earth and water. The wail grew, and a melody began to mesh with the thunder they were approaching. They could see the river fling itself toward the cliffs, the white froth climbing the walls and bucking over the black rocks. The haunting voices seemed to call it on and drive it to a wild white frenzy. Aranur did not know how long they stood there, listening to the song of the dead while the moons rose over the Spirit Walk. It was a long time before he realized that the song had faded and that all he was heard was the cry of the river itself, leaping and twisting to destroy the walls that held it in.

It was early dawn when Aranur awoke. No one else was up, but the healer was gone. She had asked about bathing the previous night, and he thought he knew where she had gone. "She should've taken someone with her," he muttered, pulling on his boots. "This country is too dangerous for a woman to be wandering around alone." Gamon, awakened by the sounds of dressing, raised his eyebrows at the younger man, but Aranur just said, "I'll be back in a bit."

Buckling on his sword belt, he jammed his warcap on his head and silently stepped over the sleeping form of Tyrel. The boy was going to develop a first-class snore in a few years, Aranur noted. Maybe sooner if he got his nose broken again—which reminded Aranur that he needed to talk to his cousin again about needling the trader. They were supposed to be a team, not a pack of snapping dogs, and Tyrel had responsibilities to live up to. Although Aranur was not sure that the boy had the skill or stamina to face the dangers he knew were ahead, the Lloroi wanted his son to learn that he had to start taking his position in Ariye more seriously if he was going to be Lloroi after his father. That meant getting some firsthand experience in the kinds of problems he would be likely to face. All of which meant that it was Aranur's responsibility to see that his cousin got the experience without losing his life.

The lean man sighed and broke into a trot on the dusty road. Tyrel was a little too young to be serious about anything, let alone to be considering how close he was to leading the people of Ramaj Ariye. And if the youth was not acceptable when the elders cast the vote, the council would be torn apart by the politics of choosing among the other ambitious leaders. Aranur wanted none of it. He was family—nephew to the Lloroi—so he held enough responsibility for the leadership of Ariye as it was. He knew, too, that if his sister had not been the Lloroi's niece and his cousins the Lloroi's daughters, the raiders would not have risked so much to steal the girls out from under the watchful eyes of the mountain men.

"Politics." He grimaced, spitting to the side of the road. "Let it go to the lepas. I've got enough trouble leading the venges against the raiders without having to sweet-talk a bunch of power-hungry elders into cooperating with each other. They don't even see the need for venges to the outlying districts unless they can get an extra vote out of it for their faction, and the raiders are getting worse every year."

He slowed down, looking around for the path that branched off to the bathing pools. Dion did not seem the type to be careless, but she must not have been too concerned about raiders, either, if she was going off on her own in the early hours of morning. Hells, he thought, we don't even know who lives in this area. There are raider bases all along the Phye, and it'd be just our luck that we run into one here. Although, he told himself, it would be unlikely that the raiders could keep anything hidden from the Clan Celilo for very long.

He glanced at the path and saw the healer's faint footprints along with those of the wolf. At least she had taken the Gray One with her, though he had thought that the wolf had started overland already. He glanced at the tracks again. As long as the Gray One was with her, the woman really did not need anyone else, but still, Aranur hesitated. Finally, knowing it to be an excuse to talk to the dark-haired woman, he strode up the path toward the pools.

"Come on, Hishn." Her soft but exasperated voice came from somewhere ahead. "Don't mess around like this." There was a pause, then the wolfwalker spoke more sharply, though she was laughing, too. "Give them back, now. No, I don't want to play keep-away. *Hishn!*" There was some scuffling, then the wolf crashed through the brush and lunged past the man, a mouthful of clothes covering most of the Gray One's face. He had the impression Hishn was laughing at him as she passed, her yellow eyes daring him to call out. Then the woman was running his way, her soft feet padding in the dust, her voice half laughing, half irritated. "Moonworms! Get back here, you mangy thing. I—"

She broke through the brush and froze on the path. Aranur stood rooted. She was naked as a water nymph, damp from the stream, her black hair twisted back and dripping from her face. The dawn light angled across her taut body and lit it like golden fire. He stared as the shadows accented her breasts and outlined her slender hips. Not even the stitched line of red that ran from her thigh to her knee took away from the impact of her blazing body in the dawn. She blushed deeply red and opened her mouth to say something, but Hishn's padding feet sounded softly in the dust behind him, and he turned to retrieve her clothes. But the wolf slipped by, and the woman took the chance to melt back into the brush without saying a word. The path was silent.

When he got back to Tramis's stilted house, Dion was already there, helping Tramis's wife with breakfast as their two girls ran around underfoot carrying things to the table. The wolfwalker must have gone back through the brush, he realized with brief regret as he came through the open doorway, because although he had walked slowly and looked sharply before and behind him, he had not seen any sign of her. At least Gamon and Rhom were not just talking about her woodskill, he thought with some relief.

"Easy," he said, catching one of Tramis's daughters before she crashed into his long legs after she whirled from the table. He steadied the pitcher of the hot drink of rou in her hands and stepped around her, winking at her open-eyed gaze of awe.

Dion refused to look at him, but Aranur felt smugly pleased when her cheeks flamed at his voice, and the memory of her wet body in the sun stayed with him and colored his view of her as she worked. He wondered how it would be to kiss her, and his eyes followed her lazily until her brother entered, sent him a sharp look, and sat down to breakfast.

"When do we leave?" Tyrel asked his cousin, the note of his excitement escaping in his voice.

Aranur raised an eyebrow at the youth. "Are you that eager to feel the cold claws of the canyon?" He twitched the raised brow in an almost sinister imitation of an earth chanter.

The boy fidgeted with irritation. "Well, we're packed, the sun is up—what are we waiting for? We have raiders to catch and debts to pay."

The leader drained his cup of rou before setting it down. "We can't rush the shadows from the water by wishing, Tyrel. Tramis said it'd be at least another hour before we could go."

"Since you're so antsy, boy," Gamon suggested slyly, "why don't you take our gear down to the wharf."

Tyrel made a face.

"And while you're at it," Rhom added, "find out who makes the best arrows—I need to fill out my quiver."

The boy made a longer face and opened his mouth to retort but met Aranur's eyes and shut it again before saying what he would regret.

"One more thing," his cousin said, adding to the growing list of tasks. "Make sure there's enough of those air vests for each of us. I don't look forward to fishing your too-eager body out of the drink in the middle of a run."

The sandy-haired boy took the rebuff with good enough grace, though he muttered to himself as he stalked stiffly out of the hut. They heard his feet hit the rungs twice on the way down the ladder, then the telltale thud as he jumped the rest of the way to the ground.

"Ah, sweet youth," Gamon said, rolling his eyes toward the ceiling.

"Sweet youth, my foot." Aranur snorted. "Yalimi," he said, turning to the older woman, "Bentol said you'd set aside trail rations for us."

The woman nodded absently toward Dion, took the pitcher of rou from her daughter's hands, and pushed another plate into the other little girl's hands.

"I already packed them," the healer said quietly, finishing her rou while she leaned on the counter. She nodded toward the packs. "You'll find them on the top of each packroll."

Aranur frowned slightly. It disturbed him that Dion took it for granted that she should pack the rations, but he shook himself. It was absurd to be irritated by her thoughtfulness—he would have been pleased if Shilia had done it instead. Not sure what to say, Aranur simply nodded his thanks and hefted his and Gamon's packs, striding to the door and tossing them out on the wide porch. His pack was worn again, he noted as the scuffed leather turned up when it tumbled. He would have to make a new one when he got back. Or convince Meri to do it for him, he thought with a grin, remembering the last time the rather well-endowed woman had asked to do something for him back at home.

Dion cleared her throat. "Excuse me, Aranur."

He jumped guiltily. "Sorry," he said, recovering himself and stepping aside as the woman tossed her own pack out onto the porch. Rhom followed her out, carrying two bags of trail rations to pack into his and Bentol's packs since they were still over at Elunint's hut, and as he swung down over the ladder, Aranur took the chance to lean close to Dion and whisper, "Moonmaid."

She jerked but quickly hid her expression behind her violet eyes, avoiding his casually leaning form in the doorway, like a whisper of a breeze that he could not quite catch. Aranur smiled. "When you're ready," he called inside to her and Gamon, "meet me at the docks. I've got to find our trader before he backs out on us again."

Thirty minutes later he lashed the last of the packs onto the kayaks. "Let's see those air vests, Elunint," he said, straightening up. The water was cold, and in spite of the hot rou in his belly, by the time he finished examining the kayaks for sturdiness and lashing the packs on with wetroot, his fingers were chilled. "If it's this cold in the canyon," he said, slapping his chest with his hands to get the circulation going again, "I hope you filled those vests with hot air."

"So they'll be just like you," Dion said under her breath as she passed.

Aranur gave her a long look and the beginnings of a grin, but Elunint tossed a vest at him before he could return her comment.

"They're made of otter gut," the Celilo man explained. "Like sausages of air sewn together. Keeps you afloat if you fall out." He grinned. "And I'll bet that half of you do."

Aranur raised his eyebrow. "Five silvers says you'd lose that bet."

Elunint's grin widened. "Five silvers? Agreed." He picked up two paddles and handed them to Aranur, but the gray-eyed leader shook his head with a smile.

"I'll choose the gear, Elunint. Not that I think you'd try stacking the odds," he added as he put aside a paddle that showed a hairline crack along the handle.

Elunint just grinned again and shrugged. "Five silvers buys a lot of supplies," he said obliquely.

Aranur barked a laugh and gestured for the group to get in. When the leather aprons of the boats were drawn up tightly against their waists to keep the water out, he nodded to Elunint to take over.

The guide gave the signal, and they dug their paddles into the water and swung into the river. In a moment the current reached out and grasped the tiny craft, flinging them toward the towering walls that were still draped in chill morning shadows.

And then they were into the canyon, darting one after the other into the great V's of current that dashed over the rocks. Elunint, the most experienced, and Dion went first into the white thunder, Tyrel and Aranur next. Aranur had time for one quick glance behind at Gamon and Rhom, and both were grinning wildly, their hair already wet with spray. Tramis and Bentol came last, the guide paddling for both himself and the trader, since Bentol's hands were glued to the sides of the craft as if by willpower alone he would stay in the kayak. Then Aranur had no time for anything but an instant's fear and a wild exultation as they lunged into a wall of water that grabbed their bow and dragged them under.

They were tossed up like a stick and came down into a frothing white hole, the power of the waves closing over Aranur's head. He knew an instinctive panic that froze his lungs as the water froze his skin, but then they were out again, twisting to avoid the black shape of a rock that loomed ahead, white froth climbing its sides and spewing around it. They shot away to the right, and he glimpsed Dion's kayak just before it went under. Her craft dived into another hole, jumping out again like a fish after a fly, and Aranur could see Tyrel yelling wildly in the front of the boat. Huge waves surged over their bow, but the little kayak cut through the water like a needle through folds of cloth. They managed to follow Dion's kayak through the next froth and then had a second's respite as the current raced into a long, smooth V. Dion and the guide were desperately paddling toward the canyon wall, so he and Tyrel followed again, not knowing what was ahead but fighting to keep in their path.

The thunder seemed to grow, and back to the left Aranur could see the water drop away over an edge. But they were already caught in the run by the wall, dashing toward their own drop. Aranur saw Dion's craft go over as if dragged down. Then he could see what she must have screamed at as Tyrel leaned back against the apron, and Aranur could feel sudden fear draw his own skin back from his face. They had no time to do anything but pull the paddles in to the sides of the kayak. Then the water shot them out and down fifteen meters. The bow of the kayak split the churning froth in two as they dived straight at the fall's feet. Then they were under, and the icy thunder was trying to rip the paddle from the man's hand and pull him apart in a hundred directions. He braced his legs against the sides of the kayak as they rolled. His lungs burned. Water leaked through his taut lips. The thrash of it was driving into his eyes, and he could not see. I need air . . . He brushed by a rock upside down, and still the current pulled them aside, dragging them forward under the water. Air . . .

The kayak hit the surface again, and they twisted it upright, sucking air and gasping for breath, their paddles grabbed by the water as they thrust them in to keep the kayak straight. Water burned in Aranur's nose and streamed from his black hair. A sudden wave surged over the small craft and flung them sideways into the water again, but they whipped the kayak back under them and twisted back into the main current. Then the waves began to break over huge rocks that struck out at them. They followed Dion's kayak but had no chance to see if the others had followed them. The frozen water swept the sweat from the lean man's skin with every stroke and fed the fierceness in his heart, and he could see Tyrel screaming his young might as they dodged from one hole to the next, the crashing filling Aranur's ears so that he heard only the rocks calling them on.

They were nearing the end of the run when it happened. The waves tossed Dion's kayak up and turned it on the crest of the wave, dropping to the left of a jutting shadow. But as Aranur and Tyrel reached the crest, the water surged again suddenly and they plummeted onto the black stone. The kayak splintered. The shock jarred Aranur's knees where he had braced himself against the kayak's sides and banged his spine where the edge of the manhole was cutting into his back. Shards of wood flew. Then the force of the crash threw him into a plunging wave that sucked him under. He grabbed his last breath as he was flung into the shocking cold, the churning water crushing him under a rock. His boots slipped up along its slick stone side, and then the river grabbed like a wrestler throwing him over and shot him past, ice-cold water rushing up his nose and drowning his ears as he tumbled. He tried to right himself on his back, feet first, but the current dropped him into another hole, the white thunder exploding on his face and tearing the last breath from his drowning body.

V

Aranur Bentar neDannon:

Sidisport

The weapons of revenge are sharp
But so are hearts

Someone was kissing him with soft gentle lips, breathing into his lungs. Aranur took the breath and kissed back, his tongue flicking along her lips as if to taste heaven before he died. He felt Dion start and opened his eyes, but then his stomach asserted itself and he rolled on his side to be sick in the sand. When he rolled over again, she was sitting back on her knees, but the blush was still on her face. Aranur felt smugly satisfied.

"Thought we'd lost you for sure," Gamon joked, helping his nephew up, the worry still in his voice. "Couldn't you pick a more reasonable time to go swimming? And if you must swim, don't you think you could remember to breathe?"

Aranur coughed and spit, clearing the vile taste from his mouth, and managed a smile. "I needed the bath, Gamon. Dion was avoiding me like the plague. One quick dunking, and I've got her kissing me already."

The woman's eyes flashed anywhere but at the lean, muscular man who teased her so easily, but Aranur changed the subject when he caught the look of dawning comprehension and anger on Rhom's face. "What did we lose?" he asked instead.

"Not a thing except the kayak you grew so tired of," Gamon

said. "We're at Portage, where the Clan Celilo takes the boats back overland to the village. Tramis says there are always enough kayaks here for us to go on down to Sidisport by river if we want to."

Aranur was gingerly trying out various muscles, finding the sore spots where the river had not been too gentle. He should have some real beauties for bruises by the next day. "How'd you make it through, Cousin?"

Tyrel grimaced. "I stayed on top when you went under, and Gamon and Rhom picked me up halfway down. I hung on to the end of their boat. Got a sore bottom off a sudden rock, but I came out better than you."

"Well, you can stop hovering now," Aranur stated, brushing away solicitous hands. "I'm alive and well and intend to stay that way for a while."

"You see, Bentol," Gamon called to the merchant, whose white face still showed his fear. "We're blessed with a moonmaid to lead us through anything. Four bruises, two cuts, and one soggy fighter. That's not bad for a run like that." The trader gave him an irritated look, got up, and stalked away.

They gained a full day on the raiders by riding the white water and staying with the river to Sidisport. Halfway to the coastal town the Gray One joined them again, appearing in the morning as the wolfwalker's pillow where the night before she had gone to bed with her pack under her head. The gray wolf was rarely seen now, except at night—there was more traffic on the road, and the massive creature haunted the marshy woods they rode through instead of the widening trail that led to the city. By the time they reached Sidisport, they were only a couple hours behind the slavers, and the cold rage that had been banked in Aranur since the kidnapping began to flame into soft ice.

The wharf where they stopped was dark and grimy. Smells of sea creatures brought in for sale overpowered their noses and kept them from smelling the garbage in the gutters, but the dingy look of the warehouses could not be disguised. Bentol, talking with a street rat, was trading a copper for each bit of information he coaxed from the grimy boy about the slavers, their voices low but clear as Aranur kept a wary eye on the wharf.

". . . several on board. They've been docked since sunset."

A copper changed hands, only to disappear quickly into the ragged pockets of the dirty boy. "How many came ashore?"

The boy looked longingly at the next copper, just visible between Bentol's fingers. "Three," he said quickly. "The captain, his second mate, and a stranger."

The copper hesitated above the boy's outstretched hand. "How did you know who they were, boy? If you're making this up, I'll cut your throat before you stir two steps from this dock."

"He comes herc often. I wouldn't lie to you," the boy protested, pretending innocence, his eyes glued to the money. The copper dropped, and he caught it deftly.

"Where did they go?"

"I don't follow them into the city every time they go shopping."

Two coppers appeared in Bentol's hand. "I think you'll find it coming back to you," he suggested.

"It's no secret," the boy said sullenly. "Whenever Salmi has extra pretty ones, he takes them to the private market first. If they don't like them there, then he goes to the public market."

"We have no interest in the public market, but the location of this private market might interest us greatly." Bentol had slipped a piece of silver into his hand and was turning it slowly in his fingers. "It wouldn't be part of Pisnot's side market or the merchant Mankarr's special black market, would it?" The boy hesitated and looked furtively around. Bentol casually dropped the silver and covered it with his foot till only a glint of bright metal showed in the mud.

"The Hanging Sword," the boy whispered. "The basement. A door behind the shelves leads to a room under Mankarr's warehouse. They meet there in two hours." His voice was urgent, hurried. Bentol stepped back, and the boy dropped to his knees to snatch the silver, then darted away as soon as the words were out and the silver was in his hand.

Bentol turned back to Aranur. "You heard?"

The leader nodded.

"Why do they meet so soon?" Tyrel puzzled. "And why a private market? I thought they'd have more bidders at a public block."

"They'd have more bidders," Aranur answered, "but the private market will attract more money. And if the slaver captain Salmi doesn't want us to be able to trace the girls too easily, he'll have to get rid of them before public market tomorrow. The rich merchants get first crack at the new girls, anyway, though it isn't common knowledge. If he tried to sell such prizes at public market before letting the merchants bid first, he might end up minus his head.''

Dion shuddered. The market block had nearly been her fate, too.

"We'll have to move quickly, then," Gamon said.

"I think, Gamon, that we must exercise our minds first, not our arms," Bentol said.

The older man opened his mouth to return the trader's sniping, but Rhom cut him off. "What do you suggest? This is a private, not a public market. We can't just walk in and bid with the others for the girls."

"Why not?" the pudgy man demanded.

"It would be unexpected," Aranur admitted. "Private markets are hard to get into. Bentol, do you know Mankarr? Can you set us up as bidders?"

The merchant nodded smugly. "Mankarr is an old friend of mine, and he owes me a favor. Plus, I finally got my hands on something he's been trying to take in trade for years. The bids for the girls are probably fixed already, but yes, I think I can fix it so he would take me to this meeting, along with two servants, just to see the fun when I outbid his rivals."

"Servants?" Gamon asked. "None of us can go into a private market—in a small place like that, someone's bound to recognize us, especially since they know we've been trailing them all along."

"*We* are being looked for," Aranur corrected. "Bentol is not. And Rhom is also a stranger; no one will know who he is or where he came from."

"Rhom can be my manservant," the pudgy trader agreed, "and Dion will be the woman from my own harem who will acquaint the new girls with their master and the local harem laws. This is customary and will get us by." He looked at the woman critically, unaware of her twin's suddenly stubborn face behind him. "We'll have to get a good harem costume for you, Healer."

"No," Rhom broke in flatly, flexing his broad shoulders and narrowing his hard, violet eyes. "Me, yes. Dion, no."

Dion opened her mouth, but Gamon cut in. "I agree. The healer does not get involved in this." The older man pointed at her twin and the trader. "If you don't make it out, we could possibly rescue you two or buy you out, but the wolfwalker would be caught in someone's harem for a very short and unpleasant life. She stays here."

"Gamon, I have to have someone to settle the harem women," the trader argued. "Men don't buy for the harem without one from their own harem to agree and settle the new women. The laws are strict. If I don't take one of my own women along, I have no business buying." He raised his hand to cut off the older man's protest. "And Dion is the only one who can go," he continued. "You are well known as a weapons master, and these merchants have sharp eyes and follow the rumors. And even with a disguise, Aranur would also be recognized immediately. Tyrel has a hot enough temper to let loose when he sees how his sisters are being treated—"

"I'd be controlled," the boy broke in.

Dion tried to speak again, but the trader cut her off and turned to the boy. "You know you wouldn't. I cannot go alone, and I cannot go with only one manservant. All buyers have women with them to settle the new ones. And the merchants who attend Mankarr's sales would jump at the chance to call charter law down on me if I went against custom. If I don't bring a woman along, they're going to start looking at the timing of my own appearance and ask some nasty questions."

Bentol knows his trading well, Aranur thought. His tongue is greased like a cook's knife. The gray-eyed leader sighed. "He's right, Gamon. Tyrel, you're too rash yet. And Gamon, you know that you—and me, too—are traveled enough to be easily recognized by these men. Rhom and Dion are the only choice."

The healer opened her mouth again, and her twin started to protest, but Tyrel beat them both to it. "But why Dion?" the boy argued hotly, jealous of her position and protective of her person. "You can always say you traveled light and just chanced on this market."

A loud snarl cut through the noise and startled them all into silence. Hishn, glaring at each of them, sat back on her haunches as Dion gestured angrily for them to remain quiet.

"*If* I could speak for myself," the wolfwalker said. "Bentol makes sense. Besides I've had the same kind of training as you, and I can take care of myself well enough. You should know that, Gamon."

"Healer Dione," the weapons master said firmly and respectfully, "this is not the same. The risks are different now."

"I understand the risks, and I know my chances. I see no difference in the stakes," the woman answered steadily. "If it's not now that I risk slavery, it will be a month from now, or a season or a year. Raiders don't wait for women to come to them anymore."

The older man opened his mouth and then closed it, and Aranur had a sudden realization that she was right. Ever since the raiders had started pushing inland, women and even men were in more and more danger of abduction and slavery. For Dion, her freedom was the stakes each time she left her village, and on Journey, as far from home and safety as she was, the odds against her grew higher every day. The Gray One was her constant companion, but even a wolf was no guarantee. And her skills in Abis—she was strong and quick and lithe, he knew, but he had never actually seen her fight—if she went in with Bentol and Rhom now, it would be on Gamon and Rhom's judgment. The blacksmith would never put his twin in danger he was unsure of, and Gamon—well, the old weapons master had no equal in judging a person's fighting skills. And, Aranur reminded himself, his uncle had seen the wolfwalker fight before.

"Gamon, Rhom," he said finally, "it's up to you. You both understand what we're going into at this slave market."

Gamon's face was still stubbornly closed to the idea, but Rhom sighed. "Dion's good," he said. "More than good enough for the job, though I hate to admit it. But Dion, stay here. You don't know what it'll be like. They'll treat you as if you were on the block, too, just because you look different, unusual. If one of them decides he wants you, there may be a fight anyway. We can manage without risking you, too."

Aranur turned to the trader. "How well does Mankarr know you, Bentol? And can you trust him?"

Bentol nodded, then chuckled suddenly. "Like a brother."

Aranur frowned but let the trader's private joke pass. "Who knows you besides him?"

"Mankarr actually knows me as one Altiss Hantinn, a merchant who deals in unusual objects. Ob Clintner knows me, and Toserva Nefarg. In fact, I should know all the merchants at the sale. If Rhom and Dion came with me, their coloring would not be out of character for Altiss's exotic tastes. I could say that I'd bought Dion, then agreed to take Rhom in service so he could be with his twin."

"It could work," Gamon admitted reluctantly.

"It will work," Bentol corrected impatiently.

"Gamon," Aranur said, "we're all in this together, and the risks are shared. And," he added slyly, "think on this. While Salmi is playing the successful slaver, who is guarding his strongbox? I think it would be only fair if he repaid the ransom we'll be paying him, don't you?"

The older man shook his head. "All right," he said unhappily. "I don't like it, but I'll go along. Salmi must have collected something interesting these last few years. He's been causing enough trouble doing it."

"Tyrel will go with you," the lean man decided. "As for me, if there's trouble, I want to be ready to get Bentol and the rest out of there fast. I'll rent a carriage for our merchant Altiss and play driver instead. I'll pass for a stranger well enough in the dark. All right?"

"Agreed," the trader said with relief.

Aranur turned to his cousin. "We don't have much time to get clothes. Tyrel, find us another wharf rat to run a few errands. Bentol, you'd better go over whatever the buying procedure is with Rhom and Dion. We can't afford to slip up and give ourselves away. Gamon, while Tyrel's finding us some cheap labor, why don't we get a good look at Salmi's boat."

VI

Ember Dione maMarin:

Slave Sale

What cost your pride?
  It is free, for I can get more.
What cost your skills?
  They are low, for I am a healer.
What cost your body?
  It is high, for I am untouched.
What cost your soul?
  There is no cost, for it is not for sale.

It had been almost two ninans since Dion had worn anything but men's clothes, and the soft black velvet felt good against her skin. The harem tunic was snug but not so snug that she could not move in it if she had to, and the baggy pants were loose enough to conceal the few weapons she would take. She admitted to a streak of vanity as she examined herself critically in the mirror.

Going hunting? Hishn asked with a low teasing howl.

You be quiet, she told the wolf, adjusting her jewel pouch to hide in the folds of the pants and turning around to see if she had gotten the scarf to hang properly. *You're a plain, ordinary mutt of an animal who has as little mind as the mute I'm supposed to be.*

Supposed to be? The wolf's yellow eyes gleamed as she licked a spot on her coat. *Wait till they hear your singing voice.*

Dion made a face at her. *Be quiet and let's get going. They can't wait forever for you to finish preening yourself.*

Aranur was waiting when the two came out from the hotel room. He did a double take, seeing the healer for the first time in a woman's tunic and pants, but said nothing other than to ask if they were ready to go.

"Bentol is in the carriage with Rhom," he said, showing her to the carriage, Hishn padding softly beside them. "Remember, if there's trouble of any kind, get out of there. Don't wait for Bentol or even your brother. Just run."

"Does Bentol have enough to buy your sisters back?" she asked.

"He should. We pooled all our money, and we picked up a little more from the raiders. Too bad we couldn't have gotten into the raider's strongbox before Bentol goes in, but that can't be helped." He gave the healer a hand up to the carriage. "I'd like to see that slaver captain, Salmi's, face when he finds out we paid for the girls with his own money."

Hishn jumped in beside the woman and lay at her feet, yellow eyes following the city lights in the windows as Aranur drove the trader and his servants to Mankarr's home. There were already four carriages waiting with their drivers when they arrived. As Bentol had arranged, they were expected: They did not even get to the steps before the merchant Mankarr appeared in the brightly lit doorway of his house.

"Altiss," he cried, and Dion frowned till she remembered that the trader had said that Mankarr knew him by another name. "What a pleasant surprise. Come in, come in. You still have excellent taste, I see," he commented, running an expert eye over the small group. "But come in. What have you been doing lately?"

"Traveling here and there, collecting this and that," Bentol answered glibly, embracing the man before entering. "What do you think of my most recent acquisitions?" He gestured negligently at the three who were following him.

"Exquisite," Mankarr admitted. "Beautiful coloring. Where did you find them? One of them can't be a wolfwalker!" Mankarr took a closer look, trying to find the chain that held the wolf in bay.

"They are twins from the Randonnen mountains," the trader boasted. "Both are mute, but even though the girl cannot speak, she can sing like a ligriatia bird, and she has the wolf to protect her."

"Is that why she's still untouched?" the other man asked slyly.

"Of course not." Bentol waved the comment aside as if it were not worthy of thought. "There was a prophecy attached to her birth that when she mated, she would lose the only voice she has left: song. Since I've plenty of women to keep me happy—"

"You're only happy with a new girl on your lap," the Sidisport merchant teased slyly.

"I have no need to break the voice of the most lovely songbird I've ever heard."

"You bought them both?"

"No, I didn't need to. Their parents were in, shall we say, desperate financial straits from the father's penchant for gambling, and I, being the kindhearted man that I am,"—Bentol ignored Mankarr's snort—"agreed to buy the girl. Her coloring and singing more than make up for her muteness in conversation. As for the man, well, he insisted on coming with his sister, so though I refused to pay for both, I ended up with the two for the same price as the one. I do pay him a minimal wage to keep him happy," he added, though it was obvious that the expense was one he would rather have done without if he could have gotten a better deal out of the twins.

"A good trade," Mankarr agreed, leading them down a rich corridor and then into a comfortable room. The tapestries that hung on the walls depicted hundreds of years of history, and the rug that covered the entire floor was deeply woven with brilliant colors. Bentol gestured for Dion to sit by him.

Mankarr shut the door. "So, what brings you here, Altiss?" the merchant asked abruptly, dropping the small talk.

The trader remained casual. "I'm in the market for a few pretty girls. You wouldn't happen to know of a private slave sale I could discreetly attend, would you?"

Mankarr gave him a sharp look, then chuckled. "You sly thamrin. How did you know?"

"The streets are alive with gossip tonight."

"I know of such a sale. But it might cost you dearly. What kind of girls are you looking for? Dancers? Talented virgins?"

Bentol dropped his voice, and Mankarr leaned forward to catch his words. "High-ranking girls. Perhaps those from a Lloroi's family."

The other man frowned and spoke softly. "Ob Clintner requested those girls specially from Salmi, the raider captain. He would be very unhappy if I allowed his prizes to be bought out from under him.''

''I was not aware that you held Clintner in such high esteem.''

''I don't, and you know it,'' Mankarr answered mildly, though his mouth tightened.

''This is a cash sale?''

''Of course.''

''So the bids are already fixed, are they not?''

''For these girls, yes. The bid was fixed at the time of the order.''

''Let me attend this sale, Mankarr, and I will guarantee you some fireworks.''

The other man hesitated.

''Oh, come, you'd love to see Ob Clintner thwarted,'' Bentol urged.

''You want into this sale badly, Altiss.'' The merchant eyed the trader speculatively. ''What do these particular prizes mean to you?''

Bentol looked at Mankarr for a long moment. ''Two of the girls are the daughters of Lady Sonan,'' he said, his voice so soft that it barely reached his ears. ''The other is her niece.''

''Lady Sonan!'' Mankarr exclaimed angrily. ''The Lloroi's wife? Altiss, does Lady Sonan know what she's asked you to do?'' Mankarr stared at the trader accusingly. ''She is trading on your love for her to—''

''Shhh.'' Bentol motioned, glancing at the twins. The Lady Sonan, Dion thought with some shock. That would be Tyrel's mother . . . She met Rhom's knowing glance and looked away.

''They are mute.'' Mankarr waved the trader's protest aside. ''What they know, they can't tell, and if they're in your service long at all, they'll guess the truth anyway. Altiss, you've got to put aside your obsession with this woman. She has brought you nothing but unhappiness.''

''It is the will of the moons,'' the other man returned.

''It is not the will of the moons that you should buck both Ob Clintner and the raiders. There is some dark dealing going on here—Salmi has contracts with Lloroi Zentsis from Ramaj Bilocctar to stir up trouble here, and it's rumored that lately Clintner is getting involved in the eastern politics, as well. If you step in the middle of this for a woman who does not—cannot—love you as you love her, you will be cracked and crushed like a bug by a dnu. I will not allow you into the sale. The girls have been in the raiders' hands for a ninan. They are already lost to their parents.''

"I gave my word.'' Bentol spread his hands. "These are her daughters, and Mankarr,'' he added, his voice dropping tragically, "they could have been mine. I cannot turn my back on her. I *must* attend this sale. I have over three hundred gold pieces to bid with, and I also have—'' He paused and pulled a pouch off his belt. ''—an object worth much more than that, which you have much interest in.''

"What is it?'' Mankarr asked, unwilling to drop the subject of the Lloroi's wife but finding his interest caught instantly by the dull cloth-swathed object that Bentol drew from his pouch.

"It is something you have said you would do almost anything to get,'' the other man said quietly. "The Orb of Olatna.''

"The orb, here!'' The merchant stretched out his hands. "Let me see it.''

"I will let you have it for a mere five hundred gold pieces and the chance to go to the sale.''

Mankarr sat back, the eager light going out of his eyes. "No, Altiss. I will not trade your life for that of a lifeless jewel. Keep it in its pouch.''

The trader ignored him and unwrapped the black stone anyway. "Five hundred pieces of gold is a pittance for a jewel that would complete the Midnight collection,'' he said in a voice as hypnotic as the light that caught the corners of the cuts and shimmered into a depthless flash of infinity at every edge.

Mankarr drew in his breath. "It is as beautiful as I remember,'' he breathed. He looked away in restraint. "Put it away, Altiss.''

"I have not brought this here to torture your senses,'' Bentol said softly. "I paid dearly for this. And I will give it to you for less than half its worth.''

"If you get the payment you're asking, you are also giving away your life. Is it worth that? Is any woman worth that?''

"I would give my life a hundred times for the Lady Sonan. You know it, Mankarr.'' He hefted the jewel in his hands. "Four hundred fifty gold pieces and an invitation to the sale.''

"No, Altiss.'' The merchant's voice was sharp, but his eyes still wandered to the trader's hands.

"Four hundred gold pieces."

"Clintner has a long and vengeful arm, Altiss. Crossing him is not worth the looks you want from Lady Sonan." But Mankarr's eyes could not leave the stone, and the trader continued to turn it so that it seemed to mesmerize the very light in the room.

"Three hundred fifty in gold, the matched pair of ivory bracelets in that cabinet, and the favor."

"Altiss, you know what you are asking me to do," Mankarr almost wailed.

Bentol went on relentlessly. "Three hundred pieces of gold, the ivory bracelets, and the favor. I will not go lower, Mankarr, and you'll never have this chance to hold the orb again."

Mankarr looked at the black orb once more and was lost. "I—I will take the orb, Altiss, but know that you make me pay also for your love with your life." He sighed. "Three hundred pieces of gold and the matched pair of carved ivory bracelets." The merchant shook his head. "They are yours," he said, "though how the Lady Sonan will receive them when you're dead is beyond me."

"There is the matter of the sale."

Mankarr took a deep breath. "You may go."

"And the *approximate* amounts of the bids and a list of who will be buying what."

The dark-faced man looked at the trader. "You want to invoke the rule of ignorance to allow you to bid for the girls? You were always more clever than the others, Altiss, though Clintner and Nefarg would never admit it to themselves." He sighed. "Why you chose to—well, it's not my business." He looked back at the orb, then nodded. "You'll have the information."

"Then this," Bentol said, turning the shimmering jewel in his hand once more, "is yours." He tossed the orb from his hand, its flawless facets absorbing the very light of the moons as it seemed to flow through the air to Mankarr. The merchant caught it and palmed the jewel, rubbing it and staring into its infinite depths.

"Ob Clintner expects to buy three girls." The merchant spoke without inflection, as if passing sentence on a man already dead. "They are being sold in a group for a sum of over two hundred gold pieces."

Dion's eyes widened. That was enough gold to buy all the

land her father owned. Bentol was nodding, staring at the ceiling as if cataloging the information in his mind.

"Clintner always carries an extra hundred pieces in case he sees something else he wants," Mankarr continued. "Aldor Copiandi expects to buy two virgins from the coast and a pair of young boys for his cousin's home. He'll spend about 135 gold pieces on the four of them. He rarely carries extra money." Mankarr paused, thought a moment, then went on. "Toserva Nefarg has put in no bids, but he will bring upwards of a hundred pieces to tease the bids of the others.

"Edihana Metrinadon seeks a new bevy, and the bids for these girls are the only bids not yet frozen. He has also been promised five dancers from the halls of Cortin and at least two pretty faces to keep him company at night. He will buy the dancers on the basis of their performance tonight. The man has never been predictable; I would guess his money pouch at two hundred pieces for the night.

"Newton Donquoan is not buying tonight. He usually carries thirty pieces to pay for his pleasures. You remember Bart Llewellin?" Mankarr asked the trader, and when Bentol nodded, he continued. "He is buying the daughter of Truss Edithewton for revenge. He's willing to pay at least one hundred gold pieces for her stolen body, and he'll be carrying about forty extra pieces of gold, maybe fifty, in case the bid is prompted higher."

"Who is buying last?"

"Clintner. He wants to make sure none of the others have money left for bidding when his prizes come up. This deal is important to him."

Bentol nodded. "As I figure it, I only need to cover bets over five hundred pieces of gold in case Clintner borrows from the extra money that'll still be floating around. I have more than enough. The Lady Sonan emptied her purse to see her daughters again."

"I didn't know Lloroi Dannon was so well off."

"He isn't." Bentol smiled grimly. "But with my funds also and the help of a few careless raiders we met on the way, we have more than enough to finish here." The two men rose. "By the way," Bentol mentioned, "the street has it that there is a door in your basement that leads to the cellar of the Hanging Sword Tavern."

"Oh?" Mankarr looked thoughtful for a moment. "I'll look

into it.'' There was the sound of another carriage in the court-yard, and Mankarr looked soberly at the trader. ''There is just one other thing before we join the sale: I lied when I said the raiders had marked the girls already. They have not been touched. It was part of the deal.'' He rose and gestured for Bentol to follow. Bentol, furtively relieved, made the sign of the blessing at Mankarr's words, then motioned for Rhom, Dion, and the Gray One to stay in the room.

''Rhom,'' Dion hissed. ''Did you hear that? Bentol and Lady Sonan?''

''I heard, but I can't believe it.''

''It explains why Bentol and Gamon are always fighting.''

Her twin nodded briefly and got up to pace the room. After a minute he paused and looked around. ''I bet it's why Bentol doesn't stay here in Sidisport. Look at this place—he's got plenty of gold to set himself up like this if he wanted, but then he wouldn't get to see Lady Sonan every quarter year. Have you ever seen so many things in one room? There must be a dozen paintings in here alone.''

''I'm still looking at the tapestries,'' she returned softly, her violet eyes wide as she let them roam. Hishn, turning her yellow eyes around the room, projected only the desire to go out the window and back into the fresh air. ''Wait, Gray One. We'll be out of here soon.''

Suddenly the black-haired man halted. ''Hey, look at this.''

''Rhom, we really shouldn't be nosing around. Hishn's getting nervous, and it just doesn't feel right.''

''I know, but this is incredible. This is a page from the original Dharvin Tsuma—the philosophies of the ancients.'' The young blacksmith peered closely at the first of the framed documents that lined one wall. ''I can almost read it, too. Moon-worms, but this must have cost Mankarr more gold than our entire village is worth.''

Unable to resist, Dion glided to where her twin was squinting at the ancient words. ''It must be over a thousand years old,'' she breathed, looking over his shoulder. Behind her, Hishn whined; she shushed the wolf with an absent gesture.

Rhom fingered the gilt of the next frame. ''Look at this one. This is a copy of the Sundown Statements.'' He ran his finger along the wall, glancing at each in wonder and going on to the next. ''By the moons, Dion, look at this one.''

"Which? I'm still reading the *Biologist's Guide to the World*."

"Drop it. You've seen the translation." He shook his head and stared more closely at the poorly preserved parchment that taunted his eyes. "I'm not sure I should tell you this, but I think this is a page from a manual describing Ovousibas, the internal healing of the ancients."

"Here?" Dion looked at her twin in startled wonder. "A whole page that escaped the Purging? How can it be?"

He stepped back as if it would bite. "Read it yourself."

She stood on her toes and peered up at the frame. "I wish I dared take it off the wall . . ."

"Better not to. What if they come back?"

The wolf whined again, louder this time. *Healer,* she sent unhappily, *there is the smell of a trap in here.*

Well, we've got to wait till Bentol gets back, the woman returned absently, *and it won't hurt to read some of this while we wait.* She glanced over the parchment, then read it more closely. "Ovousibas," she whispered. Then she shook her head. "This doesn't make sense. It says you just look to the left and drop into the patient's body."

Her brother frowned. "You sure you read the letters right?"

"Uh huh. Look—it even mentions the wolves. Says they're the key to the whole thing." Her voice trailed off, and her eyes got a faraway look.

"Look, Dion, don't go getting any funny ideas. You're a good enough healer that you don't need miracles to pull a patient through."

"Don't worry. I'm not about to risk Hishn in an experiment." She tore her eyes away from the ancient parchment. "But Rhom," she could not help saying, "what if I could do it? Just spread my hands over someone and make them well again by thinking it out."

"Ovousibas is death, Dion."

This place is death, Hishn broke in even more strongly than Rhom.

The wolfwalker pulled herself out of her reverie and looked at the Gray One as if seeing her for the first time. "What are you saying?" she demanded. "Why?"

I smell blood. Old. And new blood. And the windows are small and far away from the ground.

"Rhom," Dion said in a low voice. "People were killed in this room not long ago."

Her twin looked at her sharply, his eyes suddenly still. "Did you bring a weapon?"

Dion nodded. "Four short knives and a pouch of throwing stars and moons."

"Wish you could've kept your sword." He strode to the door from which Bentol and the merchant had left and put his ear to the wood. "Can't hear anything," he muttered when he turned back around.

The wolf snorted and padded balefully back to the window. "Hishn says there's no one to hear. Not in the corridor, anyway." She frowned. "Rhom, where did they go?"

"Probably just to check out the sale before taking us in."

She nodded, unconvinced, and glanced toward the parchment that beckoned on the wall.

"Leave it, Dion."

"I just can't help thinking—"

"Every healer who's tried Ovousibas since the plague is dead, Dion. And their wolves with them. And dead is where we might be, too, if we're not careful here. So keep your mind on the business at hand."

She shot him an irritated look. "I've not forgotten what we're here to do, Rhom." She glanced to where Hishn was sniffing at the thick carpet near the window, and her twin followed her gaze. *What is it, Gray One?*

The fear scent is strong.

The dark image of the room made Dion shiver, and Rhom put his hand on her shoulder. She jumped. "Don't worry, twin," he said with a grin, though his eyes were serious and his hand hefted his sword to make sure it would slide easily from the scabbard. "Don't forget, we've got one weapon no one ever counts on. We've got violet eyes. If you get scared, just pull out your knife and flash those eyes. Those merchants will think the moon warriors have come back to Asengar for the Purging. All we have to do is look at them and frown, and their hearts'll chill in their chests."

"Glad you've got confidence," she said shortly, "because between Hishn's pacing and your nosing around, I'm starting to get paranoid."

"Relax," he advised. "There's nothing else we can do for now."

Healer . . .

"Rhom—somebody's coming!"

They dodged back to the sofa, and Dion plopped down just in time before the door opened and Mankarr and the trader came back in. The Gray One stood at the window, her paws up on the sill and her nostrils flaring as if she could breathe easier by sucking in more air.

"Come," Bentol gestured. Obediently, though with a side-ways glance at the wall on which the parchment of Ovousibas hung, Dion glided into place and bowed her head, trying to look subservient as she shoved the thoughts of Ovousibas out of her mind. In formation, Rhom marched slightly before her, and Hishn, with a silent snarl, fell in behind.

The house seemed quiet as they walked through its halls, but there was an undercurrent of excitement that hit them as they descended the stairs into the basement. They passed through three rooms, each soundproofed against the noise that grew as they walked, and finally they reached a small, dark, incon-spicuous door at the back of a storeroom. Mankarr paused, looked meaningfully at Bentol, then pushed open the door. As it opened, there was a lull in the noise, then it picked up again. Dion tried to keep her eyes down but could not contain her curiosity.

It was a huge room. Five men and women twirled and danced on low tabletops, the men dressed in sober colors and the women in opaque veils and scarves that tantalized the hungry-eyed mer-chants while musicians beat at the room with wild melodies and primeval rhythms. Sweet smoke filled Dion's nose. Her nostrils flared as she caught Hishn's impressions of the expensive drug and coughed. Each man was surrounded by servants and some-times as many as four women of his house, the women dressed in bright but discreet clothes. Amid all the color, the somber black of Dion's costume attracted too much attention. She sud-denly wished she had listened to Rhom and stayed with Gamon and Tyrel.

Mankarr led them to a low table surrounded by embroidered cushions and left them there. Bentol looked completely at ease. There were startled murmurs behind the group as the people noticed the wolf, and speculative glances were cast in their direction. Dion could feel her cheeks flushing at the hard stares. Hishn's lips pulled back in a snarl, and the eager hands that reached to touch her fell away as their owners shrank back. Rhom stood close till she knelt in the cushions beside the trader, then he dropped to sit behind them both, guarding his twin from lecherous looks with hard glares of his own.

"That's an interesting pair of servants, Altiss," a man said as he leaned over from his own table. He eyed the twins. "How much did you pay for them?"

"Too much, Metrinadon." The pudgy man smiled lazily. "But I have not been displeased with them."

"It takes much restraint to leave the girl untouched," Metrinadon said, referring to the black velvet Dion wore. His soft, pale hands tapped out the dregs of his pipe and scooped them from the table before him. "I might be interested in picking up a virgin with looks like that if she's not already spoken for."

Dion could feel her brother tense, but Bentol turned the man away easily. "She's a mute," he said, "but she can sing as long as she doesn't mate. I enjoy her voice enough to take my pleasures with the others in my house." He paused and lowered his voice conspiratorily. "For now, that is."

The other merchant chuckled, his paunch rolling with his laugh. "You're as lecherous as any, Altiss. I'd wager ten silvers you won't keep her untouched for another ninan."

"I'd take you up on that bet," Bentol said with a smile, "but I'm leaving tomorrow night, and it would be several ninans before I could collect."

"Next time," the man said, turning his attention back to his pipe.

Another man moved to speak to Bentol, having watched the interchange between the trader and the overweight merchant. "Altiss," he acknowledged, inviting himself to sit at the trader's table. "You've been making quite a name for yourself lately. I understand you got the better of Cransti in an unusual trade last month."

Dion's attention wandered. Hishn was nervous, catching the impression of many minds and making the healer edgy with them, too. They watched the dancers and glanced discreetly at the men and women in the room, and then her attention was brought back to Bentol's conversation by the other man's words. ". . . I would pay handsomely for the girl," he was saying.

"They are a pair, and much too expensive for your tastes, Donquoan. Besides, I am fond of the girl right now."

"I happen to have a hundred pieces on me right now. I would part with it for both of them if you threw in the wolf."

Bentol chuckled. "It would be a poor day in Sidisport if I sold all three for that. The girl does not go for less than a hundred pieces by herself."

Donquoan snorted. "That is far too steep for a mute virgin with a pet."

"Ah, but she is not just a virgin." Bentol leaned back against the cushions and gestured lazily at the healer. "She is mute but can sing songs to turn the hardest heart. She is also a wolf-walker."

Bentol, Dion thought nervously, you shouldn't have said that.

He has a purpose, Hishn returned softly, but the undertone of worry just added to Dion's own. *He is feeling out the thin one's greed.*

But Donquoan was looking at her, surprised, his thin, sharp face set off by the bushy eyebrows that hung over his cold blue eyes. "A wolfwalker? Come now, Altiss, you can't expect me to believe that. You are trying to pass off a trained wolf as a legendary beast."

"It's true enough. I promised to respect the girl when I bought her, else she would not have come. So you see, she is much above your price range."

"I will give you 110 pieces of gold for the girl and the wolf, untested."

Bentol considered it. "Hmm. But you would still have to pay for the man."

"I'm sure I could find a use for a personal guard. Twenty pieces plus wages is a reasonable price for such," he said.

"The man is worth much more. Look at the pair they are together. Their coloring is exquisite. They would make a beautiful addition to any household."

Bentol, Dion wailed silently, beginning to feel panicked, you better not be serious.

"I will give you 140 pieces of gold for the three of them."

The trader hesitated.

"One hundred and fifty pieces of gold." Donquoan pulled two heavy jeweled rings off his thin but wiry, strong fingers, the lust eager in his eyes as he stared at the healer. "And these. Think on this, Altiss. I am being generous."

The trader opened his mouth to say yes but then shook his head as if with great effort. "No, Donquoan. Your offer is generous, but I cannot take your gold in trade. I cannot give the girl up yet. I . . . have a certain fascination for her myself," he admitted. Dion was so relieved that she almost did not mind when Bentol stroked her hair for a moment, showing the other man his claimed affection.

The other merchant took Bentol's refusal with good grace. "I'm willing to wait for such a prize. If you care to sell later, let me know. I'll make sure the offer is agreeable to us both."

Their talk turned to smaller things, and as the man stayed at Bentol's table, no other merchants could approach. Soon Mankarr brought the music to a halt, and Donquoan returned to his own table.

"There will be much extra gold floating around tonight," Bentol whispered without moving his lips. "But we should still have enough." Dion fingered the jewel pouch she had taken from her boots and hung from her belt on a whim. It contained the total wealth of the twins—the sum of the healing she had done in the last three years since her Internship, the money Rhom had earned in the smithy in the same amount of time, and the payment for a tract of land beside their father's. There was some gold, two cut and two uncut sapphires, a deep black ruby, three emeralds, a yellow taliv gem, and a few strange carvings of rare stones done by the Ethran people. They could add those if they had to, she told herself, questioning Rhom with her eyes and relieved at his barely perceptible nod when he saw her fingering the pouch.

"The appraiser has arrived," Mankarr finally announced. "The sale is open. First bids are for—"

"Wait a minute, Mankarr," a slender man interrupted, a curved pipe in one lazy hand and a sneer on his darkly handsome face. "This is a closed bidding." He pointed the pipe at Bentol. "Why is that dour-faced tamrin here?"

"It is indeed a pleasure to bid with you once again, Nefarg," Bentol said smoothly, oiling his voice. "Do you not remember that I am always welcome in this house?"

"This may not be the time to exercise your poorly perceived rights, Altiss," a richly garbed man warned with contempt.

"Why, Clintner, you are the wealthiest merchant of us all. What have you to worry about?" Bentol asked in mock surprise.

Clintner's face darkened, and he turned back to the front and ignored the trader. "I have no objection. Let us begin the bidding."

Mankarr nodded. "First bids are for two coastal virgins." He turned the bidding over to a small, almost unnoticeable man in gray and gestured for the two girls to be brought out. Cheeks flaming, dressed in nearly sheer tunics and pants, the two girls were chained together. They would not raise their eyes from the floor as they hunched their shoulders against the appraising looks of both men and women in the room. A raider hauled them forward and struck them sharply on the back to stand up straight; Dion's eyes flashed as she saw how young the girls were. Why, they're no older than Kabrun's daughters, she thought in shock.

"These two lovelies are only fourteen," the raider said, forcing them to pivot in front of the men. "Good teeth, beautiful long hair. With ebsin not mature enough to carry a child, so they're guaranteed to give at least three more years of undisturbed pleasure."

Ebsin, Dion thought in shock. If Aranur's sister had been given such a drug and he found out about it . . .

But the raider had stepped back, and the bidding had begun.

"The bidding starts at twenty pieces," the small man said quickly, his voice droning quickly into an indecipherable pitch. "Twenty pieces twenty pieces doIheartwentyfivepieces . . . Ihavetwentyfivepieces twentyeightpieces doIhearthirtypieces . . . lookattheirlovelyfacesandvirginalbodies Ihavethirtypieces-thirtypieces . . . doIhearthirtyfiveIhavethirtyfivedoIhear . . ." The voice buzzed on, finally pausing and snapping Dion's attention back to the front. "Thirty-eight pieces. Do I hear forty?" His voice slowed as he sensed the end of the sale. "For thirty-eight pieces. Do I hear forty pieces? Do I hear forty? Thirty-eight pieces. Forty pieces. I have forty pieces. Do I hear forty-one?"

Dion looked around, but it was not until Rhom nudged her and directed her attention to the malevolent glare that passed from one of the men to Clintner that she figured out who had just bid the first man up again. Clintner smiled indulgently. The other man, with a barely contained gesture, angrily signaled the auctioneer. "I have forty-one," the small man droned on. "Are there any more bids? Going for forty-one pieces of gold each, two virgins from the coast, forty-one pieces. Going. Going. Sold to Aldor Copiandi, cash up front." The small man nodded to the new owner, whose servant rose and carried a heavy purse to the front.

Mankarr gestured for the next girl to be brought forward, and the auctioneer went through the same pitch. Bentol bid a few times, never seriously, just keeping the drone of the auctioneer going, while people shifted and stretched as the bids went on. When it came to the dancers, the musicians played again, and each dancer showed herself off for several minutes before the bidding started again. Dion watched in fascination as the men and women contorted wildly to the music. One woman writhed obscenely like a sand sucker and was sold for forty-two pieces of gold. By the time the dancers had been sold off, the wolf-walker's eyes were burning with the smoke and Hishn's nose was clogged from the smells. They both felt dizzy with the cloying drugs that wafted through the room, and Dion wished she could wear a veil, too, so she could filter out some of the smoke. Hishn coughed and pawed at her nose. Dion could do nothing. The bids went on. Ob Clintner bid two men up as high as they could go, infuriating them and then waving off their protest as if it were not worth a thought. Finally Mankarr announced the last sale. Clintner remained in his lazy pose, but his eyes sharpened when the three girls were herded onto the stage.

The girls stood as the first had done, their faces red with mortification and the thin chains on their arms and legs dragging them down. They would not look up, and the raider had to yank their faces forward for the men to see. They were beautiful girls, and the healer felt pity for them, wishing she could give them some comfort.

Beside her, Hishn growled deep in her throat, and Dion caught her uneasy thought. *This place smells more and more like a rabbit trap,* the Gray One warned.

But the auctioneer was still talking. ". . . such beauty already in girls so young. They are as yet untouched, except by the light of the moons. These two are the daughters of the Lloroi of the Ramaj Ariye, this one his niece."

"The three girls are offered as a group," Mankarr added. "Bidding starts at thirty gold pieces each."

The auctioneer took over. "Thirty pieces. Thirty pieces, thirty-five, forty pieces of gold, forty-two pieces." The bids rose quickly as the men got into the excitement of the sale, even knowing that Clintner would take the girls anyway. The tallest girl's eyes focused on Bentol at one point, but her surprise and joy died; suspicion and despair replaced them when she saw strangers with him and not her brother. Dion wondered what rumors flew in her village about the pudgy trader. "Fifty pieces. Look at their beautiful faces. The flash of their silky hair. I have sixty pieces, sixty-two—" Bentol discreetly showed a closed fist. "Sixty-five pieces of gold." Clintner looked around to see who was bidding him up, and when his eyes met those of Bentol, they darkened. "Sixty-five, sixty-six, sixty-eight pieces of gold. Look at those gorgeous green eyes." The auctioneer's voice caressed the room, singling out Clintner as he noticed the other bidders dropping out and leaving the battle to Bentol and the merchant. "See the fire that flashes there. Such spirit is—seventy pieces of gold!" The voice was triumphant. "I have seventy pieces, seventy-one—"

"Let us hold for a moment under the rules of the charter." Clintner's angry voice broke through the auctioneer's drone.

Mankarr stood up, unsurprised, and calmly looked askance. "What is it, Clintner?"

The man glared at Bentol and gestured angrily at the trader. "It is against the charter to bid above the fixed price. We have all agreed—"

"Agreed on what?" Bentol broke in with apparent unconcern. "I was not aware that the prices are fixed."

"You were not invited, either," Toserva Nefarg put in.

"But I am here and was accepted before the sale began." Bentol waved his hand negligently. "I am most sincerely"—he smiled lazily—"apologetic if I have bid above the fixed price, but—"He paused and looked around the room. "Since this is a cash sale and I was not told the prices before the bidding began, I have the right to offer my gold freely for those prizes that catch my eye."

"You should keep your eye and your gold to yourself or you might lose them both."

"Clintner," Mankarr warned.

"And you," Clintner accused the merchant. "You set this up. It is your responsibility."

"The one who requests the sale is responsible for naming the bids," Bentol stated firmly. "And, Clintner, you requested the sale—and accepted my presence."

The merchant's face darkened. One of the others, gleeful at a chance to snipe at Clintner, put in, "Let us get on with this. The matter is settled."

Clintner looked murderously at the man, then sat back. "I will offer seventy-five pieces of gold apiece for the girls."

The auctioneer glanced at Bentol. "I have seventy-five pieces of gold. Seventy-six. Seventy-nine . . ." The room began to murmur. Clintner looked around and gestured for Toserva Nefarg to lean toward him.

"He is borrowing from Nefarg," Bentol whispered out of the corners of his mouth, "but he will pay dearly for the favor. Nefarg is one of the men he bid up to the limit earlier."

"Eighty pieces of gold," the auctioneer continued uncertainly. "Do I hear more?"

Nefarg nodded to Clintner, and the merchant signaled the auctioneer. "Eighty-one pieces of gold for each girl. Eighty-one. Eighty-eight." His voice raised the tension in the room as much as Bentol's bid had. The noise level rose suddenly and fell as quickly as Clintner looked furiously toward another man. "Eighty-eight," the auctioneer repeated anxiously.

Metrinadon, another man Clintner had bid up to the limit, shook his head. Clintner made a signal that spoke volumes, and Metrinadon finally nodded, a malevolent smile on his face as he contemplated the interest he would receive for the night's loan of his gold. "Ninety. Ninety pieces of gold." The auctioneer wiped his brow. "Ninety-eight." Clintner turned to two other men he had previously angered. One made a gesture, and Clintner's face darkened further, but he nodded; the other glanced at Bentol, then smiled viciously and nodded also. The auctioneer nervously raised his voice over the murmuring. "One hundred. One hundred pieces of gold for each girl. One hundred and one. One hundred and two. One hundred five."

The amount of gold they were betting staggered Dion's mind. I could buy that entire tract of land, she thought, incredulous, for the price of one of these girls. But Clintner and Bentol were not bidding just for the three girls who stood so ashamed in front of the room; the two men were bidding to beat each other. "One hundred eight pieces of gold—" The auctioneer's voice broke, and he cleared his throat. "One hundred ten. Do I hear more?" Bentol finally raised his hand. "One hundred fifteen." Clintner gestured angrily. "One hundred twenty." The auctioneer looked helplessly back at the trader, and Bentol signaled again. "One hundred twenty-five pieces of gold. One hundred thirty. One hundred thirty-five." There was a pause, and Clintner looked down at his hand. He viciously pulled off a signet ring and held it up. "One hundred forty pieces of gold for each of the girls before you." The auctioneer looked as if he were going to faint when Bentol calmly raised his hand once more. "One hundred fifty pieces of gold." The auctioneer's voice trembled. The lines of sweat ran down the side of his face, but he did not notice. Clintner looked slowly around at Bentol, then sat back, a grim look on his face. "One hundred fifty. One hundred fifty. Going, going, sold," the auctioneer announced, his voice hoarse, "to the trader Altiss Hantinn, three girls for the sum of—" He swallowed loudly. "—one hundred and fifty pieces of gold each, cash up front."

Bentol rose and moved to the front, followed by Rhom with two small bags. He dumped the bags heavily on the appraiser's table, and there were a few moments of confusion while the gold and jewels were sorted out. In the meantime, while Hishn's hackles rose and a growl began to grow deep in her throat, Dion was studied by Clintner. Bentol was just sitting down, his purse much lighter, when Clintner's voice rose above the murmuring once again.

"Since we have been discussing the charter rules tonight, I would like to bring up one more." The room quieted down, and Bentol looked at Clintner, his eyes narrowing. "Uninvited guests must expect to show equivalent wealth for the prizes they bring with them, which can be bid upon by any interested party. Altiss—" He paused malevolently. "You have brought with you some very unusual prizes. I would like to bid for them now."

The trader's face tightened. "The sale is over," he began.

"The bidding has not yet been closed," Clintner corrected.

Bentol turned to Mankarr with a gesture, but Mankarr shook his head. "Clintner is right, Altiss. You must allow the bid. If you cannot show comparable worth, you must give up your prizes." Mankarr gestured for the auctioneer.

Bentol turned to Rhom and Dion. "This is a show of wealth," he said in a low voice. "I must be able to top Clintner's final offer or sell you to him for his last bid. If I match him piece for piece, he keeps his bid and I keep the prizes—in this case, you two and the wolf—neither of us loses. If I best him with a higher offer he can't match himself, he will lose half his bid to me." Bentol tried to wipe the worry from his face. "Clintner can still use the four hundred and forty pieces he borrowed, and he may do this for revenge. I have less than two hundred in gold left— not enough to match him if he is serious about buying you just to humiliate me in spite of the price he would pay. We might have to break for the door. Mankarr already sent the girls upstairs." He gestured toward the curtains that hid the slave chambers. "They'll be ready when we leave. If we get out of here."

"The bidding," Mankarr interrupted, "will start at a hundred pieces for the girl, the man, and the wolf." The auctioneer nervously cleared his throat again. "A hundred pieces . . ."

Dion listened to the bidding as if in a dream, Hishn's growing fury like a fire that burned her thoughts. She felt Rhom's tension as if it were her own, her eyes flashing each time Clintner bid up the sale. For it was a sale. Since the twins had come in as owned servants, nothing they said now would make the other merchants believe they were there of their own free will. Papers got lost, others were forged; in the case of Rhom, Dion, and the wolf, previous sale papers would be completely overlooked. And if Bentol could not match what Clintner bid, Rhom and Dion—and Hishn—would legally belong to the merchant. The price rose to two hundred pieces. Rhom's hands were on his belt as he stood behind his sister, ready to use his sword and the knives hidden at his side. Hishn's mind was ranging, trying to sort out the hostilities and excitement in the room. The bidding rose again. Bentol faltered. Clintner seemed to pounce. "One hundred eighty pieces." The auctioneer's voice wavered. "One hundred eighty-one pieces. One hundred eighty-five." Bentol glanced at the twins desperately, helplessness in his eyes. The auctioneer looked at Bentol one more time for a bid, but the trader could not signal to bid what he did not have in cash. "Going. Going—"

A pure sweet trill broke the tension, and everyone stared. There was a confused murmur, but the auctioneer stared straight at Dion until all eyes were on her. The healer rose slowly and glided to the front, bowing to the appraiser. The auctioneer held his breath. Bentol held out his empty hands. Clintner held his temper, but just barely. Finally Dion reached into the folds of black velvet and produced a small green emerald that flashed in the light of the lamps. The appraiser took it lovingly, holding it in his hands as he examined it under the glass. "It is flawless," he announced. "Thirty-one pieces."

The auctioneer cleared his throat. "Two hundred eleven pieces." Clintner closed his fist. "Two hundred twenty-five pieces." Dion did not leave the appraiser's table, and Bentol leaned back, deliberately casual though his eyes were tight, and smiled at Clintner. "Two hundred twenty-five," the auctioneer repeated, looking at Bentol, then at the woman who stood so quietly before him. She bowed, producing another green stone. The appraiser took it as he had the first, and the bidding rose again. Dion brought out the stones one by one, matched each time by Clintner, till she had nothing left. Clintner leered at her and smirked at Bentol, and the healer could feel her face flush. "Four hundred and twelve pieces of gold." The auctioneer's voice cracked as he repeated Clintner's sum. She hesitated, then drew out a carved silver knife she always carried for luck. It was not worth much, but it was something. "Four hundred nineteen pieces of gold." The auctioneer looked at Clintner. "Four hundred twenty-five pieces of gold." The auctioneer's voice seemed to stick in his throat as he repeated Clintner's last and leering sum. Dion bowed her head. Had she nothing left? But Clintner still had fifteen pieces of gold to bid with. She clenched her hands over the blade still hidden in the baggy pants. "Going," the auctioneer croaked.

Healer, Hishn's thought broke through the woman's, *your headband.*

"Going . . ."

The healer trilled once more, the clear tones interrupting the auctioneer as he opened his dry mouth to close the sale. And Dion reached up and removed her headband, setting it before the appraiser and making a sign. There was a murmur, and the room was silent. The intricate silver and blue stood out soberly among the random gold piled in front of the appraiser. She did not know how much the band itself was worth, but on the slaver's scales its bare ornamentation meant much more than earthly metal. With the healer's band itself, Dion was offering herself and her skills. If she lost this bid, not only Rhom, Hishn, and Dion but Dion's healing skills would belong to Clintner, to be used however he wished, for good or evil.

Moons of mercy, she prayed, Clintner doesn't have more than fifteen more pieces. Let this be worth the sixteen pieces of gold that were paid to have it made . . .

The appraiser turned it over and examined it minutely. He finally turned to the auctioneer. "For the band, three pieces of gold. For the healer's skills, for a term of four ninans as outlined by the skills listed in the charter, sixteen pieces of gold, four silvers," he announced. Dion's knees felt weak with relief, and her heart started beating again. The appraiser handed her jewels and headband back, and she tucked the first things back into their pouch after setting the band over her glossy hair.

Clintner had nothing further to say. His face raged dark red, for Bentol had beat his best offer, and there were sly smiles among the other merchants. Ob Clintner had just been disgraced twice before them, had been beaten at a deal he had set up himself, and had lost half his borrowed wealth to a mere trader. If ever eyes could give death to a man, the power was there in Clintner's face.

Mankarr started the musicians, sending the dancers leaping to the tabletops, breaking the last bits of tension with exotic music. Clintner gestured furiously for his manservant to give Bentol half his bid, and the trader saluted the merchant lazily.

"Leave," Mankarr ordered in an almost imperceptible whisper as he passed Bentol.

The trader made no response, but his small group rose, making a casual way to the door. Rhom watched the movements of the merchants from the corners of his eyes as the dancers whirled on; the music beat at his twin's consciousness till the door shut mercifully behind them.

Hishn lunged up the stairs in relief, ignoring Dion's cry until she had escaped the smell of the drugs below. *The hunt is on,* she sent, slinking across the hall past a startled servant. The man hesitated as if to stop the wolf, and she whipped around, slashing at his calves while he shrieked and ran.

"Control your pets, Altiss," Mankarr snapped. But Dion was already soothing the wolf, calling her back from the windows, where the Gray One ran from one to the other, snarling and baring her teeth at the bars that covered them all.

"The girls are in here," the merchant said in a low voice. Rhom, with a backward look down the hall, waited outside the room as Dion took the heavy cloaks from the merchant and went in to help the girls into them. The eldest girl, taking one look at the healer and the wolf, went pale. She drew the heavy garment closely about her, then did the same for the youngest as the wolfwalker helped the middle girl into the other wrap. Dion was glad of the lighting—she was not sure it was appropriate for a woman of the harem to blush at such scanty clothes. At least they had slippers on instead of the bare feet the dancers had used downstairs. They would be silent on the steps. She hoped.

"Now, go quickly," the merchant warned, hastening them to the door. "Clintner lost money tonight that wasn't his and has nothing to show for it but a foolish face. He'll be a devil till he gets his revenge." Mankarr opened the door and began talking in a normal voice for the benefit of the drivers in the courtyard. Dion, who felt as if there would be a knife in her back at any moment, glided smoothly down the steps, leading the girls to the dark carriage that awaited. She glanced back only once; Clintner was there at the door, gesturing angrily after them at Mankarr, the man's sharp and furious eyes following them with vengeful intent as they drove away.

VII

Aranur Bentar neDannon:

Lost Again

Flee while the night is still dark
Fly while the fog hides your tracks
Fight when their breath warms your neck
Kill when their blades near your heart

Aranur had been waiting for three hours, his sword loose in the scabbard and his ears strained for noise within the house as he paid scant attention to the talk of the other drivers.

"Last I heard," said the short one with the too-long cloak, "Ramaj Caflanin was going down."

Another laughed, tossing his copper to land close behind the first man's coin. "Not a chance, Mick. Even Zentsis wouldn't waste his time on that land."

"It has value," the man insisted. "It borders more of the coastline than any other Ramaj."

The other driver tossed his coin against the wall. "Worthless land, worthless sea. You can't squeeze out taxes where there's no people to pay."

The tallest one chuckled.

Eyeing the way the coins had landed, Aranur rubbed his thumb twice along the edge of his own copper and almost missed the sharp, sidelong look he got from Mick. Aranur hesitated, then kept his voice lower than usual when he spoke. "Whether Zentsis moves in or not, Caflanin is his."

"How do you figure?" the tall man asked, squinting at the coins and then at Aranur. "This one's yours again, Mick."

Aranur shrugged, pulling his cloak in tighter as the wind tried to pry it from his chilled fingers. "Zentsis uses the roads through Caflanin to keep Prent's old rule controlled. He owns the borders on all sides except that of the sea, and the Cliffs of Bastendore keep the people from settling out on the coast, so where would they get supplies or help from if he decided to cut them off?" He dug in his pocket for another copper as the drivers started another game. "Better to take the crumbs of trade he gives them than deny him access and force him to make it an issue."

"You've got more brains than you look," one of the men said with a grin, peering at Aranur's shadowed face as if he were trying to place his voice.

"Your throw, Borden," the short one prodded. "Can't you tell he's not a man to let anger skew his toss?"

"Doesn't hurt to try."

The other, stockier driver studied Aranur, too, as if he thought the lean, dark-haired man familiar, and Aranur let his hand rest casually closer to his sword hilt. "How long's Altiss in town this time?" the man asked.

Casual. Too casual, Aranur thought. He shrugged easily enough, careful to let the light behind him catch on his shoulder and leave his face in deeper gloom. "He hires the carriage; I drive the dnu. He doesn't tell me much."

"If he's like Nefarg," one man said slyly, "he tells you enough to tease your dreams but not enough to appease them."

"As if he'd ever let you sample his wares," another snorted. "Nefarg is the last one to—"

He bit off his words as if a sword had cut his tongue, and they all moved, like shadows shrinking when a light is turned on, back to their carriages, for there were voices in the hallway near the door and the clank of chains to keep the voices company.

But it was the merchant Mankarr with Bentol, and he had three girls in tow behind the healer and her wolf. Aranur could see the attraction the women of the harem had for the slavers of Sidisport: In the dark folds of the harem pants and the tunic of an untouched one, Dion was beautiful, and he suffered a few thoughts of her in a harem of his own.

Namina—and Ainna—and, moons be praised a hundred

times, Shilia was there, too, dressed in scanty clothes that could be glimpsed beneath heavy cloaks, shamed and showing it with cheeks still burning, but by the gods, Aranur thought, carefully relaxing his fists with a wary glance toward the other drivers, safe. She still did not know—none of the three knew—that he was already there, that Bentol and Dion and Rhom were friends; he wanted to shout and grab her and run into the house and kill the raiders he found. But he moved no muscle, showed no part of his fierce joy except the imperceptible shaking of his body, where he held his relief and rage clenched tight. And then Rhom appeared, striding behind the girls, his sword out as if to slap them should they move too slowly. Their small chains clinked thinly in the damp evening while despair dragged their shoulders down as much as the chains did.

". . . fortunate for me that you dropped by," Mankarr was saying. "I hope you enjoy your bargain, as well."

"My bargain? Ha!" the trader snorted. "You already have twenty-five percent of my bids as the house take, you old tamrin, and you wouldn't hesitate to try to skin my back in another deal, too."

"You're too kind," Mankarr mocked. He looked up and changed the subject. "The weather is getting stormy. There's an inn with a good reputation near the south end of town. You may want to stay the night instead of trying to travel the main road in the rain."

"Oh? I'll consider it. Pleasant trading, Mankarr."

"And you, Altiss."

Dion glided silently to the carriage and waited while Aranur opened the door and helped the first girl in. It was Namina, Tyrel's oldest sister, and as she took Aranur's hand, she looked up and gasped.

"Quiet," he whispered savagely, gripping her wrist hard as he thrust her in. Namina, stunned, barely choked his name back before Ainna joined her in the carriage. Aranur's own sister, Shilia, was last, and he had to pry her fingers out of his own to step back and give Dion room to get in with the wolf and Bentol.

"To the east side," Bentol directed him quietly, as if the trader did not want anyone to hear but was too pleased with himself to keep his voice down. "Over to Quarterlain's house," he added jovially.

Rhom swung up on the driver's seat and settled without a

word till Aranur slapped the traces and the clacking of dnu hooves hid his words. Then, glancing behind him, he murmured, "Take a right at the next wellcourt, then straight two blocks."

Aranur complied without comment. Ah, Shilia, he thought, you'll be home again in two ninans, gossiping with the girls and flirting with those I disapprove of. But home again, and safe. And, he added grimly, it'll be a dark day in the seventh hell before I let the hooves of a raider's dnu ring in the pass again.

Left, then left again at the squat house of the Sequent, and then past the glibben trees along the square. Straight another mile, then a quick dodge right, left again, and down through the lane by the old woolen mill—Aranur sent the dnu twisting through town to hide their passage, merging with the traffic on the busier streets and then darting away again to drive pursuers out into the open, where he could see them if they dared to follow.

When the carriage pounded across the waterfront to the dock, Tyrel and Gamon were waiting, dripping wet under their cloaks but with grim smirks on their faces. Gamon gave his nephew a glimpse of the raider's money bag he was holding under his cloak, and Aranur flashed him a quick grin before they swung into the carriage. He heard a muffled squeak, then a lupine yelp, and wondered who had sat wetly on whom, but there was no time to find out. Salmi's payroll coffers must have been very full, Aranur thought with satisfaction. For the first time in two ninans, his smile touched his eyes and the tension around his jaw relaxed—Shilia, his sister, was safe again. Moonworms, but he had missed her, feared for her, raged that raiders could ever have touched her—he forced his hands to relax again as the dnu picked up his sudden tightening on the reins and broke into a faster trot, pulling them to a slower, less obvious pace and letting the six-legged gaits drum the damp night into his head while he held to his calm like a desperate man clinging to a plank in the sea. As the docks came to an end and the road roughened into a less-traveled way, he finally slapped the traces and urged the dnu into a rhythmic lope toward the south end of town, where Mankarr had directed them.

The inn was still lit as time moved into the early hours of morning, and the singing inside was still loud as they approached. Aranur pulled up at the side of the inn, and Rhom swung down. Bentol and he went in, the door loosing a shaft of light like a spear that split the courtyard and the noise quieting momentarily till those inside judged the visitors and let them be. Aranur fidgeted. The dnu, placid as usual, hardly picked up the uneasy mood that clung to him like a cloud hugging a mountain, but they stamped their feet as the traces twitched, eager to get to the stable and start on their dinner. "It's about time," he muttered as Rhom and the trader were silhouetted in the doorway again, followed by the shape of the merchant Mankarr as the yellow light dodged around their legs and stretched out as far as it could before the innkeeper called it back and shut the door. "Use the running boards," Aranur ordered the three men, already starting the dnu around to the back of the inn. The sudden sway of the carriage told him that they had caught the edge of the roof, and he did not look back, too busy guiding the dnu at a fast pace through the barrels and stacks of goods waiting for pickup and the small sheds for storage.

Rhom jumped down to open the stable doors while the firmhanded leader held the impatient dnu stomping and snorting in the cold. They could smell the dry hay inside, and they were hungry.

The stable was dry inside and smelled of clean, musty hay, but Aranur felt another twinge of unease—it would not be hard for anyone who had overheard Mankarr to stake out the few inns on that side of town while they were at the wharf. And Mankarr himself could have been followed. "It's been too easy," he muttered to Bentol. "Too damn easy to get this far without a squall out of the raiders."

"Hah," the trader whispered back as Aranur tied the traces onto the driver's seat and swung down to open the carriage doors. Rhom and Mankarr closed the stable doors quickly behind them. "If you'd seen the market block," the trader continued, "you'd cut your own tongue out before saying that again. Mankarr says that Clintner's out for blood."

Whatever else the trader said was lost as Shilia burst from the carriage. "Shilia!" Aranur caught her from the step.

"Oh, Aranur!" And then she was in his strong arms, her arms choking his throat in her relief and tears, and Aranur felt the protective urge rise in him and feed his fury at the slavers. "Oh, Aranur, we thought we were lost. We thought no one would ever come for us.'' Her silent sobs cut off her words as she cried out her shame on her brother's shoulder.

"It's all right, Shilia,'' he whispered back. "I'm here. You're safe now. Tyrel,'' he said over his shoulder, "get their clothes out from the bags.''

The trader had removed the girls' chains on the way to the inn, and now Gamon threw the indentured slave links violently into the hay with a grunt. "Disgusting things,'' he said, helping Ainna down from the carriage. There was a sense of urgency in the air, and they all moved as stealthily as thieves. "You girls change now,'' Aranur directed in a low voice. "That way we'll attract less attention when we go into the inn. Tyrel, haven't you got those bags yet?''

"It's dark under here,'' the boy complained softly from under the carriage. "I can't feel the knots.'' The girls climbed reluctantly back in, Ainna taking a moment to squeeze her brother's calf where it stuck out so awkwardly from under the wheels.

Suddenly Aranur tensed. There was a flash of dim light on metal inside the carriage. It was Dion's blade, drawn and ready, while the wolf's fangs gleamed dully in the shadows. "Aranur,'' she whispered urgently.

The hay rustled, and he swung around, startled. Two figures leapt to the carriage driver's seat and grabbed the reins. There were sharp cries from inside the carriage and a terrible snarling as the doors were instantly bolted and the girls were trapped inside. Mankarr and Aranur were closest to the carriage and leapt for the traces, but they were beaten off brutally. Swords sliced in the air before them as other men charged from the darkness of the dnu stalls, and they fought back to back, the night lit with the flash of swords where the metal blades clanged together. Aranur, Rhom, Gamon, and the two traders were suddenly fighting for their lives.

"Aranur!'' Shilia's despairing cry was flung back as the dnu burst through the open barn doors, the carriage careening past the inn and onto the street. The inn was too noisy for anyone to take more than a passing glance at the wildly driven coach, but in the light that spilled from the windows across the courtyard the gray-eyed man caught a glimpse of a figure hanging on underneath. *Tyrel* . . .

He parried and thrust, his attention brought sharply back to the man lunging at him from across a bale of hay. Aranur's well-timed blade slid easily along the other man's too-eager strike, and the soldier dropped with a bloody sigh, convulsing on the hay. Then Mankarr was beside him, parrying a blow aimed at the man's heart from behind. There was no time to thank him. Aranur could not see Gamon or Rhom; so many figures were clashing in the dark hay that they got in each other's way as they attacked.

Bentol had been cut off, his back to a stall, two men before him. Aranur could see the sweat gleaming as the trader tried to keep one of them between him and the other man. Bentol slashed, then ducked and tossed hay into the man's face, cutting down across the man's sword arm as he moved. The man cried out and lunged into the trader, a blade flashing momentarily in the poor light. Bentol slapped it down, but not soon enough. Aranur jumped across a hay bale and brought his own blade down, a hideous spurting sound indicating where the soldier's blood shot against the stall, and now he could see Rhom weaving wickedly to hold off three attackers and Gamon leaning against a stall with one hand pressed to his side and the other holding his sword in bare defense.

The lean man jumped on the back of the one who was stabbing Bentol's still shuddering body and fairly ripped the soldier's head off with his sword. Another man thrust his dripping knife at him, and Aranur felt cold steel slide along his arm. The soldier's eyes shone in the torchlight, but Aranur's rage was fiercer. He growled and threw himself into the soldier, both men crashing to the floor. Legs scrabbled against one another. The man from Ariye grabbed something and brought it down across the other man's neck as hard as he could; it was a wooden bar for locking the stall doors, and the soldier's struggling stopped as his neck snapped and his body went limp.

Aranur rolled to his feet and stood, panting harshly, the sweat still stinging his eyes and the dust from the hay beginning to settle. Mankarr had joined Rhom and had beaten down two of the three who found themselves flanked in the corner. The last one stood, backing away from the circle of blades, knowing he was now alone against at least three.

"Hold that one there." Aranur's voice grated against his heavy breathing. He could feel the sting in his arm as sweat ran into the slash and the edges of the gash scraped against his shirt.

"Altiss?" Mankarr asked, peering into the shadows from which the tall man had stepped.

"I did what I could," Aranur said harshly. "I'm sorry, Mankarr. He is dead. Gamon?"

"A little cut, a little bruised." The old man sucked in his breath as he straightened, his voice hardening as he added, "But strong enough for revenge." He wrapped his side with a cloth torn from a stable banner; the cut was long and nasty, not too deep, but he had lost a lot of blood.

Aranur nodded and turned to the man before them. "Drop the sword," he ordered. The soldier looked at the four hard-bitten men circling him and obeyed, the steel falling into the hay at his feet, and shifted nervously from foot to foot, looking first at Aranur, then at Rhom and Bentol.

"All right," Aranur said quietly, holding his rage with barely concealed control. "Where did they take the girls?"

"You'll be a long time in the second hell trying to find out," the man growled in mock courage.

"Cut off an ear for the first two wrong answers, Mankarr, then start on his eyes." It was not difficult for Aranur to make his voice hard. His fury was cold like the steel of his knife.

"Now, wait a minute," the soldier started, tensing up.

"You're going nowhere," Rhom snarled, jumping him and dropping him into the dust so that he choked.

Mankarr let his knees fall with a heavy thud onto the man's thighs, splitting the muscles beneath him and pinning the soldier's legs while Rhom forced his arms back and up. "You're not a mute," he said, startled, to Rhom.

"Nor a slave. And neither is my twin."

Mankarr nodded and wrenched the soldier's arm again.

"Ow—gods dammit, you're breaking my arms!"

Rhom forced his arms higher behind his back. "We'll break more than that if you don't start talking."

"Clintner'll get you for this." He spit the words out between clenched teeth.

"What he'll get is a pair of ears," Mankarr whispered. The merchant's knife gleamed at the soldier's ear and gently, very gently, began to cut through. "I think I'll send them wrapped," he added softly. "Wrapped in your skin from, let me see, what should I cut next, Rhom?"

Rhom looked slightly sick, but he forced his voice to be as

cold as the chill air that clutched at their skin. "The eyelids, I think." He wrenched the man's right arm up over the left so that the left was pinned by the soldier's own body and Rhom's hand was free. "Then the eyes."

The man froze when he sensed the steel sliding across his skin, the heat of his own blood panicking him.

"This was none of my doing," the soldier choked out. "I was just following orders."

"Orders to enslave young girls? Orders to cheat a merchant out of his fair bid?" Aranur laughed harshly, the sound a mockery of humor. "Those are orders to die if you don't tell us where our little birds have gone."

"Dammit, Clintner'll have my hide!"

"I already have your hide now," Aranur snapped. "The girls—where are they being taken?"

Mankarr's blade moved deeper, and Rhom turned the man so that his blood ran bright red down his neck and stained the hay before his eyes, drop by drop.

"For moon's sake—" the man gasped.

"For your sake," Aranur corrected. "The girls—where? Now!"

Mankarr gave a decisive slice, and the man shuddered. "Clintner—" he gasped. "It was Ob Clintner and that captain, Salmi. Believe me, they had it all rigged. He'd been promised the girls from the start. The others were just there to bid him up."

"How did you know where we were?" Aranur's voice was as sharp as the blade Mankarr held, ready to start slicing again if the man's words came too slowly.

"His driver overheard Mankarr sp-peak of the inn. He sent men to follow you when you left; Salmi helped pay for them—"

The man was nearly sobbing. Mankarr had cut nearly halfway through his ear, and it was getting very messy. Aranur's stomach roiled, but he thought of his sister and hardened his heart. "Where are they now?" he demanded.

"Ob Clintner's," the man gasped as the knife moved again. "Ob Clintner's!"

Mankarr pushed the man away, and Rhom released his arms. The man scrambled back, but Rhom's pommel caught him along the temple and laid him out cold. "Ob Clintner," Mankarr said, his voice grim as he wiped his blade in the hay, "has the biggest harem in town. He lets his guests sample his wares."

"But taking the girls to his own place?" Aranur shook his head. "He must have a lot of confidence."

"He can afford to," Mankarr said quietly.

"What do you mean?" Rhom demanded impatiently, tightening the cinches on the saddles of the dnu he had gathered in the gloom.

"Just that Clintner knows his business. I was as surprised as you that Clintner took the girls to his own home, but when I think about it, I don't know why not. He has over twenty men on the grounds at all times, and the place is built like a fortress. If he wanted to . . ."

Aranur looked at the merchant with gray eyes cold as ice. "If he wanted to?" he prompted, stopping momentarily from wrapping his bloody arm with a spare cloth.

The other man looked uneasy. "He could easily hold us off long enough to mark the girls for his harem. If so, there's nothing you could do to get them out again. He could have started in on them already, and from the way he looked at your twin," he added with a nod to Rhom, "I'd say she's the first to go in."

"No." Rhom shook his head decisively. "No, Dion is in no danger yet."

Aranur raised his eyebrow, and even Gamon looked sharply at the younger man.

"I *know*," Rhom said fiercely, as if to convince himself with his vehemence. "She is safe for now. If we go quickly . . ."

Aranur put his hand on Rhom's arm, trying not to think of Shilia. "We'll go now," he promised grimly.

Leaving the bodies where they lay, Aranur took Bentol's limp form and carefully tied him to the saddle of the fifth dnu. They would return him home, though it was a sad burden they would bring.

As they slipped quickly out the rear of the barn, Mankarr sat stiffly, his eyes unseeing, and Aranur rode closer and put his hand on the merchant's arm. "Is it Bentol?" he asked.

The other man nodded.

"Mankarr, who was Bentol to you?"

"Not Bentol. Altiss," the merchant corrected unsteadily. The tears were running down his dirty face, but he did not notice. "He was my brother."

VIII

Ember Dione maMarin:

Fly by Fire

Luck flies with bold hearts
Like Aiueven on the wing

Three guards roped Gray Hishn and dragged her away snarling and lunging, their ropes taut in different directions to keep her fangs from them all. Dion could feel the wolf's rage color her own emotions as she beat on the ground, wailing and moaning like the semimute Bentol had proclaimed her to be. He embellished the story of Rhom and me a little too much, she thought angrily. It's fine for a flash appearance, but how well would it stand up to the sharp eyes and ears of a slimy tamrin like Clintner? A mute who could sing and not talk? He had not even asked if Dion had a good voice. She was afraid that Clintner, whose eyes had lusted on her as well as on the girls who had stood before him on the block, would want to sample her, too. As she loosed another ear-wrenching keen and Hishn emitted a three-tone howl, doors slammed and suddenly the good master himself had come to the courtyard to see why his prizes were making such a racket.

"It's the mute and the wolf, sir," the lieutenant shouted, directing the men dragging Hishn off. "The moment we split them up, they went crazy."

"You." Clintner pointed at Shilia, who had at least maintained a face of calm. He, too, had to yell over the noise. "What's the matter with her?"

"How should I know—" The girl's voice dripped the next words sarcastically. "—good master." She shrugged disdainfully. "When they are together, the girl is an imbecile and the dog is a babe."

Dion got the feeling that if it had not been for the laws that protected women of the harem, Clintner would gladly have had the healer knocked out to shut her up. As the din showed no sign of diminishing, Clintner made an angry gesture. "Bring the wolf back," he ordered.

"Sir!" The lieutenant whirled and gestured for the men to return. Reaching Dion, Hishn lay beside her panting softly while Dion knelt and scraped the ground toward Clintner over and over. Shilia coughed, smothering a laugh. It's all very well for her, Dion thought sourly, trying not to sneeze. She's not the one who has to rub her nose in the dust.

"Get the mute off the ground. She looks like a beggar with convulsions." Clintner gestured to the lieutenant. "And put the others with the women. Tell Marash to prepare two of them for me tonight. I'll put my mark on the other one in the morning." He turned back to the wolfwalker and hesitated, frowning at the ropes that were still taut around the wolf's neck. "Since that one loves her dog so much, put her in the blockhouse with it till I call for them." He did not spare so much as a glance back at her when he had finished, and since the soldiers hurried to obey, Dion had no chance to signal or even give a comforting look to Ainna, closest to her and most frightened.

At the thought of the other girls' panic, another question suddenly poked through the commotion like a mud serpent sprouting from a bog: Would Clintner leave Dion alone? If Bentol's story had convinced him—and Dion was not at all sure that it had—he might not touch her for a while, at least until he realized that the story was untrue, but as she glided smoothly beside Hishn, patting the wolf like the idiot Shilia had told him she was, the wolfwalker felt a chilling unease grip her hard. *Once marked as a harem wife, never free in life.* The saying was not one Dion needed to think of right then. If Clintner tried to mark her, there would be the witnesses, not just the merchant to take care of—the head of the harem and two others from the women's quarters, then two of Clintner's men, and Clintner himself. Not good odds. "Oh, Rhom," she whispered. "Please hurry."

For the first few moments she had not worried about her brother, Aranur, or anyone else—the shock of the attack had hit her with sudden fear and fury, and she had been more concerned about where her knife would land than with where her twin stood left behind. But now, as her feet padded across the hard stone of the courtyard and the silver flash of soldiers' spears prodded her toward the stone blockhouse, Dion had second thoughts about the attack. Clintner had not struck her as a man who would indulge in a grab-and-dash raid. In fact, she realized, Clintner must have begun making his plans as soon as Bentol had bested him in the bidding for the girls—Clintner's attempt to take Dion and Rhom from the trader had merely motivated the Sidisport merchant to get a bloodprice out of Bentol instead of making a simple revenge trade.

And she had been stupid not to see it coming. If she had not been crooning to the Gray One at her side, she would have spit her disgust on the shiny black boots of the soldiers who were leading her across the stones. Hishn had been nervous enough, and even Dion had felt the unease—why in the second hell hadn't she listened to what the moons were trying to tell her? And now? The wolfwalker looked surreptitiously around and had to admit that Clintner had planned his home well for attack or siege. A well-planned raid, a well-armed base; she was surprised for the moment that Clintner had taken them to his own place since it seemed so obvious, but then, it would not matter how obvious it was if there was no one left to come after them. Her crooning faltered. *Rhom?* She sent the frightened thought out with Hishn's amplifying power. *Rhom!* It struck her again that Clintner would not have taken risks of losing the prize and having the plot come to light; the authorities did not look kindly on anyone who disturbed the peace, whether he—or she, Dion reminded herself—was attacking or defending.

The fact that she kept her head bowed let her use the shadows to hide her anger, but now they were standing in front of the blockhouse, and the bright torches that burned bravely on the gray walls were creating a light that haunted her face and forced the wolfwalker to control herself. Hishn, picking up the woman's fear as the foremost guard unlocked the first door, growled and flattened her ears, the bristle on her shoulders rising imperceptibly at first.

There is more to handle now than vague thoughts and uneasy smells, Hishn said with a nudge that almost unbalanced the healer. *This place is cold like the heart of a seven-day corpse.*

Now, that's a comforting thought, Dion retorted, thinking of a hundred ways to break free and not one that would get her out of Clintner's clutches without a spear in her back or an arrow in Hishn's. The Gray One ignored her thoughts and snarled more clearly as the soldier pulled the heavy door open so that the darkness emerged almost like a nameless evil. The flickering torches fought it back, holding it at bay in the blockhouse, but Dion had no urge to enter.

It's cold and dead, the wolf sent. *Scents of old boots and worn leather, old blood and dust.*

Dion shuddered. As the soldier stepped back and gestured for her to go in ahead of him, she balked. The cell was dark, with only a small barred window in the door for light; inside, the stone looked as cold as the empty courtyard. An abundance of steel and stone, she thought, with only a drop of blood to warm it. But she paused. Maybe, just maybe, a keening voice could bend its bars.

It had already kept her out of the harem for the night, and at the least, she thought, if they did not lock her in a stone cell, she would have a better chance of escaping—lock picking was a skill she had never learned, and unless she could steal a key, she would be stuck there till Clintner called for her, and the moons help Shilia and the other two in the meantime. But, she reminded herself, the moons helped those who help themselves, and the guise Bentol had spun for her might help her more with the harem laws behind it than she had thought at first it could.

Dion kept up her crooning until the guard stepped aside to push the two in, then began wailing and moaning again while Hishn took the cue and began to howl. A long, mournful howl that raised the hair on the back of their necks, the healer thought with satisfaction. One that'll make them plug their ears a ninan from now when they wake to the sound of the wind and think it the wolf come for their blood.

"Sssh," one of the guards hissed, looking around nervously. "Be quiet now." He put out a hand to half shove Dion into the

cell, but she dropped to her knees and he snatched his hand
back.

"For moonsake, Jontis, you'll lose your arm doing that,"
one of the others said.

"She went down by herself," he replied defensively. "I didn't
touch her. Dammit, woman, shut up."

She took a perverse pleasure in wailing louder; she had to
resist a sudden temptation to laugh while at the same time she
was resenting Bentol's imagination more and more.

"Maybe she's afraid of the blockhouse," another one suggested.

"Well, why don't you put one of the torches in it and make
it homey for her," Jontis snapped sarcastically over Hishn's
howl. "With a voice like that, Clintner'll want her as far from
him as possible when she isn't in his bed."

The stocky guard beside Jontis was nearly jerked off his feet
by Hishn's lunge at the ropes, and he staggered, giving the wolf
room to back up another meter from the cell. He motioned the
two inside again, pushing up behind them though trying to stay
as far away from Hishn as possible, and Dion turned her terrified
face to the guards, wailing to turn the stomach of even the most
tone-deaf person while Hishn added an increasingly amazing
repertoire of forlorn howls to the sky and pulled against the
ropes to keep them all off balance.

"Hurry up," the tall guard yelled angrily over the noise. "If
the noise drags Clintner out here again, we'll all be dnu meat."

Jontis made a gesture as if he were going to strike the other
man, then jerked back on the ropes Hishn was yanking around.
"What would you like me to do, Gordy? Grab her and throw
her in?"

I'd like to see you try, Dion thought smugly, knowing that
none of them could touch her without losing his hands to the
judge's ax.

"Why can't we just let them stay at the door?" the one with
the berry-stained fingernails shouted. "They're quiet enough
there," he added, "and Clintner's going to want them soon
enough, anyway." He stepped back, and Dion and Hishn settled
down on the stones again, her hands petting the wolf and her
voice crooning again. Dion was going to go hoarse if she had
to keep it up much longer, and she kept telling herself not to

laugh. It was like opening a door to a carnival band, she thought. On, off.

"We could watch them right here," the other suggested, breathing hard from struggling with Hishn and clenching and unclenching first one hand and then the other while maintaining his tight grip on the rope. "I'd bet five silvers that Clintner's business will be done within half an hour."

"Moonworms, can't anything go right tonight?" Gordy shrugged angrily. "Go ahead, do what you want, but I won't be responsible. You three stay and watch them. You sit out here all night, and it's your heads if they go anywhere." He stalked back to the gate and let himself out into the main courtyard.

"Guarding an idiot and a cur," Jontis scoffed.

"This was your idea, Jontis. We're stuck with it now unless you want to interrupt Clintner's business trying to get them inside."

"She's got a voice that could bend steel," the first one snarled. "If you want to think of a way to get them in without disturbing Clintner, that's fine with me."

The argument was degenerating quickly, so Dion just kept crooning to the wolf, lulling them into ignoring her and waiting for her chance. But fifteen minutes later her voice was already getting husky—she had not had a drink in hours, and she was getting tired of playing the idiot besides—and with the cold creeping through her cloak to her buttocks, it would only be a matter of time before she was too chilled to act. She shifted uncomfortably, then shifted again to cover the startled glance she could not help as a dark shape appeared at the top of Clintner's gate wall, silhouetted against the city-lit clouds. She blinked, and it was gone. Rhom? No, the shape had been too skinny. But Tyrel? The boy? Aranur would never allow it.

But then, Aranur might not be there. The thought that the boy was alone sobered her. No one else flitted over the wall. Dion thought at first that he had dropped into shadow on her side of the courtyard, but the dark was misleading, and she was not sure until she caught a glimpse of his cloak fluttering at the gatehouse corner. As if her look had called his attention to it, the cloak suddenly disappeared, snatched back into the shadow he was hiding in. Dion crooned with more intensity, slipping into one of the haunting lullabies that characterized the mountains of Randonnen.

There was one other guard in the courtyard besides the three watching Hishn and Dion so carelessly, and that one was lounging by the gate that led into the main yard. Tyrel's figure slipped up behind the gate guard as the healer started to sing softly, huskily. Watch me, she ordered the guards in her mind. *Watch me, Hishn. Keep your ears turned to me,* Dion silently commanded the wolf. The two shadowy figures merged, and the gate guard disappeared.

Hishn's nostrils flared as she caught Tyrel's scent and sent the woman his mental image. But Dion did not need it. The youth was coming across the courtyard in a crouching run, using the shadows and stacks of boxes as cover. She began swaying slowly, hoping the movement would distract the guards even more. One of them frowned and started to turn.

Tyrel clubbed the center guard over his head, and he slumped forward with a sigh. Dion's boot knife had already sunk deep in the throat of the guard to her left, but the one to her right was jumping up, drawing his sword and a breath to yell with. The boy and the wolf leapt at the same time, and the guard's startled cry stopped suddenly as his head cracked sickeningly against the stone.

"Moonworms, Dion, are you all right?" Tyrel whispered urgently.

"Yes." Hishn was darting from one to the other, snarling and snapping at the dead man and the two who were still breathing. Dion had to pull with all her strength to get the wolf away from them, but by the moons, it was hard to believe it had been so easy, so complete. She realized that two of the guards were still breathing and pulled her knife from the flesh of the third before starting to shake. Suddenly she could not hold the knife to clean it. Her hands seemed to blur before her eyes as the blood continued dripping from its blade. Tyrel gave her a sharp look, then pulled her to him and held her tightly for a moment, the pommel of his sword digging unnoticed into her side and his lanky bones hard against her shuddering body. "Just take a deep breath," he whispered awkwardly. "We'll be out of here in a couple of minutes."

Dion gulped, sucked in a breath, and held it against the sobs that shook her ribs; then, embarrassed, she pulled free and wiped the knife clean, careful not to drop it as she put it unsteadily back in its hidden scabbard. "The others—" She wished she could spit out the nauseating taste of the man's death—it sickened her like rotted meat. "The others are in the women's quarters, somewhere in the back of the house."

"I know," he said, dragging the guards into the blockhouse. "I caught a ride on the underside of the carriage and heard the whole thing. Here—" He started tugging at the uniform. "Wear this. We might be able to pull this off yet."

So he was alone. "Tyrel, only women can get into the harem. Hishn can go with me since they know who I am now, but we won't be able to get near the girls if we're dressed as men."

"What do you suggest? I could never pass as a woman, even in those baggy pants."

"You put the uniform on, and I'll stay like this. We'll just walk in as if we belonged. Take Hishn and me to—what was her name?—Marash, and tell her Clintner wants to see all three of the girls now."

"It sounds all right," Tyrel said uncertainly. He hesitated, and she realized sharply that he was only fifteen. "I don't know what else we could do," he admitted. "Through the side gate?"

She shook her head. "Kitchen. It should be empty by now, and if it isn't, you could always say you just wanted something to eat before going on guard duty."

But fortune shone with the fourth moon, and the kitchen was dark, closed for the night. Hishn was a ghost by their sides as they slid inside and sneaked down the hall toward the main house. Footsteps— The wolf warned them an instant before the sound reached their ears, and they swung into the shadows of a dark room and waited. The soldiers passed. Tyrel and Dion breathed again. Hishn, glancing disdainfully back at the two men who guarded the halls, snorted softly and headed on toward the back of the house. Tyrel looked out, and then the two slipped along the wall after the Gray One, where the sound of giggles, then laughter, and then the cruel cause of the mirth became clear. Tyrel's youngest sister, Ainna, was crying. The women were having some fun with the new girls. The youth tensed, and Dion put a hand on his arm, then stepped out behind him to the left, gliding submissively as they turned the corner and faced the harem guard.

"What do you want?" he growled. The guard was over two meters tall and easily weighed as much as Tyrel and Dion together. We're not getting out of here without a fight, the wolf-walker told herself.

One leap, Hishn sent. *One jump and he is mine . . .*
Wait, Gray One. We cannot risk raising the alarm.

"This one is to be prepared," Tyrel stated with casual confidence. "Clintner wants the others now."

The guard opened the doors and gestured for Tyrel to wait. The woman who must have been Marash came quickly to the door, her hard, jealous eyes belying her soft voice and flaying Dion's face with a look of scorn at the younger woman's beauty. "The two asked for are ready, good sir." She turned, and Ainna and Namina were brought up, their faces burning with shame. The healer was shocked. The girls were dressed in veils sheer enough to see completely through, and the heavy jewelry that masked their faces dragged their shoulders down as well. They had been sprayed with perfumes so that the scent of flowers lingered as they walked, and Shilia was receiving the same treatment from others. There must have been twenty women in the rooms.

"These are only two. I was told to bring all three," Tyrel stated with a frown. The girls recognized his voice, and their eyes widened, then dropped again with shame as they realized that their brother had seen them undressed for Clintner's pleasure.

"That is not what Gementel said," Marash contradicted. She took a closer look at Tyrel. "And I have not seen you before, have I?"

The guard at the door turned at her words and began to draw his sword, but Tyrel moved first. The butt of his knife smashed back into the guard's solar plexus, stunning him upright, then the boy struck him again on his temple. Dion jumped at Marash, drawing her blade and twisting the harem woman to stand in front of her, the knife poised against her throat. Hishn lunged forward, a snarl on her face and death in her eyes. Marash was frozen in the wolfwalker's grasp.

"A sound, and she dies, and the wolf will brand the rest of you on your faces," Dion threatened them harshly in the terrified silence that followed. "Tyrel, go, now!" Shilia slapped away the hands that reached to hold her down and darted toward her cousin, hesitating only as she passed an alcove and leaned inside to grab some heavy cloaks.

"Dion," the boy cried. "Come *on*!"

But she could see some of the women opening their mouths

to wail or scream. "The moment I leave, they'll bring the house down on us. Go! The Gray One is with me. We'll catch up." Tyrel hesitated, torn between rescuing his sisters and leaving Dion alone in Clintner's house. "Go!" she cried again.

Namina flung one of the cloaks about her shoulders, and Shilia did the same for herself and Ainna. Tyrel looked once more and said fiercely, "I'll be back for you." He turned and raced down the hall with the girls, their feet padding softly in the deep carpet as they escaped out through the dark kitchen. The women of the harem began to lose some of their terror as they realized that it was just another girl and what looked like a large dog that was holding them all there.

"And how long will you hold us so?" Marash whispered, her voice hateful. "I don't think you will do as you say."

"Oh?" The wolfwalker pressed the blade into the harem woman's throat, and a thin line of red appeared on her pale skin. "I think I will. And if I don't feel like draining all your blood away, I can think of other more unpleasant things to do. How much would Clintner or anyone else want you if your nose was slit like the hooves of a dnu, Marash? Or your eyes torn raggedly from your face by the Gray One's claws?" She gestured with her chin at the rest of the women, some of them barely girls. "And what I do to this one, I'll do to the rest of you, too."

Marash paled, and Dion saw that she had shocked them into silence for the moment. But someone would notice the guard at any moment, and the door was still open. "Everyone on their stomach on the floor," she barked. "Now!" Harem training took over, and they obeyed quickly. Dion struck Marash on her left temple, and the woman crumpled while Hishn growled and held the other women at bay. One woman made as if to rise. The massive wolf, glaring balefully, snapped at her hand, and she stifled her scream, snatching her fingers from the Gray One's well-fanged mouth. At the door, Dion dragged the guard inside. By the moons, he weighed as much as a dnu. She did not think she could have done it if the adrenaline had not fed her arms, and even then it was a struggle. No one had come down the hall yet, so unable to think of anything else, the wolfwalker grabbed the nearest oil lamp and dumped it on the floor. Someone cried out in fear, but the flames were already digging into the carpet and racing around the door. Dion called, and Hishn leapt to her. Then they were out the door, the heavy bar dropping easily into place, and down the hall into the first dark room they came to. Dion panted, adrenaline coursing in her veins and tension tightening her lithe form. She grabbed one of the soldiers' cloaks that hung against the wall and flung it around herself. In the dark, her black pants would pass for a soldier's uniform long enough to get her out of there. She hoped.

They would have to go out a window—even with the night shadows, the shape of the wolf was too easy to recognize. Moonworms, she swore silently. The screams from the harem could be heard now. Pounding footsteps were muffled in the carpet, and two men ran by. It took only a second to open the window for Hishn to jump out, and the wolfwalker was about to follow when three figures rounded the corner below and, startled, shouted at the wolf and gave chase. One of them got too close and went down beneath the Gray One's slashing fangs, but the other two drew back, yelling for more soldiers to help catch the beast. Even with the men in the court below, Dion was tempted to jump out and take her chances with the wolf, but behind her other voices starting yelling "Fire! Fire in the harem!" and the place exploded in action. Too many men were running into the main courtyard now—she would have to chance escape in the melee inside the house. A confusion of bodies raced back and forth in the hall. Women were thrust down the hall, and no one noticed that Dion, in her borrowed cloak and hurriedly crammed-on warcap, did not belong.

"You there, and you!" the lieutenant yelled at her from the stairs. "Man the pumps from the barn! You, Pent, make up the line! Fall *in*!"

Dion raced out, bumping against another man. She reached the door and hurried down the steps past the two soldiers who were running up. But one of them brushed open her cloak as he passed and realized that she was wearing harem dress.

"Stop, you!" He grabbed the wolfwalker's arm. "Where do you think you're going?" He turned to the other one as if to justify his touching her. "This one's trying to get away."

"Well, mark her and bring her back inside. Clintner'll deal with her later."

She let her shoulders droop as if in submission, but her leg flashed out as she turned and kicked him viciously, first in the knee, then the groin. *Gray One, where are you?* she called frantically in her mind. The man gasped and doubled over, and she brought her hands down across the back of his neck and slammed her knee back up into his face at the same time. His teeth were hard against her kneecap, but his nose crunched and his jaw snapped, and then she was staring fiercely into the shocked expression of the other man.

"Hey!" He snarled, lunging at her after a second's disbelief. "You bitch!"

But her knife flashed, and his wrist disappeared in a streak of crimson. He gasped, and her other hand clubbed the man across his neck as she thrust the pommel of the knife back into his solar plexus. It stunned him momentarily, but it was enough time for her to trip him down the stairs with his friend. Breathe, she commanded herself, and turned and fled from the now-immobile bodies into the darkness and confusion.

She was at the gate, her cloak flapping like a bono bird, and had just glimpsed the dark shadow of the wolf across the yard when another figure reached out from the shadows. He opened his mouth to shout, and then she was on him. She clubbed up with the hilt of the knife, hidden blade down against her wrist. But he seemed to have a sixth sense that the blow was coming and blocked it instantly, cuffing her across the cheek. "Hey—" His cry was cut off as she punched into his throat, but that blow slid away, too, weakened by his smooth movement to the side. He's too good for me, she thought desperately as they struggled, her mind calling out for help. *Hishn!* The man grabbed her shoulder and twisted her toward him, and she went with the motion, dropping down at the same time. She threw him over her, but he got hold of her hair, yanking her with him. Heavily, they crashed to the ground together. Her knife flashed again, and he brushed it away, trapping her arm in a controlling hold. She pretended to slump, then twisted instantly out of the hold as he relaxed, and he was not quick enough in the dark to stop the kick that caught him in his rock-hard gut. "Dion!" he hissed, finally smothering her struggles with her cloak and trapping her in the cloth that had protected her earlier.

Her second kick brought them both up against the courtyard wall, jarring her back and bursting the air from her lungs as he fell heavily on top of her. "Aranur?" she panted. "You? Here?" He lifted her to her feet, cloak and all, and swept her up into his arms. He was already striding to the wall as he said, "We have to hurry. The gates are locked, and they're going to light the courtyard any minute now.''

''I can walk, you know,'' she returned tartly, since he had not put her down yet. She could not help blushing as she remembered the other times he had touched her. But his arms were protective, and she was just beginning to realize that the pounding of her heart was only part of the throbbing she felt. Her leg burned where the muscles felt torn again.

''Wouldn't you rather ride?'' he asked, ducking into a shadow as men ran by. They both held their breath.

''I'd rather fly,'' she whispered, still clinging to his neck. The soldiers disappeared around the corner. She drew a ragged breath.

He glanced after the soldiers. ''We're not going to get through the courtyard now unless we run for it with something other than our legs. This way, milady.'' He set her down in the darkness cast by the blockhouse, and they fled through the shadows to the stables. They slid inside.

''Aranur—the carriage. And our gear,'' she cried softly. The packs were piled to the side where they had been thrown, and the carriage still stood ready to be hooked up again. Clintner had not had time to order things put away yet, or else he was expecting to use the carriage again that night.

Aranur gestured at the door. ''We can pick up the others—I left them below the main gate. Quick, get the packs. I'll get the dnu and harness.'' He hurried to the stalls and led two dnu to the bar, grabbing the traces as he passed the tack wall. Dion threw the packs inside the carriage and ran to help him hook up the dnu, but Aranur grabbed her arms and practically tossed her up into the driver's seat. ''Can you drive?'' he whispered, throwing the reins up next.

''Yes.''

''Then do so. I'll fend off the soldiers. But wait a moment.''

''What are you doing?'' She held the traces in her nervous hands. Every second they waited pulled her tension higher and tighter. They could be discovered any instant. *Hishn?* she called.

Where are you? The Gray One's thought reached out in confusion and frantic worry. *Your trail is as scattered as your thoughts. There is danger—too much danger for you . . .*

We're in the stables, Dion sent back quickly. She twisted at the sounds behind the carriage. ''Aranur, come on. We've got to get out of here *now*." The dnu were getting nervous, catching the edge of her excitement.

"I'm just loosing a few friends to add to the confusion," he called back softly. There was more stamping, then the back barn door creaked open slowly. As Dion watched nervously, the lean, powerful man shoved two of the too-eager dnu back until they crowded around the carriage.

Hishn's impressions came to the woman as Aranur swung up beside her on the seat: *No one is looking in the barn yet. The others are too busy with the fire. I can smell the meat burning already.*

Throwing two of the heavy lanterns into the now-empty hay, he smiled grimly. The spontaneous blaze began to eat at the barn. "Now we can go."

Without waiting for him to settle on the wooden seat, she slapped the traces on the dnu and let out a wild yell. The dnu, startled by her voice and panicked at the fire, jumped forward and raced out the door into the already smoke-filled courtyard, the carriage swept along in the middle of their stampede. They careered past two of Clintner's men running for the house and flung a third out of the way before the free dnu scattered, and then Dion drove straight for the opening gate that led to the entrance courtyard. *Hishn, where are you? Get out of the yard!* she sent urgently. Aranur, his sword gleaming dully in the moonlight, hung on, ready to beat down any who tried to bar their way. Four men raced out of the shadows to jump at the carriage. Aranur cut gruesomely at the hands of the first who tried to swing up on the running board, and the man screamed as his wrists were suddenly bare. Dion slapped the traces and yelled at the dnu. The other soldiers were already climbing up the back of the carriage as Aranur scrambled up on top and tried to balance through the unsteady ride. Sparing a glance at the fighting, Dion concentrated on the tall, barred doors of the courtyard as if she could make it there by will alone. *If we can just reach the gate . . .* There was another scream and the heavy thud of a falling body. Aranur was grappling with the third man while the last one swung along the side of the carriage toward her, his sword gleaming in his hand. *Hishn!* she screamed in her mind. The Gray One's thoughts were already lost in the hunt. *. . . dust, breathe softly. They come. Tense and leap. Ah, the taste—hot flesh, stringy meat . . .*

Aranur lost his footing and crashed forward, both fighters tumbling over the luggage rack to fall into the healer's lap. Dion nearly lost her hold on the traces as they fought back and forth. The man on the side tried to stab around the corner at Aranur, and she screamed. "Aranur, behind you!" She tried to swing the dnu to throw the man off balance, racing near a lamppost, and Clintner's man grunted as his shoulder was struck against the metal, but he held on till a gray shadow tore him from the carriage side. *Hishn!* Four more men were directly in front of the carriage, their arrows about to be loosed at all the struggling figures indiscriminately. Dion jerked the snorting dnu to the side, and the sound of metal hooks going into wood followed them back into the courtyard. Aranur's muscled arms gleamed with sweat through the rips in his shirt as his hands slowly forced the knife toward the man's panting chest. Just before the blade went in, he released the knife with his left hand and punched the man in the jaw, throwing him off the carriage to land heavily in the dust.

Dion circled wildly back toward the gate. Aranur beat off two more who tried to swing aboard. Just ahead of the snorting dnu, three soldiers rose up and jumped for the traces. *Hishn!* Dion shouted again. The gray shadow tore one man's gut wide open as he flung himself on the dnu. The man screamed thinly. His hand held his guts in disbelief as he knelt in the dirt. But the momentum of the wolf's strike carried her over, and she braked violently as the massive beast was thrown under the thundering hooves. "Oh, moons of mercy," she gasped. But the Gray One flashed like light from under the powerful feet of the dnu and hamstrung the man who jumped at Dion as she hesitated. "Gods . . ." She thrust an awkward kick at his head. Her foot hit his face, and he grabbed her ankle and jerked her down. "Damn you to the seventh hell," she snarled in fear and sudden fury. She ripped at his eyes but caught his nostrils instead and jerked his head back, his mouth hanging open at her expression and her heel catching him unexpectedly in the throat. He dropped to the ground with a choking sound, his trachea crushed and his lungs gasping for air that could not get in, the gargling noise lost in the rattling wheels that thumped over his arms and broke them with sickening cracks.

. . . *blood lust, hot and sweet* . . . Hishn's thoughts were no longer coherent, and the wolfwalker cried out in her mind.

"Get going!" Aranur yelled at her.

Hishn—to the gate—

. . . lunge. Take to the shadows. Slink. Pause. Now—fast and low, rip the legs and turn—crack the spine . . .

Gray One! Dion shrieked, unsure if she was speaking out loud or in her mind.

. . . blood hot, blood scent . . . Healer? I am with you . . .

Hishn, get out of here. Get away from the archers—they'll have you in another minute. The soldiers were already mounting the beasts they had herded back toward the barn.

"Aranur! Dion!" It was Tyrel. The gate guard was gone and now Tyrel stood tensely at the metal-braced door to shut it after the two passed through.

Aranur's breathing was harsh, and his hands were red with blood. He threw a knife at an archer who stood taking aim in the open too long, and the man toppled slowly back to sit uncomprehendingly on the ground, his life shocked away by the blade. The fleeing carriage made it to the gate, a gray shape racing beside it, now behind, now in front of the wheels as arrows skittered across its path. By the moons, Dion swore silently, if even one quarrel so much as bruised Hishn's flesh, she would go back and kill them all. But then Tyrel jumped for the carriage, and Aranur grasped his arms to yank him up from under the racing wheels.

"That way!" The boy pointed to the outer gate, where a mounted figure detached itself from the shadows. It was Rhom, hauling the dnu around and spurring it on to match their pace and give them some protection.

"Dion!" he cried as he saw his sister driving the traces.

"I'm fine! Let's go!"

The archers followed them out, arrows chasing the fleeing forms down the drive. Aranur, Dion, and Tyrel could only duck lower on the driver's seat. The woman twisted the dnu around the corner of the gate and had almost yanked them to a halt when she saw the other shadows pounding toward them. They were mounted, three riding double. Hishn lunged up onto the driver's seat, her claws scrabbling for a hold till the wolfwalker hauled the Gray One into her lap by the scruff, the sense of urgency still clinging to their fear-sped limbs. Traces snapping again, they raced into the streets, the carriage swaying frighteningly with the haste of their ride. The smoke and shouts were disappearing fast in the morning fog as they thundered away from the dark streets of Sidisport.

IX

Aranur Bentar neDannon:

There Will Be a Way

Watch the shadows, watch the lights;
Never shoot till they're in sight.
Hold your rage down, calm your fears;
The end comes soon enough for tears.

They ditched the carriage at a dark crossroads, bundling the last of the packs onto the saddled dnu and throwing blankets over the others from the carriage. Aranur's side ached where Dion had kicked him twice, and his arm burned where dirt and sweat had gotten caught in the slash he had taken back at the inn, but there was no time to stop—they had no way of knowing how soon Clintner would be on their trail. He caught Mankarr's attention. "We need clothes and gear. Is there someone discreet enough to trade with at this time of night?"

"There is one Ethnen Rambuntin. He was always one to smell out a sweet deal."

"How soon could we reach him? Clintner may be on our trail even now." Aranur boosted his youngest cousin up on one of the bareback dnu ahead of its middle legs and steadied her till he could give her the makeshift reins Gamon had cut from the carriage traces.

"A five-minute ride, going quietly. But be prepared to leave him with your purse considerably lightened."

"It's not my purse I'm worried about," Aranur returned

144

grimly. "We filled that at Salmi's expense. How discreet is this Rambuntin?"

"As discreet as money can make him." The merchant hesitated. "He has a code of honor, but it's a twisted one. If you pay him to keep his mouth shut for, say, one day, he would probably consider it worth his while. Longer than that, and he would just take your money and run straight to Clintner to make another deal as soon as he figured out who you were running from. I sent word by carrier bird to one of my ships on the coast. If you can make Red Harbor before the tides turn tomorrow afternoon, you have passage south along the coast. It'll be a near thing, though; you haven't much time."

And if they missed the ship, they would be stuck with nothing but trouble and nowhere to turn. If the rumors were true, the merchant Clintner had strong allies and an even stronger urge for revenge. They could not go back through Sidisport, and to go east, directly into the heart of Ramaj Bilocctar, would be crazy, since Ramaj Bilocctar was Lloroi Zentsis's county, and The raider captain, Salmi, and Clintner were allied with Zentsis. On top of that, barely four years before, Lloroi Zentsis had invaded and taken over Lloroi Prent's rule, the county next to Ariye. And Zentsis's laws over his new citizens were harsh and unfair. Strangers were always suspect. Word had it, too, that Zentsis was looking to add another county to his rule.

Aranur looked down the road, straining to hear any sound of pursuit. So. They could not go east because of Zentsis. They could not go south overland because of Clintner. And they could not go west because of the marshes that stretched along the low side of the river—impossible to travel through if a person did not know the way, and even as late as it was in the spring, the bogs would be as treacherous as a pack of worlags. As far as he could tell, their only chance was to make Red Harbor and catch passage on the ship.

"Are you staying or going with us, Mankarr?" Gamon asked as he swung up on his mount. "Things are going to be hot for you here."

The merchant shook his head. "I have my own ways of dealing with Clintner, and there are things I must do. Local law sets inheritance through the male line," he said grimly. "Since Altiss never took a wife, his property falls to me. I'll be staying to settle his accounts and arrange the—the Moonsong." His shoulders bowed a moment, but he straightened. "Go quickly," he warned soberly. "You haven't much time to beat the tides, and I can't guarantee that the captain will wait for a pack of strangers."

"Thanks," Aranur said simply. "Good trading!"

The merchant pounded out of sight, disappearing in the dim fog till only the sounds of the dnu's hooves were left to fade away.

"Rhom, Tyrel," the gray-eyed leader said, turning. "Brush the tracks from the roadside. With luck, no one will find the carriage till midday or later." He helped his sister, then Dion, mount, ignoring Rhom's glare as he held the healer's hand a moment too long. Rhom did not seem to have gotten over his resentment of that kiss by the river. *I'll have to explain to him,* Aranur thought, *before we end up fighting. And then he thought, Explain what? That I find his twin attractive? Sexy? Hells, she's his sister, not his Promised. He's going to have to let her go sometime.* He pushed the subject from his mind resolutely. He had better things to do than get involved in juvenile jealousy over a woman who did not even seem to care for him overmuch.

With a change of clothes, the girls were more comfortable, and with the four saddles Aranur bought for the carriage dnu, they made better time, as they could ride harder. They were too large a party to go through small towns unnoticed, especially with the wolf loping ahead like a running shadow, but they were more interested in making it to the coast by the next evening than in tracking carefully through empty brush to avoid curious eyes. So far there were no signs of pursuit. But there was more than one way to the waters, Aranur reminded himself.

The countryside began to come out of the morning mist as the sun rose from behind the hills. Tyrel's eyes were closed, and he snored softly, his head lolling with the steady gait of the dnu—the dumb creatures would follow a trail till it ended without changing their gait—and while the others nodded off, Aranur took the chance to study the height of the river. The Phye still lay sluggish between the early gray pastures, backed up like a sleeping mudsnake by the tides that flowed inland. Tides were a tricky thing, with the nine moons pulling and pushing every which way. Legends said that the ancients had known only one moon and that that moon had been half as big as Earth, the first world, but Aranur always found that hard to believe. If there was only one moon and it was that big, all the water would bunch up and flood half the world at each tide.

His arm had begun to bother him badly, so he looped the reins over the saddle horn to free his hands. Using knee pressure, he guided the dnu at a rolling gallop while he pulled up his sleeve and unwrapped the bloody bandage.

"Let me," Dion said, startling him. She matched pace easily, throwing one knee over the horn to brace herself as she leaned across. The exposed wound looked worse than it was, but she frowned.

"It's just a scratch," he protested as she gestured for him to stop.

"There's a good place to stop here," she said, ignoring his words and pointing to a small clearing.

He sighed and pulled to a halt. "Be quick, then."

The others woke as they slowed down, dismounting and stretching when they stopped. "Can I help?" Ainna asked as the healer examined the slash in the tall man's arm.

Dion nodded. "Cut me some strips of cloth about this long," she said, measuring the distance in the air with her hands. She pulled two pouches off her belt and mixed some of the herbs in a small mortar she dug from her pack. Adding water from her boata bag, she spread the paste gently but quickly on Aranur's arm, expertly dressing the wound with the strips Ainna had made for him.

"Almost as fast as Ovousibas," he said. He flexed his arm experimentally. "And as good." He grinned. "Thanks, Healer."

She nodded, then hesitated. Ovousibas. There it was again. "Aranur," she said, stopping him. "What do they say of Ovousibas in Ariye?"

He finished giving Ainna a hand back up on the dnu, then turned to Dion with a speculative look. "Why do you ask?"

She sighed, shrugged, and leapt onto her six-legged mount as gracefully as a cat. "Guess I'm just curious."

"There are legends," he said softly, watching her closely. "But every county has its ghosts."

Dion shivered. Aranur, swinging up into his saddle, motioned for the group to break into an easy lope. There was little chance to talk as they cantered through the hours, moving easily through the small valleys toward the coast. The pounding sound of the dnu in the heating dust of the day made it hard to hear and harder to speak against their rhythm. It was nearing evening when they finally stopped for supper at an inn, a comfortable place half-filled with serious eaters. Their exhaustion was obvious as they trudged in and dropped to sit at the eating tables. Hishn, irritated that there was no hunting close by, snarled as she slunk by the wolfwalker's feet to stretch out under the table. The two pairs of feet that had been there before were hurriedly drawn back as the wolf shoved them aside, and the two heavyset men who shared the table swallowed nervously, their eyes darting from the cold, gray-eyed man, to the burly violet-eyed fighter he strode in with, to the mass of thick gray fur at their feet.

Hishn, Dion sent with a sigh, dropping into a seat on one of the benches. *Don't scare the locals. We've trouble enough without you giving someone a heart attack.*

They smell rancid, the gray beast returned sourly. She sneezed, woofed, then stuck her head up between the two men, glaring first at one and then at the other. The two locals froze, one with his spoon halfway to his mouth and the other with both hands on the table as if they were glued.

Hishn, Dion snapped. "Excuse her, please," she apologized to the men.

The two men looked at the wolf's fangs while Hishn ran her long, pink tongue over her gleaming teeth, and one of them gulped.

Dion, tired enough to have little patience with her partner's jokes, stood suddenly and glared at the wolf. *Hishn!* she sent angrily. *Get back under the table or I'll rap your nose so hard you'll hear your teeth click all the way into the next ninan.*

"Don't worry," Rhom said with a grin as he plopped down next to his twin. "She doesn't bite."

The local men looked from the snarling wolf to the furious woman, and one of them was brave enough to ask, "The wolf or the woman?"

The young blacksmith chuckled. "The wolf," he returned slyly. "I don't guarantee anything about the woman."

"Rhom," Dion said over her shoulder, "I can whack you just as easily as her." She continued to glare at the wolf until the Gray One rumbled her protest in her throat but pulled her head back under the table and laid it on her massive forelegs.

"Sit down, twin," her brother said. "Dinner's getting cold

in the pot, and we're getting cold waiting for it. You don't have to leave," he said to the two men who hurriedly got up from the table.

"We were just finishing," the first one said. They looked back only once before they were out the door of the inn and lost in the night.

"How long is the ride to the coast from here?" Gamon asked the innlady while she served them, her plump figure leaning over the table to reach their bowls with her stew ladle.

"If you ride like you eat, no time at all," she said sharply, eyeing the speedily emptied bowl Gamon casually set back under her spoon while she finished filling everyone else's dishes.

"Now, good lady, such fine stew demands a man's full attention." He winked slyly at Rhom from beside the woman's well-filled dress. "As do your bounteous proportions." He righteously pointed at his bowl, now heaped again with stew meat and vegetables. Aranur choked at Gamon's sly words, and the old man slapped him on the back.

The innlady shook the ladle at the weapons master. "You keep a civil tongue in your head. I'll take no guff from the likes of you."

Aranur broke in, turning his laugh into a cough. "We've got friends waiting for us at the coast. If you could just tell us how hard we'll have to ride to meet them before tomorrow afternoon."

"It's a long day's ride and a rough one." She turned away to the hearth even as she spoke. "But if you ride fast and take the low trail so you can run the dnu out, you might make it there on time. *If* you can keep that one's tongue shut in his head to keep you out of trouble."

Namina and Ainna were giggling behind their napkins. Shilia's eyes were dancing in her tired face as Aranur explained, "Trouble follows him like a dog. When we can, we try to keep his mouth full so he can't talk himself into more scrapes than we can get him out of."

"You!" She gestured at the older man quickly, seeing him open his mouth to respond. "You be quiet." She dumped another ladle of stew into his bowl. "And eat."

Gamon flourished his spoon, bowed from the bench where he sat, and made a great show of devouring his meal. Aranur was always amazed at how much food his uncle could put away.

A guffaw rose from a group of men in the corner near the fire, and Aranur glanced over at them. He did not like their looks. As his uncle had remarked when they had first entered, the strangers looked a little too hard-bitten and traveled for the area.

"Dion." He turned to her and spoke in a low voice. "Find out from the innlady how long they've been here and, if you can, whether they've followed us here. Maybe we shouldn't chance it, but we've got to rest the dnu or trade them for others, and we've all gone too long without sleep. We may have to take rooms for part of the night and go on early in the morning." He passed her one of the smaller bags of money.

She nodded and rose, turning questioningly to the innkeeper as if to ask her for a favor. The lady nodded, and both of them disappeared into the kitchen.

"Aranur, the dnu are pretty much done in." Rhom was worried. "They won't last through the day tomorrow without more than a few hours rest."

"We put them together in the stalls so we could get at them in a hurry," Tyrel added, "but Rhom's right. We'll have to have fresh mounts if you want to leave early and set the same pace."

"There's Dion, too." Ainna spoke up softly. "She's been hanging on, but she's about done in from all the riding."

Shilia nodded. "Aranur, she almost fell from the saddle twice. Rhom wasn't riding so close to us just for my conversation." She blushed, but embarrassment was quickly replaced by worry. "Dion won't be going much farther without a rest."

"Why didn't you say so?" Aranur turned to the blacksmith angrily as he realized how close to collapse the man's sister was and how close to his own sister Rhom had been riding. He did not examine too closely which made him angrier: jealous worry for the healer or protectiveness of Shilia.

"We're all tired, Aranur. And I didn't say anything about it because she's as stubborn as you are and we both know it." The younger man's antagonism flared suddenly. "She wouldn't stop if it meant slowing you down and placing you in danger."

"I didn't mean to start anything, Aranur, Rhom," Shilia interrupted as the two men glared at each other. "I was only pointing out that we all need a rest."

Aranur took a breath and relaxed, forcing the other fighter to do the same. "No offense meant, Rhom."

"None taken," the younger man said stiffly.

"Rhom, how many dnu do you think we could get in trade tonight?" Tyrel asked.

"Some. Not enough for all of us unless we want to play a few games with our worthy friends in the corner." The other man rolled his eyes in that direction.

"What do you mean?" Shilia asked.

"A little judicious gambling," Gamon said in a low voice as if she were not supposed to know. He winked at Ainna. "If I catch our friend's gist, he means to make use of our four-footed friend to tip the scales in our favor on the trade."

"You're too clever for me, old man." The black-haired smith grinned. "Dion can loan us Gray Hishn for a few moments. Enough time to do the job."

"Enough time to do what job?" the healer asked as she slid back into place between Gamon and Namina.

"Oh, a little trading, a little persuasion . . ." her twin said vaguely.

"Uh huh. And you want Hishn."

"Well, you have to admit it would go much more quickly with her than without her."

"And just who were you going to scare out of their hard-earned wealth?" Her voice was mock serious. Aranur guessed that her brother had "borrowed" the Gray One before to read the cards on the pokerstar tables. He wondered what the wolf said to Dion, because he saw the wolfwalker's leg jerk slightly and heard a solid thump, and then the wolf grunted from under the table.

"The gentlemen in the corner there, who are so happily immersed in their bottles." Tyrel directed her attention to the group.

"As long as you don't lose *all* our shirts, dear," she said with mock solicitousness. Her twin grinned at her as she leaned toward her hands on the table as if examining her nails for dirt. She spoke softly. "They arrived shortly before us, from a back road that leads in from Sidisport. They said they'd ridden in from the coast, but their dnu were fresh, and the innlady recognized two of them from stables a few kilometers from here. She remarked on it—as she seems to remark on everything."

Gamon grunted agreement at that, and Ainna poked him in the ribs.

"She mentioned that they must be in a mighty hurry to keep going if they traded mounts before they reached the inn," Dion went on. "They told her to keep her mouth shut or lose her tongue."

Aranur considered that. "Would she be willing to help us?"

"Actually, I persuaded her to let me add a few ingredients to their grog. If they wake up before late morning, I'll be surprised."

Gamon chuckled. "That grog of yours is going to get us in trouble someday, Dion. It's not quite so strong this time, is it? I'd hate to have to carry them all to bed because they didn't make it out of the dining room."

"It will put them up just fine." She grinned at him. "Not that you couldn't use the exercise."

"But what about our mounts?" the boy asked.

"Well . . ." The wolfwalker shot Aranur a look from under her long lashes as she set the much smaller money bag back in front of the man. "Seeing as how they had fresh mounts and we didn't, I took the liberty of asking the innlady if we could trade mounts with them. She found the handler's fee acceptable."

"Legal?" Aranur asked skeptically.

She nodded. "It's late, and the stable hands are getting mixed up with all the travelers coming through. There's one out there now accidentally putting the fresh dnu in the trade corral. There'll be no fault to us."

"So now we're safe enough to get some sleep?" Namina begged.

"Go! Sleep. Snore if you like." Gamon shooed her and the other girls away. "Just be ready to ride in four hours."

Five of the moons were floating in the predawn dark when they led the dnu from the inn the next morning. They mounted down the road, where the sound of the hooves would be far from the inn's ears, and sped away to the coast. A good day's ride, the innlady had said.

It was still dim and cool when Dion rode up beside Aranur. "I haven't thanked you yet for coming after me night before last," she said.

He caught a dark look from Rhom before answering and bit back the comment he was going to make about catching her in the dark. He smiled instead. "Luck. Rhom took the front gate, and I took the back. But even knowing that you run with all nine moons' blessings, I wasn't expecting you to be ready to go when I came in."

"It was pretty close," she agreed.

He nodded. The wolfwalker must have done some fancy stepping to get out of that house without a scratch. Tyrel told his cousin that he had had to leave her alone to get the other girls out. "You must get a lot of fighting up in Ramaj Randonnen."

"No." She smiled apologetically and spread her hands. "Actually, I've never been in a real fight before this Journey."

Aranur stared at her for a moment, then he could feel the smile on his face grow into a grin, and he started laughing. The woman looked puzzled for an instant, then irritated as he could not stop. "It's not you," he managed to gasp between chuckles. "It's just that here's Ob Clintner, a mansion full of guards, a pack load of raiders, a band of worlags, and a healer who's never been in a fight in her life—and who comes out on top but the healer!" He laughed so hard that he started to cough.

The violet-eyed woman started to smile, then to laugh with him. "I hadn't thought of it like that," she admitted when they had both calmed down. She did not smile enough, Aranur thought. She was too reserved, too quiet, and then, her twin was always hovering over her like a lepa over its mate.

"How long have you been training in Abis?" he asked.

"Since I could walk," she answered. "At first Rhom taught me what he learned, but after a while everyone gave up trying to keep us apart, and I joined the regular classes and trained with our weapons masters as Rhom did. What about you?"

"It was always my dream, my ambition to be the best weapons master on Asengar," Aranur said quietly.

"That's a strong goal." She looked out over the plains. "I could be happy just to take away pain and give back joy in life."

"I'm sure you've already done that many times," he said lightly, glancing at her healer's band.

She looked at him, her violet eyes suddenly shadowed and unreadable. There were ghosts in her past as well as his. If not for the loss of Ovousibas, the legendary art of internal healing, would those she had lost have lived? If she had had the ancient skills, could the three boys found after the rock slide have been walking the plains now instead of the path to the moons? Her face suddenly withdrawn and remote, she said abruptly, "Tell me about your family."

He noticed her change of expression but only shrugged. "There were four brothers," he began obediently. "Tyrel's father, the Lloroi Volan; Gamon; my father; and another we always called Uncle Fastfoot."

"Didn't he have a name?"

"Yes, but he was ten years older than the others, and no one remembers what it was before he was called Fastfoot. Fastfoot and Gamon never mated, though Gamon was always pursuing and Fastfoot always pursued by the women." That won a smile from her. "Lloroi Volan and Lady Sonan had their three: Tyrel, Namina, and Ainna; and then there are Shilia and I. The Lloroi was too busy to bring Tyrel up as he wanted," he continued, "so Gamon raised both of us. He made sure that Tyrel had the right kind of teachers to prepare him to follow his father and then made sure of the same for me, just in case."

Dion nodded her understanding. If Tyrel died before becoming Lloroi or before leaving a male heir, Aranur would become Lloroi. Aranur shrugged. "Lloroi is not a job that appeals to me," he said simply. "Playing council politics is good experience for everyone, but I'd hate to make it my life. Anyway, with one of our best weapons masters teaching me and Tyrel Abis, we were able to take care of ourselves fairly well. Gamon encouraged us to be good at whatever we did." He glanced back at the old weapons master. "We owe him a lot."

She nodded. "And your parents?"

He hesitated, then shrugged. "Both dead."

"I'm sorry," she said.

There was no pity, just empathy in her eyes, and Aranur heard himself open up as he had not done in years. "It was a rockfall from a raider attack," he said slowly. "Mother, Father, Shilia and I, Uncle Fastfoot, and two other women were out for a late harvest of loban berries. My father was by the cliffs, helping my mother, and the other women were just starting out along one of the rock paths with Fastfoot for another patch of the berries.

"I remember hearing my father shout and my mother scream. I turned . . ." His voice faded away as the memories came back, dim and dreamlike. "I saw the rocks crush my parents and knock one of the women from the path. She broke like a doll on the stone below. Fastfoot screamed at Shilia and me, but the raiders started shooting then. An arrow stuck out of his shoulder, but he grabbed the other woman and pushed her toward the dnu. Shilia and I were just standing there, staring at what was left of our parents. I remember an arrow went between my legs, and I just looked up at the raiders like it was a dream."

He shook himself and let the gait of the dnu bring him back to the present. "Fastfoot grabbed Shilia and me, but I started screaming for him to let me go and help my mother and father. He slapped me. I remember what he said, the blood all slippery across his arm. 'Aranur, you've got to protect your sister now. You've got to be a man.' And then he threw Shilia and me up on our dnu—we were young enough to be riding double still— and then mounted his own. There must have been half a dozen raiders, and they shot him again, twice in the back, to try to stop us, but he held on and got us out of there. We rode like a field on fire, but it wasn't fast enough. My uncle died before we got back to the village."

"I've never known what it was like to have a mother," Dion said slowly. "She died after Rhom and I were born, but we've always had our father. It's a hard way to grow up, without both."

Aranur gave her a half smile that did not quite touch his steady gray eyes. "We were lucky, Shilia and I," he answered. "We always had Gamon and Lady Sonan and the Lloroi. And Gamon always treated us as if we were his own children."

Dion turned wistful eyes toward the hills. "I wish I could send word to my father now," she said softly. "Just to say that we're all right."

"This is your first time away from home?" he asked quietly.

She nodded, sighed, and shook herself out of her own wishful thinking. "I took one of my Internships back in the hills with the Ethran people, but I was close enough to home to be able to meet Rhom and father halfway in the forest in one of the Safe Circles every few ninans."

"I remember the first time I took off from home," he said with a smile. "I was with Gamon and my best friend, Lioton. I don't know how my uncle tolerated us—we were lucky he brought us back, the way we behaved. We must have played every prank ever invented on him." He grinned wryly. "So what was it like, living with the Ethran? I've never seen more than two or three of them together at a time.''

"They're very gentle people in some ways," she answered slowly. "In others, they're like animals. There was a lot of work to do. I was lucky to be chosen to go—they ask for a healer maybe once every two or three years.''

"Is it true that they pay for what they need with carvings?"

She pulled out a small pouch and displayed two small carvings. "These were made by the Ethran. I carry them for luck. They gave me others, but I left them at home with my father.''

"Are they really all as short as a clumpbush?''

"That's one of the reasons they chose me instead of an older healer. I was young, so I was shorter than the adults, but I was already ready for my first Internship. Moonworms, but I wanted to go.'' She smiled. "I traded my scheduled Internship with another healer—one who didn't like to leave the comforts of home—for the chance to go with the Ethran.''

"How long were you there?"

"Three cycles." She smiled suddenly as if at a private joke. "Three very long cycles.'' Aranur raised his eyebrows, and she laughed. "They wanted me to stay and become one of their clan," she explained. "The ninan before I was supposed to leave, they had a huge meeting. At first they sent me into the woods so I wouldn't hear what was going on, but the little ones kept running back and forth telling me everything that happened, word for word. The adults didn't really mind—they can't keep secrets, anyway. When they finally called me back, they tried to present me with an Ethran headdress.'' Dion made a face. "I didn't really offend them by refusing—they would have had to rebuild half their village for me to be comfortable—but they still tried to insist that I carry half their carvings away with me.'' She laughed. "I had to accept one from each family just to keep peace in the village.''

"It was a small village?"

"It was a very large village," she corrected.

Aranur chuckled. He could just see her as a girl, weighed down with stones, trying to travel the sixty kilometers back home again.

By midafternoon they had passed several parties on the road but were still kilometers from the coast. Dion was still riding beside Aranur when they heard a "Damn."

Looking back, Aranur called them to a halt. "What is it?" he demanded, twisting his dnu around and riding back to Tyrel, who was dismounting.

"Picked up a rock," the boy muttered.

Aranur gestured for Rhom to help the boy look. He wanted to tell them to hurry, but there was enough tension in the air without his adding to it. "Well?" he asked finally, shifting impatiently in the saddle. The Gray One, appearing suddenly from the brush, startled him, and he almost swore himself. The wolf looked at him with its yellow eyes. He could swear the beast was laughing at him again. "What's the problem?" he asked the young blacksmith.

"It's a Siker barb," Rhom said slowly. "Not a rock. We'd have been better off with a rock." He put the beast's foot down carefully. "It's worked up into the foot—we must have picked it up when we took that shortcut across the fens—and even if I cut it out, the dnu won't run again soon."

"Why not?" Tyrel demanded.

"The nerve damage is already starting," the smith explained, lifting the placid dnu's hoof and pointing to the radiating purple lines. "It's probably why it ran so long with the barb in there before you noticed."

Aranur frowned and looked back at the hills. "Tyrel, strip your pack and take Ainna's dnu. Ainna, ride with Namina. It won't be comfortable, but we're losing ground every minute we hang around here." He barely waited for the switch before spurring his mount back to the fore and picking up speed again.

They crested another hill, and Rhom dropped behind, away from his twin's side. He had been gone only a few minutes when he reappeared.

"They're back there, about five kilometers," he said over the noise of the hooves as he rode up to Aranur. "They must have found fresh mounts on the way, because they're riding hard."

"We'll have a race for it, then."

"That's not all. I have a feeling that the bunch behind us is only half of what we'll find when we take the turn to Red Harbor. There's that higher road to worry about, and I could just about see a dust cloud behind one of the closer hills."

"We still have three kilometers to the coast and then another kilometer around to the harbor. And," Aranur said with a gesture, "look at the river. This is the second high slack tide. The tides are starting to turn out on the coast now, and there's no guarantee that the ship's there at all, let alone that it's still waiting, if there's a cross-tide today.''

"We just have to chance it. What else can we do? We're going to have to fight anyway.''

The tall man agreed. "One thing's for sure,'' he said flatly, brushing dark hair from his cold eyes. "We'll give them a run for their gold.''

They lay against the dnu's backs and urged them on. Beside them, the gray wolf loped across the ground just off the trail, where its feet landed silently in soft sandy grass. The Gray One was excited by the smell of the sea, and Dion had to quell the shadow emotions that spilled from the wolf's mind to hers. The sea. Neither of them had seen it before, but the salt scents that raised her nose and the stale dampness that invaded the air gave a sullen impression of the coast. And the band of pursuers was gaining on them little by little, inexorably, like the tide creeping up on sand-trapped men. The dnu that Ainna and Namina were riding held them back since it carried the heaviest load, but they had no other mount to use, and on the second kilometer Ainna changed across the saddles to the healer's dnu to shift the burden and give Namina's mount a rest. The ride took on a surreal quality. Each time they topped a hill Clintner's soldiers appeared closer. They were almost on the coast when they could see what Rhom had feared: the second party thundering down the hill road, their dnu foaming in the afternoon heat as they pushed them on to cut off the fleeing group.

"We have to make the harbor!'' Aranur shouted at his uncle, the wind tearing the words from his mouth.

The old man nodded and yelled back. "If we can just beat them to the crossroads, we stand a chance of not being flanked by the second group. There are too many of them for us to charge through.''

They spurred their mounts on. Both groups of soldiers knew they had been seen. Ainna had shifted again, this time to Shilia's dnu. They topped another rise and tore past more hay wagons. Aranur suddenly yanked his dnu to a halt by two of them and yelled, "Twenty pieces of gold to dump your wagons here!'' The farmers looked astounded, but as the tall rider yanked one of the pouches from his tunic and pulled a handful from it to show them, they grabbed the reins and turned the wagons so sharply that both vehicles shuddered and began to jackknife over. Aranur threw the bag to them and wheeled to pound after the others, a rising cloud of dust marking the "accident" that had mounded hay across the road. The farmers got down to discuss the situation, the bales still tumbling across and off the road into the thick brush. Aranur caught his uncle's grin and waved to him. He wished he could have seen the soldiers when they topped the hill like a swarm and thundered down on the confusion of hay. Their dnu must have gone off the road like marbles bouncing off a stone step.

But the soldiers coming down the hill were only a half kilometer away and still coming strong. The fleeing party would beat the soldiers to the crossroads by a quarter kilometer, but the soldiers would gain on the group till they either caught them on the road or chased them into Red Harbor and tried to take them on the streets by the docks. The tides were changing, and Aranur could see the sails dropping on a ship that had turned to catch both tide and wind. It must have set sail from the docks almost an hour earlier.

"That's our ship!" he shouted at Gamon. "We missed the tide. We've got to make a stand here, where we have a chance of defending ourselves."

"There! Beyond that dune, there's a hollow. We can pull in and fight from behind the logs." Gamon pointed. "Quickly! Or the others will be down on us, too!"

They thundered from the road, crashing through low brush and sharp beach grass to drop into the hollow. Hishn loped beside them, winded from the long run. It was a faster pace than she held naturally, and her lungs sucked the damp air from between the dune grass as she regarded the hollow distastefully.

A hole with no exits is a trap, she snarled, catching the healer's clothes with her teeth as Dion jumped from her dnu and started to lead the beast into the depression.

The wolfwalker tugged free. *We need a place to defend.*

The wolf growled deeply. *Healer, come with me. There are better places where you can lie in wait and leap when the prey come to you.*

The woman turned and knelt by the wolf, burying her hands in the thick fur. "Hishn," she whispered. "By the moons, I love you, friend." She glanced back to see the clump of dark riders top another rise and clenched her fists. "But you're right, this could be a trap for us all. Go now. Find a place to hide, and when you can, tear at them from behind.''

I cannot leave you to the worlag's claws again.

"You're not, Gray One. This time I've a few claws of my own.''

"Dion, hurry up," Tyrel cried, vaulting a log and grabbing the reins of her dnu from where they trailed on the ground. "Get down.''

Go, Gray One, she sent, touching her cheek to the massive bones of the wolf's face. *Your fangs are only sharp when used.*

The hunt, the beast sent with a flash of heat that almost blinded Dion. *The hunt is on.* The Gray One's hot tongue licked her nose, and then the wolf was gone.

The dnu, their sides heaving for breath, were antsy and stamped their feet as they caught the tension that was tangible in the air. "Ainna," Aranur ordered, "speak softly to them, get them to lie down. We've got to keep them out of the way of the swords." He looked around. "Shilia, Namina," he said, pointing sharply, "drag those two logs closer together. It'll make a good wall we can shoot behind.''

Shilia nodded and ran across to grab at the branches and pull. As her cousin helped her, a gust of wind rose and caught their cloaks in the limbs, tangling them until Tyrel tore them free.

"Get down now," Aranur snapped. "Rhom, cover the right. Gamon, the left.''

Tyrel waited beside his uncle, shifting restlessly. Scant minutes. That was all it would be before Clintner's men thundered over the rise. The wolfwalker was motionless beside her brother, tensed for sight of the soldiers. Rhom flexed his arms. Like the gray-eyed man they followed, the twins had arrows notched and ready to fly, and from where Aranur was crouched, the one looked like a slender shadow of the other.

"Wait for them now," he said softly. "Make them come to us.''

The soldiers charged over the rise like a black thundercloud. Nine figures dark in the afternoon. And suddenly there were eight. A massive gray shape hurtled up from the ground and tore one of the soldiers from his mount, any sound or scream of death drowned in the din of the hooves. Aranur's group shot as one and then two other riders dropped like stones, the second one trampled under the sharp, driving hooves as he rolled to his death. Then they swung low on their dnu's backs, shooting under their mounts' necks. Aranur heard the young blacksmith grunt in pain, and then he was shooting again. The soldiers charged, and another one dropped. As the wounded man's dnu sidestepped, it threw off the aim of the man next to it, and the arrow notched for Aranur's eye whapped by his side into the log.

And then they were in on the group, and Aranur rose up to meet them. He ducked under a dnu and dragged a man off his mount. The soldier pulled out his sword as he fell, but Aranur cut into his thigh, and the man screamed, writhing on the ground as his life's blood spurted from between his fingers. Gamon was wrestling with another, and there were too many bodies to figure out who was where. Aranur felt a man leap at him from a charging mount and jumped to the side. They crashed to the ground, struggling to bring their knives to each other's throats. A gray body suddenly shot across into the man, and his hold on Aranur's wrist was broken; the wolf laid the soldier's arm open to the bone as she passed over, and the soldier jerked back with a cry. Behind Aranur, Ainna screamed. And in the back of his head something snapped. Skin gashed open beneath his knife, and blood rushed from the soldier's face as Aranur separated his neck and rolled free. A huge figure in leather mail jumped at him from another dnu. He parried the blow, though his arm was jarred to the bone. Then he dropped as if tripped, and the soldier roared with victory and lunged forward. He got less than half a meter. Aranur's blade struck up as he thrust with both feet against the other man's legs. The soldier fell toward him, blade outstretched, but Aranur's sword slid right into his chest as his arms swung out for balance and found death instead. The hollow was still reverberating with the sounds of blades and sobs. Aranur looked at the small party that was left from the melee. Tyrel was on his knees with Ainna in his arms, her head rolling limp against him. His face was terrible as he cried out.

"Help her, please, Dion!" His voice broke even as his sister's life drained away in his arms. Her eyes were already glazed. The blood that flowed from her side showed the slashed skin split open where the girl's guts gleamed dully gray. "Dion, please . . . don't let her die—you can't let her die . . ."

The healer clenched her hands. "I can do nothing, Tyrel," she said gently, her eyes tragic. "She is dead already."

"No," he cried out. "No!" He smoothed the hair from his sister's sightless face. "Oh, moons of mercy," he anguished, crushing her limp form to him and then sobbing in horror as her side opened farther and the hot steam from her guts spilled across his hand. "You can't let her die."

The healer turned away, hiding her grief. "Oh, gods," she whispered, looking down at her stained and helpless hands, "for the gift of Ovousibas I would lay down my life."

Hishn looked up from her side and met her eyes with a yellow gaze still rimmed with the hunter's black. She licked the blood from the fur around her mouth, and her claws were red as well. *Ovousibas is death,* she sent. *Like this. Death for you and me.*

Dion choked back a sob. *I know, Gray One, but this—*She gestured helplessly at the bodies. Only ten meters away two men cried out terribly. At her feet, the young girl whose smile had come so readily even when she was scared was dead, her body cooling in the damp sea air, and the slackness of her lifeless muscles was somehow obscene. *This, Hishn, is also death.* She wiped her hands shakily on her pants and worked her way to Shilia, who was holding Namina. Shilia's hand was pressing hard against the girl's arm where the blood ran down her skin. Namina had taken a deep cut across her forearm as she had tried to protect Ainna from the raider's blade, and as she looked around, Dion realized that her own twin was bleeding from a tear in his shoulder where an arrow had caught him as he shot.

"Tyrel." Aranur touched him gently. "You have to help Namina now." The boy's eyes were blind as he turned to face his cousin. Aranur gripped the youth hard on the shoulder. "The moons call whom they will, Tyrel. Namina needs you now. Go to her." The tall man straightened up, feeling suddenly old and tired, then started rolling the soldiers' bodies out of the way to meet the next attack.

Dion wrapped Namina's arm quickly. The girl did not seem to notice, her face numb as she stared at Ainna's still form while the healer worked. Finally Dion leaned back against the wolf, glad of the emotional and physical support, and turned to her brother. "How is it?" she asked.

"Just a scratch," he lied, his teeth gritting against her gentle fingers.

She looked into his eyes a long moment. "I can fix it so you can shoot," she said finally and flatly, binding his shoulder tightly against the motion of his bow arm. He nodded and stood to move back to the logs, where Aranur expected the next attack. The wolfwalker hesitated as if there were more she wanted to do for him, then shook her head. "No time to be true to the band," she quoted softly to her twin as he shrugged back into his jerkin. She fingered the healer's silver and blue headband and then resolutely dropped her hands to her sword.

Go, Gray Hishn. There are more coming in for our blood.

The wolf grinned hungrily. *There will be fewer who ride to your claws than you see at first.*

Just don't lose your teeth in their hides. They're tougher than they look. And stay out of the path of the arrows.

The wolf sent a hard shaft of blood lust for answer and then was gone. Only a slight wave in the grass told Dion where the creature had gone, though she followed the Gray One's silent steps in her mind as the wolf slunk out and around again.

"Tyrel, Rhom," Aranur said, breaking into her bleak thoughts. "They're coming now. Get ready."

"Be careful." Shilia's whisper was almost a sob in her brother's ear. The tall man ran his hand through his hair, then squeezed her shoulder and pushed her away.

They came with a rush, charging like the first group but already hung over so far on the sides of the dnu that Aranur could not shoot at them directly. He had to shoot the soldiers' mounts to drop them and managed to take out only one before the soldiers were on them. Blades flashed, and the attackers dropped into a defensive circle, letting their dnu run on through or collapse in their midst.

Aranur's rage rose in his throat. Rhom was having trouble with his shoulder and had switched his blade to his other hand. Dion was defending his back, and both lunged and parried with Tyrel as they were forced slowly back in front of Shilia and Namina, facing four of the soldiers. Their pattern was slowly breaking up as the fight degenerated into separate battles. Two men jumped Aranur, their swords flashing. They fought back and forth till the Ariye leader dispatched them and turned to see another man falling to his knees behind him, a haft protruding from his blade-choked throat. The soldier's arm was upraised to plunge his blade into Aranur's back, but it went no farther. Dion's knife had sunk deep; his eyes bulged, and his mouth spit blood.

Aranur scrambled to help Dion, who was now weaponless, pressed against the logs by a long-armed swordsman. The soldier stabbed at her, sure that he had the wolfwalker trapped, but she somehow managed to turn the blade, lunging to the side and striking his elbow with her palm. She stunned his nerves, and the sword dropped, but he twisted and grabbed at her jerkin. As she went with the pull, he flew over her shoulder but yanked her to the side and grabbed her arm, his quickly bared knife stabbing. She fell. His blade seemed to pass through her side, and her eyes were wild, and then the wolf was on him, too, tearing the leather of his mail and ripping the tendons of his other arm. He screamed, throwing up his arms to protect his face, but she twisted his knife from his hands and brought her arm down to his chest twice, and he was finally silent, only his body thrashing in his mortal throes. It was a hard death.

"Are you all right?" Aranur shouted through the noise, lifting Dion to her shaking feet and looking for the blood that should have been spreading across her stomach.

"Yes! Help Tyrel!"

She dived for her sword, which had been dropped in the brush, and Aranur turned to see the youth thrust back by two of the soldiers, ganging up. Shilia and Namina—there was no one to protect them, he thought with sudden fear. Rhom was down, wrestling with a burly man in the branches of a log, their struggles crashing them back and forth as their blades flashed and jammed together. Aranur jumped another dnu huddled on the ground and cut at the nearest man. But the soldier turned and parried the blow easily. A master swordsman, Aranur thought with grim certainty at his movements, to make sure we don't escape. Clintner must have realized who the fleeing people were. The man from Ariye lunged suddenly, pressing the other fighter back against the logs, but the swordsman stepped aside and then he was on Aranur, the blade flashing at the tall man's head as he twisted and turned. The swordsman's snarling grin held the joy of a fight, and Aranur could feel the rise of his own battle exultation in his chest.

His arm turned a blow to land heavily against a log. He could feel Gamon fighting behind him and Rhom getting up from the side; the air seemed alive with limbs and metal flashing and snapping in the light. Behind him, the Gray One snarled and someone else screamed. Then the swordsman feinted, and Aranur stepped in, anticipating his blow. The other man twisted. Aranur swung. His opponent parried. Aranur lunged. He smashed his fist against the swordsman's chin unexpectedly, and the other man's eyes widened in shock as he staggered, but Aranur brought his blade up against the underside of the man's arm. It slid off, and the swordsman's elbow jammed into Aranur's ribs.

Aranur sucked in a ragged breath. Pain stabbed his stomach where the man's pommel met his gut again as he smashed his knee into the man's thigh. The swordsman staggered, his muscles cramping up from the attack, and Aranur brought his boot back down on the swordsman's instep, their long blades useless as they closed the distance. They grappled. The ground came up suddenly, and they fell, Aranur's shoulder jarring hard against a log. The man tried to kick Aranur's knee, but Aranur trapped his neck in the crook of his arm and squeezed the soldier's carotid arteries. The man's breath was harsh, and his eyes bulged in panic. He realized that Aranur was not trying to choke him; the icy-eyed leader meant to shut off the blood to his brain. The man's fear strengthened his hands to rip at Aranur's face. One, two, three . . . Aranur twisted him to trap one of his arms and keep the soldier from tearing his eyes out. Four, five . . . The man's legs thrashed, but he was slowing. Six, seven, eight . . . The muscles began to relax at last. Nine, ten, eleven . . . twelve. The man's body was limp; Aranur's breathing was rough in his throat.

Aranur rolled off the lifeless carcass and slowly got to his feet, his face and side so bruised that he could feel the new swellings rise under his probing fingers. Namina was crying; Shilia was pale. Dion was kneeling by Rhom, binding another pad of cloth over the one that already was soaked bright red— his shoulder had broken open again when he had wrestled Clintner's man down—and even from where Aranur stood, he could see the healer's hands shaking so that she had to try twice to tie the bandage down. Around her, the wolf paced like a lepa over its brood, the baleful glare spearing first one, then another of those who still lived. The creature's fangs were red and dripping, cloth was still caught in her claws, and when Gamon stood up, the wolf almost took his head off, stopped only by Dion's sharp command. The Gray One went back to pacing, but her eyes did not lose the ring of black that darkened the yellow into death.

And the soldiers' bodies lay like scattered lumps of cloth, the seabirds already circling, landing, stalking across the small dunes to pick out still-open eyes and peck at soft, open throats. And among them—Aranur swallowed and closed his eyes—Ainna. Dead and limp as the soldiers who had bled out around her.

He forced himself to finish the tally, hating himself for doing it with such cold control and terrified that the pressure that had built up in his chest would cut loose and flood even his lungs with tears as big as blocks of ice. Moons give him strength, he prayed. He counted. Three of the dnu were still, the others huddled around them, bleating softly in their nervousness. There were at least four more dnu close by, but the rest had scattered across the dunes like the jumper bushes that grew so haphazardly in the sand. At least six of the soldiers who had attacked were still alive, groaning and writhing with their separate pains, and the bleak-eyed leader watched as Dion moved resolutely to attend to them after she had seen to her brother and the others in their group.

"No! Dion, don't—"

"Tyrel—what are you doing? Get away!"

Dion's shocked voice startled Aranur, and he jumped toward Tyrel. The boy swung his bloody sword at the wounded man she had knelt by.

"Don't help them, Dion—you fool—"

"My gods, Tyrel, but they're hurt, too. Tyrel—no!" She warded off his blow instinctively, sheltering the wounded man with her body as the wolf, on the edge of the clearing, whipped around and, with a terrible snarl, leapt to put her fangs between Dion and the boy. "No, Hishn!" she screamed at the wolf.

But Aranur was already there, grabbing the boy's sword arm and forcing the blade out and down.

"Aranur, let go or I'll—"

"Drop the blade, boy, or I'll break your wrist, cousin or not." The lean, powerful man twisted, and Tyrel cried out. "What the hell do you think you're doing?" he snarled at the boy. Shilia stared at her cousin, her eyes wide as the moons, and Gamon caught Rhom's arm as he jumped over a log to help Dion. The wounded soldier had scrambled back, groaning as his gaping leg wound gushed fresh blood, and fainted; Aranur was furious. "She's doing her job, Tyrel. She's a healer."

The boy struggled frantically in his older cousin's inexorably strong hands. "Don't let her help them—the bastards—they killed Ainna . . ."

Aranur slapped the boy so hard that the youth's teeth rattled and his mouth dropped open. "It doesn't matter anymore, Tyrel. She can't come back. Now let Dion work."

"Moons damn you," the boy cried. "They killed my sister—they're the enemy—"

"They're men, Tyrel," healer cut in, shocked and scared at the boy's reaction. *"Men."*

"They killed my sister," he sobbed.

"Would you kill them now?" Aranur asked harshly. "In cold blood? They're down and dying already, Tyrel. If you put the sword to their throats, that's murder." He gripped his cousin's shoulders hard and shook him. "You're not a murderer, Tyrel. Much as you'd like to bring Ainna back, you never will. She's already on the path to the moons, and killing in cold blood will never make up for that."

The boy stared at him, and Aranur felt the weight of twice his years settle on his shoulders. "Put the sword away and go help Namina," he said quietly. "The living need you, not the dead."

He looked at the hollow that was now a shallow gravesite, then turned and watched the sails taut in the wind on the ship they were to have taken out to sea. The tides had turned, and the wind blew their hopes south without them.

It was sunset. The sky was as bloody as the day was long, and Aranur found himself on the decks of the last ship in Red Harbor, watching the captain shake his head as Shilia, Gamon, and the others waited below. Aranur could see Dion talking desultorily with his uncle, her hand absently tugging at the wolf's ear as they waited for his return.

"Dammit, man, give us a chance," he said harshly to the captain. "If not for me and the men, then at least take the women through to Randonnen. We'll pay double the normal fare."

The captain shook his head. "The weather's shaping up for a hurricane roundwind. Only a suicidal fool would be caught out in those swells." He turned away and yelled at a sailor who was lounging by one of the unbattened hatches.

"Triple fare. In gold."

The captain did not even hesitate. "Sorry. Even ten times the gold wouldn't be enough." He turned back briefly, noting the desperate gleam in the weary man's eyes. "You'd have better luck going out over the South Road, even with the flooding coming up."

"Damn you," Aranur swore. "Damn you to the second hell. Isn't there one man brave enough to sail through to Randonnen?"

The captain looked at him measuringly. "You won't find a sober man in Red Harbor to take a ship out now. I'm sorry."

He turned, and Aranur was left standing at the rail, his face haggard and his eyes bleak with the realization that Clintner's net was closing in and there was no way out. He almost staggered with weariness as he swung onto the gangplank and barely caught himself before he fell. They would have to take dnu again, he thought, then dismissed the idea as quickly as it had come. They had already run into two patrols in town, barely escaping from the last one as they fought their way through to the dark alleys of Red Harbor's slum.

Slinking from one block of the town's ghetto to the next, Aranur had already paid dearly for the scant time spent hiding. He rubbed his thigh absently where the muscles were stiff and swollen from the blow he had taken from a dnu's hoof and forced himself to land quiet and catlike on the dock, ignoring the shooting pain that tightened his jaw. That Salmi had called in his own raiders and added them to Clintner's force was a move Aranur had hoped the raider captain would not make for at least another day, but Clintner must have wanted them more than the gray-eyed man had supposed—the word was out, and even the barrio folk were interested in the reward.

The lean man spit. As if he could rid his mouth of the dank smell of rotting seajel, he snorted, scraping his boot on the dock. The purple-green slime was everywhere. It was just as well that he had sold the dnu, he thought, since chancing the overland route would mean risking a fight every kilometer. And dnu could be outdistanced by message pigeons, he reminded himself. He closed his eyes suddenly as the vision of Ainna's body rose before him with the spray from the slapping waves. How many more of his family would die before he got them home?

"Aranur?" Dion asked quietly.

He shook his head, clearing his thoughts and answering her question with one short, bleak motion.

"Damn," Gamon swore. "Clintner must know where we are by now. He'll have warned the garrisons already."

"The overland route was cut off a hour ago," Rhom said, his voice almost as quiet as his twin's, and for a moment Aranur stared at the man without seeing him. "I bought the news just ten minutes ago," the smith added as the other man said nothing.

"It was too obvious, anyway," the leader said wearily, gesturing for them to gather their packs so he could lead them from the docks. "We'd have been shot down before we made it two kilometers."

"But what can we do?" Shilia asked hopelessly. She stood without moving, staring up at her brother and trembling with unshed tears and exhaustion. "Where can we go?"

Aranur shook his head. "I don't know," he admitted. "But we'll find a way." He slung his pack up onto his shoulders and stood for a moment, bowed as if the load were too heavy even for him. Finally he straightened, staring out at the wild white-caps that slapped the barely sheltered bay and listening to the rising howl of the roundwind that whipped the trees down to the gray beaches like serfs bowing to their lord. "There will be a way," he repeated softly. "Even if I have to make the way myself."

X

Ember Dione maMarin:

The Cliffs of Bastendore

Blow, blow, you winds of the sea
To counter the currents carrying me
The black cliffs of Bastendore call me to die
If the sails do not lift from the masts where they lie.

Cold, cold, the waters are wroth
To stir up their waves in a hurricane froth
The boat tilts to meet them, its bow on the reefs,
And the waves take me down in the dark Koldor seas.

Twelve hours later Dion found herself clinging to the pilot-house of a fishing boat while the small craft plunged up and down on the roiling sea, and Rhom and the other men worked as deep-sea apprentices to the bellowing Captain Mannoa. Her twin and Tyrel were knee deep in seajel, trying to guide the bulging net up the boat's ramp and onto the deck, but every few seconds another glob of seajel oozed through the net and splattered over their deckhoods, blinding them in an acidic spray of slime. Her brother had taken the last splash: It hung off his hood over his face, its oozing, transparent threads slapping to and fro as he turned; he did not dare let go of the net to sweep the slime from his hood, as the winch was at its most critical pull and the captain was screaming at them fit to burst his lungs.

"No! No! Don't pull faster than that, idiot, or the net twists. You've got less brains than the bono bird. You! Speed it up. By all the worms that fill a curry's flesh, winch! Can't you see the net's going to drop back over the ramp?''

It was not luck that had given them a way out of the raiders' eager jaws. After trying for six hours to find passage through to the town, they had realized that word would soon be back to their hunters that they had survived the attack, and Aranur had watched with growing desperation as their margin of safety dwindled with each passing hour.

Even though they had found a temporary refuge on the fishing boat, Dion was still uneasy, idly scratching the scruff of the Gray One and soothing her with a mental croon she wished would do as much for herself as for the wolf. After watching two raider vessels slink by in the growing fog, she knew she would not feel safe till there was firm ground beneath her feet and a hundred kilometers between them and Clintner. How could Aranur be so confident? They could be stopped and searched on any raider's whim, and fishing boats did not even carry catapults, let alone have space for the racks of caged bird bombers used to drop gases and poisons on other boats. The wolf echoed her wish for dry land, but for a different reason—the Gray One was getting seasick in the increasing swells.

Sorry, Hishn. The woman grimaced. The shadows under her eyes made them seem even more violet than the massing clouds that sullenly colored the darkening sky above what was left of the sun.

". . . stuck with an idiot crew of damn farmers and a round-wind squall on top of it all. Bring it up faster, you friggin' lazy dogs!" The scroungy captain waved his arms wildly at Aranur and Gamon. "We'll lose the whole catch if you can't put your brains together to get enough of them to do a job a dead dnu could do. Damned idiots . . ."

Gamon's silvered hair was plastered against his forehead, the fish slime thick on his pants as he and Aranur cranked the winch and the silver-purple bellies of the fish started sliding around each other as the net was gathered in, fins and scales meshing with the sea slime. The four men were all slipping and swaying with the deck as Mannoa tried to keep the bow pointed into the waves. The boat plunged suddenly over a deep swell, Rhom lost his hold on the net in the sickening drop, Tyrel flattened himself against the rail in a crouch as the deck shot abruptly up again, and a dozen silvery fish slid back into the gray roiling sea. Mannoa let out an ear-splitting roar.

Shilia came edging her way around the pilothouse to cling to the rails beside the wolfwalker. "I never thought of my brother as a sailor before,'' she said soberly, watching Aranur, "and now I know why. They look like slime monsters.''

"Something from the depths of a swamp city's cesspool,'' Dion agreed. She brushed the wind-wild hair from her cheeks, making a face as the salt-encrusted strands scratched her skin. "But if they didn't play fishermen, those raiders would be down on us in a hot second wondering what we were up to.'' The boom swung toward the two women, and they ducked instinctively, though it was over their heads by a good half meter. "We were lucky to find someone willing to take us through to Stattinton. I guess we can't complain about the ride.''

"Yes, but I don't think Aranur expected to have to learn the ropes,'' Shilia punned; then she sobered, looking at Mannoa. "I don't trust that man. He baits us every chance he gets.''

"I know what you mean. I get the feeling that he's good for his money for now—and he should be, the way we paid his boat mortgage off, thanks to that slaver captain's strongbox—but I'd bet twice on the eighth moon that if we got in a jam, he'd toss us to the worlags, or the raiders, as it'd be in this case, before he'd even draw a second breath.'' The women watched Tyrel and Rhom set the net out again, the water running in sheets across the plunging deck to drain from the scuppers.

"Namina's still sick,'' Shilia said hesitantly. "She's not taking the ride well.''

The healer's jaw tightened. "There's nothing more I can do for her, Shilia. What good are my skills when the wounds are in her heart?'' But seeing the younger woman blanch, she sighed. "I can give her something to put her to sleep.'' The image of Ainna, bloody and limp in Tyrel's arms, was still with her. *Ovousibas*, she whispered silently.

A dream, Healer. A bad dream that brings an ancient wrath.

Dion looked down at the wolf and smiled crookedly. *What would you know of Ovousibas, Hishn? Of a myth eight hundred years old?*

The yellow eyes blinked once, twice, and then Dion's mind filled with an image: *steamy brains . . . screams that echo in the past . . . an agony that burns the blood and sanity till all that's left is a gray wisp that cries out through the centuries . . . the healers, the Gray Ones . . . Gone . . . all gone . . . broken bones lying brittle in the dust of years, and only echoes, echoes calling for home . . .*

"Gods, Hishn," she whispered raggedly. "What do you mean?"

Ovousibas, the wolf snarled softly, a deeper pain remembered from ancestors long silent in her mind. *Ovousibas is death. Death to us all in time.*

Dion stared long into the yellow eyes, but Hishn did not repeat the thoughts. Racial memories, she acknowledged. But the Gray One rarely called them up. That the dim images spoke of myths, she knew, but not what in the myths was truth, and that was what was most frustrating of all. Those who tried internal healing died, and died a hard death, but Dion was not thinking of that. She was thinking about the framed page on Mankarr's wall and Ainna's limp body bleeding sluggishly in the dirt by a mercenary's dnu.

"Dion," Shilia said again, "can't you do something for her?"

The healer started and flushed slowly. "I'm sorry, Shilia. I wasn't listening."

Aranur's sister looked down at her feet, then met Dion's gaze with troubled eyes. "She hasn't eaten or drunk anything since we left Red Harbor. She wouldn't even have come in from the rain to get a coat if Aranur hadn't bodily carried her inside."

Dion closed her eyes helplessly. "Namina's in shock, Shilia. Being kidnapped, slaved, watching her sister die—she's young to face it all at once, and she's not as strong as you or Tyrel. Even so," she said quietly. "Even so, she has to face it by herself. No, I don't mean alone, I mean by herself. We can support her, but the strength to go on must come from within, not without, or it crushes instead of building up the heart. Can you understand that?"

The other girl's lips trembled, and Dion said softly, "Your strength is not enough for two, Shilia. Only Namina can give herself the courage she needs." A wet nose nudged her hand, and the healer tugged on the Gray One's ear, ignoring the silent admonishing comment that Dion's own strength was not enough for two, either. *Ovousibas* . . .

The younger girl nodded slowly. A healer's wisdom was always law, no matter how young it was learned. She looked toward the gray bank that closed in on the small boat from the horizon and changed the subject. "Did you hear what Mannoa said about storms? I didn't catch it in the wind."

"Something about hurricanes," Dion returned, relieved to

be talking of something else. "I thought he said they circle west—might drive us into Ramaj Bilocctar, Zentsis's lands."

Shilia frowned. "But that could be trouble."

"Why? Lloroi Zentsis isn't involved in this."

"Aranur said that Zentsis has been making deals with the raiders lately, and Mankarr said—I overheard him when he was talking to that raider captain, Salmi, at the slave sale—that even Clintner was starting to ally himself with the Lloroi of Bilocctar."

"Zentsis must pay well," the wolfwalker said with a snort of disgust. As she paused in her scratching, the gray wolf butted her demandingly, thrusting her nose under the woman's hand and lifting it with a soft whine.

"I don't know which I'd prefer," Shilia said slowly, "Zentsis or the raiders. At least with the raiders, I'd know where I stood. Indentured slavery isn't my idea of living well, but at least it's living. They say that Lloroi Zentsis likes to use his prisoners for sport."

"Not the women, surely?" The twins had not heard much about Zentsis except the occasional rumor, news that had to travel the hundreds of kilometers to Randonnen was often discounted as exaggeration. Still, Dion could not believe that anyone would actually use people for sport in a public fighting ring.

But the brown-haired girl shook her head. "I don't know for sure—I don't know if anyone really does—but there've been stories about women and even children being put in the rings as prizes, if they weren't fighting themselves. And it's said that Zentsis likes the fights to go to the death."

"That's disgusting. It's one thing for fighters to play war games for practice and learning, but it's something else to pit people against each other in life and death battles just so some bloodthirsty warmonger can get his jollies watching people get hurt."

Wolfwalker, I have an itch, Gray Hishn reminded her again, leaning against Dion's legs and throwing her off balance on the slippery deck. The wolfwalker flicked Hishn's ear but dropped her hand obediently to the gray scruff.

"They say he's more violent every year," Shilia continued. "Some say it's because he wants more and more power, but lately they're saying that he's only got a couple years to live and he's growing desperate for a son to take over the ruling from him. He must have a dozen daughters now, but he's never gotten a son.''

Dion absently wiped dirty water from the rail. "The justice of the moons. There's nothing so capricious as truth.''

"I wish the moons would shine through these clouds," Shilia said, looking up at the darkening sky. "I hate rain.''

"If rain could wash the heart as it does the skin.'' The healer thought of Ainna and her sudden, raider-spawned death, and of Namina sitting huddled and broken in the cabin while the dark clouds pulled more tightly together, thickening the way they did on the peaks in Randonnen. "I don't mind the rain," she said wistfully. "At home, Rhom and I used to go into the mountains during the storms and climb the canyons. When the waters built up and ran off, the waterfalls thundered as if the whole ocean was hiding in the hills and coming down on the rocks.''

"I wonder if it's raining at home." For a moment Shilia looked as if she were going to cry.

It was time to change the subject. They might both be homesick, Dion told herself, but at least she had left home of her own free will. Shilia had not even known if she would see home again till her brother had plucked her from the raiders' hands.

"At least a rain would wash the slime from the decks," she said, scratching Hishn's ears absently. The wolf was getting more and more uncomfortable on the bucking ship, and Dion debated sending her inside. At least outside there was fresh air blowing across the decks; inside, the whole cabin stank of fish.

Shilia was silent a moment, then asked hesitantly, "Dion, why do you Journey with your brother?" At the healer's curious look, she added quickly, "I don't mean to pry, but you, well, you're a woman. Internships are for women; Journeys are for men. How could you go? How did you learn to fight in time to go along? I mean, did you actually want to go?''

Dion regarded the girl for a long moment. "We're twins, Shilia. There's a bond between us that holds us closer than what brothers and sisters normally feel. What Rhom trained in, I trained in. What I trained in, I showed him—if he was interested. He wasn't much interested in sewing, but then, neither was I unless it had to do with stitching people back together.'' She paused and stared out over the sea, letting the surges of water wash over her feet and splash on her pants. But I couldn't help Ainna to save her life, she thought. She was too cold to shiver and too old to cry. How could I not understand death before? she berated herself. All the wounds, the illnesses, the plagues—the aftermaths, she admitted. Never the reality till now. Oh, gods, may the moons curse me if I was callous to those in Randonnen.

Not callous, Healer. Never unfeeling, the wolf sent.

Oh, Hishn, that I could believe that.

What you feel, I live also, the wolf reminded her. *If you were ever insensitive, I would not have run in your shadow so long as a moment of night.*

Dion's expression softened. *You honor me, Gray One.*

As I should, Wolfwalker.

"So they just let you go?"

Shilia's question brought Dion back to the present, and she shook her head. "Let a woman go on Journey? Without argument? No, when the elders cast the fortunes for the Journey, it was cast that I go with him."

"But you already knew martial arts?" the girl persisted.

"I am a fourth in Abis. I've trained since I could walk." She was puzzled at Shilia's insistence.

"Dion, Namina and I, well, Aranur said you're good, and we were wondering if maybe you would—if you had time—teach us how to fight." She got the last words out in a rush and added hastily, "If you wouldn't mind."

Ainna's death was hard on us all, Dion thought bleakly. She looked out over the swelling ocean. Fighting for fighting's sake and fighting for their lives. And she remembered how many times she had asked herself the question that everyone asked: Could I kill another human being? And now she had killed, not just once but several times, and her hands still felt dirty, her sword unclean.

She knew there were truths and ideals to be preserved by fighting, but the price of life had hit her hard. How could death justify life? Just the day before, Ainna had died in Tyrel's arms, and now the pain in his heart, not the principles of his mind, would guide his sword. If he fought, he would not be fighting for the living but for the dead. And Dion—why was she fighting at all? She was a healer, sworn to protect life, not take it. I have taken men's lives from them, she cried out silently, her hands clenching the rail as she tried to close Gray Hishn out of her mind.

The Gray One's thought came unbidden: *You have saved them, too.*

She stared at the sea, remembering, thinking ahead. There were times when the choice had to be made, not just in fighting but in healing, too, she remembered harshly. She had never thought a healer would have to make that decision, but now she knew better. She still planted flowers every spring on Kari's grave. The dead woman's ashes reminded the healer that she had made a choice and would never know if it was the right one, but that she had decided and that one woman had lived and one woman had died because of it. Teklia's son trained with Dion to become a healer like the woman who saved his mother, while Kari's daughter's dark eyes still haunted her in the night. And now Shilia stood before her asking to be taught how to make that decision, not with her heart but with a blade.

Her voice was harsh and cold when it came. "Can you kill a man, Shilia?"

The girl looked at the healer deliberately. "I can kill," she said, the underlying vehemence answering the question more than mere words could ever have done. She was Ainna's cousin, and Ainna's death drove her as much as it would the dead girl's brother, Tyrel.

"And can you love yourself after you kill a man and see his blood and guts painting the ground around you? Can you face yourself each morning, knowing that the wife and babies of the man you just killed will cry over his ashes and go hungry this winter?"

Shilia looked down at her feet. "I could kill," she said in a low voice.

"What are you going to say to yourself when you see the man's children? Do you tell them that you killed their father with your knife? What do you tell his mate? When you pray to the moons, will they still listen to your voice? Or will they turn away behind the clouds and let your empty prayers fall on the rocks and shatter like the family you destroyed with your sword? Look at me, Shilia," the healer commanded. "Can you kill a man, or a woman, or even a child to save your own life?"

The girl looked at the wolfwalker, then dropped her eyes again. Her hands trembled. "Dion—"

"Death is ugly, Shilia. Death is the last and the most lasting thing you'll ever see on this world. Can you give death and take life as lightly as you say you can?''

The younger girl did not answer.

"You've seen death, but it's been others who've killed for you. The guilt for that is on their heads, the blood of that is on their hands. Can you kill for yourself now, knowing what you're doing?''

The other girl clenched her fist on the rail. "Dion, I can admit that I hate the raiders and Clintner and Salmi. I can't deny that I want to get back at them for shaming us and killing Ainna, and I can't say that I don't want to see them die the way they murdered my cousin.''

The healer said nothing.

"Anger and hate aren't very good reasons for killing someone,'' Shilia said finally, her voice low.

"There's never a good reason to kill someone,'' Dion said slowly, remembering, wondering if there was a way she could have avoided the times her own sword had slid into a body. "Can you understand that in your heart?''

"I understand what you say,'' Shilia said, her voice so low that Dion could hardly hear her over the sound of the swelling ocean. "But I still hate them. I still feel what's in my own heart.''

Dion put her hand on the girl's arm, and Shilia looked up at her, two tears sliding down pale cheeks. "Then,'' the healer said gently, "I will teach you what I know of Abis.''

Shilia's eyes widened, spilling the tears left there. "But—''

"Abis is not for vengeance, Shilia. It's not for anger or hate or temper or frustration or even for fun. It's a skill you should use only to save your life or the life of someone else. Or to protect yourself or something you own. You must not abuse it, or you abuse yourself. If you can understand that, and I think you do, then you are ready to learn Abis.''

Shilia nodded soberly. "I won't let you down, Dion. You won't be ashamed of me.''

"I know that.'' Dion gestured toward the pilothouse. "Does your brother know you want to learn? Or Gamon? Since he's your weapons master—and your uncle—he should be the one to teach you, not me, unless you prefer for me to do it.''

"Gamon hasn't said no,'' the girl said. She gave the violet-eyed woman a sly look and added, "And although Aranur feels a little funny about your rank in Abis, I notice that he doesn't think you're any less a woman for it." She tossed her head, regaining her confidence. "If I want to learn Abis, that's my business."

"All right. When do you want to start?"

"As soon as we get off this boat."

"We could start now if you want." Dion nodded toward the pilothouse door. "Let's go inside."

The cloud bank grew heavier. By the time the men had finished their last set with the fishing nets, the sky had become a solid gray-black and the sea was swelling hugely under the decks. They could barely see the ocean under the creeping fog; it surprised them each time it leapt up on the decks and thrashed the wood with its thunder.

Mannoa stamped his feet as he entered the cabin, stripping off his rain gear and hanging it on the hooks by the door. "Take the wheel while it's not too rough, Gamon. I'll take over again as soon as I've had something to warm my gut. Looks like we hit one of the roundwinds," he said to the group in the cabin. "We'll be driven back west for sure."

"Can we make for some harbor?" Tyrel asked.

"There isn't a harbor this side of the marshes till we reach Stattinton, and if we try to anchor here, we'll be driven aground on the bars. The water's going to build up and roll in, flooding the coast."

"What about making it back to Red Harbor?" Aranur pulled off his borrowed fishing gear and dripped across the floor as he reached for a steaming mug of grog. "I take it we can't head out into the ocean in this weather and try to ride it out."

"This is a small bottom-dragger, not a cross-sea trading vessel," Mannoa said, surly as he drank his grog in a few gulps. "The deep sea waters would tear us apart. We'll try for the harbor and hope we don't get blown past the mouth of the channel."

The steaming brew warmed their insides, and they ate hungrily, except for Tyrel. The boy's face was getting greener by the minute as he sat miserably on the bunk, trying manfully to ignore his heaving stomach. Namina was getting used to the sensation, and her pale face was a little better than his, but Dion could tell from the way she swallowed that she was just as uncomfortable as the rest of them. Poor Hishn whined and rubbed her head against the wolfwalker's hips. It was worse when they tried to sit, and lying down was the fastest way to throw up that they had discovered so far. Even though she was careful not to focus her eyes on anything close, Dion felt the uneasiness herself and had been trying to remember a remedy told to her by an old healer several years before. It was some sort of heated poultice applied behind the ears, where it would settle the balance centers. Since she knew nothing of the sea except what she had picked up from others' talk, the healer mused on the poultice and listened only vaguely to the discussion of harbors, currents, and winds that began to rage in the cabin as the storm had begun to rage outside.

Aranur was gesturing at the water-washed porthole as he argued. "The problem with Red Harbor is the soldiers. Clintner's men will know by now who we are out with, and they could very well be waiting at the harbor for us to run back to shelter when the storm blows in."

"Well, I could order the weather from the moons themselves, but they rarely listen when I ask," Mannoa growled. "If we miss the harbor, we stand a good chance of wrecking on the cliffs to the west. I'm not taking my boat onto the rocks just because you're in trouble with the locals."

Ah, I have it, Dion thought. Three leaves dried vanset, a fingernail of rubsam root, nine crystals of garvenov, and one bruised leaf of fresh ansil. She started digging through her herb stores. Heat into an orange paste the color of wild lody flowers with a few drops of water, then apply warm behind the ear . . .

"Can I help?" Shilia offered.

"You don't happen to have any ansil with you, do you?" Dion asked absently. She was trying to remember what she could substitute for ansil when it was mixed with garvenov. "I should have thought to find some before we came out."

"Mannoa might have some in the cupboards for cooking."

"It has to be fresh," the healer returned, frowning and tucking a loose tendril of hair up into the warcap she still wore. She had begun to doubt that in the dingy, greasy cabin the captain had any cooking stock at all. "Maybe I can use souie powder and kobah stems instead." She shook another pouch out and found the right packets. "We should have done this before the sea got rough, but it will still help. And Tyrel looks as if he's going to need it soon."

"What is it?"

"A poultice to counteract seasickness."

Mannoa twisted in his chair, bracing himself against the tilting decks. "You a coastal healer or something?" he accused.

The dark-eyed healer suppressed her instant irritation. "Not coastal, no. But I know the remedy."

"Dion's one of the finest healers in Ramaj Randonnen," her brother stated proudly.

"Pretty damn young to be a finest healer," the captain growled rudely.

Dion's twin got slowly to his feet, anger building hotly in his broad shoulders as he flexed his hand above his knife. Hishn, echoing his temper, pulled her lips back in a snarl. But the captain just leaned back and smiled grimly.

"Just making talk, boy," he said insultingly, prodding the young man to attack.

"Make talk with less fighting words," Aranur commanded him, his hand on Rhom's arm. The younger man shook him off coldly.

"Do you need a healer, or were you just curious?" Dion asked in the short, strained silence that followed.

"Yeah, I need a healer." Mannoa rolled up his pants leg. "I got bit by a hansruck a week ago. The local healer was all for cutting off my leg right away, but the hole is still small and I didn't want to stop walking yet. So I went to this other guy, one of the priests of the Mooncult."

Dion stopped and looked at him in distaste. "The Mooncult priests are a bunch of faith healers who do no real work except that of taking money."

"Well, I wouldn't know, Healer," the captain said in a slow, insolent drawl. "But the local healer wanted to amputate, and this other guy said he could take away the pain for a handful of silver. So I done it, and he kept by his word. I haven't had any pain for the last two ninans." He stretched his leg out to the bunk.

"Let me guess, he told you to stare at a spinning crystal, waved his hands, asked you if you believed, and said, 'By your faith and by the moons, you're healed.'"

"He did more for me than the licensed hacker." Mannoa gave her a cold look from under his salt-crusted eyebrows and tugged at the knot on the bandages. "Probably more than you can do now, unless you know some other fakery, like Ovousibas.''

Dion's eyes flashed. "Ovousibas is real," she snapped. And suddenly realized that she believed what she said.

"Then prove it."

She stared at the man for a long moment. No one spoke. Then a low howl crawled into their ears, and the captain glared at the wolf.

The man snorted. Spitting to the side, he deliberately unwound the dirty bandage so that the girls saw the mess first. Namina let loose her stomach and retched into the sink; Shilia's face blanched, and she turned away to sit on the bunk, looking out the porthole. Even Dion nearly choked at the sight of his leg. After controlling her instinctive disgust with the skill that comes from years of practice, she leaned close to examine the gory wound impartially. At a place about two fingers' width from his knee, the man's skin was rotting away from the edges of a hole the size of two gold pieces across, and maggots were feeding on the dying flesh. Angry red and purple lines radiated out from the hole. He must not have cleaned the wound in the week since he had been bitten, and even the healer swallowed hard before touching the gaping hole.

"Set your leg up here," she commanded. "You've been lucky. The maggots have been cleaning out the dead flesh and preventing gangrene. These hansruck are venomous? Or did you get something in the wound?''

"They're venomous, all right. Most people have to have the limb amputated eventually, but it was such a little bite . . . and then I found that Mooncult priest . . ." His voice trailed away. He was enjoying the attention and the effect of his ugly wound on the girls.

"How big was the bite originally?" she asked. The spread of infection made it difficult for her to guess.

"About so big." He held his fingers about three centimeters apart.

She revised her image of a meter-long fish. "Just how big exactly is a hansruck?"

"Tiny. No bigger than my thumb. But they have five tentacles with mouths on the ends. When they bite fish, they paralyze and kill the flesh and attach themselves to the spot. As the flesh rots, the hansruck feed."

"Shilia, if you would boil some water." Dion turned to her twin and gave him quick directions for making the seasickness poultice. May as well do everything at once, she thought. It was not a gentle or pleasant job to clean and treat the swollen wound, but Mannoa stolidly made conversation with Rhom and Aranur while she worked.

". . . Storms stir them up from the shallows, and they come over in the nets. I didn't notice it hanging on to a silver webber's fins when I grabbed the fish. I'd ripped my pants open on the winch earlier and figured I could finish the set before getting new gear on, but I was wrong. The hansruck bit me when the webber slapped against my leg."

"How many get stirred up in the storms?" Tyrel asked nervously, thinking about the recent hours on the deck handling the catch.

"They don't school. They're more like seajel, floating around until they find a likely host. They get thrown up on the rocks all the time, but they just crawl back in the water. They don't last long out of the sea. Like the tidal areas, though. Lots of things to feed on."

"Dion," Rhom interrupted from the small stove, peering uncertainly at the heated pile of orange paste in the small pan. "This stuff is the color you wanted. Now what do I do with it?"

"Bring it here so I can make sure," she said. "I need to finish this first, but you can put the paste on everyone for me. Smells awful."

He made a face. "Everything you make smells awful."

"Who made what this time?" she retorted. "Here, look. Smear about so much like this behind the ear. You should feel better in a half hour to an hour. And don't forget Hishn. She needs it, too. Only put hers deep inside both ears toward the back."

The blacksmith smeared the poultice awkwardly behind Namina's and Shilia's ears while Aranur watched unsmiling. Dion wondered if the two men were getting along all right. They had seemed hostile to each other lately. When he finished, Rhom went out on the deck to keep Gamon company, taking Aranur's sister with him to the pilothouse. Inside, Dion had just finished treating Mannoa's fish bite.

"There's nothing I can do besides keep this clean," she said to the stocky man. "The poison is already in your blood. And as far as I know, there's no known counteragent I could give you that wouldn't kill you.''

He snorted. ''About what I figured. I'd have been better off to find me another Mooncult priest and hand out another piece of gold.''

''All a charlatan like that will give you is a quick death,'' the woman said shortly.

''And you can do better? There's stories that say a healer with a wolf can do Ovousibas if she wants.'' He rolled his pants back down over the new bandage she had put on the poisoned wound. ''If she wants,'' he repeated.

Dion said nothing, but her jaw tightened and her violet eyes looked suddenly haunted. Whether she believed in it or not, the one thing she did know was that Ovousibas was death. Hishn, sensing her distress, rumbled in her throat.

''Mannoa,'' Aranur said softly, ''you're riding a narrow trail and pushing a heavy wind. You're going to fall off, and fall long and hard, if you're not careful.''

The healer's face was taut and pale. ''If the leg had been amputated even a ninan ago, you'd keep your life,'' she said finally. ''Now there's nothing I or anyone else can do.'' She turned away, sitting down on the bunk beside Shilia. But even when she closed her eyes, the look on Mannoa's face demanded an answer—an answer she was not prepared to give.

The afternoon was darkening with the storm's false night, and Mannoa left to take over the wheel from Gamon. With the sea thrashing the small boat, the rest of them huddled cramped in the cabin while the other men took turns helping Mannoa with the sails. At the moment, Aranur had dozed off. Tyrel was still too uncomfortable to be much use and was simply sitting, wedged in one of the bunks, his face turned to watch the ocean surge up over the window and down again. Beside him, Namina was silent, and Shilia huddled, wet and cold. Watching the others, with their bleak, hopeless expressions and the rat of guilt gnawing at her guts, Dion sat on the cramped bunk with the upper bed cutting into her hunched shoulders and her arms around Hishn's neck and realized that Mannoa had the right of it, after all. Ovousibas. The healing art of the ancients. She had told him it was real, and he had told her to prove it, and it had suddenly occurred to her that she believed what she had said. In fact, she had as much ability to do the internal healing as had any of the ancients. And she was a wolfwalker, too. "Look to the left," the piece of parchment had said. Ovousibas.

Gamon glanced at her face, then at Namina. "There's stories of healers who've tried to do this thing called Ovousibas," he said softly. "They have a common theme."

The slender woman met his gaze squarely, but in her eyes was the shivered reflection of a ghost that crawled over her grave.

"Ainna would have died anyway, Dion. Or you and the Gray One. Either way, it's not worth it."

"Gamon, I—"

"All legends have a core of truth, Healer. And the one thing that legends of ovousibas have in common is that the healer always dies. The wolves go insane, and the healer always dies."

Dion stared at her hands, but Mannoa stomped inside then, leaving Rhom at the wheel and preventing the older man from saying more.

"She's torn it now," Mannoa snarled.

Aranur stirred and looked up. "The sail?" he asked.

"A lot of good a sail does in this wind." The captain threw his rain slicker across the deck, where it splatted angrily against the bunks. "We missed the harbor by a good half kilometer, and the drag anchor's barely slowing us down. Now it's wherever this whore of a wind takes us, that's where we'll go."

"But won't the wind die down?" Shilia asked timidly.

Mannoa opened his mouth to snarl at the girl but, seeing the expression on her brother's face, thought better of it. "I've been caught in roundwinds before, but this early in the season they last longer. The winter winds still back the storms into late spring, so instead of dying down quickly, the roundwinds just hang on."

"So what does that mean for us?" Aranur asked.

"It means we're heading for the Cliffs of Bastendore," Mannoa snarled. He grabbed his slicker, slung it back on so that the water sprayed them all, and slammed the cabin door shut behind him as he went back into the storm.

Aranur looked at Gamon, and the weapons master looked back.

"Bastendore," the old man said quietly.

"There's still a chance that the storm will die out before we're driven onto the rocks," Aranur returned. "The cliff currents are strong, but we may be able to beat them if the moons give us a chance."

"A rabbit's chance in a lepa hunt," Dion could not help saying.

Gamon smiled sourly. "You've got that about right, Healer."

"Well," she sighed. "I think I'd rather put my money on swimming to shore from here than seeing the Cliffs of Bastendore and living to tell my grandchildren about it."

"We're not dead yet," Aranur said, irritated by their pessimism. "And Bastendore's still a long way off."

"You're always so damn calm, Aranur," Tyrel burst out. "Don't you ever stop thinking? Don't you ever get afraid like the rest of us?"

The gray-eyed man looked at his young cousin. "You think I'm not afraid?" he countered with a slight smile. "Fear is something you grow up with and grow into, Tyrel. Whether you're a coward or a brave man is just a matter of whether you control the fear or let the fear control you. Moonworms, Tyrel, the first time I met a worlag face to face, I pissed in my pants, just like a lot of men." He glanced at Dion, but she was not going to enlighten him at the moment about her own first experiences. "Fear's a natural reaction. It pumps the adrenaline up so you can run faster and hit harder and not notice the pain as much. A lot of people mistake that for bravery, but it's not. It's a survival trait, just like anger and laughter and everything else we feel. Everything has its purpose," he said. "All you have to do is figure out what the purpose is and use it to help you get the job done."

The boy opened his mouth to say something, but another bout of seasickness forced him to turn his face to the side and try to control his stomach.

Dion shifted to pull up the sweater behind her so that her head did not bang against the wooden cabin walls while the boat plunged sickeningly over the waves. "Tyrel's right, though, Aranur," she said, bracing herself against a sudden lurch of the boat and grabbing Hishn by the scruff as the wolf scrabbled across the slick planking. "If you were facing a hundred raiders in the fighting ring, I bet you wouldn't waste a minute praying to the moons—you'd be pulling out your sword and figuring out how to beat them all and still get away without a scratch."

"Maybe," he admitted with a smile. "I sure wouldn't go down without a fight. I learned that from Gamon."

"You learned everything from me," the older man agreed, "but I swear almost all of it slipped right back out of your ears." He aimed a cuff at his tall, dark-haired nephew.

Aranur merely grinned at the old weapons master and leaned back as the boat lunged through another set of swells. Hishn put her head on the healer's knee and looked mournfully at the woman as Dion stroked the wolf's fur. The Gray One's mind was agitated with the rolling boat and the confinement of the cabin, and the only thing she cared about at the moment was getting to solid ground.

Even facing two worlags is better than this, she told the wolf-walker as her stomach roiled.

Think of it as if you're just running over hills and the ground's uneven, Dion advised. *And don't focus your eyes on anything.* She had already discovered that if she tried to look closely at anything, the sickness got worse. She wondered briefly if it could get any worse than this the closer they got to the cliffs of Bastendore. Bastendore was a legend even in the Randonnen mountains, and one more ship wrecked at the feet of those ocean cliffs would not be noticed among the hundreds that had already met that fate.

But the night drew on, driving the small craft faster and farther to the west as the swells deepened and the skies dropped down on the boat. Mannoa was sailing merely by feel, the ropes holding him to the wheel so that he would not be swept overboard as rain lashed at the wooden sides of the vessel and drilled into the decks. The boat slammed into waves and dropped sickeningly from the crests; the sails were rolled so that the canvas would not tear in the storm. Mannoa and Rhom were fighting the wheel to keep them turned into the currents, and inside, the ride was too rough for the passengers to do anything but brace themselves against the bunks and wait for their stomachs to catch up to them. None of them slept. Hishn had no way to brace herself against the motion of the boat and would have been flung back and forth except that she was wedged between Shilia and Dion on one of the bunks.

The healer could feel the power of the sea beneath the decks as it lifted them and flung them forward with each wave. There was a knot of fear in her stomach. They could not see where they were going, the portholes showing nothing but the dark froth of the sea as they plunged through the water. Being from the mountains, she was awed by the sea's power. The deep quiet presence of a mountain lake was a puddle compared with this, the thunderous force of a flash flood merely a trickle across the decks. There in the midst of crawling mountains of water and cresting sweeps of ocean, Dion saw, met, felt true power.

Hours later the black night lightened to a gray dawn, and the rain eased up on the sea. They were still being driven by the currents, but they had passed around the western bulge of land and were heading north. Mannoa grimly told them to make their peace with the moons because the Cliffs of Bastendore would be off the starboard bow in an hour.

"Can't we steer away?" Rhom shouted through the wind.

"Currents meet and mix there," Mannoa yelled back. "The wind always drives straight into the cliffs, then circles and dies. If the storm doesn't last long enough to pass us beyond the cliffs, we don't have a chance."

"What about anchoring in one of the little bays on the charts?" The wind whipped the words from Rhom's mouth.

"Those bays are there, sure. But they're guarded by reefs that angle into the water and explode the waves fifty meters in the air." Mannoa twisted the wheel to counter another wave, water streaming from his rain gear and rushing away across the tilted deck. "Even if we got into one of those bays," he yelled back, "we'd never get out again. The waves might push us over the reefs, but they'd trap us inside, too."

"We'll die anyway if we don't do something!" Rhom shouted. "The wind's dropping, and the storm is passing us by."

And as the wind slowed, the clouds lifted and unmasked the doom that held them in its grip. Each crest carried them in another rush toward the towering black walls of rock. They could see the water hitting the reefs and blasting up into the air, creating huge clouds of spray that rained back down on the cliff tops. Fifty meters? Mannoa had told them a barefaced lie about the power of those wide geysers. The cliffs themselves were a hundred and fifty meters tall; the water shot up an easy forty meters more above them.

"If we can get into one of the bays, we can climb out, perhaps," Aranur told Dion. She did not ask what their chances were of getting into one of the bays. Not noticing her look, he added, "It'll be difficult with the rocks wet, but it can be done. Tyrel is not as experienced in climbing as Gamon or I, and Gamon is out of practice," he mused, thinking out loud. He looked at Dion. "Does Rhom climb?" She nodded, and he continued. "Shilia and Namina have never actually climbed, but they know the techniques. They'll be all right if we set a rope and haul them to the top. How about you? Have you done any climbing?"

She just nodded. The boat crashed into a trough, and she caught herself against a bulkhead before being flung from her seat. She liked rock climbing and mountain climbing, but she was also stupidly afraid of heights—the result of a natural phobia on top of a bad fall she had taken a few years earlier. Part of a cliff had broken off, and the metal pitons hammered into the rock had been yanked out one by one as she had shot past on the way down. Rhom had called it a zipper fall. In a fall like that, with luck, the person died quickly when the rope snapped the body from terminal speed to zero. Dion had been more lucky. She had caught a loop of slack rope on the way down and managed to wrap it around her arms and hands three times before the rope reached the last two pitons. There had been so much sound in her ears that she had not been able to hear what Rhom was screaming, or had it been her own screaming that had filled them? She had not been able to tell. She had braced herself for the jerk that would break her back. If the rope did not snap. If the last piton held. If her arms were not torn off by the force.

When she had come to, Rhom had been cradling her against the cliff. The pain had not been so bad at first—only one arm was broken—but the rope burns where the wrapped cords cut into her skin had begun to fill her mind with incoherence. She remembered little of what had happened after that. Rhom set up a bivouac camp on the side of the face, let the distress flag fly, and set loose a flare. He locked his twin into a sling and set her arm after she described how to do it in one of her more lucid moments. But after one night hanging on to the cliff face, they both knew she would not last another day before the rescue team arrived. The cold and shock had stripped her of most of her energy, and they had rations for only one more day. So she told Rhom to strap her arm tight to her body and bandage the burns on the other, and they started back down the cliff in the longest climb the woman would ever make. She was one-armed and halfway in shock, the fingers of one hand almost nerveless as she tried to use what was left of her skill to get down the cliff. Rhom was exhausted from leading the way and helping his twin down, lowering her hand over hand when she could take no more. Dion slipped and fell again as the exhaustion took its toll—a short fall, mere seconds, but in her mind it was a fall three months long. Even after they finally reached the ground, she could not stop shaking. She just sat there on the sloping dirt and grabbed a handful of it in her fist while the tears ran down her face.

After her arms had healed, she had had to rebuild the muscle she had lost, along with her confidence, because the fall had affected her deeply—every time she tried to go up, she shook so badly that she rocked off every hold she managed to get.

She did finally climb again, but the fear had become an integral part of her. She began to lose all focus for anything but the rocks; once she started up, if the fear took hold, she could not stop until she reached the top of the climb or the end of the rope. She, Ember Dione, was the only person ever to have climbed the north face of Dountuell, but she had done it only because she had been too terrified to stop. She had had to leave the rest of her climbing party behind when they could not go farther and she could not go back—she had unhooked herself from the rope and free-climbed the rest of the face. And ended up spending two days walking down the back side of the mountain, her hands so scraped from the climb that she could not use them for a ninan afterward. The odd thing was that even though everyone knew she was afraid of heights, they still wanted to climb with her. Her skills were guaranteed to get almost any climb up a challenging route—if she could control her fear. But now, sitting in the cramped cabin of the fishing boat and bracing herself against the wooden bulwark, Dion could feel herself getting nervous just thinking about climbing out of the grip of the sea into the grip of that fear. I'd rather spend a ninan being seasick on this boat than climb forty meters off the ground, she told herself, ignoring Hishn's snort of disbelief. But she said nothing to Aranur. Don't embarrass yourself before you have to, she told herself. Maybe he'll want to lead the climb.

"How well does Rhom climb?" Aranur was asking.

She started, then nodded. "He's very good."

The tall, dark-haired man put his arm around her shoulders

and pulled her close, and she suddenly wanted to lean against him and tell him how scared she was and how much she had started to depend on him. But then he said, patting her knee, "Don't worry, then, Dion. Gamon's still a pretty good climber, though he's not gone up a mountain in years, and Tyrel is okay, too. If Rhom's a good climber, we've more than enough people to see us safely to the top."

Probably thinks I've never climbed anything more than the ladder to the upper barn, she thought sourly, and sighed.

Since the rain had stopped, Mannoa had already begun to steer the boat crossways to the current to find a lower spot in the reefs. The charts were not much help because no one had ever gotten close enough to measure the depth there and return with the information. But the fishing captain just kept driving the boat beside the current.

"If you're going to climb the cliffs, you won't have much time to do it," he shouted. "The bays are just as rocky as the shore off the cliffs. I'll have to hold the boat steady while someone crosses to the rocks."

Aranur agreed and turned to Rhom. "Dion says you climb. What kind of climbing have you done?"

"I've never climbed Dountuell, but I've done Hoxher twice." Rhom glanced at his twin and smiled slyly at her if he were going to say something about one of their last climbing escapades, and she thought, Don't you start in about me, Rhom.

Aranur, who did not notice, nodded appreciatively at Rhom's admission. Mount Hoxher was a rough climb and was famous because of it. Climbing Hoxher put Rhom among the top climbers in the world. Of course, the twins' home, Ramaj Randonnen, had some of the finest climbing, too, so it was a more popular activity there than in other counties. Even Randonnen's worst climbers were better than some of the best in other places.

"You climb about the same as me, Rhom," Aranur continued. "From here it looks as if we could do the cliffs in one pitch, but without protection and with the weight of one of these fishing ropes instead of a light climbing rope, we'll have to go up leapfrogging. It'll probably take four pitches. I'll lead first, then you pick up and take the second lead. I'll take the third again. Tyrel—" He turned to his cousin. "See if there are some hooks or spikes we could wedge into the rock. We'll need some kind of piton to hook the rope into."

Tyrel nodded and then pointed with excitement. "Look there! A hole in the reef. You can see the water rushing through on the crest."

Mannoa squinted and nodded. "We'll have to time it, or we'll drop on the rocks."

They gathered their gear quickly. For the last hour Gamon and Shilia had been knotting one of the lighter ropes so that it would be easier to climb with, and Tyrel had found some heavy santeril fishhooks that might work for spikes. Rhom attached wire loops to the hooks so that the rope could pass through the loop and be drawn up once the hook was wedged into the rock. As the waves tossed the small boat up and down, they could see into the bay, its tiny hollow surrounded by the cliffs. A small rocky ledge leaned into the water on one side.

"Look—if we could make anchor by that ledge." Dion pointed.

Her twin squinted. "Where? Midway along that dark streak? Yes, that looks good."

She nodded. "Getting the gear and us up to that ledge would shorten the distance to the top by twenty meters."

"And climbing with this," he said, hefting the heavy fishing rope in his hands, "even that distance will make a big difference. I'll tell Mannoa."

The woman was relieved. She did not like the captain and had avoided speaking to him when possible. He seemed as slimy a character as his fish. But he did get us this far, she admitted.

It's not far enough, Hishn returned. The wolf looked wistfully at the cliffs as if they were a thick and juicy steak just out of reach.

They washed closer to the reef. The waves rose and fell with the thunder of a thousand six-legged dnu while the gap in the reef showed briefly and then disappeared. Mannoa, the sweat glistening on his face, forced the boat to hesitate. Dion's fingers clenched. The spray from the wind-whipped waves crusted her hair with salt when the curling swells of the ocean lifted the boat to dart forward again. They were just outside the reef. The boat twisted slightly, and Mannoa spun the wheel to counter; the gap showed, and he let loose on the boat. They dashed at the streaming rocks.

At the last minute the swell of water rose under them and carried them almost over the drowning rocks as if they were surfing. But they began to crash down again too soon. A god-awful tearing sound shrieked through the decks and shuddered the boat like an earthquake. The back of the craft caught on the reef, and the rudder splintered into the hull. Groaning off, they slid into the water with the next swell, the wheel tearing from Mannoa's hands when the rudder went, and the boat turning aimlessly as the current swept them gently toward the cliffs of the tiny bay.

"We're going to have to swim for it," the captain growled. "We're taking water in the hold."

"We need to make that ledge." Aranur gestured. "We can get a purchase right off the deck of the boat if we get close enough."

"I'm friggin' doing the best I damn well can," Mannoa snarled.

They had all come up on deck and watched as the boat moved more and more sluggishly in the water. The current pushed them into a thick bed of seaweed driven there by the storm, and they slowed further.

"We won't make it if that seaweed traps us away from the ledge," Aranur said. The wind was light in the bay, and they could talk at a normal volume, though their voices were still rough with tension.

"We still have the dinghy," Mannoa stated, staring intently at the bed of purple weed. "We don't want to swim here if we can help it. Look at the seaweed." They looked but saw only purple shadows under the wide leaves.

"What are they?" Tyrel asked, leaning against the list of the boat.

"Rastin. They'll eat anything—even wood if they get confused. A school of them must have followed some fish into the bay. They'll eat a man to the bones in a few minutes. They're stupid, though, and slow. They don't move out of their school, and a fast swimmer can sometimes beat a school to the shore." The shadows moved away toward the ledge.

"Comforting thought," Gamon commented, "for anyone who can swim fast in a jungle of seaweed."

"The dinghy only holds five," the captain snarled with a grim look as he lowered the small boat from its hooks. "And the decks will be swamped in ten minutes." Dion had the feeling that he would have tried to take the dinghy for himself if he had not had to face down five swords and a mouthful of wolf fangs to do it. He did not trust his passengers, but they did not trust him, either. "Boy," he said insultingly to Tyrel, "get the floats from the nets and the mattresses from the bunks. We'll have to sit on a raft till the dinghy returns."

"Rhom," Aranur began, changing his mind about the first pitch. "You go first. Take Namina, Shilia, Dion, and your gear. Gamon will anchor you for the climb and then bring the dinghy back."

"Dion can climb," the younger man said quietly. "She can anchor me. That will give Gamon more time to get back to you."

Aranur raised his eyebrows but nodded, and Rhom jumped down into the boat. He helped the others down from the deck, which was sloping like a slide, and grabbed the gear to stow it under the seats. Gamon settled at one side, Rhom at the other, each with an oar. They had to use them like paddles at first to sweep the purple weeds aside. Dion edged up into the bow and started pressing the seaweed down under the hull with a loose plank so that the dinghy could move forward without dragging. She looked back at the boat. Aranur, Tyrel, and Mannoa were quickly tying the mattresses under the hatch cover to make a rude raft, lashing net floats to the sides.

The dinghy had reached the rocks. They could almost take it right up to the cliff, but the seaweed bed covered a ridged bottom, as if several fault lines had ridden out into the bay, and they did not want to risk splintering the boat when Aranur and Tyrel and Hishn's lives depended on it's making one more trip. Dion got out and gasped as the cold water swallowed her up to her waist. With the uneven bottom and the purple slime that made the rocks difficult to see, she and Rhom kept sliding off and splashing into deeper water as they dragged the dinghy as near the cliff as they could. Careful as they were, they both twisted their ankles several times slipping between the ridges.

"That crack there." Rhom pointed. "It runs through to the top."

"Uh huh. If we can rope down from the ledge, we can haul everything up and go from there to the top of the cliff."

"Hurry," Namina called, the fear in her voice making it shake. "They're almost underwater."

Dion waded back to the dinghy, her leather leggings stained

purple with the weeds. Gamon passed her the rope, and she held it over her head to keep it from getting wet. Something brushed against her leg, and her heart stopped for an instant, but it was a gray flatfish, not a purple rastin. She was too nervous at the thought of climbing. Calm down, she told herself. This is ridiculous. It's only twenty meters to climb. She forced herself to smile at Hishn's unamused howl fifty meters away when Aranur's makeshift raft settled in the water and the wolf got her feet wet.

Her twin was hanging from the cliff face already, and Dion passed him the rope's knotted end. He climbed quickly up the cliff, slipping only once when he reached into the crack and came out with a clump of weeds instead of a handhold. Giving herself a second to feel proud of her twin's smooth climbing, the wolfwalker looked back toward the swamped decks of the fishing boat: The raft they had made was already shifting over onto the seaweed.

"Okay, Namina first." She turned to the dinghy and gestured for the younger girl to wade over. She could not let go of the rope to help the girl or it would drop in the water, and climbing with a water-heavy rope would be just too much. "You'll have to wade over here, then go up the knots. That's it. Keep coming. You're doing fine." The girl gasped and cried out in terror as she slipped off the rock into a shallow hole. "You're okay, Namina. It's just a deeper spot between the ridges. There, you can grab my hand. Now, can you climb the knots? Good. I'll hold the rope steady down here so you don't twist about. Careful of your arm, now." The healer kept talking to comfort her as Namina hauled herself up the rope. The water was cold like mountain runoff, and Dion's shivering hips began to ache with numbness.

"Shilia, now you come across. Good. That's right. Grab the rope like this; just lean out from the rocks and walk up. There you go. Don't stop; just keep going and you'll have no trouble. You're doing fine." She lashed one of the two packs Gamon had tossed her to the end of the rope and sent it up, keeping the other on her back to keep it out of the water. The older man had already turned the skiff and was heading back toward the raft. The edge of the pilothouse was still visible in the water, but the raft had floated free and the men were steering it slowly toward the cliff with boards ripped hurriedly from the door.

Mannoa shouted suddenly and scrambled into the center of the raft. The whole thing tilted, sending one of the packs into the water to sit sinking slowly on the seaweed bed. They all scrambled to readjust their weight, Hishn snarling and balancing precariously on the slick surface, and Aranur grabbed at the floating pack.

"What in the nine hells of the moons are you doing, Mannoa?"

"Our splashing has drawn the rastin. Look!"

"Holy mother of all nine moons." Their voices carried clearly over the water, and Dion could hear that quiet shocked statement as if it were in her ear. "How many are there?"

"Thousands. The whole bed here must be a breeding ground. Keep your hands out of the water, boy," Mannoa said edgily to Tyrel. "And don't anyone lean. If we go off the raft here, that's it. You won't be outswimming anything in this stuff."

"Dog's worms," Gamon exclaimed suddenly, and held up the oar he had been using. A bite-sized chunk was missing.

"They're hungry," Mannoa cried, his voice thick with fear. "Hurry up. The fish in the hold are drawing them to the boat."

Shilia had made the top of the ledge, and Dion had found a precarious purchase on a slippery stone near the surface. Water lapped her knees. She shivered, her wet clothes cold against her skin and the constant wind stripping the heat from her body. She lashed the last piece of gear onto the rope for Rhom to draw up.

Gamon had reached the raft, and they passed the packs carefully across, shifting with each movement to keep the raft balanced. Even from where she stood Dion could see the dark purple shadow gathering under them in the water. The activity on the raft was acting as rastin bait, and the smells of the fish in the hold were exciting the rastin to bite anything. Hishn was in the dinghy now, and the raft tilted farther as Tyrel crossed carefully.

The raft wobbled again, and Mannoa cried out with sudden realization, "They're eating the mattresses!" He lunged past Aranur and tried to grab Tyrel from his uncle's reaching hands so that he could make it himself into the dinghy.

"Mannoa! You'll kill us all!" Aranur grabbed at the captain's legs to keep him from upsetting their barely floating raft. It tilted anyway with his sudden weight, and Tyrel and Mannoa both slid into the sea between the swamped raft and the dinghy. Gamon yanked the boy by the arms, dragging him over the side of the dinghy in a flash as he screamed and two purple shapes slid back into the sea from his torn legs. Mannoa was not as lucky. As he slipped, he grabbed the side of the skiff and tilted it dangerously toward the water, but his legs were stripped in seconds, the water churning slowly around his body as the fish fed. He screamed, but Gamon could not unlock his hands to pull him over the side. "Let go, man!" the old man shouted hoarsely over the captain's screams and the snarling of the wolf, "Gods' sake, let go!"

The tortured screams finally stopped, and Mannoa's eyes turned up into their sockets. He slid down into the gather of gloomy purple, which turned vaguely red.

Aranur was flat on the water-swept raft, batting away the flat purple shapes that tried to swim across. "Aranur, if you take one step and jump, I think I can catch you," his uncle said harshly in the silence. Tyrel was shaking as he tried to staunch the flow of blood from his legs.

"All right." Aranur's dark hair made his face look even more pale in the morning light as he rose to his knees and carefully shifted till he was balanced on one leg. He stepped, and the raft was instantly flooded with the purple shadows of rastin, but Gamon already had his arms and yanked him across.

Back at the cliff, Dion breathed—and looked down at her feet. None there yet. Gamon and Aranur were bringing the dinghy back, the oars getting chewed at almost every stroke. Parts of the purple shadow spread to follow them, and the woman shivered again as much from fear as from the chill of the water and wind.

"Dion, go on up," Gamon called. "Get out of the water, now!"

Her voice shook a little, but she had to ask. "Does Tyrel need me?"

"The bandage will hold for now. He'll have to go hand over hand. Go on, woman. We're going to drag this skiff right up to the cliff and climb from there."

They were almost to her, and Dion did not want to take up time on the rope that they could use when she could climb without it. Rhom had drawn it up so that it was not dragging in the water, so she pulled for more length and then tossed the end of the cord out to Gamon. She climbed the crack Rhom had used, going up the sheer wall as easily as if it were a stairway. Her breath caught in her throat when she was halfway up, but it was a simple climb and she was only twenty meters off the water. Below her, Gamon was already attaching two packs to the rope.

By the time she swung over the top of the ledge, the packs were on the way up, her twin hauling them like sacks of ripe potatoes. The wolf had to be hoisted, too, complaining bitterly the whole way, but Dion told her to shush. At least she was not feeding the fish. Tyrel came next, hand over hand, as Gamon had said. The older man sent the other four packs up while the healer looked at Tyrel's legs. The boy had been very lucky, but the bites of almost all sea creatures were poisonous, and Dion was not sure how well they would heal. Gamon arrived then, and Aranur was last, bringing up the rear and carrying the rope. They huddled then on the ledge and breathed the wet air. None of them mentioned Mannoa.

Dion pushed the image of the dead man out of her mind, studied the cliff instead, and shivered, this time not from the cold. The climb would be difficult: The face went sheer about halfway up.

"Nice climb," Gamon remarked soberly, noticing her look.

"Uh huh," Aranur returned. "Real nice." He was looking up at the face of the rock speculatively and judging the distance to the top. "The rock's pretty solid, hmm, Rhom?"

"Not much vegetation," the blacksmith agreed. "I had to scrape the crack free only twice. Our makeshift protection isn't going to work well, though." He was turning the hunks of metal in his hands and comparing them to what he could see of the cliff's face. "Most of the hooks are too big for the cracks, and the others are too small to hold much weight. Plus, there's a lot more ledges than cracks." He smiled grimly. "We'll just have to make sure we don't fall."

"Just remember that old men can't play cliff-hanging games like young boys," Gamon warned. "It looks as if you can make the top in one pitch, but you won't be sure till you get up there. You may need an extra length of rope that we don't have."

Aranur nodded. "Rhom, I watched you climb, and you're good, even with your shoulder, so as long as the wound isn't bothering you, you're climbing as the anchor man. If the rope isn't long enough, you'll have to get the girls up to where they can reach it and tie them in. I'll take this pitch with Gamon. Tyrel's legs won't stand the strain.''

"I'm afraid you'll have to do the pitch with someone other than me or Tyrel, Aranur." Gamon opened his shirt and showed the blood-soaked cloth still bound around his middle. "My side opened up again, and I'm not going to be good for the climb. Sorry, Dion, I ripped out the stitches already."

"You'll do anything for attention, won't you?" She tried to joke as the fear sank her stomach. Oh, moons of mercy, I'm going to have to help lead this climb.

Rhom glanced questioningly at his twin. She shrugged helplessly. "You'll be okay?" he asked in a low voice, gripping her arm as she looked up at the cliff face.

She nodded. "Got to go up sometime. Might as well be first."

He turned to Aranur. "Dion can take the climb."

"Dion?" the lean man asked in surprise. "Just how good are you? I saw you climb to the ledge, and that was smooth, but this is going to be one sheer climb."

"I can do it," she said shortly.

"She's better than both of us, Aranur," Rhom said flatly.

Aranur looked skeptical but nodded, trusting her brother's judgment, so Dion got ready to climb. Aranur was going to go up in his boots, but Dion's did not fit snugly enough to keep her footing solid on the face, and she could not afford to slip because of sloppy footwear. He watched her take off her boots and stack them too carefully by one of the packs. Her hands shook, and she steadied them before she turned back around. But Aranur had noticed. "Exactly how well do you climb, Dion?" he asked, looking from Rhom to his twin sister and back.

Rhom answered for her, worry and pride in his slow voice. "She's climbed the north face of Dountuell. Alone. And a free climb. No protection."

Aranur stared.

Gamon let out his breath in a low whistle. "You've got the moons watching over you, Ember Dione. We'd heard that it had been done by a Randonnen man two years ago, but you? We thought it was just a wild rumor."

She said nothing, just looked at the rock face in front of her. It's only 130 meters, she told herself. I can walk up and down twice before breakfast. But the fear was already collecting in her gut as she looked at that dangerously smooth face. Most of the climb would not be too bad, but the crux looked rough. The face became glass-smooth about twelve meters below an overhang, and the overhang stretched out almost six meters into the air where the wind had eaten away at the cliff. That wind would be a problem, too, she warned herself automatically.

Rhom gathered the rope into a coil to keep it from getting tangled as it was fed up the cliff. Aranur and Dion would trade off, climbing one above the other. Fishing rope was a lot heavier than the climbing ropes used in the mountains, and this one weighed too much to haul up over their shoulders, so Aranur would climb first, taking one end of the rope up twenty meters or until he found a good spot to stop. She would climb past him, taking the end from him. Then they would repeat the pattern. That way they would leapfrog up the face, and neither would have to climb with more than a portion of the rope weighing him or her down at any time.

"Ready?" Aranur's voice broke into her thoughts as she studied the face and planned her climb.

She took a deep breath. "Climb on."

He reached up and found a notch with his fingers. His left foot stepped up into a small crack running horizontally across the face a half meter up. His dark hair brushed back against his shoulders, and he swung up, moving swiftly, smoothly up the face, the rope tied to his belt like a long tail. Dion fed him more length as he moved so that he would not have to tug to pull it up. When he reached a spot about thirty-two meters up, he swung off to the side and perched on a ledge about the width of his foot. His right hand was jammed into a notch above his head to keep his balance, and his left hand began to coil up the rope over his shoulder. He was a good climber.

"Okay, Dion," he called. "Whenever you're ready."

Be calm. Breathe easy. It's me and the rock now, she told herself as she reached for the first notch. Just up to the top and then it's done. Her right leg began to shake ten meters up, and she stopped for a few seconds to calm it. The rock was hard against her fingers wedged into the face. She stretched to reach a small knob the size of her toe. Aranur was taller than the slender woman by almost a quarter meter; his reach was about half a meter more than hers. She could not even get to the holds that had worked for him, so she climbed a zigzag path beside the one he had followed up the face.

She reached him, her breath slightly ragged.

"All right?" he asked, a slight frown on his face, doubt in his eyes.

She nodded, trying to control her breathing.

"I'm rested now," he offered. "I can take the next lead, too."

She shook her head. She knew and he knew that he might not make it through the crux coming up. He would need small hands and a low center of balance to climb the cliff, and Dion was the only one who had both of those along with the skill. But not the fear. She did not need the fear. She reached for the end of the rope he was holding out. By twisting on the face, she could turn her back to him so that he could knot the rope in her belt. She tugged it to make sure it was tight and then swung back across to the path she had chosen from below. She brushed some dust from a small notch, jammed her foot into a hole pecked out by some cliff worm, twisted her foot in the hole, and stood up on it.

The next part of the face had few cracks. Instead, it began to run with tiny ledges no wider than her fingers but plenty wide for her to stand on. Her fingernails broke against the rock as she pulled herself up. She hardly noticed. The fear was sickening in her stomach. Her focus narrowed.

Keep calm. I'm all right. It's me and the rock now.

She caught her breath as her foot shook off its ledge. Her fingers pulled her up against the face, and she caught a new foothold.

Rhom always said I looked good on the rocks. Just keep moving easy. Keep moving smooth.

She lay back away from the cliff so that she could see the face above her, her fingers and toes holding to the bare stone as if glued. Yes, I can use that. The dust sprayed out in the slight wind from the edge she caught in her fingers. She moved smoothly for another ten meters, her breath short and harsh in her ears. Aranur was calling something from below, but she could not understand the words. Her stomach was a tight pit. Don't fall, don't fall. There was a ledge just after a small layback two more meters up. She was about twenty-five meters above Aranur, fifty-five meters from the small ledge where the others waited, and over seventy meters from the rocky water. She was in the crux of the climb. The roaring in her ears blew away the other voices.

"Dion, stop there . . . don't take the crux . . ." She could feel Aranur's voice beat around her head, and Rhom's voice joined in. ". . . there's a crack opening to the right . . . pass the layback and . . . four meters . . ."

She climbed on, swinging by touch across the face and twisting her fingers into the crack. Good holds, she thought. Her throat was getting hoarse, and she could feel the scream beginning to rise from her stomach. Her legs shook. She jammed her little finger into the irregularity and pulled up again. Smooth, sure . . . She went up the meter the crack ran before it angled toward the overhang. A knobbin beckoned a half meter from her reach. She lunged up off the crack and caught it with her thumb, immediately pinching her fingers down on top of it to build a stronger hold. Her legs swung free. A sob tore from her throat, and she carefully, slowly pulled herself up by the one hand to find a foothold against a small indent. Breathe! she reminded herself.

"Dion, what are you doing . . . hold on there . . ." The anguished words flew around her head like birds. ". . . I'm coming up . . . with you in a moment . . ."

And from below: "Got to climb now . . . can't stop . . ."

Rhom, my brother, who always said I could outclimb a cliff-hanger.

". . . wait till she's through the crux . . ."

She set her palm around a small bulge and pinched it while her left foot inched up the face and stood on her thumb. The drag of the rope was beginning to tell on her. She was forty meters above Aranur and in the center of the crux—she tried to keep her thoughts from screaming too loud. She had to wiggle her fingers from beneath her foot to reach for a new hold. Standing, slowly edging her body up beside the cliff, her breasts and thighs brushing the face as she moved. You have no protection, no protection—you'll fall, you'll fall. The voice beat against her confidence, numbing her mind. She found a notch under her seeking fingers and jammed a pinch hold with her thumb and forefinger into the hole. The crack widened about a meter up where part of the face had fallen off, and she twisted her fist into its off width. Her foot found the first notch, and her big toe wedged into it so that she could stand, shaking, the flesh crushed around the jammed bones of her foot.

Me and the rock, Ember Dione. It's me and the rock.

Her world shrunk to the face of the cliff around her. She could feel the wind brushing her as it swept the face, her breathing echoing its wake.

"Dion, above you . . . opens up on the right side . . . only a few more meters . . ."

She crept up under the bulge and began to edge out upside down, her hips hugging the rock and the rope falling away into air as she climbed out away from the face. Her thumb and pinkie found a strange pinch hold gripping two divots in the overhang. She reached out toward the sea as the bulge set her face to the sky. Upside down. She caught at a knob on the edge. Her feet peeled off their hold and dropped like stones to dangle in the air; her arms jerked, and her fingers were almost yanked off the rocks. She heard a scream far below. Hishn's desperate howl drifted up. Her arms burned with the strain. The wind twisted her and blew salty hair into her mouth.

Slowly, slowly. Don't lose the grip.

The sea was dark and shallow with the rocks below, and the purple weeds that choked the bay called to her like a soft bed. She could feel her little finger beginning to slip off its pinch hold. She doubled her feet up under her in the air and set first one, then the other back onto the roof of the overhang. The pinch hold was going. She released the hold and reached out for, then around, the bulge. Her fingers scrabbled at the rock, dust flying away in the wind as if to scour her eyes. Searching, shaking as they ran along the edge looking for something—anything—irregular to grasp. Her breath fell away as if dropped from the cliff. She could not hold any longer. Her fingers seemed to melt away from the rock as she began to fall. She sobbed and grabbed once more desperately at the bulge—

—and got it. A ridge no wider than the edge of her broken fingernail, but it was enough. She dug what was left of her nails into it and let her legs swing free again, out into the air. Turning her arm so that her elbow lay flat against the slab that smoothed the top of the overhang, she pulled up slowly. Scraping her arm on the rock, she brought her right foot up level with her shoulder and dug her bare toes into the top of the wind-smoothed bulge.

She could hear nothing from below as the overhang cut off

their calls in the sounds of the wind and sea. The face stretched the last thirty-five meters above her, half of it smooth as the blade of a knife. But a crack opened halfway to the top—she could use it if she could get to it. She moved to the face. Her legs were shaking so badly that she was rocking off every hold she managed to find.

Keep moving, just keep going.

Her right foot was bathed in red, and the scrapes on her fingers had spread blood across the backs of her hands. She reached up and found a small series of ledges about as wide as a silver piece was thick.

Move smooth, move sure . . .

She went up fast, her feet slipping off each hold as she reached for the next one, her breath ragged and sobbing. The base of the crack appeared, and the little finger on her left hand wedged in. She reached up and got a good jam with the right forefinger and middle finger as the crack widened just a little. The knuckles were crushed together as she hung her body from their tiny bones and hauled herself up.

Twenty meters, that's all . . .

The crack widened enough at the top for her to use her elbows; she tightened her arm muscles to swell out her flesh into the crack and hold her in place. It was too wide now to use her feet for jamming, and she went up twisted, elbows holding and releasing, then her feet scraping the crack to follow her up. Her face was wet, the wind tightening her cheeks as her tears dried. Three meters. The wind grew stronger, and the rock suddenly sloped away from the face as she approached the top. She got her hands at the top of the crack.

As she pulled her shaking body up through the crack, she could see the great expanse of plains stretching away, the sky huge and low above her and the sea thrashing itself against the cliffs as it reached up from below. She rolled onto the top of the cliff and crawled away from the edge. The only sound in the wind was her sobs echoing down the stone.

XI

Aranur Bentar neDannon:

Rumors, Reason, and Myth

My people, I led you through valleys of death
Through sorrow and heartbreak of war;
We fought for our rights and we won them again,
But the battle will never be done.

My son, now I feel my heart faint in my chest
And my time on this earth is near done.
My life has been given to further our cause,
And yours must go too for the same.

The headband of leadership weighs like a stone,
And decisions will have to be soon.
My son, do you give them dishonorable death?
Or the glory that rides with the moons?

Aranur's heart stopped as he watched Dion slip from the overhang and dangle helplessly in the wind. Shilia screamed from below, and the terrible howl of the wolf added a chilling ghost to the wind. Above him, the slender woman doubled up, pulling in her legs and somehow setting them back on the roof of the bulge as she hung upside down. She seemed to hang there forever, one hand searching the edge of the overhang, the other beginning to slip. In his twenty-eight years in the Ariye mountains, Aranur had never seen such climbing. The face was sheer, with holds too small for his fingers to wedge into, and blood marked the tiny cracks and scrapes across the minuscule ledges where her bare feet jammed in. He caught sight of her face once and saw the terror deep in her eyes; she did not recognize him. All he could do was keep feeding her the line as she disappeared around the bulge and pulled the dangling rope taut.

There was a cold line of fear crawling into his gut as he looked at the face and saw that the crux she had just anguished through was beyond his skill. If she can't find something to tie off to, he thought with a chill, I will take her with me when I fall. The others won't stand a chance in all nine hells. His fingers cramped, and he shifted his hands, then shifted them again. Then, when he thought himself beyond hope, two tugs pulled sharply on the rope, and then two more snapped the line taut. Relief flooded him. The sick feeling in his gut relaxed. He had been straining to hear the girl scream when she fell, waiting to see her outflung body as she hurtled past.

He took a deep breath. "She's at the top," he called down, seeing Rhom's pale face turned up for word of his twin. Then he wrapped the rope around his hands and leaned out. It was not difficult to walk up, but it was tiring; the wind buffeted him more and more strongly as he went up.

When he neared the overhang, his feet slipped from the face, so he let them swing free and hauled himself up hand over hand until he reached the edge and pulled himself up around the bulge. The rope was already chafed from where it rubbed against the edge of the overhang, but he could not stop to fix it—he did not know if Dion had the rope tied off or if she was simply braced and holding it while he climbed. The sea swept out distantly below him.

Sweat ran between his fingers, and he wiped them on his pants. He slipped twice, but once around the overhang he went quickly to the top. He need not have worried about Dion taking his weight—the rope was tied off to a huge stone column sticking up from the cliff. She sat, backed up against another column as far as she could go, wiping her eyes with the back of her hand and trying to control the sobs that still shook her chest. Her pale skin was stained with the blood that was welling from her torn fingers, and the tear tracks smeared the dirt further on her face until she looked as forlorn as a lost child.

"Oh, Dion . . ." He dropped the rope and put his arms around her. "You're okay now. It's over." She buried her face in his firm shoulder and burst into tears, her soft chest pressed tightly against his, her hands locked around his neck while he stroked and kissed her hair and soothed her as he would his own sister. "It's okay. Is it always bad like that? Don't worry," he said tightly, "you won't have to do it again." Damn Rhom, he thought. He would not put a dog through something like that. And Dion was Rhom's own sister! The lean, gray-eyed man controlled his anger and instead held the sobbing woman closer. He kissed her forehead, then, without thinking, his lips followed the salty tears to her mouth and he kissed her gently, then deeply, his desire sudden and charging him up as the wind blew the dust around them and the ocean fell away below.

"Mmmph," she mumbled finally. He released her and sat back on his heels, his hands still on her shoulders, her face flushed deep and her lips bright red. He reached to tilt her face to him again, but she ducked away and asked unsteadily instead, "Do we need to readjust the rope? I didn't look to see how far it reaches down."

"They need another couple of meters if we have it, but I'll do it." He straightened and carefully began coiling up the rope. He would have to drop it again, but he did not want it falling down before he reattached it, and he still had to put something around that chafed spot.

"Does this happen often?" he asked, and she knew what he meant.

She hesitated and then shrugged. "I'm afraid of heights," she answered in a low voice.

He stared at her. He was incredulous. "Afraid—and climb like you do?"

She shrugged, looking down at her torn hands. "I've always been afraid of heights, but then I took a bad fall a couple of years ago. Now, when I lead a climb, everything seems to focus down to just me and the rocks. Sometimes I can't stop climbing till I'm done or the pitch is finished and I can't go any further. I like climbing," she said simply. "I'm just scared."

Aranur shook his head and took a section of leather from a spare belt pouch to wrap around the rope where it would rub against the overhang. Tyrel would climb first and help bring the others up, and the girls would be tied on so that if they were not strong enough to come up hand over hand, they could be hauled up from the top. The rock he tied into the rope's end would keep the rope from swinging away in the wind as he let it down again. After a while he felt three tugs, then three more. Tyrel should be coming up. Dion moved beside the man to help with the rope.

"I can handle it," he suggested. "Why don't you rest." She was still too pale.

The tentative smile died from her face. "I'm strong enough to help bring Tyrel up," she said a little sharply. "If you waste all your strength hauling him up alone, it will be that much harder to bring up the others."

Moonworms, he thought with a flash of irritation. What a waste of a kiss. He leaned into the wind against the dead weight that pulled the rope down. By the time his cousin's face appeared around the overhang below, Dion was gasping for breath, and even Aranur felt the strain in his arms. The youth was doing what he could to walk up, but even so, it was a job; the wind could not quite dry the hot sweat stinging Aranur's muscles, and he hauled the boy up the last meter by his arms. "Took you long enough," he growled, breathing deeply.

"Good to see you in such a fine humor, Cousin," the sandy-haired youth retorted, though his face was red with the effort of the climb. "I guess you want help with the rest of them."

"You've had your break. You just rode all the way up here, didn't you?" Aranur coiled the rope again to let it down for his other cousin. "You want supper, you have to bring up the rest of the cooks."

The boy tactfully said nothing to the wolfwalker about the tear marks on her dusty face, just took his place between the two to help with the rope.

An hour later Aranur stood and looked over the scraggly plain they found themselves on. Now what? he asked himself, the words of that ancient poem coming to mind: *My son, do you give them dishonorable death? Or the glory that rides with the moons?*

He looked out from the Cliffs of Bastendore over the sea, watching the tide drop lower and lower. The reefs no longer washed with water. They exploded with each wave, the white water reaching up past them and dropping back like a freestanding waterfall. If they had been even an hour later going though the reef, they would have been shattered like old china on those rocks.

Inland, under the heavy gray sky, the cliff grass worked its way into a scraggly forest. Thin here, thickened there with the twiggy brush of the coastal clime, and then suddenly bare where lightning had burned into fires that finally died away in the damp—the dark line of growth was as uninviting as an unkempt house. At least there were flatwood trees in the forest, he noted. Their variegated leaves and ugly, scar-striped wood were hard to miss even at that distance, and the sparse spread of their thin canopy was too distinctive to be mistaken for something else. Flatwood trees. Then there would be rootrocks, too. The spring berries would be hardening with summer, he knew, but they might still give enough fruit to flesh out a meal that would otherwise be gamey meat and soggy, leftover bread. Soon enough they would be eating nothing but meats and greens anyway.

Beyond the forest, the hills built up into a mountain range that disappeared under the overcast sky. Jagged fingers of rock stuck up every which way except at a strange smooth peak from which the fog slid like a slow-motion waterfall. The white snow of late spring had not yet melted on the mountains, but that only meant that the snowfields would be soft and treacherous. There would be passes, but without a map, how could he choose one that was safe? He picked up two packs and started moving them to the dubious shelter of the trees as he mused. The few charts they had taken from the fishing boat would not help them figure out where they were; sea charts rarely penetrated the shoreline by more than a kilometer except for known estuaries and rivers, which were all too far away.

"Well?" his uncle asked, sitting with a comforting arm around Namina's shivering figure. "Where to now, O fearless leader?"

The tall man squinted at the peaks and then squatted by Gamon, where he cleared a patch of dust with his hand and set a pebble down. "Here's where I think we are. From what Mannoa said, these cliffs line the coast from Riner to Newonton with no towns in between." He made a line of the peaks with several twigs. "Here's this mountain range. It's unpopulated, but there are supposed to be some abandoned mining sites and a couple other places of the ancients. If we were more than lucky, we could find the roads that lead to them and follow across this valley into the next range, but I doubt that the moons will grace us that much."

He pointed to one of the lines of twigs. "The first range here is only 50 kilometers across. Then there's this valley, about 260 kilometers wide." He made another mountain range of random sticks. "The second range is not as high as the first, but it's another 100 or 110 kilometers wide. From here, where we are—'' He pointed from the pebble across the two ranges. ''—to this valley, where Caflanin actually starts being populated, is over 400 kilometers. It's rough country, and it'll still be cold this time of year. At this point here—'' He pointed to the pebble and traced the line up the twig mountains. ''—the ranges stretch along the coast till they merge and drop into the sea near Obrador, forming the Reef of Coal.''

''That range gets higher the farther north you go, as I recall,'' Gamon mused.

''Uh huh. Home of the snowbears. They're about the size of a dnu,'' he explained to Shilia at her puzzled expression. ''Anyway, as I figure it, we're about 340 kilometers from Sidisport and 220 kilometers from Riner.''

His sister frowned. ''But it's just a matter of picking the shortest way home.''

''Pretty much,'' he answered. ''Except I've no way of knowing which way will end up being shortest. The rougher the country, the less distance we can cover each day.'' He scowled at the forest. ''Although, with the raiders out of our hair, we've time enough to decide.''

In half an hour every bush around was strewn with clothes, packs, and other gear, drying in the muggy afternoon warmth. Aranur tossed the two depleted money bags they had left into a pile and was standing near the fire, thinking about the best way through the mountains. From where he was standing, there were three possible passes they could take—

''Hey, Aranur,'' Tyrel called, breaking into his thoughts. The boy, having worked his way down to the bottom of his pack, was tossing things every which way, including at his cousin. ''Catch.''

Aranur looked up as the boy threw a packet of papers toward him. He reached without thinking and caught the bundle, but not before it had leaped through the flames of their lunch fire. ''Moonworms, Tyrel!'' he exclaimed. Hurriedly he pinched out the flames that already had flared on the edge of the packet. ''Did it never occur to you that paper burns? Next time send it over, not through, the fire.''

''Sorry,'' the youth said, contrite and paying more attention to where he threw the few clothes he had left to take out of his pack.

"Tyrel," Aranur said slowly, looking at the packet more closely. "Where did you get this?" He undid the string that tied the bundle together, but there was no seal or signature on the outside to hint at what the letters held.

"Salmi's strongbox. I just grabbed everything I could and stuffed it in the bag. Figured it was probably just his payroll or a bunch of love letters but thought they might be interesting anyway." The boy shrugged. "I forgot to tell you about them till now."

Letters kept in a slaver's strongbox? Aranur's interest was instantly kindled. That would not be a payroll, but it might be transaction records—orders and sales. He would give a lot to know who was behind the sudden increase in slaver activity. When he opened the first letters, he was not disappointed: They were records of raider activities to the north, and he read several pages, correlating what he knew of their forces with the information in the letters before something caught his eye. "By the gods of all nine hells," he exclaimed.

Gamon looked up with a frown. "What is it?"

"I'm not sure," Aranur said slowly. Unfolding the next letter, he glanced at it and then the next before passing them to his uncle. "Here, Gamon, look at the signatures on these letters."

The older man examined them slowly. "That seal is private—I've seen it only twice before. But I do know that it's used by only one man: Longear, the head of Lloroi Zentsis's secret service."

But Aranur was already reading the third page of the letter. "By the moons!" he exclaimed. "No wonder we were chased to the second moon and back. They don't want us, they want these letters back. Listen to this: 'Bounty paid for every farm destroyed,' " he read, unbelieving. " 'Five extra pieces of gold for every woman taken from a Lloroi's family . . . three extra pieces for women from other high-ranked families.' " Gamon and Rhom leaned closer to read over his shoulder, so after scanning the letter, Aranur passed it on to Shilia and Dion. "This explains why you three were taken by the raiders when there were dozens of other girls easier to kidnap for slave markets."

"But Aranur, this says—this says that we were supposed to be taken to Zentsis, not sold in Sidisport."

"Salmi must have been trying to make a double profit on you." The gray-eyed leader thought of the raider captain's private slave sale. "He would probably have told Zentsis that you'd killed yourselves rather than become his legal concubines. Not a bad story, since Salmi and Zentsis both come from coastal towns where that's standard procedure. So Salmi keeps half profit from that deal, then sells you at that private market for a sweeter slice of the pie. You're never heard from again, but Salmi gets enough money to finance another slaver boat and repeat the process."

Gamon looked up, his face grim. "Aranur, you're missing something here. The slave runs aren't the main point of these letters."

Aranur met his uncle's look with one of his own. "I know, Gamon. I read between the lines. I just can't believe we've been so blind to this for so long."

"Blind to what?" Rhom asked quietly.

"These bounties," Aranur explained slowly, "these directions for strikes—these aren't just letters telling the raiders where and what to strike for profit. These are the early plans for a war."

"Be serious, Aranur," Shilia said derisively. "We haven't had a war for decades."

But Rhom frowned. "He's not joking, Shilia."

Her brother nodded, disturbed. "Look at these references: organized raider attacks, supplies being shipped up the Phye. There's a definite pattern to the areas the raiders are concentrating on: Look at these orders for command posts—we know several of these are already set up on the coast and in the lowlands. As sure as these letters don't actually say it," he said, "these are preliminary war plans, with the raiders being organized as the advance guard."

Gamon looked grim. "The raiders have gotten more daring lately," he admitted, reading the rest of the letter and glancing at other pages Aranur passed him. "We never considered the pattern of their movements other than noting that we had to strengthen the borders. And none of the elders—not one of us," he said with a snort, "made the ridiculously obvious connection that those borders were the ones closest to Zentsis's lands."

Aranur resisted the impulse to smack his fist into his palm the way he wished he could do to some more of those self-styled slavers. "We assumed that when Zentsis took over Prent's rule, he overextended himself and the raiders moved in under his weaker rule. None of us considered the alternative—that the raiders moved in under Zentsis because they worked for Zentsis.''

''But that means,'' Rhom said, looking up, his eyes smoldering with violet fire, ''that Randonnen, too, is being set up. By these plans, after Ariye falls, then Randonnen will take the brunt of the raider attacks, then Diton and Yorunda.''

''Ariye will not fall,'' Aranur said flatly.

His uncle nodded grimly. ''Ariye must not fall. But this plan is subtle, clever. Zentsis has quietly organized the raiders into a wide ring of destruction that will not be recognized until too late.'' He paused, his face dark.

Aranur nodded. ''We think of raiders as unorganized looting bands of murderers. And we think of Zentsis as being too far away to be a threat to Ariye. We wouldn't have understood this pattern of attack until Zentsis marched in and offered us release from the raiders by joining with him, under certain conditions beneficial only to Ramaj Bilocctar, of course.''

''But a bounty for every farm destroyed, rewards for stealing women . . .'' Shilia was shocked. ''What is Zentsis trying to do to us? He'll have nothing left to rule if this is followed.''

''He'll have enough,'' Gamon answered her soberly. ''This will wear us down and destroy our morale just like he did to Lloroi Prent. We'll be weak and disorganized from fighting off bands of raiders. Right now, all Zentsis has to do is sit back and wait for the raiders to do his work for him. Then, when he does finally come in with his army, we'll fall like rabbits before a horde of hungry lepa. Hells, we may even welcome his forces as a solution to the raider problem.''

''The Lloroi—my father must know,'' Tyrel said in a troubled voice. ''The elders must be told.''

''Yes, but it's not going to be easy. Damn it!'' Aranur smacked his fist into his palm. ''We thought the raiders were just getting unruly, greedy. No one thought to plot their movements across Ramaj borders.'' He turned to Rhom. ''Exactly how much raider activity has Randonnen seen since last fall?''

''Our village hasn't had trouble yet, but we're farther from the coast and the main river than other towns.'' The smith thought a moment. ''It's not safe to travel on the roads alone anymore, and their attacks are more frequent to the west, where the Lloroi's village is. Last fall the Lloroi sent out two hunter venges to track and take care of the raiders that have been a problem; this spring he's already sent out six.''

"And each venge lost more men than they usually do," Dion added. "And the men's wounds were more serious.''

Her brother nodded. "They reported that the raider groups were larger now than before. Early this spring, one venge nearly didn't come back, so now when the Lloroi sends one out, twice as many men go along as they think they need. And still they could use more swords.''

Aranur looked grim. "It is as Zentsis says here to Salmi: 'With money to back them, the raiders will become the vanguard of my army, preparing the land for my rule.' ''

"We have to get back," Tyrel said hotly. "These letters—''

"The letters must be shown to the elders. But there is more risk here than you perhaps realize. Think, Tyrel. If anyone in Ramaj Caflanin suspects that we have these things, Longear and the rest of Zentsis's secret service will soon know, and our lives won't be worth half a copper. By the moons, they've already shown us what they're willing to do to get these letters back.'' He glanced at the crude map drawn on one of the letters.

The wolfwalker looked at the mountains, then at Aranur's determined face. "We're very close to Bilocctar now, aren't we?" she said obliquely.

Aranur met her eyes and smiled grimly. She had seen through him in a second. "One of us should take the chance to find out more while we're in his backyard," he admitted.

Gamon gave his nephew his own grim smile. "Count me in. I'd like to put a stone in the pie myself." He looked at Namina's sagging shoulders, the dark circles under her puffy eyes, and the bandage strapping her forearm tightly. "I figure we owe Zentsis something already.''

Aranur slept heavily that night. The strain of the last few days and the peace of the woods combined to close his eyes in deep dreams that shuddered with sounds of battle and dim cries of the dead. It was all he could do to drag himself out of the bedroll again to stand watch when it was his turn, and his bleary eyes opened late in the morning when the crackling heat of the fire wafted breakfast smells his way.

He decided to cross the mountain range and make for Caflanin first. By then Salmi's raiders would know they had taken a sea route and would have sent word to the ports to look for the fleeing party. If they stayed away from ports and kept inland, the raiders might think they had wrecked and drowned. That was half-right, anyway. And Caflanin was not a rich enough county to tempt Zentsis to exploit it. Even with Zentsis's meager occupation of the county, it was still the safest overland route to Ramaj Ariye, and with luck, Aranur's sister and cousin would see home again in four ninans. A long time to travel—Namina would turn seventeen, the age of Promising, by the time she saw her father again—but, the subtleties of Zentsis's plans forced his raiding armies to a slow beginning to build up their momentum. Aranur had time enough to get back and warn Ramaj Ariye to prepare.

To Aranur's irritation, Rhom took Shilia with him when he went hunting for supper. She must have been more interested in the dark-haired blacksmith than Aranur had suspected, because she surely did not know how to hunt. The two did come back with five furry rabbits, but it took them a long time to find the creatures, and Shilia had a telltale blush on her cheeks when they returned. She avoided her brother's stern expression, while Rhom went around camp with a smug look on his face. And Dion ignored both men, treating their cuts, bruises, slashes, and bites without speaking till she came to Tyrel. The boy's legs looked bad when she unwrapped the bandages she had put on earlier.

"Infection?" Aranur asked as she examined the youth with a frown.

"No. It's something else. Almost all sea creature bites are venomous. You can see from the swelling here and here—" She pointed to the angry red lines radiating away from the raw edges of the wounds. "—that something in the rastin bite is causing the skin to puff out. I'll have to lance and clean them right away, Tyrel."

The boy nodded and turned his face away so he would not have to watch as he endured the process. He gasped only once. Namina took one look and hurried out of the clearing. As for Aranur, he would not have believed there was that much fluid in the wounds, but when she had lanced both bites, he swore the boy's legs were two kilograms lighter. By that time the sun had stumbled over the mountains and left them with little light to work in.

"I'll take the first watch," Aranur suggested as they relaxed around the fire. "Then Gamon, then Rhom." His two young cousins were already asleep and would stay that way if he had his say.

"Then me."

He looked at the wolfwalker and opened his mouth to protest, but Shilia cut in first. "And me," she said, sitting down by Dion. Aranur just looked at her. "If we watch, too," his sister suggested brightly, "everyone will get another two hours of sleep."

"Gray Hishn will tell us if anything approaches," Dion added mildly.

He gave up. Women, he said to himself, exasperated. "All right." He leaned back against a log and listened to the others talk while the evening darkened the sky into night. If the moons were with them, it would not rain till the next day, maybe even blow off completely if the storm front passed them by.

Later, when Gamon relieved him from watch, he still was not sleepy. He was trying to concentrate on the letters Tyrel had stolen from the slaver, but thoughts of Rhom's sister kept disturbing him. She should not keep her hair up in that warcap—it should be loose like his sister's. Glossy . . . he wondered what it would feel like brushing against his chest.

"Stop frowning and get yourself to sleep," his uncle ordered, settling down beside him for the next few hours of cold watchfulness.

Aranur sighed. "I don't know what's the matter with me, Gamon."

"I could give it a guess."

"And with your one-track mind, I know what you'd say, too."

"Dion's a beautiful lady," the older man said obliquely.

"She wears the clothes of a man." The gray-eyed leader shifted irritably. "She fights like a man. Hell, she fights better than most men."

Gamon snorted. "You've got a thick skull, Aranur. She's on Journey with her brother in a county where women are stolen and sold like dnu. You expect her to wear Shilia's clothes?" He chuckled. "You'd have more men following us just for her than for those letters we stole."

"Speaking of Shilia," Aranur said sourly, "she seems to be getting to know Rhom a little too well."

"Good for them. It's about time the girl found herself a good man."

"And Rhom?" Aranur asked, hiding his irritation.

The older man was unruffled. "It's time he realized that his attentions should be on women other than his own sister."

"What about your women, Gamon?"

His uncle chuckled at his unsubtle attempt to change the subject. "I dream about them all the time," he said slyly.

"She's just so damn different from what I thought I wanted," the tall man complained.

"Dion?"

"Moonworms, Gamon, but I think about her half the time I should be concentrating on other things. She's driving me crazy. One minute she likes me; the next minute she thinks I'm pond slime. Every time I think things are going okay, she ups and gives me that gods-but-you-are-a-scum-ball look, and I'm back in the doghouse. I'm going nuts, Gamon."

The old man chuckled. "I can tell."

"I've never found a woman who could hold my interest before."

"Ha. What about Wylonia? You acted like you were never going to look at a woman again when you stopped seeing her."

"I lost interest in her fast enough when she started hanging around with Marco," he retorted.

"And for a while," his uncle teased, "I thought Ammyn had caught you for a mate."

"Ammyn." Aranur snorted. "She has a tongue like a lepa and the disposition of a dnu."

"That's not what you said the day after she kissed you in the caves."

"The caves were dark. I couldn't see her true colors."

The old man laughed and leaned back, picking his teeth with a sliver he had split from the log. "Reminds me of a woman I courted back, oh, ten years ago. When I was around, she was the sweetest, kindest woman, but when my back was turned, she changed into a worlag's bitch. I found that out just in time." He grinned and gave his nephew a sharp look. "What is it exactly that you want in a woman, Aranur? Have you thought about that?"

"I don't know." Aranur leaned back and stared at the sky. "I suppose I want everything. I want someone who's beautiful and gentle and exciting and unpredictable. I want a woman who will keep me company for the rest of my life and understand what I do, not just listen to what I say. I want a woman who will be a mother for my children but will still excite me thirty years down the trail."

The older man nodded. "I used to be taken with a woman who lived in Conceton, about fifty kilometers away—used to dig up every excuse I could to go see her. I courted her for four years, trying to convince myself that I wanted to stay unmated. Then I finally decided to ask her to mate with me, and I rode into town, all spiffed up, with my bouquet of blue and white flowers, and she met me at the door with another man. She looked at me and said, 'Four years is a long time to wait for a man to make up his mind.' I just turned around and rode away. And I've kicked myself every ninan since." He looked over at his nephew. "If I'd been riding straight in the saddle instead of going around in circles with myself, I'd have seen what she meant to me before it was too late. She was the only woman I ever wanted." He sighed again. "She has two boys now, old enough to learn sword fighting."

"Do you wish they were yours?"

"Every day," the old man admitted. "Now you, Aranur—" He pointed at the younger man with his sliver of a toothpick. "You're young and strong, and the women, only the moons know why, think you're handsome. You can still pick and choose."

"Why would I want to choose now? I'd rather face a dozen raiders every day than mate a woman I wouldn't be able to stand in a year."

"I hear you there. And now's the time to play around, while you're still young. But someday it's going to hit you like a sand-bag that you're in love. And when it does, you're going to realize that one particular woman is half your life. She may be moody or temperamental, she may be a nag or a bitch or a shrew, but you're going to want her like you've never wanted anyone be-fore. And I'll be waiting for the day, too, because I'm going to enjoy watching you squirm before her with your blue and white flowers, just begging her to take you."

"Gamon, you're a damned romantic."

"Aranur, you're a twice-damned romantic because you re-fuse to recognize the same thing in yourself."

"Hah!" the other man snorted. But his dreams that night were sharp and clear, and it was Dion, not another, who lay in his nebulous arms.

The next day was as quiet as the first. Rhom, Gamon, and Tyrel cut some flatwood and started to make skis. As unpre-pared as they were, the trek across the mountains was going to be rough, and they would need the skis, crude as they were, to get across the snow that still lay thickly in the lower passes. While the other men went out for flatwood, Aranur spent the day sharpening and oiling their weapons, since the salt air had not done the steel any good. Shilia spent the morning practicing some of the martial arts Dion had showed her. Aranur was im-pressed: The wolfwalker was a good teacher. His sister had already grasped the principles behind leverage and power, things that could not be considered too important for someone of her small size.

He wished Namina would spend some time working out with the other two girls, but his cousin seemed to have lost interest again. She spent hours silently drying the extra rabbit meat over the fire. It was tedious and mindless work and allowed her to withdraw farther from him and everyone else until he wanted to shake her and tell her to snap out of it. "Everyone is called to the moons sometime," he told her gently. "But you cannot reject your life because of another's death." But she just gave him a hollow look and turned back to the fire, and Aranur had to swallow his frustration and try to think of something else to keep her alive inside.

With Shilia working at Abis, Namina dragging about the camp, and the wolfwalker gone into the woods, Aranur's de-pression took over. He moped, desultorily sharpening his knives and then doing it again, hoping that Dion would come back so he could talk to her about Tyrel, but she did not come back till the evening's dusk brought dinner. After she had been gone an hour, Aranur had become irritated, but after six hours, he had worked himself into a black mood. He was breaking wood into chunks that would fit their fire ring when the shrubs behind him rustled quietly, and a lupine sneeze announced her arrival with the Gray One.

He swung around sharply. "Dion," he said sharply, stopping

her. He noticed the healthy flush on her cheeks and was even more irritated at his reaction of sudden desire than at her lateness. "I don't want you going off alone anymore."

"I wasn't alone," she said, surprised. The wolf, who had trotted in with her, yawned lazily and rubbed her side. "Hishn was with me."

"Hishn—no offense, Gray One—is not enough to protect you. We don't know what dangers are out here yet."

The Gray One growled, pulling her lips back from her teeth and stepping forward so that he realized how big she really was. "Aranur," Dion said with puzzled irritation, "Hishn is as well aware of the dangers as anyone can be. I am safer with her than with you."

He took a breath. "I'm just concerned for your safety and for that of the group," he said shortly. "If you got in trouble, we'd have no idea where you were, and I might have to place the others in jeopardy to help you."

She gave him a sharp look. "I appreciate your concern, Aranur, but I'd never place you in danger if I could help it. You know that. And I can take care of myself in most situations."

"And what about the other times, when you can't take care of it yourself?"

"Then I'll call you," she said with a sudden smile.

The expression lit her eyes like violet fire, and Aranur realized that he had rarely seen her look like that. He forgot why he was angry with her and, nodding, turned away, but not before he caught a smug look on Gamon's face. He had a feeling that Dion had somehow gotten the better of him in that conversation, but he was not quite sure how. He frowned and sat down.

"Shilia, let me see those letters again," Gamon said to his niece as he finished gnawing on a rack of rabbit ribs. He absently set them down by his side in the pile of bones that had grown there, but the ribs never reached the ground; a gentle set of fangs took them from his fingers, and he did not notice for a second until he realized that the wolf was lying beside him, chomping noisily. "Moonwormed mutt of a misguided dog," he muttered. The wolf tilted her head and regarded him from her wide, innocent yellow eyes; he grumbled, tossed her another bone from the pile beside him, and wiped his hands on his dirty pants, accepting the packet of letters the brown-haired girl dug from her pack.

"Uncle Gamon, I don't understand why Salmi has to kill us to get these letters back," Shilia said, slipping over the log he was leaning against. "Why don't we let him have them, then go slip away home again?" She plopped down in the soft dirt and nestled against the old man's toughened body, wishing she had a bed to sleep in that night instead of the ground.

"Girl, you're a smart one sometimes, but other times I think you've been sheltered from the world too long. The absence of those letters is the only reason Ariye and Randonnen and the other counties haven't banded together to confront and fight the raiders—or rather, I should say, Zentsis—directly. No one believes that there's a grand plan to their activities. But those documents are evidence. With them, everyone will know what's coming. Hells, it's spelled out like a first-year primer. Without the letters, even though we know the important points of Zentsis's plan, we'd have only half of Ariye behind us, and half of the other counties, as well. That's enough to fight a battle, girl, but not enough to win the war."

"And with the letters?"

The old man chuckled. "We'd have ninety percent of all the counties aligned with us. And that's more than enough to light a fire under Zentsis's britches and then keep fanning the flames."

"I still think if we gave the letters back they'd not try so hard to find us."

"Girl, taking something from Zentsis is like stealing from Aiueven," he said quietly. "You might get away with it for a while, but you won't survive the experience."

Dion, only partially listening to their conversation, frowned at the mention of the bird people. The legends surrounding the Aiueven, the original inhabitants of Asengar, were even more morbid than those of Ovousibas, the double-edged gift the birdmen had given the ancients.

As if he could read her mind, Gamon gave the healer a deliberate look.

"Take Ovousibas, now. The ancients took internal healing from Aiueven but got the plague along with it."

"That's just speculation, Gamon," she said.

"Is it?" The weapons master regarded the woman seriously. "Every healer who's tried Ovousibas since the plague is dead. That's eight hundred years of death, Dion. Almost a millennium. Even two hundred years ago in Ariye, there was a healer that tried it to save the Lloroi's mate.''

"I've never heard that, Uncle Gamon," Shilia said.

Gamon nodded at his niece. "It's an old tale. One of tragedy, as all stories of Ovousibas are.''

Shilia's eyes were wide and eager, but Dion made a gesture of dismissal.

"Don't be so quick to scoff, Wolfwalker," the older man said warningly. "Listen. I'll tell you the tale, then you decide for yourself.

"The Healer Malc and the Lady Ibirni had been childhood sweethearts, and it had always been understood that they would Promise and mate. But they had an argument, and a month later, she Promised to the Lloroi.'' The weapons master shook his head. "Healer Malc left the village. Within a year the Lady Ibirni fell ill. It was a serious disease—a fever that sapped her strength until she had nothing left to fight the disease with. No one could do anything. She was going to die," he said softly. He gestured at the Gray One. "But Healer Malc was a wolf-walker, like you, Dion, and he listened to the legends.'' The old man shot the woman an odd look. "Much like you're doing now. Well, Malc went to see his sweetheart three times, and the third time he got it right.''

Shilia frowned. "Got what right?''

"Ovousibas," the old man whispered.

"So what happened?" Shilia asked impatiently.

Gamon's eyes were on the healer. "Ibirni lived and bore the Lloroi a son." He paused. "Malc died.''

Dion shivered in spite of herself.

"He became feverish, went comatose, and died two days later. The wolf who ran with him went berserk and had to be destroyed.'' He glanced at Hishn. "The Gray Ones did it themselves. They formed a ring in the hills and began to howl, and then there was silence, and Gray Ramosh was gone.''

Hishn looked up, troubled. She nudged Dion's hand, and the woman scratched the Gray One under the chin. *It is true, Healer?* the beast sent.

That the Gray Ones take care of their own? I knew that.

No. The wolf hesitated, and Dion was puzzled.

It's just a story, Hishn. Gamon's always telling stories.

The wolf remained silent.

Shilia leaned back against the log watching the stars crawl around in the darkening sky. "Did he leave notes about it? Tell anyone how he did it?"

"Uh huh. But the papers were destroyed in a fire. Another message from the moons."

Rhom snorted. "If you believe that, you probably think that our shipwreck was a message, too."

Gamon grinned. "No, but the ancients did call the Cliffs of Bastendore the step to the Yew Mountains. And that's what we've used them for, so it must be some kind of sign."

"I've heard that story too," Shilia put in. "They said that the moons would bathe in the sea, then wash their feet at the base of the cliffs before they climbed the Yew Mountains and stepped back into the heavens."

"It's supposed to be where the ancients first landed," the old man said. "In fact, many legends center around this wilderness. That's about the only thing Caflanin is rich in—legends."

"What legends, Uncle?" the younger girl teased. "More tall tales of yours picked up from the taverns?"

"Would I tell a tale that wasn't true?" he said in injured innocence, though his eyes twinkled.

"More likely you wouldn't tell a tale that wasn't tall," Aranur put in from where he was lounging at the edge of the clearing.

The old man laughed. "I know just about every story that's come out of these hills, and I'd have to agree that there's no one to say whether the myths are true or not. Unless it's the wolves."

Hishn's eyes gleamed at him, and she cocked her ears.

"I wonder what the old ones saw in the stars," Shilia mused. "Different worlds, different peoples."

"Different peoples, surely. Just as they found when they came to this world." The old man leaned forward into the fire so that the shadows threw evil-looking lights on his grimy face. "Remember the Aiueven. Why would the ancients have brought those far-reaching claws and tooth-lined beaks to Asengar with them? No, the birdmen must have startled the old ones—maybe stolen some souls before they were discovered and forced to retreat to the northern lands."

"Oh, Gamon," she said with a laugh, "that's a child's tale. You frighten the village boys and girls with it every year at winterfest."

He made a gesture with his hands. "Ask yourself this, young

lady: Who sent the fever that swept the wolfwalkers into death? What happened to the secrets of internal healing? And why do the wolves die out even now? Listen to the wind, and when you hear the hunting cry of Aiueven, who still want revenge on the ancients for the loss of their homelands, you'll know." He turned his head from side to side so that the orange shadows from the fire seemed to crawl across his face.

Gray Hishn's eyes gleamed yellow in the firelight. Dion was silent, listening to the words that echoed in her head long after the old man had stopped talking. In the dark, the night creatures rustled while the others slept, and the muted thunder of the reefs called out the song of the southern sea.

XII

Ember Dione maMarin:

Into the Cold

Blue wings brought peace, then death;
Wolves run now where dawn was once a science;
When the nine moons spin silver lines on the mountains,
Howl with the wind, Wolfwalker.

It was chilly when they woke, though the day promised to get warm. The storm front seemed to have passed in the night, leaving a heavy gray bank across the sky. Dion squinted at the clouds, then back at the group, where Namina and the others were packing their rucksacks.

I can smell her despair, the Gray One told the healer, sending the strange image of Namina's shrunken inner form. *She does not believe she will see her home again.*

The wolfwalker looked at the gray beast for a long moment. The wolf was just over two years old—had not even had the chance to false-mate yet, let alone true-mate and raise a litter— but her thoughts were already mature with the wisdom of a grown wolf. That she spoke of death now was sobering, especially after the nightmares Dion had had that night of climbing an endless cliff. In her dreams each time she had climbed the towering wall, as she reached the top, Mannoa's skull had split out of the rocks and turned into a worlag's beetle jaws that threw her back down the cliff to fall those endless kilometers to certain death. Each time she was sure she would hit the rocks and die, the waves had rushed in with the captain's teeth as their crest and the rastin as a huge purple tongue. And flung back onto the cliff, she was forced to climb and climb again.

A thought struck her suddenly, and she wondered what would have happened if she had died in her dream. She frowned at the wolf. *If I died,* she said softly, *where would you go, Hishn?*

The moons do not call us yet, the Gray One said, troubled at the way the healer had picked up the thought. The wolf's eyes yellowed, and she sent the woman the smells and sights of the forest through her nose and eyes, an assault of images that dropped Dion into her more primeval world. *I would run with my brothers and sisters in the woods,* she answered finally. *Perhaps I would run with your man,* she sent, adding an image of Aranur watching Dion walk into the clearing, at which the healer blushed, *but I would not give up as she has.* And with the Gray One's words, the twisted and stooped image of Namina lingered in her mind over the stronger image of Aranur. The wolf saw the young girl not as a simple visual image but as a total image with her heart and mind. She did not usually send the whole image of people, only when she was troubled or concerned, looking deeper than she could through her nose and eyes.

"Oh, Hishn," Dion said softly, burying her face in the Gray One's fur. "What would I do without you?"

The wolf cocked her head and licked her chops. *Probably find a baby lizard to carry around with you when I'm gone,* she said, mocking the wolfwalker's sudden attack of sentimentality.

Dion laughed. "All right, you mangy thing, you've made your point. Go find a trail for us to take through the mountains."

The Gray One trotted past Gamon, who was pouring cold water over the hissing remnants of the breakfast fire, and howled deeply just as she got behind him. The older man started and spilled the water everywhere, mostly on himself, and Dion caught the echo of lupine laughter in her head as the wolf took off, dodging the weapons master's too-accurate aim.

"You worm-bitten dog!" he roared after her. "Wait till I get my hands on you! You'll be sorry then, you howling gray tamrin!"

Tyrel, who had been waving branches to scatter the thick smoke that rose from the streaming fire, doubled over laughing till Gamon threw the last of the water on him.

It's a good thing you're fast, Dion sent after Hishn's fading mind. Her only answer was the wolf's image of a smile. She hefted her pack off the ground and groaned. She had just gotten over the bruises and sore muscles of the worlag attack fourteen days before, and now her whole body felt beaten again, sore from the fight with the soldiers and torn down from the climb up the cliff. Even two days rest had not rid her of the stiffness that plagued her like a fever. She should have trained for days before trying to climb a rock face like that, she told herself, stretching her arms with a wince.

Noticing his twin trying to ease on her pack, Rhom stepped over and helped settle it on her sore shoulders. "A cliff-hanger's got nothing on you but wings, Dion," he teased, lifting his own pack easily with a wink. "Bet I can outrun you today, old lady."

"I couldn't outrun a two-legged dnu, the way I feel." She tightened the stomach straps of the pack and gave him a sly look right back. "You want someone to pace you, go run with Shilia. I'm sure the two of you will find something to talk about."

He made a face. "Just as long as you don't run with our long-eyed leader."

"And what's that supposed to mean, brother of mine?" She could feel herself blush. Did Rhom know that she and Aranur had kissed on top of the cliff?

"I'd say, judging by past experience, that he's got his eyes on you. Not that I blame him," he said, noting his twin's telltale pink cheeks, "but this isn't the time to get yourself Promised."

"Promised!" she exploded. "Who's getting Promised? I've spent more time tending Tyrel or talking with Gamon than I have with Aranur—"

"And don't think he hasn't noticed, either," her brother teased. "You just can't keep the men away, can you, twin? Lucky we got you out of Sidisport. You'd have had all the harems in the city after you."

"You better watch your own warcap or you'll be changing it for a flower band before the sixth moon sets," she warned.

He laughed. "Shilia's nice, don't you think?"

"Very," she answered shortly.

"She's an excellent weaver, you know. Make someone a good mate."

"You're just digging for information," she accused, then gave up with a smile. "She's not Promised," she admitted, "but she's got four boyfriends back in Ramaj Ariye."

"No competition." He grinned, dismissing them with a wave.

"They're back in the hills a thousand kilometers away, while I've got her here in the woods with me for at least another couple of ninans." He flashed another grin and became serious. "Dion, about yesterday, how are you? You shouldn't have had to take a climb like that in your shape. Is your leg all right?"

She glanced down at the leg that had taken such a beating from the worlags and shook her head. "I'm okay. Like all wolfwalkers, I heal quickly."

Rhom frowned. "I've never been able to figure that out, Dion."

"Neither have I." She shrugged. "It's probably just some weird carryover of her strength to mine. In any case, I'm still more sore than if I ran the Intessin River Rapids on my behind," she said with a rueful smile. "Which reminds me, your own stitches will have to come out in a few days."

He nodded, but he tensed as he remembered how he had gotten the arrow wound, and the momentary flash of Ainna's lifeless body sobered the healer suddenly. She almost glared at her bruised hands as if they should somehow have given the girl's life back even as the moons took it away. But it's too late for miracles now, she reminded herself harshly. Even if she knew the secrets of Ovousibas, she could never bring Ainna back.

"We've blown enough wind," she said abruptly to her brother, though she managed a smile to take the sting from her words, "and I'm tired of talking to someone I've seen all my life. Let's go." They jogged up to join the rest of the party already starting off through the forest, Hishn leading. After only a few meters Rhom winked and dropped back to pace Shilia.

Cool scents of creatures in the dirt; deer footfalls moving quietly away in wind-rustled leaves—Hishn's images were like soft noise against Dion's thoughts. Twigs caught in the glossy hair that fell loosely from under her warcap as she ducked under the spindly branches. The branches reached for each other over the game trail and made a brushy arch that dipped and turned beneath the taller trees so that she felt as if she were jogging down a path in a garden of the moons. Then a blue lizard crossed the path and stuck its tongue out, mocking her fancies, and she smiled to herself. It was a hopeful morning, and they moved quietly through the forest and into the foothills of the mountains, where they camped below the snow line that night.

The crisp air that met them the next day belied the look of snow that hung in the heavy clouds. "Well?" Aranur asked his uncle, who was rubbing his shin. "What does the weather-wise leg say about tonight's sky?"

The old man pretended to feel his shin seriously, then frowned and turned to the sky. "Temperatures in the twenties going to the low teens tonight; pressure dropping before the front that's moving south-southeast at about fifty kilometers an hour. I'd say rain below the timberline, and snow above 1,500 meters tonight sure as the lepa fly."

Tyrel snorted. "You old faker! That's what you said last time, too."

"Ah, but I was right, wasn't I?" The old man grinned, scratched a piece of moss from his silvered hair, and stood up. "If the moons are with us, we should make it through that pass before snowfall tonight, or at least get through to the timberline on the other side."

By the time the snow was deep enough to ski on, their feet were getting moist even through the waterproofed boots most of them wore. Their own sweat dampened them further. Tyrel did not complain, but Dion knew his legs were hurting him; he was glad to get on the rough skis and trade trudging for the smooth gliding motion of cross-country skiing.

The snow smothered the world around them, their breath frosty clouds that split around their faces and hung behind them in the air. Hishn bounded beside them, her wide footpads breaking through the crusty snow as she loped and sinking her chest deep in the spring-softened drifts. In the distance they could see pockmarks in the snow, tracks of other creatures, the mounds where smaller trees became hugged by drifts of snow till they were round, not conical. Aranur directed the group toward one of the closer pockmarks even though Hishn snarled and pulled back.

"What's with her?" Shilia asked in the cold quiet.

Rhom glanced over. "Danger. An old one, perhaps, but danger all the same. Watch her hackles. When her ears come up and her hackles rise, there's something close by."

"Glacier worms," Aranur said from where he was studying the crumbled snow. The worm had attacked a hibernating creature, and the tall man pointed to a frosty two-meter hole where the worm had thrown up the powder as it dived back into the drift. Careful not to get too near the edge, he leaned over the underground passage. "We won't stop till we get near the next snow line. It's still deep enough for the glacier worms to be active. Sound doesn't usually attract them, unless they've already scented warmth, but warmth attracts them like treesuckers to sap. If one found us, we wouldn't know what hit us till we gathered again in its belly." He looked at his younger cousin. "Tyrel, I know your legs are hurting you but . . ."

"I'm all right, Aranur," the boy said bravely. "You set the pace, and I'll keep up."

They skimmed on, slicing through the thin white crust that held the mountains through the summer. They had to stop only once where a wide stream had cut through the snow and made a deep draw. Aranur, who was breaking trail, studied it carefully for a few minutes while the others came to rest on the banks, then went down to make sure it was frozen solid enough to hold the rest of the group. The mountain chill was already starting to strike through their damp clothes as their warm sweat grew cold while they waited on the banks. Below them the lean man came to rest on the snowy surface in a spray of white powder and stamped a few times to make sure the water was solid, then went on, tracking up the opposite bank like a huge bird till he reached level ground again. One by one the others followed, cutting the bank further into a switchback with each pass. Shilia passed the previous night's leftovers down the line for lunch, and they munched as they skied.

The afternoon shadows began to thicken as the sun moved behind the mountain, and the snow rumbled ominously now and again as the glacier worms hunted. Hibernating creatures were the mainstay of the worms, but in summer they had to make do with the creatures they caught in their snow dens. In spring, when snowy sleeps were broken by melting snows and warmer temperatures, the worms retreated to the higher altitudes and entered their hungry larval phase, when they roamed the packs incessantly.

Once the group turned aside and dodged around a hillock when two glacier worms attacked a snowbear feeding on a winter hare. Another time they were harassed by a swarm of snow stingers until Aranur lit some oily rags and drove off the persistent insects with smoke. Snow stingers lived off what the glacier worms processed, and their bites were venomous, irritating skin and muscles into swollen hives that bubbled with fluid. Swatting at a last persistent bug, Dion wondered if the venom of the snow stingers was similar to that of the sea creatures. If it was, maybe she could make an antidote for Tyrel's rastin bites out of stinger poison . . .

They barely reached the snow line before dusk required them to make camp. Aranur insisted on spending the time to find a good site, and though Tyrel grumbled irritably, he was glad enough of it later when he rested his torn legs on soft needles instead of hard and icy rocks. But Dion was worried. She had not been able to keep the swelling down in his wounds. She had already tried two different poultices, but neither one had worked, and she just did not have the facilities to experiment or the herbs to keep treating him as she had been doing. And if the poison changed composition or crossed the blood-brain barrier and brought the fever into the boy's brain, there would be nothing she could do besides take him back above the snow line, pack him in ice, and hope the swelling that would squeeze his brain did not kill him. Hishn, sitting beside her and looking distastefully on the wound, whined low in her throat. Every time Dion treated Tyrel, the Gray One's instinctive and unexplained unease rubbed off on her until she was as irritated as the wolf. If Hishn would just tell her what was wrong, she could try to do something about it, but the Gray One did not seem able to put her subtle fear into images the wolfwalker could understand.

"Why the frown?" Aranur asked, dropping to sit beside her after she had finished treating the boy's legs.

Dion sighed, looking across the fire at the space where the youth was restlessly sleeping. "Whatever the poison in the rastin bites, it's gone into his veins—like a mild blood poison—and is keeping the bites from healing. Unless his metabolism adjusts to it, there's not much more I can do." She made a face. "The stuff tastes vile enough that I'm surprised I haven't gotten sick from sucking it out of his wounds."

"How much is it affecting him? He's keeping up, but we have a long way to go, and there are more mountains on the other side of that valley."

"Frankly, I don't know. It's sapping him—you can tell by the way he reacts to all of us—and forcing his body to use up its reserves dealing with the toxin instead of letting him spend his energy sleeping or walking or eating.'' She gritted her teeth in frustration. ''I need herbs, chemicals that I don't have.''

''Could you find them if we slowed down?''

''Some. Three of the herbs I need grow in the snow climes, and four grow in temperate areas. If luck rode my back like a demon, I'd be able to locate half of the herbs in that valley.''

''Do what you can.'' He frowned. ''Time is on our side right now, so we can spend as long as you need in the lower altitudes. If you don't find what you need,'' he promised with a smile that did not quite touch his eyes, ''I'll carry Tyrel back to Ariye myself.''

Dion did not put into words the grim thought that if the boy did not get better soon, none of them would have to worry about him because the moons would take him for their own.

After the snowy cold of the mountains, the valley was a pleasant change. The muggy air was heavy with coastal rainfall trapped between the ranges, but with the mild heat of early summer, the land was green, steep, and beautiful. Dion's first glimpse of the valley brought a gasp from her lips, and Aranur, who had taken her to the overhanging cliff, watched in pleasure.

''It's beautiful,'' she breathed.

He nodded. ''Like a hidden paradise.''

''It must be dense in those canyons. And look at those valleys—it'll take a long time to cut through all that just to get to the other side.''

''We've time.'' He gestured at the pristine expanse of deep green relieved only by threads of darker hues where streams edged their way through the valley and rock heights jutted up suddenly like lookouts. ''This is about as remote as you can get from Zentsis. The man never took his troops anywhere there wasn't gold to be had, so we won't have to worry about fighting anything here but the brush.''

She glanced at the tall, black-haired leader from the corner of her eyes. Standing there, one foot up on a rock and one hand unconsciously on the hilt of his sword, he made a rugged picture. His profile was strong—as strong as those clear gray eyes that seemed to see right through her and leave her blushing every time. His hard, muscular body was as worn as his thin boots, made lean by trail running and scarred by the blades of raiders, his mail stained with old blood and dirt, and his once-clean leggings the easy color of the earth. But as she stood next to him, she felt curiously comfortable—protected—as if she were standing by a massive wolf. He was taller than her brother and not as wide in the shoulders, but Dion knew that his quiet strength was more than a match for the bursts of furious violence her twin could erupt into. That, then, was the major difference, she realized. Where Rhom used anger to fuel his sword arm, Aranur used experience. He lunged, he blitzed, and he cut as quickly as a sand cat could strike, but even when furious, he never let the rage turn his blade too soon or move his arm too slowly out of a slaver's blow. Instead, he let the other men make the mistakes, and when the smoke cleared and the swords were cleaned and counted, his was one of the blades still ready to fight again.

"Which pass are we heading for?" she asked curiously, gazing across the valley with him.

He nodded toward a low saddle between two snow-strewn peaks. "One of those streams seems to run straight toward that low spot. Probably on a fault line. I figure we can cut a raft and take to the water—might save days of hacking our way through that jungle."

It would save Tyrel a great deal of pain, too, she knew. The boy had not voiced a word of complaint, but he moved more and more slowly; soon he would not be able to jog at all, something that Aranur had realized a day before. "How long will it take to build the raft?"

"A day. Maybe two. Depends on how hard the wood is and how rough the water."

"I'll run out of two of the herbs I need by tomorrow."

He stood down from the rock and turned to her. "I'll help you look for them. It'll give me a chance to scout the area." His gaze lingered on her figure for a moment, and she blushed.

"I can take Gray Hishn," she protested ineffectually. He merely looked at her, and she flushed more deeply. "So you could help with the raft," she added quickly. By the moons, she berated herself silently, what was wrong with her? She was acting like a girl who had never gone walking with a man before.

The wolf sneezed slyly. *Well, have you? And if not, isn't it time you did?*

Hishn! She was shocked. But as Aranur helped her down from the cliff's edge and led them back to the main trail, their hands brushed and a shiver ran up her spine. A lupine chuckle filtered through her thoughts, and Dion glared into the brush. *Go find your own escort,* she sent, *and we'll see who has the last laugh.*

The wolf, sending only a last burst of mockery, faded away, leaving Dion with the impression that Hishn's potential mates far outnumbered Dion's tall escort. But the Gray One was happy. In spite of the worry she was picking up from her healer, the wolf was finally out of the cities and back where the ground was cool and soft under her feet and the brush was full of game. And everywhere there were tracks of other wolves. She had already met the three unmated males of the pack that ran in those foothills; the soft gray thoughts of the creatures echoed like the sound of a distant rain in Dion's head. It had taken the wolfwalker a full day to realize that the dream images distracting her from her work and filling the tedious hours of travel were from Gray Ones that ran as strangers to herself. But even though they were strangers, she sensed them like lonely voices. Pacing silently, hidden in the growth of the forest, the wolves padded after the small group of humans and wondered at their presence.

They're curious, Hishn told her that evening. The two were sitting in a clearing eating what was left of the smoked rabbit Namina had prepared the day before. The wolf shared Dion's meal politely but took little, since she had already eaten and was not hungry. No one else was awake in the near dark. It was Dion's turn to take first watch, and the already sleeping bodies of the other humans were curled into comfortable positions against their packs or one another.

The woman picked up a rotting stick and examined the odd moss that curled around its end. *Curious about what?*

They haven't seen men in a long time. They feel your thoughts as I do. Hishn's ears perked up, and she looked to her left. *It is Gray Sholishen—calling me to play,* she said eagerly. She nudged the woman quickly before taking off into the woods, giving her a toothy grin as Dion caught the echo of a male wolf's interested thoughts.

Well, Dion thought philosophically, Hishn was not a yearling anymore, and it was time she went into the false heat of adolescence. Happy for her, too, that her hormones were taking hold in that playground of wolves. She was a good-looking wolf, bigger than most because of Dion's care—she would have as many mates as she wanted easily enough, and they would overlook her capricious ways, whereas the wolfwalker had to live with them. She sighed, tossed the stick away into the brush, and looked up to see another Gray One across the clearing. Its yellow eyes reached her own, and she felt a different, deeper, older voice in her head.

Wolfwalker, he said with respect.

She was startled. *You honor me,* she sent quickly, her awe making her hesitate but a moment. But the wolf had already melted back into the trees. Dion stared at the spot where the Gray One had vanished, but he did not reappear. Only a tendril of thought, gray as the creature who had sent it, floated through her mind.

"Dion?" It was Rhom, leaning up on one elbow and looking at her with a frown.

She shook her head, hoping unreasonably that he had not seen the wolf. Had the Gray One sensed him waking? Rhom was her twin, but this was somehow private, and she guarded the Gray One's honor with an instinctive jealousy that startled her.

As they pushed into the valley the next day, the terrain became thicker with growth and damper with the scent of a marsh. The rock formations that split the soft ground so abruptly showed evidence of high water, while others looked as if they were sinking. Twice they crossed obvious fault lines, the first time dropping down over a vegetated ridge that broke cleanly in two and began again twenty meters away.

"It'll get worse before it gets better," Gamon said to Dion as he took her pack while she climbed smoothly over a nest of boulders. He tossed it up to her, and she then caught his to do the same for him.

"Still, it's a lot easier to stay with the rocks than to try hacking our way through all that," she returned. She caught her breath as she gestured into the swampy forest. "Hishn says the whole thing's a marsh."

"She's been talking with the other wolves?"

"That, and—" Dion hesitated. "She remembers."

The older man looked askance. "That mutt's not been out of Randonnen before this, has she?"

She shook her head and stepped over a rotting log that lay against the rock. "No, but the Gray Ones' memories stretch far beyond a single life. Sometimes I think they remember everything that's happened to them since the ancients."

"I'd think they'd remember only their own bloodlines."

"I don't know," she said slowly. "I asked Hishn what she remembered about this place, and she said 'men.' Not one or two men but many—hundreds, going back and forth on white roads that cross the valley."

"Well, there's no roads now. And the only evidence of the ancients themselves are the ruins of some of their buildings."

"I wish we could explore," she said wistfully. "Hishn said there were a couple of broken buildings to the east, but she was taking about a two-day journey, not an hour's diversion."

"Her memories are that clear?"

"Uh uh." The black-haired woman ducked under a spiny branch and shook her head. "It took a good half hour to figure out the distance she was talking about. The memory of the ruins must be five hundred years old. It was as fuzzy as a dust ball under a dark bed." She pushed on, catching only a glimpse of Shilia in front of her but following the ragged trail easily enough. Their tracks sank deeply in the treacherous earth, and Dion's boots were already muddy up to her knees. "Strange," she said with puzzlement, "but when I asked her about it, I got the feeling that there were other, larger places around here that weren't broken down at all. At first I thought she was talking about the domes in Randonnen, but the scenery was like this"— she gestured around her—"only a little different. Drier. More like a forest than a swamp. Think of it, Gamon, whole buildings of the old ones we could look in."

The old man ducked under the same branch and calmly shook off a crawler that had dropped on his hand. "Don't know as I'd say that's strange, Dion. There's at least five places of the ancients in Ariye. It wouldn't surprise me if there were some around here, too. After all, some of the ancients were supposed to have dropped from the moons to the Yew Mountains."

Something about the idea made her shiver, and Dion glanced quickly over her shoulder, sure that she would see a ghost but meeting only the dense, waving branches of the low-slung trees. I'll ask them, she promised herself. I'll ask the wolves what they saw back then.

On the second day they reached one of the streams that Aranur had judged to be large enough and straight enough to cross the valley on in a raft. They used the smudges constantly now, for the stingers in the valley had a vicious bite, and they were all sporting at least two or three swollen spots where the insects' venom had caused them grief. Finally, as they found a tiny inlet where the spring rains had flooded the bank and left a rocky beach, Aranur called them to a halt.

"Rhom, you and I will look for logs we can use for a raft. Shilia," he directed as she dragged herself into the muddy clearing where he stood, "go with Gamon. The rope we have isn't enough to lash everything together; we'll need another hundred meters of braided vines." He looked around, scanning the bank for tracks and nodding with satisfaction that there were few to catch his attention. As directed, his uncle, after dropping his own pack, set off with Shilia. In the meantime, Tyrel and Namina straggled into the area, and Aranur looked them over sharply. The boy was exhausted, and Namina was depressed enough that the trek was nearly as difficult for her as for her brother.

"Tyrel, set camp up straight back from here. We'll want to be close to the raft but far enough from the water so that other creatures can drink. Namina, he'll need your help." He looked around again. "Where's Dion?"

"She said she'd be back in a bit," Rhom said, unconcerned. "She took off with Hishn. Saw some herbs she wanted."

Aranur frowned. "Why didn't you tell me?"

"Didn't see the need." The younger man unstrapped his pack and swung it to the ground on a relatively dry spot. "She can't get lost, and she's not in danger. I'd know." He shot the other man a faintly challenging look. "You'd know, too."

Aranur scowled. He wondered how Rhom knew he could sense the Gray One that Dion ran with. It was nothing concrete—Hishn did not speak to him, and the images he picked up were not clear, but the soft gray voice that whispered in his mind was like a soothing thought that pierced his irritation and reminded him of it. Abruptly he cleared his head. "We'll find her first, then look for raft logs," he said shortly.

"Aranur, she doesn't need—"

"I don't want us split up without knowing where everyone is. If something happened, how would we find her, or she us?"

The younger man shrugged, accepting his reasoning, but Aranur had the feeling that the burly smith thought it an excuse. Moonworms, he thought irritably, it was not Rhom's business, anyway. He gestured back along the muddy path. "Come on."

They trudged back a full kilometer before finding the place where Dion had left the path. She had left only a faint trail in spite of the muddy ground, and Aranur was surprised. She had stepped lightly, careful to place her feet where they would leave the least noticeable marks on the ground, something he expected from a woodsman, not a healer.

"She is a woodsman," Rhom said with a grin. "What she didn't learn from Father or me, she learned from Hishn in the last couple years. Started spending ninans in the forest by herself— well, her and Hishn. We used to track each other for practice."

Aranur nodded. He found where she had slipped between two thick chello shrubs. "This way."

"Aranur, I still think she has a right to be alone—"

"Shh—there's something up ahead."

It was only a brown hare. The creature darted off the dim trail as they moved by, staring at them from the uncertain safety of the brush. They followed the faint marks of Dion's passage until Aranur paused, stepped around a thick shrub, and abruptly found himself in a clearing. The three figures in the sheltered meadow started and whirled—the two massive wolves baring their teeth and Dion whipping around with her hand on her hilt, the sword sliding into her fist as easily as if it were the needle she had been holding an instant before.

Aranur and Rhom stared. That another Gray One would come to her—that she could treat the wounds of another wolf . . . The tall man took a step forward.

Dion made a choking sound, then found her voice. "Go!" she snarled, putting herself between the men and the strange wolf whose hackles had risen into a stiff brush of wiry hair. "Leave. Now!"

Her twin grabbed Aranur's arm and yanked him back. Aranur staggered, caught himself, and shook Rhom's hand off, then realized that Dion was crouched to lunge. Her lips were curled back like those of the wolves, and her eyes were strange in the dim light. Violet? Or did a hint of yellow touch their depths?

The next thing he knew, Rhom had jerked him back behind the bole of a tree and spun him around. "Get back," the smith hissed savagely, dragging the other man with him. "We've got to get out of here. Now." Aranur glanced back once, but at the naked fear and strain on Rhom's face, he changed his mind and melted swiftly into the brush with Dion's brother.

"What was going on?" he demanded of Rhom as soon as they were far enough to be out of earshot even of the Gray Ones. "What was she doing back there?"

Rhom shrugged. "I don't know, but you don't argue with her when she looks like that." He shivered. "No, don't go back there. You don't mess with the Gray Ones. You don't go to them unless they first come to you."

Aranur shook his head. He had never heard Dion use a voice like that. Almost as if she were speaking through the wolves themselves. "She drew her blade," he said, casting a look of disbelief back through the brush. "She was ready to fight."

"You don't know Dion very well, Aranur. And you sure as hell don't know the Gray Ones. Come on. We can wait back on the trail."

"She actually drew her sword."

"So she was feeling protective. She's a wolfwalker. She has a special relationship with the wolves. Forget about it. Let's get back."

"You don't understand." The tall man still looked amazed. "She was ready to fight me. *Me*. I'm a gods-damned weapons master—" He cut himself off, seeing the speculative look on Rhom's face. "We'll wait for her here," he decided suddenly. "She'll be by soon."

Rhom pushed on through the brush. "Don't be a fool, Aranur. She'll come when she's ready, and I'd as soon be as far from here as possible by then." He glanced back through the growth and tensed as he heard a faint crackling, then flushed at the other man's expression. "Aranur, you've never seen a mad wolf. I have. I'd rather face two worlags than a Gray One with eyes like that. And Dion—well, I'd rather face two Gray Ones than my sister. She's got her own temper that can kill a lepa before it leaps."

The gray-eyed man's face was silent. "Is she in danger?"

"Not unless we do something stupid."

"All right." Aranur gestured for Rhom to lead back to the trail, though he glanced back twice to see if he could catch a glimpse of the Gray One Dion had been treating. A healer who worked with the wolves—who would believe it, anyway?

They had gone only half a kilometer when Aranur heard the sound of something behind him. He signaled Rhom, who silently got his own sword out, and they waited. But what burst through the brush was not a beast but a woman. And Dion was still furious.

"How dare you," she snapped, confronting the men with her violet eyes blazing. "Who told you to follow? Rhom, I told you where we went—did you think it necessary to risk everything to interrupt like that?" Her chest heaved with her anger and the strain of running through the forest, and Aranur had to admire her shapely fury in spite of himself.

"I'm sorry if we interrupted something important, Healer. But I did not and still do not understand what is being risked here except your life. I told you I didn't want you wandering off alone—"

"The Gray Ones are not a threat until threatened, Aranur," she retorted hotly. "And you threatened them. Didn't you listen?" she demanded. "Didn't you sense them?"

He frowned. "I sensed nothing I could tell was you."

She glared. "Hishn says you can hear her better than Rhom."

"Sometimes," he admitted with a slight smile. He really did not see what she was so upset about, but she was beautiful when her eyes flashed like that, and he enjoyed the way her breasts filled the leather jerkin she wore so well.

Angrily she clenched her fists, two red spots remaining in her pale cheeks. "Men," she muttered, pushing past the two of them and stalking down the path.

Aranur looked after her. "Women," he said sourly under his breath.

"I think she likes you."

"Shut up."

In the next six hours they dragged four logs back to the rocky beach and set to breaking them up. They had only one hatchet, so Tyrel took it and gathered wood for a fire. When he had it built and blazing comfortingly, they lay the logs across the pit so that the flames would burn through them and save the travelers the chopping necessary to cut them down to size. In the meantime, Shilia and Namina braided the vines they had gathered into ropes. As they worked, Tyrel twice stoically endured having his wounds lanced by the healer. She cleared the purple-black flecks of toxin from the angry yellow and red holes, but by evening the boy had lapsed into a semistuporous state anyway, talking quietly only when necessary and forgoing the cruel teasing he was wont to do.

The thought of being mortal must have hit him hard after Ainna had died, Dion realized. It was if he had grown up in the last four days. Being the son of the Lloroi of Ramaj Ariye could not be an easy position, but in the trials they had been through, Tyrel had finally started to take his responsibilities seriously. She had been doubtful at first of him learning to be the kind of leader a Lloroi must be, but now, seeing him find strength in his pain, she prayed that the moons would give the boy time to show his father how he had grown.

Thinking of the boy kept her mind off the valley. She appreciated the calm, the peacefulness, but there was something about it that was setting her on edge. The previous night her dreams had focused onto the image of a white building that squatted just around each ridge of the mountains on the horizon. Ice dripped from its clear windows—the windows that looked out over the valley as they walked. Packs of wolves ran wild in the woods, singing at the moons and circling the dome, while ghosts looked out the windows and walked in silent halls.

When they camped that night and settled down to sleep, the images were stronger again, the dreams more intense; she woke in a sweat with Aranur shaking her and the wolf together. "Dion," he whispered urgently. "Wake up. Snap out of it."

She gasped, clinging to him as the dream faded from reality to a dim pull in her mind. The Gray One simply opened her eyes and stopped grunting, kicking her legs as if running and pulling her lips back to attack in her sleep. But Dion shook her head. Hishn lost the images as soon as Aranur spoke, but Dion could not clear them away. Something was calling her, drawing her to it. She shivered.

"It was just a dream, Dion," he repeated, pulling her blanket up around her shoulders and holding her gently in his strong arms. "Go back to sleep now."

It had been a dream. Nothing more. Looking around the dark camp and seeing nothing but sleeping bodies and worn packs, Dion flushed and pulled away from him. It was bad enough that he did not think much of her in the first place. Now she had gone and acted like a fool in front of him over a bunch of wolf eyes chasing her around in the dark. She pushed the blanket away and Hishn, disturbed, got up and trotted off to sniff the night. They had both been having too many dreams lately, Dion thought. Ever since they had landed on the coast she had been restless and wandering, searching for something she could not find or figure out. "I'd just as soon be up for a little while," she said shortly, looking into the shadows. Was that a pair of yellow eyes still staring at her? She pretended to rub the sleep sand from her eyes, and the image disappeared. "It's my turn for watch now, isn't it?"

"Rhom's, actually," Aranur said quietly.

"Well, I'm up, so I might as well take it," she said, rolling out of her blanket. "He can take the one after me."

Hishn? she called when Aranur lay back down and dropped quickly off to sleep. The only answer she got from the wolf was quickly growing faint, a dim excitement communicated through the night that spoke of a potential mating, something that Dion would rather tune out than listen in on. She glanced at Aranur's lean body, resting easily on the soft earth. With the darkness pressing in and only the coals of fire glowing like a bank of red eyes, she wished she dared curl up next to him and let his strength feed her failing spirits. What was it about this valley, anyway? A body would think she was seeing ghosts.

She stopped suddenly. Ghosts. Not the Gray Ones—those she could sense around her even then—but ghosts. The images that Hishn planted in her mind took shape as she concentrated.

Wolfwalker, a Gray One said softly.

She hesitated. *You honor me,* she returned. The old female was invisible in the night shadows, but Dion saw her image anyway. *Gray One,* she sent finally. *Who are the ghosts you send to my dreams?*

The yellow eyes glowed. Scents of men and women filled her head suddenly, and she reeled. The power in the old wolf was twice what Hishn could send. *Feet splashed through puddles; faces floated, dipped, and smiled . . . Hurry . . . A Gray One romped with a young man, falling off the road into the thick brush . . . The smell of fresh crushed grass, ground dirt . . . A* thousand images fled through her mind, and the woman clutched the blanket she had shoved away a moment before.

Gray One, she said weakly as the flood tapered off, *I do not understand.*

The old wolf shrugged mentally.

Who are these people?

Again the answer was a crush of images that told Dion only that once there had been thousands where now there were none.

Then where did they go?

The old female paused and regarded the wolfwalker silently. A strain of despair touched her mind, and Dion shivered. It was not only the anguished cry of humans that reached and touched and slid inside her ears but the silent agony of the animals, shivering, burning, and dying in the flames of a fever they did not understand. Pups that died at birth and were discarded with the dead young of other beasts. Piles of rotting rabbits, then mounds of lepa chicks, fallen from their rookeries as their parents pushed them away from those still alive. Rocks overturned to display the husks of many-legged insects once active in the soil but now dead and hollow from a virus even they could not withstand.

"Gods," she whispered, beginning to understand what the old one was telling her. She stared unseeing at the wolf, horrified by the pictures that lay dimly in her mind like twisted nightmares that refused to fade, and she did not notice when the Gray One left and Hishn lay back down beside her.

Her eyes were dark and sleepless the next day. Rhom looked at her face, noticed the different tracks that sank into the mud where she had been sleeping, and frowned slightly but said nothing. Dion rubbed the tracks out carefully when no one was looking.

Over the next three hours they broke the burned logs into sections and lashed them together into a crude frame. Dozens of smaller logs made the deck, and then Rhom built a small splash guard around the edges so that their gear would not wash overboard. With the sky overcast and gray, there was not even a glimpse of the moons or a telltale shadow to indicate the passage of time, and Dion's shoulders were tense with the feeling that she was trapped in a timeless swamp that circled and circled with the stream, never leading to the mountains but only to a deadly hole in its center. So much did the tension show that finally Shilia stopped her and asked her what was wrong.

"You don't smile, you haven't said a word all day. Between you and Namina, I think I'm already walking with the dead."

Dion shivered. She looked away and broke a twig off a bush, twisting it in her fingers. "I've just been on edge lately." She shrugged. "Been having bad dreams."

"Sure it's not something you ate?" the other girl teased lightly.

Dion shook her head. She could feel it, though, closer and closer, like a test, like a threat. The danger of deep coils trying to snare her senses. There were voices in her mind, echoes of other wolves crowding her memories and doubling her vision, urging her on to some unknown despair. She felt them brush by her on the paths, felt their fur on her legs and smelled their breath. But there never was anything there. Just her own nervous eyes, flitting to and from the dark growth, and Hishn, growling with an irritation that fed Dion's unease.

"Dion, give me a hand, will you?" Rhom called from the bank of the stream.

She shook herself, nodded, and gathered an awkward armful of the poles he had cut to steer their raft down the river. He stowed them on the crude craft, then held out his hand for the packs. As he passed them on, he noted the tense set of her mouth but said nothing. If it was Tyrel or Namina who worried her so, he could do little he was not already doing, but if it was Aranur who had caused her this pain, he would take the man aside and speak with him that night. Jaw line grim, the blacksmith helped Shilia, then Namina on board, letting his sister leap lightly on by herself, proud of the graceful way she moved even when she was tired. Gray Hishn, snarling and whining, paced back and forth across the boulders that jutted into the inlet before taking a leap that set the whole raft shaking and sliding in the water.

"Moonworms, twin, can't you get her to settle down?" Rhom said sharply.

"Hishn!" Dion grabbed the massive beast by her scruff and shoved her down on her belly, holding her there until she calmed down enough for Tyrel and Gamon to board. She hoped the wolf would quit whining soon. Otherwise Aranur would probably throw her overboard and tell her to make the rest of the trek overland by herself.

"That everything?" Aranur glanced around their small camp. The fire was out, their gear stowed. He shook loose the rope that bound the small craft to the boulders and jumped to the raft from another one as it slowly spun by. "Gamon, Rhom, Dion, and I will steer," he directed, picking up a pole. "We cut extra wood to steer with, so if you get a pole jammed, let go. It's not worth risking sand suckers to save it."

They nodded. Even though the stream ran through the swamp, there was little current in the water, and poling the raft through the forest was more like meandering along the banks of a lake than like following a river. Dion watched the edges of the bayou flow by quietly, ignoring the harsh cries of the marsh birds that were startled into an uproar by their odd passage. But it gave her no peace to see the swamp in all its brilliant greens. Instead, rotting bones crowded her sight where there should have been only branches, and the image of the white dome sat like a tombstone on the hills in her mind.

XIII

Ember Dione maMarin:

Death Trek

In valleys of fear,
Do I walk with head high;
The weakness that threatens,
My courage belies.
And when it is courage
That fails me as well
It is hope and my faith
That save me from hell.

The second mountain range was wider than the first, but the foothills were easier to go through. With spare and leafy underbrush that did not catch on their clothes like the dense growth of the damp coastal range, they traveled more quickly, jogging through much of the day and dropping, drained, to the ground when they rested. On the first day, after only six tiring hours, Aranur decided to camp at the snow line even though they had half a day of light left. He guessed it would take six more days to cross the mountains even if they followed the pass that Hishn had shown them, and he wanted to give Tyrel a chance to rest before they went back into the cold.

"It's the weather that will be a problem now," he said to Rhom. "It hasn't rained in the valley yet, and that means it's still building up for a good one."

Rhom frowned and looked back at Tyrel. "Aranur, we can't wait forever. Dion hasn't got the medicines to treat Tyrel, and he's not getting better. He's weak now, but unless we get him to help soon . . ." His voice trailed off.

Aranur stood silently for a minute, staring at the heavy sky.

"We'll chance it," he decided heavily. "At least we still have the skis to travel on."

The pass cut through the mountains in a series of shallow valleys. In the other range they had had to ski because they would never have made it through the depth of snow; because of the wind along this pass, the snow was barely half a meter deep outside the drifts, and they skied more for speed than out of necessity. Hishn, bounding along beside them, continued to disappear along the ancient path, only to meet them ahead at another turn or twist, guiding their steps past billowy shapes and clumps of trees that staggered through the drifts with them. The first night in the range they camped under a stone outcropping where they had shelter on three sides. But even with the heat of a fire and the shelter from the incessant wind, Dion was worried about Tyrel. He was keeping up, but barely. She was afraid he was getting worse. She still had to lance and suck the poison from the bites four times a day, and even though the wounds were starting to close, the low-grade fever was taking an ever-heavier toll on the boy.

The second day saw them well into the mountains, and the cloud cover seemed to sit right on top of the trees. Gamon predicted snow. By noon, he was right. Fat snowflakes began to fall, turning the frozen forest into a softly hissing world. Small avalanches dumped snow from the ridges as the travelers warily stopped in a clear area for lunch.

"Dion, Tyrel's not feeling well," Shilia said in a low voice as she helped the healer repack after lunch. "His forehead seems hot, and his eyes are pretty bright."

Getting to her feet, Namina added, "He slept badly last night and kept trying to scratch the bites and grab at them. I tried to keep him from doing it, but he tore at least one of the bandages off."

Dion was concerned. "Tyrel," she called. "I'd like to look at your legs one more time before we go on."

When he turned toward her, his face flushed and his eyes glassy, Dion saw immediately what Namina meant. The weather had brought his fever up to a dangerous level, and she glanced at the sky with foreboding. The clouds had not lightened one gram, and the pressure was still dropping. In spite of the harmless appearance of the flakes that smoothed their tracks behind them, a summer snowstorm in those mountains might keep them holed up for days, and the way the boy looked right then, he might not last if the fever did not break and give him some relief. And where was Hishn? The Gray One could look inside the boy and tell her how strong he really was—how much farther he could make it—but the creature had disappeared that morning after making some comment about the hunting being good for snowtee that season. Dion suspected that the wolf was just avoiding having to deal with Tyrel. Each time Dion sucked the toxin from his wounds, the Gray One got so uptight that she was starting to avoid the healer, as well. But it was as much memory that disturbed the gray beast as it was the reality of the present. At least, that was what Dion guessed from the images the wolves had sent the last three nights in the valley. But what Hishn and the others had shown her was visions of diseases that came and went with the seasons to creatures of the woods—they could not be related to the fever that gripped the boy, and the healer was more and more frustrated at the reluctance of the wolf to help.

"Aranur, could you come over here for a minute?" she asked as she checked the boy again.

"Is that lazy cousin of mine causing trouble again?" he asked with a teasing smile. The smile died as he looked at their faces: Dion's so serious and Tyrel's heavily flushed. "What is it? Is he worse?"

"He's soaked. The fever is high now, and he's sweating." She took the last of the hot water and made a quick tea for the youth before the fire died in the falling snow. "He needs warmth, meat broth, medicines that I don't have, and rest. Every hour we travel we risk his getting worse. If the dehydration doesn't bring him down, the exhaustion from fighting off the fever in this cold, wet atmosphere will."

"Warmth and rest—we can have both of those if we stop here and build a shelter," Aranur said slowly. "But we risk being snowed in deeply by the storm. As for meat broth, we can soak some of the jerky. But medicines? Not a chance. Maybe, if the moons bless us with luck, we might scare up a winter hare, but don't count on it." He thought for a moment. "If he can last one more day, we'll be out of the worst of this range."

Dion hesitated. "He might make it. He's not very coherent right now, but he's on his feet and will be until he collapses."

"And you don't know when that will be?"

She shook her head soberly.

"The problem is this, Dion. We could build a snow cave here, but look at those ridges." He pointed to the snow-hung cliffs above them. "With more snow, they may collapse and bury the whole valley. And we haven't got food to last out the storm in this cold."

Tyrel looked at his older cousin, his eyes brightly glazed and his words slightly slurred. "It's okay, Aranur. I can follow you. You always get me out of trouble. I'll be fine."

Aranur smiled, but there were worry lines around his gray eyes. "Sure you will be, but you're going to have to work for your fire tonight. Think you can make it out of the valley? There may be caves or fissures we could use for shelter on the ridge."

"You just set the pace, Cousin." The boy frowned. "Dion, my ears are ringing."

"It's all right. That's the fever," she soothed. "You're not going to hear very well for a while, and your eyes may hurt from the light, but it'll be over soon."

Aranur decided to try for the next valley and hope that the ridges were not so precariously hung over. With the summer melting, all the snowpacks were dangerous. They had already seen signs of avalanches in other parts of the pass, but this valley made them all whisper and ski as silently as possible. Tyrel skied between the twins, where Dion could keep an eye on him and Rhom could lend him a hand where he needed it.

But they had gone hardly three kilometers when the boy pulled up. "Dion," he said fearfully, reaching up to his head and shaking it as if that would clear the fog from his brain. "My ears are going numb."

"Shh," she said, motioning him to keep his voice down. "They're not numb—it's going to be hard for you to hear for a while. It's the fever."

"But I can't hear anymore," he protested, his fever-shrill voice ringing against the white walls of the valley. A clump of snow fell with a *thwump!* from a tree branch.

"Shh." Rhom moved up close and put his hand over Tyrel's mouth.

Aranur and Gamon, who was leading, stopped and waited for the three. But Tyrel was too feverish. Scared, he twisted out of Rhom's grasp and called loudly at the healer. "I can't hear, Dion? Aranur?"

Rhom tried to sidestep over the boy's ski tracks and grab him to quiet him again, but Tyrel slid forward and fell in the snow. "I can't hear anyone—I can't hear!" His voice was rising into a scream, and Aranur looked up at the hanging snowpacks. Was one of them cracking?

Namina tried to help Rhom get Tyrel up without scaring him further, but in his fevered state he was convinced he was deaf. He struggled wildly. Aranur finally got him firmly and held him as the boy cried, smothered against his cousin's shoulder. "I can't hear you, Aranur. I can't hear you. Namina? Gamon? I'm deaf."

Some sudden, dangerous stillness in the air froze them all in that tableau for a long, dooming moment.

"The snowpack," Shilia whispered, her frightened face turned up. "Oh, moons of mercy, it's going to go."

"Move!" Aranur's whisper cracked like a whip on their backs. "Go! Follow Gamon! I've got Tyrel."

Gamon sliced ahead, leading Namina, Shilia, and Dion. Aranur and Rhom were on either side of Tyrel, urging him on. The air began a low rumble, and the crack on the snowpack widened. They cut around a few lone trees that poked out from the snow like old fence posts. Snow fell from their branches like rocks. A minute went by, and the rumble grew. Another minute, and the skiers were strung out, their swift feet fed by fear as they skimmed through the drifts. Ahead a thin stand of trees opened into a clearing and then darkened again in the thick alpine woods they were speeding toward so desperately. And then Aranur could see the ridge that marked the next valley. The ground began to tremble.

Dion tripped up on a snow-hidden branch and tottered on the awkward skis. Rhom was by her in an instant. "Keep on!" They were in the first stand of trees, but the trunks seemed too thin and too widely spaced to protect the group from the avalanche.

Gamon and Namina flashed out into the light. Shilia was about to follow when the avalanche hit. All three were swept away instantly. Shilia clung to a branch as the wash of snow sucked at her and shook the tree. Her skis were torn away. Then billowing powder obscured the very air before them.

The roar of the thundering snow filled Dion's ears and shook her bones so that her body seemed filled with nothing but sound. The boy collapsed against her where Aranur dropped him and raced to help her brother. When she finally dared to look up, clouds of ice vapor and snow flurried the air like fog till the roaring died. Miraculously, the sparse woods they had stopped in had sheltered them, the snows having split around them on both sides. Aranur looked, disbelieving, at the rough expanse of snow that had taken his uncle, his cousin, and his sister.

"No," he whispered. He flashed out onto the new snow.

Rhom struggled to wrap his skis back on. "Dion, stay here with Tyrel. There may be more slides." He darted after the other man.

The avalanche seemed to call not just the ridges but the heavens down, too, because the snow was falling faster than ever. Flurries began to build as the wind grew into a whipping, twirling dance of white flakes. Dion finally got Tyrel into a sitting position and wiped his eyes, cradling him like a child while she tried to make him understand that they had to go on. It was slow going. They followed the men's fast-fading tracks till they could see Aranur and Rhom half a kilometer away down the new slope. The two were digging. They half pulled someone out—it looked like Shilia—then they slid to another spot and began again. When she got closer, Dion could see that it was Aranur's sister. The girl was struggling to free herself from the ice before it froze up again, trapping her legs.

"I'm all right," she called. "Help them with Namina and Gamon."

Dion pointed Tyrel toward his cousin and left him with the girl. Rhom was cutting away at the ice with his sword, lifting out the chunks as fast as he made them. "We haven't found Namina," he cried as his twin skidded up to him. "Gamon's down here. We made him an air hole, and he's reciting a drinking song, so I don't think he's hurt."

Aranur stood, searching. Uprooted bushes and trees cast shadows across the ice, smoothing out in the falling snow and misleading his desperate eyes. "There!" He took off toward the spot with Dion close behind. It was the girl's ski—but not the girl. They scrambled over a broken tree half-drowned in the snow, and then they found her. At the edge of the flow, where huge ice boulders had churned like a tumbler, she lay white and still, blood slowly melting and staining the snow away from her head.

"Oh, gods," Aranur said hoarsely. He levered the frozen boulders from his cousin's legs and torso as if they were pebbles.

When he had thrown them off, both he and Dion were struck silent. The compound fracture that had split the girl's right leg had bent it back under her at an impossible angle.

"I will need splints," Dion said without inflection.

Aranur turned without a word and skied to the nearest tree. His face was so bleak that Dion did not know what to say. If the moons had blessed them earlier, they had turned their backs on them now. *Gray Hishn,* she called out to the wolf. *Hishn, I need you.* She did not know if the Gray One had heard. Hishn sent no answer back. Dion looked out for a long moment at the blank snow and then turned back to Namina.

They used their skis to rig a sled for the girl, then made snowshoes to replace the skis. The shoes were more than crude—they had little material and less time to work with—but they were better than nothing. Aranur redivided the packs, lighter now since they were wearing almost all their clothes and the makeshift sled was taking up their blankets. Dion fretted, hoping against hope that Namina would be warm enough. The girl had not come to yet, thank the moons, for the healer had had to set and splint her leg without a painkiller. By the time Dion was finished, her own hands were white with the cold and her fingernails were purple. The snow scurried faster around their heads.

Aranur thought he spotted a cave in the ridge above the valley, but no one could see more than a hundred meters anymore. "If we can just get to that, we might stand a chance," he said.

His cousin made it only half a kilometer before he collapsed, and Aranur slung the boy over his shoulder and trudged on, sinking deeper in the snow. Shilia and Dion followed, breaking the trail further for the other two men, who dragged the sled behind. The cold bit deeply through their clothes, and their cheeks burned from the frozen air.

Two gray shadows plunged toward them between the trees, and Dion felt Hishn's call in her head. *This way,* the soft voice said. *Come this way.*

But the ridge is over there. She pointed with her chin, her quick breaths steaming in the cold.

The den is this way, the wolf insisted.

"Dion, where are you going?" Shilia grasped Dion's arm as she veered off after the wolves.

The healer shook her off. "Hishn says shelter is that way."

Another gray shape appeared through the flurries and flanked them on the left. "Aranur!" she shouted in the wind. "Aranur! This way!"

The white-swathed man stumbled and fell, dumping Tyrel into a bank, but two more wolves moved in and gave him the leverage he needed to get the boy back on his shoulders. "What?" he gasped between his heavy breaths.

"They're leading—us to—shelter," she called back, breathless, as she tried to break trail for the others through the deepening snow. "Keep on. It won't be much farther." *Will it?* she asked Hishn doubtfully. She struggled in the drifts only a few minutes before Aranur moved up beside her slender form.

"Stay behind me," he yelled, his words disappearing in the flurries like the white wind around Dion's face. He plunged ahead. The snow gathered on Tyrel's back as he hung limply from Aranur's broad shoulders. Dion was having a hard time, but Shilia's light pack was too much for the smaller girl to struggle with when she fell. *We can't afford to lose those supplies,* the wolfwalker told herself desperately. Taking the pack, she tossed it over her shoulder on top of her own thin one and struggled on beside the younger girl. The wolves moved in and let them both hang on to the gray and icy fur. The other two men simply dragged the sled, leaning into the rope across their chests as they forced each step in the snow.

It's almost three more kilometers, Hishn sent, her acute senses making Dion twice as cold, twice as tired, but her tone giving the woman confidence.

The white sky became gray as the clouds thickened. Late afternoon? Evening? They could not tell. Bitter cold chewed mercilessly at Dion's face, her cheeks seemingly splintered by the icy particles. It was hard to keep her eyes open in the mesmerizing swirls that turned her head and made her dizzy. Hishn was beside her, supporting her, pushing her on, but she was already cold and wet and tired. She could hardly see Aranur a few meters ahead. The storm was growing worse.

Wolfwalker, a soft voice said, urging her on.

You honor me, she sent, as she had done so many times before, the effort making her stumble again, her crude footwear settling awkwardly over an icy patch in the snow. Her feet were numb. Her hands had stopped burning in the wind that had stripped them bare of heat, and she could not feel Hishn's fur beneath her fingers. Bad sign, she thought vaguely. Her ankle twisted as she hit a soft pocket, and she suddenly floundered up to her thighs in snow.

Keep on. Hishn shoved her hard. Three more wolves were running ahead of them, plunging through the snow like dnu through deep water. They broke the trail, trading off to spell each other, and Aranur pushed on in their wake, but behind her Dion heard a cry. *Keep on,* Hishn commanded.

"Gamon? Rhom?" she shouted into the blinding white air.

"The sled . . . slipped, but Namina's okay," Rhom answered in a hoarse voice.

The falling snow hissed. Dion finally realized how cold the silver band was against her forehead and removed it, stuffing it inside her jerkin after knocking the ice off its edges. Her face was numb. She was shivering in spite of her sweat. The darkening forest struck its icy chills into them like a driller putting nails in an empty house. They stumbled more often, their heavy breathing bringing the cold more quickly into their lungs and their numbed minds slowly succumbing to hypothermia.

Hishn, Dion sent. *We've got to stop now and build a shelter before we're too cold and tired to survive the night.* Aranur, carrying double his weight, was moving more and more slowly. He had not removed his pack, or Tyrel's, either, and Dion did not see how he could keep up his stubborn pace. Even he was not that strong.

Keep on, Hishn commanded. *Soon you can rest.*

Keep the pace, Wolfwalker, the soft voices chimed in. *Run with us. Sing in our dreams.*

The white wall before the woman blurred, and her face and feet and hands began to feel relaxed. It was too much effort. She struggled more slowly. *Wolfwalker, keep going.* Voices in her head. Images of large gray bodies lay warmly beside her. Dreams of dark warmth in a shelter, the smell of old dust and closed rooms.

The snow had wet, then frozen her hair where it hung out of her cap, and the ice particles on her clothes weighed her down like stones. Her teeth chattered so hard, she thought they would break off. Finally another wolf moved to her side and closed in, guiding her through the blinding flurries. *Cold, so cold,* she sent without realizing it. She fell. It was so comforting to stop moving, to rest.

Get up! Hishn shouted in her head. *Get up and keep moving.* The wolf nipped the woman's nose, hard teeth piercing the numbness, and she could still feel enough to rouse at that ungentle bite. The other wolf put his nose under her to shove her up, and Hishn tore at her jerkin, shaking the Wolfwalker like a doll. Dion found herself on her knees. *Keep going,* they commanded. *The den is just beyond those trees.*

Time. Cold hours, cold minutes. How long was it before she bumped into a motionless body and slid back down to the frozen ground? *Here,* Hishn panted. *The door.* Dion did not move. The wolf bit at the woman, but Dion did not rouse. As the snow fell further, the cold settled into her bones like an old man in an armchair, and she just lay there, sinking further into the white peace of her mind.

XIV

Aranur Bentar neDannon:

Shelter of Ice

Legends sing of truth beyond imagining;
Ancients holding the world in their hands.
You, who travel the path of mythology,
Weary beyond the distant lands,
Hold true to your heart and despair not your courage;
The old knowledge lives where the Yew Mountains stand.

Snow curled Aranur's hair, freezing his days-old beard. With Tyrel's weight dragging his feet down in the snow, Aranur could barely lift his legs to step each time. The wolves that broke his trail and shoved against his legs to keep him on it were silent; only his own harsh breathing kept him company in the sounds of the storm. His sweat was cold. His muscles burned. He lifted deadened legs and almost dumped the boy again as his foot sank suddenly in the uneven drifts. His skin was so numb that he could sense only pressure, not fur or warmth, from the wolf that gave him leverage to get up again; the feel of his clothes was lost on his frosted skin.

Only the insistence of the wolves kept him going, each leaden, snow-kicking step taken just one at a time. Shilia and Dion, he told himself grimly, they depend on me . . . Got to keep going . . . But his eyes stared at the wolf-shattered drifts before him, white swirls of driving snow confusing his gray gaze when he looked up. Cold. He stumbled again. His snowshoes spuffed into the steep bank and started tiny avalanches of sifting snow, but he forced himself up again. Before him, a circle of wolves huddled, waiting for him at a wall of ice. He could go no farther.

Is this it? his numbed mind asked. The two women had collapsed behind him, Rhom and Gamon letting the sled stop as
they fell into the snow. The wolves gathered around them pro-
tectively like gray ghosts guarding the dead. Dumping the boy
beside them as gently as his leaden hands could, the wind biting
eagerly at his body where Tyrel's form had protected him from
the cold, the man looked around, exhausted, not understanding
the silence, the drifts of hissing snow. This is the safety of a
warm den? His heart, hanging on only by stubborn insistence,
sank and froze with the realization that there was nothing there
to see. No shelter but that of a cliff of ice.

"Damn you, where is it?" he whispered hoarsely at the
wolves. There was no answer, and a sudden rage filled him.
"We'll die without shelter, you gray soul worms!" He took a
step toward one of the wolves as if to strike it but fell to his
knees in the snow. "We've followed you till we have no more
strength. We trusted you . . ." He struggled to take out his
sword, but his hands were too cold to grip the pommel, and his
voice, when it came again, was hoarse and weak. "If you've
killed us," he promised grimly. "I'll take you with me to the
seventh hell." The snow drifted high against the ice cliff, ignoring his footprints, and his eyes met those of an ice-crusted
wolf. Faint edges of thoughts that were not his own echoed in
his mind. *Door,* the impression came. *The door to the dome.*

Aranur stared at the wall uncomprehendingly, but the thought
did not come again. The wolves waited, panting in the blizzard
wind. He kicked at the snow in front of the wall as the wolves
began to melt away, back into the storm. Four stayed, huddled
close, protecting the bodies behind him in the piling snow. He
searched numbly with his hands. Nothing, no irregularities, no
bumps or knobs or handles or anything that could be a latch—
as if he could feel one if it were there. Finally, Dion's twin
struggled to his feet and fell against Aranur's leg with his sword
in his hand. Aranur stooped, the snow piled on his shoulders
falling into the trampled drifts, and took the weapon, beginning
to strike at the ice, shattering it slowly while icicles fell like
knives into the snow at his feet. The white flurries were beginning to cover the girls' bodies. His eyes met those of a wolf.
Yellow eyes. He attacked the ice wall again.

"A latch," he whispered to himself, not sure that the dark
shape frozen in the ice was what he was hoping for. He pulled

back the sword and struck again, hard as he could, letting his weight fall with the sword on the door. A heavy slab of ice broke away, knocking him down into a soft drift and baring the light color of a smooth surface. He struggled out from under the ice block. There was a latch, too, but it was frozen in place. He smashed the latch with the pommel of the sword, set his foot against the door, and kicked. Nothing. He kicked again, and the ice cracked. "One . . . more time," he grunted. The door burst open into darkness, and he fell through, carried by the force of the kick over the threshold.

"Aranur!" Rhom cried weakly after him.

He pulled himself back up on the ice so that Rhom could see that he was not lost, and then he helped the younger man inside, letting him crawl away from the doorway. It was almost more than he could do to lift the sled over the threshold so that Rhom could ease it inside and drag it back from where the icy wind clutched Namina's body. By the time he helped Gamon and the others to the doorway, shivers racked his body and his sweat had frozen against his skin. Dion's wolf, dripping ice from her fur and looking more like a snow ghost than a Gray One, leapt into the dark room as the last of the other wolves disappeared. Aranur stumbled back to shut the door.

After four tries, he had to admit that he could not do it. He sagged against the door, too cold to fight anymore. Gods give me strength . . . The fallen ice had blocked the hinges, keeping the door open for the heavy winds to drive through. He moved back, staggering on his feet, and lunged at the wood one last time—and forced it nearly shut, crushing the ice and shifting the snow drifts till the drafts were closed out. It would have to do.

The place was bitterly cold and pitch dark, and his harsh breathing seemed to echo in the space they were in, but he could not seem to move anymore. Light, warmth—nothing seemed more important than rest. A wet nose nudged his numbed face. The wolf nudged him again, and he forced himself to move, pulling himself up against the wall.

"What?" He tried to thrust the cold nose away.

Come, a voice summoned. The Gray One tugged at his icy clothes, pulling him away from the wall to follow.

"Aranur?" Rhom questioned weakly from the darkness.

"The wolf . . . is leading to something."

Hishn let him hold on to her shoulder as she padded down the hall. After the first few uncertain steps, he assumed that the floor was smooth and stumbled after her. He had no sense of direction. Once he brushed against cold metal and jerked back. The moons only knew what it was. After a while the wolf paused, then continued. The exhausted man stepped after her and stubbed his burning feet on a flight of stairs, falling into the steps as he toppled over. The wolf jumped up several stairs, leaving him to follow. Lost, he groped to the right. Yes, there was a wall, and he followed it up the flight, crawling with the last of his strength till he felt the wolf's warm panting again.

He reached out, and his hand hit a smooth surface. Wall or door? he wondered, dragging himself up and searching for a handle. When he found it, he hesitated only a moment, then turned the handle and collapsed against the door. The blast of light and warm air hit him like a heavy blanket. The air, hot with an unrecognized warmth, scalded his skin where it touched, and he fell to the floor with a clumsy thud, letting it envelop him as he stared unseeing at the two skeletons that populated the room. Must get . . . the others, he forced himself to think, knowing he would have to leave that life-giving heat. That the bones of the dead were watching did not bother him. The bones of the living were what concerned him now. "Come on, Gray One," he whispered.

XV

Ember Dione maMarin:

Dome of Death

Skill comes with a teacher's patience;
But knowledge is heavier than gold.
When the healer touches, the healer trades.
One life for the life of another:
One soul on its way to the moons.

Dion was running with the wolves, snow spraying back from her legs. The excitement of their thoughts echoed in her head as the snows melted into mud and spring warmed the ground beneath her feet. The wind whipped the fur on her face. Clear and sharp, it blew its mountain air across her wet nose and lifted the scents of the hunt to her mind. Still they ran on. She could feel the familiarity of the mountains, sense what was ahead. They ran through summer, the dust gritty in their eyes. She felt the image of a building, the echoing emotions of people she did not know. Something called. Fall cut the hot summer air with a chill knife and drained the sap from the trees. The skies grew heavy with unfelled snow. Her feet grew tough, and her fur lengthened for the winter.

Six, seven, eight times they ran through the seasons, and as many years a hundredfold filled her mind with forgotten time. The songs of human voices echoed more dimly each season till they were all but silent; the bonding between them and the song of the wolves grew thin, stretched, and the Gray Ones grew ever fewer. She could feel herself tauten as the tension of that loss held her close, closer to the wolves each season, till she could hear only the Gray Ones' voices as they ran. Running, racing, there was something up ahead, something that pulled. The wolves ran faster, calling her to keep up. She faltered. There was a danger to this dream . . . But they urged her on, howling in her head. Her consciousness wavered, inside, outside her body. Fear pegged the voices to her memory. They called, begged her to return. *Run with us . . . Run deep . . .*

She was sweating when she woke. The ceiling was yellow, the lighting was bright, and the first thing that met her eyes was a skeleton that grinned mindlessly back at her. She shook her head. Then, as she was starting to edge away, sure that she was still seeing things, a voice brought her up short.

"So," Rhom said, looking up from pulling on his boots. "You decided to rejoin us?"

She sat up abruptly and looked around. The skeleton was still there; she saw that there was another one crumpled against the opposite yellow wall. Aranur's sister, sitting by the still unconscious form of Namina, had one hand on her cousin's arm, and she gave the healer a worried half smile of greeting. Tyrel slept across the room from both of them; he tossed once restlessly, then snored in the deep sounds of exhaustion.

Dion looked back to her brother. "Where are we?"

He hesitated. "Aranur and Gamon went to find out," he said finally. "Gray Hishn went with them."

She could feel an echo of Hishn's excitement, too reminiscent of the dreaming in her mind, and she got up and went to Shilia, ignoring the skeletons as best she could. "How long have you been with her?" she asked as she took Namina's pulse.

"About an hour." Shilia was worried. "Will she be all right? She's so pale . . ."

Dion unwrapped the bandages on Namina's leg. She had reset the bone and stitched the wound closed as best she could after the avalanche, but the leg was swollen and ugly. The only consolation was that the cold and cleanliness of the snow had prevented more infection than there was already. But as she took in the unconscious girl's erratic pulse and irregular breathing, she realized bleakly that Namina was not even trying to fight the pull of the moons. The girl had not taken in any liquids in over a day, and the combination of dehydration and shock could kill her as easily as a knife in her throat.

Shilia, watching the healer closely, said hesitantly, "What is it? What's wrong?"

The healer closed her eyes for a moment, then sighed before wrapping the cloths back over the wound.

But Shilia grabbed at her arm. "Dion—what is it? She's—she's not going to die?" she asked in stunned disbelief. "Can't you do something?"

"I've done what I can already. The rest is up to her."

"But Dion—she—she's—"

"She's got to fight this one herself, Shilia. The herbs and poultices will do nothing if she doesn't care herself anymore."

"But you can't just let her die like this!"

"*I* don't have much to do with it at this point, Shilia," Dion said forcefully. Seeing Rhom's frown, she tried to contain her helpless frustration. "When Namina's sister died, well, it hit her hard," she explained as gently as she could, "and now she has withdrawn. She isn't willing to deal with life, to fight for it. I'm not a moonmaid with a basket of miracles, Shilia. I can't *make* her want to live."

The other girl clenched her hands, and her lip started to tremble. Finally, Rhom pulled Shilia to him, and she clung to his shoulder, leaving Dion staring at the walls. Shilia's only nineteen, Dion told herself. She doesn't understand how limited modern healing is. Damn the ancients for keeping their secrets! she burst out silently. When a section of the wall split open beside her, she jumped, thinking for an instant that she had called the wrath of the moons down on them all.

Rhom reached across and touched her arm. "It's okay, Dion."

She gave a shaky laugh at Aranur and Gamon as they came through the smooth doorway. This place was creepier than a walk through a worlag's den, and she wondered suddenly exactly where they were.

"Everything okay?" Aranur asked as he looked around. His gray-black eyes met her violet ones, and she found herself compelled to answer his unspoken question.

"Tyrel is stable," she said quietly. "His fever is down, the wounds have finally closed, and he's resting. Namina—" She hesitated, then said flatly, "Namina will die unless she finds the will to pull herself out of the death grip she's in."

Aranur clutched her arm painfully, staring at her with bleak eyes. Finally he dropped her arm, and she rubbed it where his fingers had left red marks. "You can do nothing?"

"Unless you found some miracle cure on your wanderings, there is nothing more I can do."

"What about your medicines, your herbs?"

"There are no herbs that will give her back the will to live."

"What about those techniques you learned from the Ethran people—the ones you got on your Internship?" he returned quickly.

"I've tried them." She cut him off as he opened his mouth again. "Look, Aranur, I can't do any more for the girl. It is in her to die, not live. If she'd just fight it, even for a few hours, she'd come through."

"What about—" He hesitated.

"Don't say it," she said quietly. "Please, don't—don't even think about it."

Ovousibas. It was in his eyes, along with the anguish he felt for his cousin. But internal healing was death. To her as well as to Hishn. Namina was like a sister to Aranur, she knew, and he would give anything to save her life, but did Dion's own life mean so little to him? What was she? Not a woman, just a means to their future? She resisted the impulse to scream her sudden, overwhelming hurt and beat at him with her fists, clenching her hand instead in Hishn's thick fur.

At the pressure, the wolf gazed up with a quizzical expression. *I am here,* she sent, but then, to the woman's puzzlement, added after a pause, *and I am here.* The second image was so different that Dion almost did not understand it.

I have been here before, the Gray One repeated. *I know this place.*

Startled, Dion met the yellow-slitted eyes. *You've never been out of Ramaj Randonnen in your life till now.*

But I have been here. As it was in the valley, it is the same here. I can feel the floors, I remember how each hall smells, I know the shadows and the back stairs before I see them.

How can that be? Dion stared deep into Hishn's eyes, letting the Gray One's consciousness and memories merge. And the wolfwalker felt it, too. That thing that called her, that sense of danger and excitement—it was in her mind and in this place, this dome, this building of her dreams. Aranur had mentioned the ancients, and he had been right, because Hishn's memories flashed her through the walls and down the empty corridors, sniffing the air for the familiar smells, squinting her eyes at the same light that had made those before her squint eight hundred years earlier. And then Dion knew. She knew what was outside the door, down the hall, and beyond. She knew where they were, and it frightened her because from Hishn's mind, from the memories of the Gray Ones outside the place, Dion suddenly realized that the legends were true. The wolves had brought them to the one place of safety they would never leave. This place was one of the domes of the ancients, a place where the old ones had lived and worked—and died with the plague brought by the Aiueven. *Hishn,* she gasped. *What have you done to us?*

Warmth, shelter. I brought you life like a mother suckling its pup, the beast panted happily.

No. Oh, no, Hishn! Dion groaned. *You don't understand. You've brought us the death of eight hundred years.*

". . . the place is deserted," Aranur was saying. "There's nothing alive in it but us."

She shivered, unable to keep herself from glancing at the skeleton that imitated Tyrel as he lay, huddled to himself, against the wall. *Leader speaks true,* the wolf's words mocked her. Maybe the plague virus had mutated in eight hundred years. Maybe over the generations people had built up a resistance or immunity to the disease. Maybe . . .

"But Aranur," Shilia protested, her face pale as she followed the same line of reasoning and realized what he was saying. "If this is one of the domes—"

"No one who's ever gone to the domes has come back," Rhom finished harshly.

Aranur shrugged. "We can do little about that now. But we also know only about the domes in Randonnen and Ariye. This is a different county. Perhaps the curse is faded in this place."

"Every legend has its feet in fact," Gamon said slowly. "As wolfwalkers are still real—" He nodded at Dion. "—so do ancient tales hold some truth."

"The question is, How much truth?" Dion said. "The fever . . ." Her voice trailed off as they all looked at her. What did she know for sure?

Aranur gave her a sharp look. "You said Tyrel had stabilized."

"Not Tyrel's fever. The other fever," she answered slowly.

"The fever brought by the Aiueven. The plague that wiped out the ancients." She shivered, trying to ignore the icy finger that touched her spine. "The virus, it's still in the air." She drew in her breath, trying to deny what she knew. "I can smell it, taste it," she said shakily.

"Dion, are you all right?" Aranur demanded.

"I can feel their memories," she said slowly, wishing she could close her eyes from the wolf-sent images that fogged her head. She knew that the walls before her were blank, but beyond them, contorted skeletons lay in rooms and lined the corridors. "I can feel the ancients through the wolves," she repeated shakily. "I know what's here."

Rhom frowned at his twin.

"It's been eight hundred years," Aranur said. "Think carefully, Dion. No one has been here in centuries—all these bones are probably those of the ancients themselves. Without anyone to infect, would a virus really survive that long?"

"It could. All the domes are the same—construction, heating, terrain—and all of them carry the curse of the plague." Dion breathed deeply to calm herself. The memories of death were echoing in her head from Hishn, from the other gray voices, the other howling songs. She could almost feel the pain of the fever contort the ancients' bodies as they died, the flames that burned the nerves of other animals caught in the throes of a death they did not understand. She thrust the images away. "It could have mutated," she admitted. "Or we could have built up a resistance to it and still be carrying it in our blood. But in eight hundred years, in Randonnen and Ariye and all the other counties I know of, no one has yet done so."

"Dion, are you sure you're all right?" Aranur looked sharply at her, trying to divine if she had caught something from being out in the blizzard too long.

She shook her head. I won't be if we stay here. None of us will if the plague is still in this place."

He searched her eyes. "I'm sure you're saying what you believe is true, but you're predicting a death that's eight hundred years old."

The healer looked shakily at him. "Death is a power that even the moons bend to."

"We'll take the path when it's time, Dion. We don't need to anticipate it now, so why don't we forget about this eight-hundred-year-old plague for now? We can't leave Diok now, anyway, so let's concentrate on surviving for the moment.''

"Aranur, you don't understand—"

"Healer Dione," he cut in harshly, "you've lost sight of the point. Namina is too ill to move. Tyrel would not make it another day in the mountains. We will stay here until they are able to travel, and then, and not before, we will leave. A fever that's centuries old and gone doesn't scare me much when my cousins are already on the path to the moons. I respect your skills, Healer," he said deliberately, "but it is my decision to stay." He shrugged, then said more gently, "And as far as getting this mythical fever, would it really make any difference if we left this place now?''

She dropped her eyes. "Maybe not," she admitted. "If we've been exposed, we could be carrying the virus already.''

"And what about other people? Could we carry this plague to other counties if we left? It hasn't been just wolfwalkers who've died in the domes.''

She nodded bleakly.

"Then we might as well get comfortable while we settle down. There's some rooms with old beds down the hall. They're musty, but it's better than sleeping on the floor with the bones. Shilia,'' he directed, "wake Tyrel, then help Rhom with the packs.''

Dion had not been out of the room she had awakened in, but her mind had already ranged through the dome a hundred times. Now, as the travelers carried their gear down the hall and set up in another room, the colors and lights had an eerie familiarity. Hishn padded beside her, excited. *This place needs you here*, the wolf sent, flashing an image of many people working in the dome. Dion felt the lupine memory, but behind it, hidden in her subconscious mind where the wolf ignored it, were the strong images of death. The woman dropped her pack inside the door and started back down the hall.

"Dion, wait!" Aranur called. He leaned back in the room and said something to her brother as she turned, then strode down the hall to meet her. "I'll go with you," he stated without giving her a chance to decline.

They walked without talking, stepping around the skeletons, and Dion let the atmosphere of the building seep into her consciousness through Hishn's mind. It was warm in that place— heated by volcanic steam, as mountain homes had always been—but she felt cold. She closed her eyes, but even then she could see what was there. She *knew*. Hishn would not let her ignore the dreams upon dreams, the shadows of death. She flinched as the nebulous image of an ancient woman walked right through her without noticing, mouthing silent words at the man who listened attentively to her echoes. A group of lab workers faded into the wall as they went through some sort of doorway. The faint lines of time stretched back in a reflection of their lives as if Dion were staring through two mirrors that echoed the dreams of the ancients a thousand times. She stepped cautiously through a faint box lying across half the hall, expecting to feel resistance and meeting none—her foot hit the floor with a real slap that echoed in the empty hall. Murmurs of ancient conversations distracted her ears while her eyes strained to find the reality in the three men by the hall's opening, brushing through their remembered minds as she passed through their faded bodies. When she opened her eyes, Aranur was staring at her.

"Dion?" he asked, his hand hovering above her arm, not quite touching.

Dion stared at him. A shadow man walked through him, blurring his face grotesquely as their expression merged and split again. The aura of despair, death. Hishn whined. Gray voices called the woman to enter, to let them in, to take away the pain, the death. *Wolfwalker, run with us. Don't leave us alone. The pain . . . the fire . . . help us. Help us . . .* They howled; her hands reached out to the door, drawn by the intensity of Hishn's call—their call—and she swayed . . .

Aranur grabbed her. "Dion." His voice cut sharply through the haze, and her eyes began to focus again. "Dion . . ." He glanced down the hall to where it ended at a broad door. There was something there—either he was picking it up from the healer, or he sensed it vaguely himself. Either way, it was a dank feeling, one of pain and darkness, and it made him shiver as well until he threw off the sensation irritably and swung Dion up in his arms. "I'm taking you back. Now."

"Put me down." She struggled, but the shaking that took over her limbs only made him grip her tighter.

"What is it?" he asked. "What happened?"

She trembled. "I don't know. I don't know," she repeated, clenching her hands to keep them from shaking so badly.

"Hishn—she opened a memory, let the Gray Ones in. And their dreams—they won't get out of my mind. They keep begging me—begging me to help them." She pointed vaguely at the double door that stretched across the end of the hall. "Hishn— I have to go in there."

He stared at her, then set her down without a word and let her lean on the wall. Stepping forward, he pressed his hands on the door and pushed gently, warily, on the surface. It slid easily into the wall, and she took two involuntary steps past him, onto the threshhold, the wolf leaping into the huge room ahead of her.

It hit her then, and she screamed, a horrible wail of despair. The skeletons, grinning and empty of soul, twisted in the death throes of those they had once belonged to. The air was stiff with the fear of a plague and the imminent knowledge of death. And still the horrible dreams of eight hundred years of lonely wolves, the images of songs and laughter, lay grotesquely over the bones of decay. Hishn howled, confused by what she saw with her inner eye and what she knew to be true with her outer sight. Aranur thrust Dion back, drawing his sword.

The room was still.

"What did you see?" he asked harshly. "What is here?" He faced the room as if a glacier worm were about to come through one of the walls. He had felt—no, he did not know what he had felt, yet the sense of danger was clear. But there was nothing alive in the room to harm them.

"But I can feel them," she whispered, trembling, moving into the room again, under his arm, as if in a dream. He did not try to stop her. "All of them," she repeated. The grinning skeletons with their empty sockets of sight did not deny it. "They live, they breathe, they die. Here. Now." She moved like a zombie past the skeletons whose dust blanketed their silent words. There were not just human skeletons there but the bones of the wolves, as well. Twisted, broken, grinning carcasses that bit at the floor and air with their ancient agony.

Aranur sheathed his sword and gripped her arms, twisting her to face him. "Dion." He shook her, as she could not tear her eyes from the bones that littered the room. "Snap out of it. What's wrong with you?"

"The dead are still breathing here," she said, her voice rising again. Aranur crushed her to him, and she squeezed her eyes shut to deny the figures she saw merging and splitting with the bones on the floor. Two men shared a shadowy joke over a grinning skeleton. A woman wrote carefully in a book while her hands passed through the arm bones lying across a counter. People shifted through each other as time lay over itself in the memorics of the wolves.

"Dion!" Aranur tried to reach the distraught woman. "Dion, listen to me." With his voice ringing in her empty ears, the intensity began to lessen, as if the emotional pressure in the room had dispersed through the open door. "It's just a room, Dion. Just a big, drafty old room with old bones and dusty floors," he said, persuading the skeletons to lie still. "Look at it. It doesn't move or breathe. It's just a room, Dion. Just a room."

She opened her eyes, ready to flinch away from the shadow of death that stood there still, but without the dreams of ancient minds to move them through the air, the massive hall stood empty, vacant of the time-lost images that had kicked up dust and fed her fear.

"Everything's all right, Dion," Aranur said softly, smoothing her hair. "You're okay." She realized her cheeks were wet and started to pull away, embarrassed, but he held her tight and touched her cheek gently. "Dion . . ." He hesitated. "Why did you come here?"

She looked around the cavernous room, and he dropped his arms from her and let her go. "This place has been calling me," she said uncertainly, still shaken by both the ancient images and the sudden heat of an unexpected passion. Hesitantly, she stepped toward one of the skeletons, unwillingly leaving the warm and real touch of the man.

"Calling you? What do you mean?" He made no move to follow, just watched her with his eyes.

"I've felt this—this dome—ever since we left the first mountain range. The wolves . . ." Her voice trailed away. She could still hear their echoes in her mind. Hishn looked at the woman from where she sat, her yellow eyes bright against her gray fur and her ears perked as if to catch Dion's thoughts with them. "The wolves have been calling me," she said finally.

"What do they want?"

"The Gray Ones? They want me to—to help them." The words stumbled over each other as Dion struggled with the thoughts that bound her to the wolves. "To . . . sing with them, become one with them. To—to let them in to their people and—and bring the ancients back. Gray Hishn knows. Hishn feels it all."

"Dion, look at me," Aranur said forcefully, turning her to face him. He tried to put one hand on her forehead, but she shook it off.

"I am not feverish, Aranur," she said sharply.

"I'll be the judge of that." He felt her cheeks.

"Aranur, I am not sick. Look around you. What I'm saying is true. The wolves—they ran with the ancients. They still have the memories of everything that happened, and they won't get out of my head. It's their songs I keep hearing, their memories."

"Dion, you know that sounds crazy."

"I can't help it." She broke free of him and gestured at the room. "The ancients died here. Died for the secret of Ovousibas. And the wolves know why."

"What do the wolves have to do with this?"

"The Gray Ones are the key. There's no such concentration of them anywhere else in the continent. Only here, where the ancients first landed, the Gray Ones are as thick in the woods as fleas. And the memories are strong. Even Hishn feels them like they were her own." She looked up at him with wide, fearful eyes. "They know, Aranur. They know how to merge. How to meld the mind into a tool . . . If I can only listen, if I could understand the images . . ."

He just looked at her. "Dion, you said the fever was still here. How do you know you don't have it already? How do you know that what you're seeing or hearing in your head is real at all?"

"I know this, Aranur." She could hear her voice rising in frustration. "I just know it. And I know what it is. It's Ovousibas," she whispered. "They know how to do Ovousibas."

Aranur gave her a steady look.

Hishn's voice was echoed by the haunting call of other wolves. *You can bring the people back to us. You can bond us again. Take the pain away. Give us back our pups, give us back our future . . .*

Hishn! she cried.

Hishn nudged her hand, and a chill crawled down the woman's spine. She stared at the wolf. But deep inside, a tiny spark of excitement pushed back at the fear. "Ovousibas is for real," she whispered. "The plague—it didn't just strike the ancients and the wolves. It hit all the creatures. It killed the rabbits one year, the lepa the next. It mutated and ate away at everything alive in these hills. It's killing the wolves even now."

"That's impossible," Aranur contradicted. "The plague killed only the ancients and, ever since then, only the wolfwalkers and wolves who've tried Ovousibas. Or those who've entered the domes."

But Dion was not listening. The pieces of the puzzle were falling into place, and the pattern was not one of life but one of death. A slow death. One that crept into the species like a tiny worm and then multiplied until they were all gone. How arrogant, she realized, they had been to think that the Aiueven would count on a single plague to rid Asengar of the humans.

Aranur glanced at her, then said suddenly without looking up, "If the wolves know how to do this healing, you could learn it from them, couldn't you?"

She laughed. "Don't be ridiculous . . ." Her voice trailed off. Aranur did not answer, and she looked at him, his face unreadable. "They are wolves. Creatures of the woods. Not human beings, Aranur. Their part in this is only a memory of death."

"Ovousibas. 'Look to the left.' If the wolves know how to do it, they must know why it has been killing them off."

"They know only the pain," she whispered raggedly. "The longing for the wolfwalkers they lost. To ask them to teach me— it would be suicide, for them as well as me."

"How could it hurt to ask? You wouldn't actually be doing it, and no one seems to have died from that. Give it a chance."

Hishn got up and padded around the room, small clouds of dust puffing up in the air at her feet. *I remember how it's done,* she offered. She sniffed at a gleaming bone that stretched across her path and stepped over it, unconcerned. *Don't worry. We would be together.*

"Hishn 'remembers,' " Dion said without inflection. "As much as the other wolves, she knows how to do it."

"Then you will try?"

"By the time I figure out what I'd be trying, we might already be dead from this cursed flu." The images from the Gray Ones' minds flashed in front of her eyes, showing her just how those ancient healers had died, and she shivered again.

Aranur spread his hands. "I'm just asking you to find out about it. I'm not asking you to do anything yet."

"Yet?" she repeated. "So when does the sword fall? When is the favor asked?" Her voice was rising, and her anger with it. "You get all these ideas in your head from tales your uncle tells when he's drunk, and then you ask me to turn myself inside out just to satisfy your curiosity." He opened his mouth to protest, but she cut him off. "Look around you, Aranur. Look at the bones. Look how many people died because of Ovousibas."

"Dion, all I'm asking you to do is look into it."

"No. It's death to us all. By the light of the moons, Aranur, we've only been here a day. What can happen in the next few days?"

"Namina can die," Aranur reminded her harshly.

His words shocked her, and she stared at him. He had struggled, fought to bring his sisters and his cousins home again. His parents and Ainna were already dead, and Namina's death was only waiting. What were her immature fears compared with his irreplaceable loss? And they were not even her own terrors—they were fears fed by the gray voices of eight hundred years of waiting. Memories that should have sifted into dust by then.

"I will think about it," she said in a low voice. He reached out as if to squeeze her arm reassuringly, but she brushed him away and ignored the hardening of his face. With a frustrated gesture, she left the hall without looking back, Hishn padding softly after her.

XVI

Aranur Bentar neDannon:

Plague

Look without, look within
All is simple as it seems
Bare your heart to the one you love
Share the visions of your dreams

Day and night passed with little notice, since the rooms stayed lit. The phosphorescence in the steam that heated the rooms gave them as much light as if they were in constant day, and with the blizzard outside blocking the sun from the windows, sleep was a thing of convenience and need, not darkness. Even though Aranur's sleep was deep and wearily dreamless, subconscious images floated through his mind and taunted him with hidden meanings. It was a relief when Gamon finally woke him.

"Aranur," his uncle said, shaking him by the shoulder. "Wake up. Come on, man, peel your eyes open."

"Why?" Aranur asked blearily. "Is breakfast ready?" He shook his legs out and popped his knuckles, then looked around. Dion lay quietly in exhausted sleep, and Shilia was monitoring Namina for any changes. "Moonworms, I feel beat."

"You look it, too. We'll get the food problem in hand shortly—Rhom found two exits besides the one we came in, which is frozen shut again, so I'll go hunting if the storm's stopped. I wanted to show you where the doors are before I go exploring with our young blacksmith."

Aranur nodded. His stomach gnawed at his ribs until he

273

shoved away the futile thoughts of food. "How big is this place, anyway?" he asked. "Same size as the dome at Blackstone?" He put his boots on and gestured toward the door.

"Seems to be a lot bigger. In fact, I'd wager a barrel of ale that this one is three times the size of Blackstone." The two walked swiftly through the halls, their footsteps clearing the dust from the floors with their passage. "Aranur," the old man said suddenly. "Go easy on Dion."

His nephew looked at him in surprise. "What do you mean?"

"Rhom is concerned about his twin's obsession with Ovousibas, and I think he's right to be worried."

"Gamon," the gray-eyed leader said slowly, "I understand the risks as much as any of us do. I know what I'm doing. I'm not throwing Dion to the worlags, but I am trying to save our lives."

"All right. I'll accept that," Gamon acknowledged. "But you should realize that she is a Randonnen healer to her very core. If you ask her to risk herself to save Namina's life—or someone else's—she'll push herself as far as she has to to do it."

"And I'll push myself to go with her."

The old man's voice was sharper. "Listen to what I'm saying, Aranur. She's a strong woman, but you're a stronger man. Don't push her past her limits or you'll lose her, and I'm not talking about love, but life, now."

Aranur ran his fingers raggedly through his black hair. "Do you think I'm pushing too hard?"

"You're a leader, Aranur. You give one hundred percent and more of yourself to get the job done and take care of those around you, but you demand a lot, too." Gamon hesitated and glanced up the stairwell they had just reached. "When you were a boy, do you remember asking me why I was harder on you and Tyrel than on the others who trained under me? And then later you asked me why I was harder on you than on Tyrel."

Aranur nodded slowly.

"I said you had it in you to be the best. I meant it then, Aranur, and I mean it now. That's why you've surpassed me. And that's why I pushed so hard for the other weapons masters to accept you even though you're barely twenty-eight." Gamon looked at the tough, steady-eyed man beside him and ran his gnarled hands through his silvered hair. "I knew I could never take the place of your mother and father and what they could have given you—and I didn't want to take that place, either—but I did hope that if I taught you to develop yourself to the height of your potential, then I could give you something that would last your lifetime. Maybe I taught you too well. Maybe I pushed too hard for you to be the best." He shook his head. "I don't think you understand your own limitations—or those of others." He paused. "You can't solve the problems of the world, Aranur. Nor can you protect everyone from the world, and that goes for Shilia, as well as Namina. About Dion, well, take it a little easier, and don't break the steel before it's tempered. Dion's a strong healer and a clever fighter, but she's still a woman, with a woman's feelings and a woman's dreams. And Rhom, for all that he'll do what you ask, is still her brother. He would make a dangerous opponent—but a better friend."

"Gamon," Aranur said finally, "I have my failings—and only the moons know how many those are—but I care about those two a lot."

"I know," the old man said softly. "Just be sure that you are a leader for them as well as for us."

Rhom's voice floated down the stairway. "Hey, Gamon, Aranur—you down there? Hurry up. The storm's stopped, and it's going to take hours to clear the ice from this doorway."

Three hours later, after breaking the broad door free of its hinges and then of the ice, Aranur got his first glimpse of the mountains from the dome. He had been smashing the hilt of his sword at the thin spot they had chipped in the melting ice, and then suddenly, with a splintering sound, the pommel, his fist, and his forearm disappeared into the brittle hole. "We're through," he exclaimed. He dragged his arm, chilled already, back through the broken ice and peered through the opening.

Rhom stepped up and took the sword, shaking it off. "Is it clear or just an air pocket?"

"It's clear," Aranur returned, "and gods, but what a view. Take a look."

Rhom handed the sword to Gamon, who took it in turn. Tearing himself away from the porthole, Aranur stepped back and warmed his fingers under his armpits before touching the cold steel again. The steam might heat the dome evenly in the inner rooms, but it did not seem to compensate for open doors or broken windows, and it was getting harder to ignore the shivers that crawled up from his hands. He just could not seem to get warm. "What do you think?" he asked Rhom with satisfaction.

The black-haired man just shook his head. After the sterile colors of the dome, the natural light of the sun had a clarity he had not expected. Ice sparkled everywhere, from the drifts in the broad expanse that lay outside the door to the glaring cliffs across the deep valley over which the dome was perched. The shoulder of another peak was just visible to the right, jutting out and then straight up and beyond his point of view. To the left, the sun cast shadows down from a snow-softened ridge. Pillows of snowfields lay across the top of the mountains, and from them, dripping quickly in the early summer heat, grew trickles that cut into the drifts and split the white piles deeply as they grew into streams. Trees were greening themselves, everywhere poking their stubby arms out of the melting snow and shaking themselves to rid their branches of unwanted weight.

"Moonworms," Rhom said softly. "I feel like I've just been reborn and the whole world is new again." He squinted at the too-bright sun. "What do you think, it's about late afternoon?"

"Uh huh." Aranur slid his sword back in its sheath. "We should get back. The girls are probably worried, and I want to see how Namina is."

"You go on back," his uncle suggested. "Rhom and I can clear this further. If you find Tyrel, send him along. We won't be getting all the way out for a while yet, and if we dump a drift down on our heads, it'll take even longer."

The gray-eyed man nodded, shivered in the chill air that blew through the hole, and made his way back down the stairs and through the halls of the dome. By the time he got back to where Shilia and the others were camping, Dion had gotten up, Hishn had gone to sleep, and Shilia had set aside the ski she was smoothing to help the healer sort through what was left of her herbs.

"Set the quadril over there and let me have that other packet," Dion directed as she opened another pouch and dumped its contents on a carefully folded cloth.

"What's this for?" The girl held up a small pouch full of tiny brown leaves.

"Helps purify the blood. Put that one over there."

Shilia carefully turned over a tiny jar. "What's in here?"

Dion laughed. "You don't really want to know. Leave that one aside with the other pouch, and I'll sort both of those later.

"Do you grow all this stuff, or do you have to buy it from an apothocary?"

"I buy some, grow a lot, trade a fair amount, and gather everything else. Hishn's great at helping me find what I need in the wild. Her nose is excellent."

"Do the other wolves help you, too?"

"Sometimes. I can't often read them as easily as I can read Hishn, but sometimes,"—her eyes got a faraway look— "especially when there's more than one together, they project so strongly that I can get wrapped up in their memories as if they were my own."

Aranur, who was digging through his pack to find a drier tunic than the one he was wearing, was not paying much attention to the two women, but his sister shook her head. "I don't understand this memory thing. How can a Gray One remember something that happened before it was born?"

"Wolves pass memories on," Dion explained. "They have a racial legacy that they hand down to each generation."

"And you can really read their memories? Their history?"

The wolfwalker nodded. "They remember everything. Oh, not details so much as general impressions, but it still helps. Like the plague. It never hit the wolves as hard as it did other species, but ever since then the wolves have been dying out. I'm beginning to think that they still carry the virus in them even now—dormant, perhaps, but there."

Aranur shot her a sharp glance, but Shilia protested. "Dion, don't you think you can relax about the fever? It's been at least two days since we got here, and none of us have shown any signs of getting it."

The healer was silent for a moment. "I think we all have it and just don't know it yet," she said slowly. "I think we're in an incubation stage, and it's just a matter of time before it catches up with us."

"Well, I think that the virus is eight hundred years old and eight hundred years gone." Suddenly Shilia stiffened. "Dion!" she gasped, staring at Namina, her eyes wide with fear.

Aranur leapt to his feet, dropping his pack and drawing his sword in one fluid motion, and dodged the waking, growling, and lunging form of the wolf, but Dion had already flung herself across the room to Namina's shuddering form. Hishn howled and cowered suddenly. Aranur thrust his sword back, stunned. Namina whimpered and arched her back, throwing her arms wide. Her eyes bulged. The fever—it had to be the fever.

"Shilia—Aranur—help me," the healer gasped, holding Namina to the bed. The young girl convulsed again, shaking them both as her legs kicked against the covers and almost dumped them off the bed onto the hard floor. Her lips were stretched back from her teeth. As her mouth worked open and closed, fluid spit and spilled from her tongue; she choked for a moment, then flung herself high in the air. The muscles of her neck stood out like boards. Grabbing Namina's legs, Aranur locked his arms around them loosely, giving her room to convulse but not enough to hurt herself. However, he did not fare so well; her knee was hard as a fist and found his gut twice. Dion grimly clung to Namina's chest, while Shilia tried to keep the girl's head from smashing into the bedstead as she thrashed in a silent rictus back and forth. "Hold on—it's lessening," the healer managed.

Namina finally gave a strangled cry and collapsed. Shilia and Aranur cautiously let go of her, stepping back, while Dion traced the girl's racing pulse and looked under her eyelids.

"It's the fever," she said quietly. The Gray One whined, and Dion sank back onto her heels. "It's the plague."

Aranur shivered. "How can you be sure? She's weakened enough that it could be a simple flu from infection."

"No." Dion shook her head. "The convulsions, the discoloring of her eyes." She carefully wiped the fluid from the girl's slack mouth. "No, it couldn't be anything but plague." The wolf crept under her hand, and she stroked the furry ears before meeting Aranur's gray eyes. "This isn't a ghost from a long-dead grave, Aranur. This is real."

He regarded her for a moment. Her eyes were fearful, her neck tense; she believed what she was saying. "So what can you do now?"

"It's the plague, Aranur." She shrugged helplessly. "If eight hundred years of healers haven't found a cure, how can I?" He shivered again, and she sharpened her gaze, looking at his eyes and then at his face. "You—you've got it, too, don't you?"

Shilia made a frightened sound, and he met Dion's eyes steadily. "I've felt cold all day. Probably just caught a chill from chipping out ice all morning."

She just looked at him. "Shilia?"

The girl shook her head. "I feel fine."

"Tyrel's gone exploring, probably won't be back for at least a few more hours. Aranur, we've got to find him."

"You think he might be affected already, too?"

"Namina's probably feeling the effects sooner because she's so weak. As for Tyrel, the poison from those bites sapped him to the point where even though the wounds are closed now, he's probably as vulnerable as she is. Where's Rhom and Gamon?"

Aranur looked at Namina's still, pale form for a long moment. "I'll get them," he said, and strode out the door.

As he left, Dion took in Namina's tremors with a sinking heart. Aranur had said the blizzard was past, but Namina was far from being able to travel; the girl's condition had them trapped in Diok till they either beat the fever—if it spread—or died. And the healer was not kidding herself. If the fever hit them as it had the ancients, what did that leave but the long walk to the moons?

Only an hour later, after he returned with her twin and Gamon, Aranur had a mild tremor. He pretended not to feel it, but she saw his hands shake and his eyes turn dark with the unexpected pain. And Gamon confessed to feeling chills when she caught him wearing his coat inside the dome. Rhom admitted nothing, but she knew him too well; the color of his eyes was strangely dark, and his jaw was tense and white. And, most frightening of all, Dion herself felt almost nothing. A chill now and then, but it did not get worse, nor did Hishn whine near her the way she did at everyone else now except Tyrel.

It was not only Hishn who was disturbed. It was all the Gray Ones. They called her to leave the dome, and, bidden by their lonely howls, she went slowly to the room Rhom had chipped the door out of. It was dark by then, but the moons lit the brilliant snow sharply against the shadows cast by stumpy trees. She stood on the old stone platform, letting the cold grind into her cheeks, and stared at the three moons that darted across the sky over the ridge until the warmth of her legs melted the drift around her ankles and Hishn curled at her feet. As she stood in the drift, the temperature dropped until the snow formed an icy crust she could walk on. And then the Gray Ones came.

Gray shadows crept and bounded up from below the balcony.

Through the snowdrifts that insulated the dome from the chill night air, they came at Hishn's call, a long, shivering howl that Dion felt in her heart as well as her ears. She dropped her hand to the gray beast's scruff.

Run with us. Run deep, they sang as they ghosted across the snow.

"Gray Ones, you honor me."

She looked at them carefully as they melted into the shadows on the ancient stone deck. There were two females, five males, and one cub. It had been born that spring, and though its tiny shape looked healthy, there was a great sadness in the mother wolf that led the pup through the snow.

"What is your memory?" the slender woman asked quietly. "Why is your mind so dark?"

The younger female cocked her head. *Warm bellies in a cold spring. A den of dirt that sheltered birth. The smell of blood—birthing blood, and the water that breaks before the first pup comes. But cold, still, the bodies slid out. First one, then two, then three. The sacks clogged their nostrils, but they did not fight to breathe. Fluid plugged their mouths, but they did not struggle to spit. I licked them, nudged them, called to them to rise; they didn't answer me. Cold. Old blood. Old bodies. Old death. An empty den.*

"You lost them all," Dion breathed. "And you, Gray One, you lost all but one?"

The gray beast inclined her head, her yellow eyes gleaming as she tolerantly regarded the single pup that tugged at her nipples from between her legs. Hishn whined softly and leaned against the wolfwalker.

"Tell me why," she demanded. "Why do you lose your pups? Is it from the plague? Tell me—what happened when the fever came to the wolves?"

The older female looked at Hishn, and the massive wolf panted softly. Something passed between them—a recognition that was too quick to follow, or perhaps a memory that belonged to neither one. The woman stretched out her hands to the shadows that came at Hishn's call, and then she was dragged into a nightmare that had no end.

The world changed and became colorless—one of shapes of black and white. Gray creatures seen from strange perspectives, scents that strangled thoughts and mind. Motion filled and fled

*her muscles suddenly as she ran, then flopped to the ground and
slept. Flesh tore beneath her claws. Blood ran hot and sweet in
her mouth. And the Gray Ones were her brothers, her sisters,
her clan, and her pack. And then a note of difference struck her
silent; a fire slipped into her blood and burned its way to her
brain. Oh, Wolfwalker, it seared her arteries and scorched
her throat till it crisped even her eyes. She screamed, and the
sound was silent. The other Gray Ones screamed, too. Coals
ate into her brain and tore at her mind until she lashed out,
slashing and biting at the dim shapes she saw through the blackening haze. Wolfwalker—why didn't he answer? Wolfwalker—
why didn't he come? Abandoned. Alone in the fire—the Gray
Ones howled. Their children died. The fog blackened further.
The pads of her feet were soaked in hot blood from the froth of
the unknown dead. The fire dived to her belly. Burned into her
womb. Scalded her eggs and then her pups. The conflagration
raged. Alone. Wolfwalker . . . The silent scream pierced her
mind once more.*

And then there was only the night.

She stirred stiffly, staring at the stars that faded with each
moon's passing and lit themselves again afterward. The night
sky's patterns of light and dark were like a slowly flowing river,
each silver shape couching the night in its own terms until it was
snagged on the mountaintops and another was spit out in its
place. One moon passed before another, and the first one's
shadow crawled eagerly across the farther face. Moons as old
as the world. As old as time itself. And the ancients . . . Who
had seen the moons with their own eyes and the stars beyond.
Who had crossed the darkness beyond the moons and flown
between the first world and this one. And with all their knowledge and all their dreams, they had not been able to cure the
plague.

"Gods," she whispered. "But why? Why?"

"Dion?" Rhom said, startling her. He leaned against the
broken doorway, cleared of old ice and slick only with the frozen
dew of the night. "Maybe you should get some sleep."

She turned and stared at him unseeing, nodding slowly.
"Maybe I should. I'm not getting much done here racking my
brains."

"Take a break, twin, or you'll drive yourself into the fever
you're afraid of." He shivered, and she glared at him, realizing

with a sudden, helpless fury that even her brother had been stricken and she could not do a thing about it. "Don't tell me what to do, Rhom," she said sharply. "Namina's out of her head, Aranur's had chills, Shilia and Gamon have felt tremors, and you're not well, either—and don't try to hide it from me!"

"I'm not," he said calmly. "Aranur's had more than just chills, and Gamon almost broke his arm ten minutes ago. He's okay now," he added, "but the convulsions are worse. Only Tyrel seems to be fine. Says he hasn't felt anything but hunger pangs, while the rest of us are throwing fits every hour."

"I should be there, not here," she muttered, swinging around.

But he blocked her path. "You should be where you can think best, Dion."

"I can't think at all anymore," she said bitterly. "So let me pass. At least I could do something for you."

"There's nothing you can do for us that we can't do for ourselves."

"I could at least try to ease the pain . . ."

"If this is the plague, will that help us live longer? No. So do what needs doing, not what we can deal with ourselves. By the eyes of a water cat, give yourself a chance, Dion. Even the moons don't expect you to make miracles out of mothballs."

"But I do," she burst out, the frustration making her want to beat on the walls as if she could crack the secrets out of them. "I want miracles. I expect answers. Why are we falling to a disease eight hundred years old? How could it live so long in the domes without infecting the people who live outside of them? Why doesn't it affect Tyrel when Shilia's so sick? Why do you have tremors when I barely have chills? I'm a damn good healer, Rhom, so why, by all those rastin-wrapped moons that ride the skies, can't I find a cure—"

"Dion, calm down. I know a hundred times less than you about your arts of healing, but I believe in you. You'll find your answers—"

"Stop patronizing me," she snapped. "You're getting to be as bad as Aranur."

"Then stop feeling sorry for yourself," he shot back. She looked at him with surprise, and he glared as if his authority had surprised him, as well. "Moping won't get anything done. If you need help, ask. If you can't work forward, work backward. Start by eliminating what isn't possible and then look at what's left.''

''I did that,'' she admitted slowly. ''I asked the wolves, I looked at all the legends, I analyzed the symptoms. I have a good idea of what it isn't. I just don't know what it is. Gods, Rhom, I just can't seem to figure out where it's coming from, where it's settled. Why we catch it only when we're at the domes or when we do Ovousibas, and why the wolves are dying out, anyway. They've got to carry it with them somehow. And us, too. There's no other explanation. But then, what is it about internal healing that stimulates it into a plague?''

''Dion, relax. Use your head.''

''That's a great idea except that my brain is already thought out.''

He chuckled suddenly. ''Then use mine. Two heads are better than one, especially when they think alike.'' He leaned against the wall and regarded his sister with a steady look. ''First off, what was here in the ancients' time that is here now that could carry a virus?''

''Almost everything,'' she said dejectedly.

''The building? The animals? The plants outside?''

''Sure, anything like that, although if it was the building, the virus would have to be living off stone.''

''But if it lived in animals or insects, it would have migrated over the mountains by now, wouldn't it?'' Rhom persisted.

''And probably the same for most plants, because these mountains run the length of the continent down almost to Sidisport, and the plants that grow here probably grow in other parts of the range, as well.''

''So there isn't much that's unique to a small enough area that could keep such a virus from spreading to other places.''

''That's true enough.''

''So, we've now narrowed the causes of this virus to things unique to the area. And ditto for each of the other domes on the continent.''

Dion laughed shortly in spite of herself. ''Rhom, I love your logic, but what am I supposed to do with it?''

''Think about it, Dion. Why does the virus affect only wolf-walkers and wolves—except you and Hishn? Is it you who's protecting Hishn, or Hishn who's protecting you from the plague?''

"Wolfwalkers rarely get as sick as other people, Rhom. You know that."

"Except when they do Ovousibas." He shrugged. "Then ask yourself this: What do you and Tyrel have in common that is keeping you from being as sick as the rest of us? What is here that could possibly harbor a virus for eight hundred years without spreading it over all five counties?"

She stared at him. "You're saying that Diok itself must harbor the virus. Well, the legends claim that's true, anyway."

"But we're not worried about legends anymore. We're worried about lives. What here could have helped a virus live that long?"

"Plants, animals." She paused, considering the images she had sifted from the wolves. "I think the virus mutated, attacked other creatures over the years. I don't think we're dealing with a single strain of it anymore."

"Does it matter?"

"Yes. Yes, it does. There's something I'm missing. Some link I just don't see."

"Look, Dion, there's not that many things you can make links out of. Hells, twin, the only things in this dome anymore are cobwebs and steam heat. So now, if you look at the complete pic . . ." His voice trailed off as he saw her face change. "What is it?"

"I looked at the dust, I studied the molds, but—steam heat . . ." She was incredulous, ready to slap herself for her own stupidity. "Of course. The domes were all built over steam vents. They have hollow walls."

He frowned. "I told you yesterday that Gamon and I'd found the vents and traced them to the hot springs. You weren't listening as usual."

"But a virus could live in steam," she said excitedly. "Especially in subterranean hot springs that stay at a constant temperature. And a virus that lived in the hot springs from this mountain wouldn't be able to migrate because the steam vents and surface tunnels run only as far as the lava flows—they're unique to Diok. The virus couldn't cross valleys or mountain ranges—the temperature changes would be too drastic for it to survive."

He shivered violently, and she grabbed him. "Stop it!" She shook him as the tremor weakened his legs. "Don't you dare die on me now!'' He clutched weakly at her, and that scared her even more, to see Rhom, her brother, who had always been so strong, leading her, helping her, rescuing her from all those childhood scrapes, groping and trembling on the floor like a night bird out in the light too long, his convulsing body racked with chills that left him as weak as a dying man. ''Rhom, please!'' she cried out. ''Don't get worse. Stay with me. Stay strong.''

''Dion,'' he said hoarsely, gripping her fingers weakly. ''Don't let yourself get sidetracked.'' He cleared his throat and clenched and unclenched his hands to relax them from the fever's grip. ''If the virus is in the steam, then why aren't you and Tyrel affected? What do you and he share that the rest of us don't?''

She took a deep breath, and when she answered, it was in a voice calm and barren of fear. ''I don't know. We eat the same things, drink from the same water you bring us—''

''There has to be something,'' he said more forcefully. ''Think, Dion. Think.''

She tried to concentrate on his words and not his taut expression. ''It can't be Hishn, because she's only with me. Tyrel can't feel her at all. Only Aranur seems to hear her well, and he hears her twice as well as you but is just as sick. It can't be the boy's physical strength, because he's too weak from the rastin poison I've been sucking out of his wounds. Rhom, the only thing Tyrel and I do—''

''Say that again, Dion, the part about rastin bites.''

''What? The boy's legs are healed over now. Have been for two days.''

''No, the part about you sucking the poison out. What about the rastin bites—the poison? Shilia never helped you with those, did she? You and Tyrel—you're the only two who've been exposed to that stuff.''

''But Rhom, that's toxic by itself—it inhibits the body's immune system already. If anything, it should make Tyrel and I weaker, not stronger against the virus.''

He slumped back. ''Dion, I just don't know, then.''

But she was hesitating, thinking back. What if the poison had changed Tyrel's metabolism? What if the toxin had forced his body to produce antibodies? Antibodies that were chemically similar to those which would attack the virus? She had sucked enough poison into her mouth that she could have gotten some of it in her bloodstream, as well. It could have inoculated her—like a vaccine—before she was ever exposed to the flu. "Rhom," she said slowly. "You may be right. If the fever lives in the steam, then we've all been exposed. If the virus is stopped by antibodies like those which counteract the poison from the rastin, then Tyrel and I won't get sick—we've already built up an immunity—or at least won't get as sick, or . . ." She paused, following the thought through. "At least will take longer to get as sick as everyone else."

"But that means you have the key to a cure, right?"

"I don't know." She twisted her hand in Hishn's fur. The Gray One kicked her legs and snorted in her sleep, and Dion stared down at the thick fur that brushed against her hand. "There's just too many ifs, Rhom. If it's the toxin that's protecting Tyrel and me, how can I reproduce it without having the fish here to take the poison from? Even if I find a way to force your immune systems to create antibodies against this fever, how do we protect all the people you come in contact with later on? There are too many questions . . ."

Rhom, seeing his twin already lost in thought, walked slowly to the door. She needed time. He just hoped they had enough to give her.

Aimlessly at first, then more purposefully, she paced the stone-chilled balcony, trying to think her way inside the plague. Tyrel seemed immune. But Dion had chills like the others—it just did not seem to take hold in the form of convulsions as it did with everyone else. Was it a mild taste of rastin that was protecting her, or was it the wolf? Perhaps Hishn could tell if there was a change in her body. She stopped suddenly. Ovousibas. If the rastin protected her, could she do the internal healing of the ancients without dying an hour later? It was an intriguing thought—after all, it was the fever that struck the healers, as well, and it might save Namina's life. But what would protect the Gray One—and why did the fever hit them only when they did Ovousibas?

The wolves. It always came back to the wolves.

"Hishn," she said finally, waking the wolf. "I need you to call the Gray Ones back." Could she stand to merge with more than one of the wolves? She looked into Hishn's yellow eyes and heard her howl waft its way up to the second moon. Did it matter? Soon they would be alone together, anyway . . .

Shadows gathered. Gray thoughts touched her more clearly than before. Could they sense what she wanted? "Hishn," she whispered. "Tell them what I need. Ask them if it's within their honor to help me."

The gray wolf panted easily, facing the other beasts in the snow. The wind, which had been still at first, rose briefly to bite first at one of Dion's cheeks and then at the other as she waited. A massive female wolf met her eyes. "You honor me," she said softly.

Run with us. Howl with the wind, Wolfwalker.

She stepped forward and greeted each of the Gray Ones that came. There were only four at first, but other shadows gathered behind those and panted with snorts of steam as they stood in the snow. The water had soaked her boots by then, and her feet were chilled, sending shivers up her legs and into her gut, but she clenched her teeth to keep their chattering still and gestured at the dome instead. "You brought us here, to give us life," she said softly. "But what we find is our death."

Hishn growled low in her throat, and the other wolves snarled back. Their teeth were as white as the snow in the darkness, and their shadows clung to them like shrouds.

"Not just ours, but your death, as well," she said. "Help me. Show me where it hides. Take me back. Not just once but twice—as many times as it takes. Show me how the fire strikes. Teach me what you know in your heart, and I'll help you kill it."

Hishn stepped forward and raised her paw. Her yellow eyes glowed.

"Help me. Let me run with you in your past." She held out her hands, then clenched them into fists. "Let me hunt with you. Let me heal with you. Let me live with you, and I will help you live tomorrow, as well."

Hishn seemed to meet each wolf's eyes with her own, and then the Gray Ones sat. The wolfwalker took a breath and knelt in the snow with them. She dug her fingers into Hishn's fur, waiting for the paralyzing strength of the images she knew would come. Even so, she reeled.

Snow crusting her fur and wetting her nose. She spun to the left and dropped. Other hearts beat against hers. Other air breathed through her lungs. She whimpered, but the gray tide had already swept in and flooded her mind. Voices broke over her in waves, battering and bashing her consciousness with each pulse of her/their blood. A hundred times she killed and a hundred times tore the carcasses apart with her claws. A hundred times she touched the minds of long-dead men and confused their thoughts with hers. Her identity fled. A memory crept in instead of familiar thoughts she would have welcomed.

Death, which clutched her gut each spring, tore her children from her womb and delivered them silently on the ground. And death jumped from wolf to healer in the tension of the moment. Touch and go. Touch and die. The fire returned, this time to burn her soul. She cried out, and a tattered gray blanket of fog whipped in the torrent of pain, anchored barely in Hishn's mind and feeding off her strength as the wolf tried to shield her healer from the agony of a Healing she had not yet learned. Whose body? How old was the memory? Did it matter? It needed healing . . .

She swept in at a headlong pace, deeper then the consciousness that threatened her sanity. Dams of blood cells formed clots and glued the tissues together. Strangely shaped molecules floated along. She touched things with ancient hands, and a patch of infection was instantly covered with white blood cells; a bubble of fluid pressing against a nerve gate was popped and the pressure was relieved; a loose ligament was set against bone, where it reached to grow back into the porous surface it had been torn from. Scars formed and faded in the span of minutes. A wickedly spiked ball of pollen swam down an artery, and an antibody smashed viciously into it, clinging to the spikes and crushing the allergen with its force. Time changed. Tensions grew. She fought to concentrate, but tissues swelled and swallowed her. A tide of molecules swept in, glommed onto cells, and ruptured them, feeding on their broken proteins. Nerves flared. Senses blistered. And somewhere in the midst of the pain, something snapped.

Aranur, looking for Dion, easily cracked the ice that had formed against the door and pushed it open. Something hit him from behind, from the side; he found himself on all fours in the snow, his paws digging into the flattened drift and—no! He had hands. And human arms. He shook his head, buffeted by a sudden gale of emotions that was not his own, and two yearling wolves tumbled past, drawing him with them into their play. He fought the pull to romp after them, wag his tail, and bite at the snow. No, he was a man—a man, not a wolf. Staggering, he forced himself to his feet, where he stood swaying until his head cleared, and he found that he was clutching the doorjamb with both hands. Hands—yes, he had hands, not blackened pads with lupine claws. He drew a deep breath, and the gray voices faded as he built a wall against them in his head. Stay separate, he told himself, and stay sane. But why was it so strong? He had never felt such depth of thought, such power from only one wolf. How many were there? And Dion—she talked to the wolves, felt them as if they were her brothers. If she was out here in this gray maelstrom . . .

He took a step, stumbled on a slick spot, and barely regained his balance in the treacherous dark. Some of the Gray Ones were sleeping near the edge of the stone balcony; others romped in the snow, but he could not see Dion's slender form among them. Hishn—if he could find Hishn, she would tell him where the healer was. He almost ran across the stamped-down snow, and then he brought himself up short. Ten, no, twelve of the Gray Ones lay in a ragged circle through which the others ran. And on the edge of the circle, between two massive wolves, lay Dion. She was on her side, as if she had grown too tired to sit, her cheek on the cold surface and one hand flung out in a curiously poignant gesture. And then a tiny puff of steam escaped her lips, and Aranur knew she was still alive. He dropped beside her, about to gather her up in his arms, but a bloodcurdling growl stopped him in his tracks. It was one of the wolves, rousing behind him. He froze.

"Gray Ones, you honor me," he said quietly. He reached again for the woman, but the Gray One snarled again. The wolf in front of him stirred, and he saw it was Hishn, but her eyes gleamed only slightly sane; the yellow depth of the hunt gave her eyes a danger equaled only by death itself.

"Hishn, you honor me," he tried again. "But release Dion. Let her go from this—this hold you have on her. She can't take it anymore."

The gray beast licked her chops and rumbled deep in her throat. She gave no sign of hearing.

Dion's face—her skin was so cold. Like the ice itself. "Hishn, listen to me," he said urgently. "If you love this woman as I do, let her go. She cannot live in your dreams. She is not a wolf. Release her."

The circle shifted, and the wolves rolled slowly to their feet. Their hackles rose, and their ears flattened as they crouched. A gray ghost rose from Dion's body and hung in the air in his sight, but he shook his head to deny it. "Gray Ones, let her go. She's going to die. Can't you see it? Feel it? She doesn't have your fur, your claws. She can't survive this cold." They just looked at him, and his anger flared suddenly. "She's a human being, damn it! Let her live as one."

Hishn, standing as tall as his chest in the snow, faced him for a long moment before the yellow glow faded and her eyes turned calm as a windless night. Gleaming, they blinked. And then she was just a wolf, and the other Gray Ones were just shadows that he had thought were beasts: The snow was suddenly empty of all but the three of them.

Aranur gathered the woman up in one swift movement and strode across the snow. He shoved the door open with his shoulder, kicking it shut again after Dion's wolf dodged inside, as well. She was too cold, he thought. The lack of food, her exhaustion, and then sitting outside on a freezing night—it was a wonder that she was not dead already. He set her gently against the wall and chafed her hands in his, breathing on them to warm them up. There was no sign of frostbite, but her skin was icy to the touch. Hishn, hovering at his back, whined softly until he shushed her, but she started up again almost immediately, and he gave up trying to keep her quiet.

"Dion," he said softly. "Come on, snap to, now. We need you."

She stirred, and he rubbed her arms more briskly, reaching down them to massage her legs vigorously.

"Ouch," she mumbled.

"You're awake. Good. It'll feel better in a minute."

She opened her eyes. "No, it won't. What are you doing here?"

"I was wondering the same thing about you." His jaw tightened momentarily, but all he said was, "Sleeping on a bed of ice isn't very practical in high altitudes."

The slender woman's eyes took on a faraway look. "I wasn't sleeping. I was . . . remembering."

"Right. It would help to remember to wear more clothes next time you decide to lie down in a snowdrift and forget to stay awake."

"Moonworms, Aranur. The wolves were watching out for me."

"The Gray Ones thought you were one of them," he returned dryly.

"I was."

"Stop it. You're a woman, not a wolf. Can you stand now?" She made a face. "Yes."

"Good," he said, pulling her to her feet. "Because I've been meaning to do this for a long time." And he drew her close. When he finally released her, she sagged against him, her heart pounding like dnu hooves on a dirt road and her breath quick against her ribs.

"What was that for?" she asked unsteadily, looking up at him with wide eyes and flushed cheeks.

"Good luck." He shuddered suddenly, and his jaw tightened almost to the breaking point.

"Aranur," she said urgently. "Oh, moons help me!" His arm muscles knotted up like cables wrapped around his bones, and his eyes turned almost completely black. "Aranur—" She tried to get him to sit down, but the rictus and his stubborn strength locked his legs in place, and all she could do was hold him while a whimper escaped the lips that had kissed her so passionately only a moment before.

"For moon's sake, Aranur, is everyone as bad off as this?" she gasped when he sagged to the floor and shakily wiped the spittle from his chin. "And these bruises?" She fingered the blackening marks across his cheek and forehead.

He brushed off her hands. "I slipped on the ice. Leave off, Dion. I'm capable of taking care of myself."

"Don't lie to me, Aranur. I'm a healer."

He stared off to the side, his fists clenched against his weakness. "To have you see me like this . . ." He pulled himself up against the wall and shook her hand off again.

"The others?" she asked again quietly.

"Aside from Tyrel," he said brusquely, "I'm the only one who can walk."

Her face paled. "Gods," she breathed, touching his arm. "I'm sorry, Aranur." But her mind was working quickly. There was no time, no way to create a vaccine, she thought. No way to test it if she made one, anyway. And no way to guarantee its results. But there was one thing she could risk, one thing that might save all their lives. The Gray Ones might never forgive her, but then, if she were wrong, she would not have long to wait before she took her case to the moons. "I'm sorry," she repeated. "But it will be all right," she said, more to herself than to him. "Moons help me, but I know now what to do."

XVII

Ember Dione mcMarin:

Ovousibas

Love crosses mountains
Where strong men fear to tread

Aranur followed Dion back to the room where they had left the others, but when they got there, she was shocked into silence. Rhom, his violet eyes darkened almost to black with the pain he bore silently, jumped up, went to his knees, and forced himself to hang on to the bedstead to face his sister.

"What happened?" he demanded harshly.

But Shilia, who had been huddling against the old man on one of the blanket rolls, looked at her as if she were a worm that needed stamping on. "Where have you been?" She rounded on the healer. "How could you stay away so long?"

Taken aback, Dion stopped short, Aranur bumping into her from behind. "I—"

The other girl went on as if she had not even tried to speak, her voice high and strained. "It's been hours since you checked on Namina, and now Gamon is worse."

"I was just up on the deck—"

"We checked every room we could find—We called and called, and you didn't answer—"

"That's enough, Shilia," Rhom said weakly.

Dion looked at them blankly, comprehension dawning as she

took them in. Their faces, so pale; their eyes, so miscolored. One side of her twin's neck was bruised so badly that she wondered how he could move his head at all, while the marks on Gamon's arms were just as dark; tremors must have taken them unawares, throwing them against the counters, the walls—anything they were near. "By the moons," Dion whispered, "why didn't you tell me this evening, Rhom?"

"This evening?" Her twin grinned crookedly, trying to lean up on his elbow but falling back. "That was eight hours ago, Dion. You've been a long time thinking."

Gamon tried to speak but just cleared his throat weakly, and the healer stared at him.

"I—" What could she say? They were dying while she watched. "I'm so sorry," she whispered.

"I'm not," her brother returned. "It wouldn't have done you any good to sit around with us, anyway. I take it you figured something out."

She nodded slowly. "The rastin's bite is poisonous to us. Tyrel got the toxin directly from the fish; I got it from sucking the poison from his wounds. It took a while for Tyrel, mainly because his exposure was so traumatic, but we both built up antibodies to the toxin. The main thing is that the virus of the plague attacks the same tissue that the toxin does: nervous tissue. The key to the plague is that the virus itself is chemically similar to the toxin. The antibodies we built up to the toxin simply mutated to match the virus." She gestured for Hishn to sit beside her, and the wolf obligingly trotted over and plopped down, but even sitting, the Gray One's head came up to Dion's chest. "What happened with you is that because you didn't have any antibodies to start out with, the virus inhibited your immune systems so that they couldn't even try to make antibodies. And all the while, the plague was eating away at your nervous systems."

"What I'm going to do," she said steadily, sitting down beside Namina, "is try to reproduce in each of you the antibody that's making Tyrel and me immune. If I can reproduce even one cell for each of you, your bodies will automatically do the rest. Namina's worst, so I'll do her first."

Rhom frowned. "Dion, just how are you going to do this? Even as ignorant as I am about your work, I know you have no way to separate one chemical from Tyrel's blood, let alone create a vaccine or cure.''

She did not look at him. ''I have something else in mind.''

Rhom stiffened. The surge of fear that replaced the worry on his face brought him to his feet, leaving him swaying against the wall. ''No, Dion. I know what you mean to do. You can't try this.''

She ignored him, gesturing for Tyrel to help unwrap the bandages that hid Namina's fractured leg.

''Dion!'' The blacksmith lunged across the room and grabbed her by the arm, spinning her around. ''You know it'll kill you. I won't let you do this.''

''Rhom—'' Aranur began, trying to hold him off.

The young man struck Aranur's hand away violently. ''And you!'' he spit, glaring at the tall, lean fighter. ''What did you say to make her try this? Do you know what you've asked her to do?''

Ovousibas. Aranur could almost see the word in Dion's mind. Gods forgive him. ''I know,'' he said quietly.

''Dion—no. The price is too high.''

''If I'm right, I'll be fine, and so will Hishn.''

''And if you're wrong?''

She hesitated. ''It's one life for five.'' Her voice was quiet, stern, and her twin fell back from the authority of her tone. ''Wouldn't you take the chance?''

''We're not talking about me, Dion. We're talking about you.''

She met his eyes steadily. ''And it's my choice, Rhom.''

He tried again. ''What about Hishn?''

''She won't be hurt.''

''How do you know?''

''The ancients melded with the Gray Ones to do Ovousibas, and the mental stress stimulated the virus to attack the blood-brain barrier. I'm not going to use Hishn that way. I'm going to do the healing myself. She will only give me her strength.''

''And what does that mean for you?'' Rhom caught at her arm again. ''Gods, Dion, please!''

She shrugged him off, and he was so weak that he staggered back against the wall, shocking them both and crystalizing the resolution in Dion's eyes.

''Dion,'' her twin cut in once more. ''At least let me help you.''

She shook her head. "No, Rhom," she said gently. "You would try to keep me safe."

Aranur blanched. And I would not, the gray-eyed man told himself. I will let her die to save us all. He cleared his throat. "Dion," he began. "Let me come with you."

She just looked at him. "You understand what can happen?"

"As well as you."

She hesitated, then nodded. He hears the wolves like I do, she realized. Not as strongly, but maybe that is better. She glanced around the room once quickly, then kissed her brother lightly on the cheek. He just stared at her. "Now, Aranur," she said quietly over her shoulder. "Hold me."

The instant he touched her, his hands tightened spasmodically on her shoulders. He was looking into the wolf's eyes, both their voices echoing in his head along with the dim and disturbing memories of an ancient death. He could feel them talking without words, just the flashed images passing from one to the other, and feel himself drawn into that contact as the wolf "remembered" how to guide her healer into Ovousibas. Other gray voices seemed to gather outside their consciousness with him, coaching them but not inside their contact. She braced herself.

Gray One, you know what I want to do?

You want to walk with this man as you walk with me.

You remember?

Yes.

But you know not to interfere. Even if it looks like I cannot survive.

The wolf hesitated but finally agreed.

Just guide me. Give me your strength. But don't stress yourself or you'll die like all the others. And Hishn, I can't afford to lose you.

The gray beast licked her hand twice.

I'm ready, Hishn. Dion's voice echoed softly. A current of fear twisted the tones beneath her images.

Then walk with me, Healer.

The wolf and the woman shifted away from Aranur mentally, as if they were moving at a distance. Then his perspective twisted dizzyingly and dropped. In that instant, before the flood of pain hit, he felt the struggling of another heart, breathed air through other lungs, and sensed the cold, slow pace of coma draw him in. And then Dion screamed.

Pain flooded his mind, and he was drowning in it. He tightened his physical grip on the healer, feeling dimly the degree of shock she was going through and not sure he could stand his own. She clung to the gray voice as the pain broke over her in waves, battering and bashing her consciousness with each pulse of blood. It was as if she were going in hand over hand, fighting flame and the raw burning of the nerves. He could feel her weakening against it.

Stay strong, he commanded, becoming a bulwark against the pain. Electrifying currents whipped his mind as she contacted the human energies of Namina's body. She went deeper, down into the fractured leg, and the nerves ground out on her mind, burning, shocking, paralyzing. The ragged gray fog whipped up around her, anchored barely in Aranur's mind but gripped firmly in the wolf's teeth. It was the wolf that shielded the healer from the foreign body's agony, but it was Aranur's strength that fed it. He tried to catch at its edges, tying it down tightly to an image of a smooth, unbroken shield, but it was the Gray One that stretched, built, spread it, and padded it more thickly around Dion's senses. Still the healer went deeper.

The fog thinned in a spot, and he unconsciously thickened it himself. *With me,* the wolf directed as his awkward patch did not mesh, threatening to break out and tear the shield. He let the Gray One's images open his mind, the fog sucking on him, sapping him, drawing on his strength and doubling its thickness as he focused his will on it through the wolf. Dion seemed to gasp at the sudden relief from pain. She flashed down past the splintered ends of bone and into the marrow, jellylike and warm, where the new blood cells struggled to come into being. She touched them, helped them, and sent them on to the lymph glands, where they were changed into an army of antibodies.

She was weakening. The fog shrouded her from the pain, but she was fighting to concentrate, trying to reach into the fracture and guide the body to do her bidding. Sluggish blood fought against her, and her hold on herself was slipping. The fog thinned, and she slid out of it, her will naked of the shield, into Namina's body, where the pain hit her like fire on the mental hands she held out to protect herself.

Healer! the wolf howled, sinking teeth into the woman's mind and dragging her shrieking consciousness back. Aranur grasped the beast by her images and braced himself for the strain. His mental arms were nearly torn off as the wolf fought Dion's pain-wrought hysteria and Namina's cold-clutching body. Hours, days, ninans, they hung on. He could not take any more. The pain—was it his imagination?—no, it was growing less, Hishn drawing the healer out little by little, fighting the currents of the body and separating their heartbeats from Namina back into each of them. There was a wrench, a bone-weary twist of perspective, and Aranur slumped onto the floor, Dion's limp form collapsed on top of him.

The roaring in his ears split into voices.

". . . breathing, but just barely. Get some water—he's coming around."

Aranur tried to open his eyes, but they cringed against the light. After the soft, cool images of Dion's mind—even the dark pain of Namina's—the room's light was as blinding as the sun.

But then Dion winced and opened her eyes. Her twin was by her side in an instant, cradling her in his arms and letting Hishn edge to the bed and lay her head in the healer's lap. "Rhom, it was—it was incredible," she managed.

"Oh, Dion," he whispered.

"I'm hungry." She struggled out of his arms. "I'm so hungry, I could eat a worlag. Raw."

Aranur nodded. "And that's an understatement."

She looked over at gray-eyed man who had gone in with her. "Thank you," she said softly.

"It was for me to do," he said simply.

"No," she corrected. "It was for us to do." She paused, with a look of wonder on her face. "They didn't—they never tried it together," she realized, thinking of the way the ancients had experimented. "They never used someone else's strength to buffer them from the pain. They could have done so much . . ." She lay back exhausted, but her eyes were lit with a new fire.

"Namina's breathing is almost regular now, and her pulse is stronger," Shilia offered timidly, her hands weak but her awe strong. "I don't understand it—you never even touched her."

The wolfwalker smiled wearily and held up her hands. The other girl gasped. Both palms were red and blistered as if burned.

"By the moons," Gamon breathed weakly, roused from his stupor by the sight. "Healer, you need some healing work yourself."

Rhom's stricken look at his sister's hands turned into daggers as he glared at Aranur.

Shilia turned the burned palms over gently, but even so, Dion flinched. "How can this be?" the girl demanded. "How could this happen?"

Dion shrugged. "The mind is a powerful weapon. The energy currents from Namina's body ground out on my mind before Hishn figured out how to shield me from them. I guess that, mentally, I was thinking of using my hands to protect myself and guide the healing, so that was where the currents actually burned." She nodded to the old man. "You're next, Gamon, after Shilia."

"Dion, you need rest," her brother protested angrily, his pale face tight as he saw the blisters on her hands.

"You'll all have an eternity of that if I don't go to work again soon, Rhom."

"If Aranur can do it with you, then I can. I will help you this time."

Dion shook her head wearily. "You and I could never work that way together, twin. We're too much alike, and you know it. You would be fighting me as much as helping me, and that could kill us both."

He slumped back.

"It'll be all right, Rhom," she said with more confidence than she felt. "I know what I'm doing now."

"Dion," Shilia said hesitantly, "I didn't mean to get mad at you."

"I understand, Shilia," the healer said, cutting her off gently. Are you ready?"

The girl nodded uncertainly.

"Aranur?" she asked. He nodded as well.

All right, Hishn, take me in, she sent.

Then walk with me, Healer, the wolf sent back. Hishn grasped Dion's mind, stepped forward, then pivoted out to the left and down again in that dizzying spin.

Lightly, lightly, the healer touched Shilia's consciousness. One instant she was dropping lightly through, and then, an outraged thought of—of pain? fear? fury? blasted her. There was an abrupt tearing as Hishn's mind wrenched them out of the girl, then her head cleared. She found herself on the floor gasping for breath, flung there by the force of the girl's rejection. Aranur was on his knees beside her, but she did not think the force of the blow had hit him the same as it had her.

"Dion!" Rhom cried out, falling to the floor with a thump as he tried to reach his sister.

His twin shook her head, dazed. "She—she rejected me," she realized. "I could feel her thoughts—"

"I could feel yours," Shilia stated defensively. "It was like you were invading me."

"I couldn't hold on, couldn't go in." Dion sat up again and looked at the girl.

"I couldn't stand it!" the younger woman cried out. "It was like her fingers were in my brain—I don't want to feel that again!" Rhom soothed her with a wild-eyed look at his twin. If it was that bad with Shilia, how would it be with the others?

The wolfwalker rubbed her hip where it had hit the other bed frame when she had been flung back. "I can't touch her without her mind throwing me off. Shilia," she said, "you have to try to relax. I'm not going to hurt you. I'm not even going to do anything you could possibly feel inside. All I'm doing to do is tell your bone marrow what kind of antibodies to make and where to send them."

Rhom whimpered suddenly and then flung Shilia away from him. The girl cried out as her arm struck the wall, but the blacksmith's back arched and he was flung off the bed, thrashing and kicking as his arms and legs tried to separate themselves from the rest of him. Tyrel and Dion dived on top of him, trying to smother him against the floor. His eyes bugged out, black instead of violet as the convulsion stole his muscle control and blood vessels in what was left of the whites of his eyes ruptured.

"Rhom!" his twin screamed. "Aranur, help us!"

Aranur, stumbling to pull a blanket from the bed and drop it over the three of them, unbalanced and fell with them. Dion tried to get the blanket wrapped around her brother as his flailing arms struck her back and forth, his burly torso bucking like an angry dnu. It was over in seconds. They lay on the floor, panting, the younger man's body tensing and tensing again as the tremor left him gradually.

"How many is this?" Dion's voice was hoarse.

"Six," Gamon answered bleakly.

"And for you?"

"We've all had four or five bad ones."

Aranur, staggering with his own weakness, helped Dion put her twin back up on the bed.

"Shilia," she said hesitantly, "I can't wait for you to learn to relax to my touch. It may take several tries to hypnotize you, and if you resist it, it'll take even longer than that."

The girl looked at her. "I understand, Healer." She sat down on the bed, her eyes big as she realized that she might die because she could not relax enough to let the healer help her. "You'll do what's best."

Aranur squeezed her hand. "I'll be there too, Shilia," he whispered in her ear. Dion reached for her neck. Pressing down carefully on the carotid arteries, she put the girl out in ten seconds, then eased her back gently onto the pillow. *Hishn?*

Walk with me, Healer.

The wolf drew her close, shifting her into a comfortable mental hold, and then pushed them out and down to the left. Dion sank into an awareness of the younger girl's body till she seemed to be absorbed into Shilia's bloodstream, whirled along with the pulse of her heart till she reached deeper—There! She caught a flash of the compound she was searching for, urging it on to the lymph gland and forcing it to mutate into the antibody the girl needed to survive. In an instant others were forming, and the original cell was hurrying for the corkscrew virus that burned into Shilia's nerves, so Dion released with Hishn to burst up and out of the girl's unconsciousness.

She trembled, tense and tired, as her eyes focused on the walls before her and brought her back to the present. Aranur was reeling. But the figure of the molecule was etched in her mind in a dozen senses, not all of them hers, and looking at Rhom, Aranur, and Gamon, she knew she had to work it into their bodies quickly. Gamon and Rhom were the worst, then Aranur, but as Dion looked at Gamon, the old man glanced at her twin. Gathering his strength, he said, "Rhom first."

"You're worse than he is," she returned honestly.

"Rhom first," he repeated. "Then you can concentrate on the rest of us."

Dion, grateful for his understanding, did not question his judgment further. Ovousibas was still too new to her. It would be much easier to go with her twin than to try it with another stranger. She dragged a chair beside Rhom and placed her hands on his forehead and chest. The sense of his inner pain was horrible, and she could already feel the muscles torn by the convulsions, the virus blistering his nerves.

Walk with me, Healer, Hishn sent soberly.

It was quick. A spin. Her twin's mind suddenly bare in a flash of images that made no sense to either one. A stiffening brief contest of wills that neither gave in to, and then Aranur shoved hard, and she dropped through. Left. Down. *In. Through the neck and chest. Heavy cords of muscle, red streaks of bulk leading to gray-white tendons. Sense, more than sight; sound, more than silence. Consciousness. Bones rising up where fibers split to cling to the porous calcium. Pounding. Heartbeats. My twin. Blood rushing by, catching, whirling me along. There's the pain. Closer, throbbing. Sluggish, dead blood cells begin clogging the muscles where nerves burn out from the fever. Huge dams of clots block the way to the ruptures. Pain, pounding pain. Deeper. I focus on a cell, merge; nerves stimulating, shocking enzymes, chemicals into action. Proteins pass back and forth. Cell membranes suck in, push out the traffic of nutrients. Tissues fall apart, torn, burst, dying. I feel the heartbeat underneath, throughout. Frantic chaos. A cell struggling to block a ruptured capillary. Here, I push. It slides into place. The flow of blood picks up—ah, the brain. Swollen tissues, torn synapses. The throb of trauma. Edge between the red fibers, pushing antibodies along. The swelling relieves, the circulation sweeps fluids away. The compound—there. My brother, my twin, I feel you. Pull, direct, build. The shocks are nerves out of control, their current grounding out on the torn tissues. Deeper again, a lessening of pain. Insulate the nerves and splice their synapses. Up again. Cells, tumbling, fluctuating, in the body fluids. Ah, there. Just past there. Build the compound into the membrane; stop the virus from screwing through; pushing is too hard now, directions begin to wander. Concentrate. Drain the fluids. Rhom—can't leave you like this . . . Heartbeats pump past. A ripple seems to wash over the membrane as it adapts to the compound. Repeat the compound stronger, harder. Black, the virus struggles to screw through again; I adjust. Membranes harden, trap, turn back on it. Shift, struggle to place another frame of antibody. Concentrate. Strength slips away. Movement hypnotizes. Cells bulge, split like overripe melons, grow again as new creatures of the body.* Get out! *An insistence, a lack of understanding, a demand. The voice shakes the grip on the compound. So much to do. My brother—you hurt so . . . Pain dulls the edge of thought. Come, now. Dole out more blood cells, match the antibodies. Weakening. The muscle, huge, surrounding, twitches; concentration breaks. Current grabs and whirls me away, crushed between the platelets. Pounding. Louder. The current is swifter, dashing the platelets together and flinging them desperately on toward oxygen. Louder. Deafening. The sense of a gale growing closer. Flung into the lungs and bursting up, away, out . . .*

Voices rang, slinging words back and forth in her echoing, dim head. Tired. So tired.

Healer? Something cold and wet touched Dion's face. She responded instinctively, batting whatever it was away. *Healer, you are needed.*

She opened her eyes, wincing at the light and feeling the tight knot of hunger twist her stomach. Answering the Gray One's concern, Dion shivered, shifted her hands to Gamon, and sent, *Okay, Hishn. Let's go on.*

Then walk with me.

They went in again, but weakened and unable to focus, she barely touched Gamon's consciousness before she bounced off.

Stay strong, Healer. Run with me, Hishn encouraged. *We can sleep soon.*

"Dion?" Rhom asked weakly, seeing her eyes open again.

She tried to stand but collapsed on the floor instead.

"Dion," Gamon protested, "rest now. I'll be fine till you can go on."

"We don't have time for that," she said as Tyrel tried to help her up. "I don't know how long it will take for the antibodies to inhibit the virus. The tremors are too bad too soon—more may—may—" she stopped and could not meet Gamon's eyes. He already looked ten years older.

We must be quick, Hishn sent. *He is close to the fire now.*

If he tremored while they were inside . . . Dion did not finish the thought. Instead, letting Hishn grasp her mind and Aranur grip her shoulders, they whirled out and down. But she almost did not make it—the shake of weariness in her physical body distracted her from their focus. The wolf pulled tightly, dropping her through the old man's consciousness so fast that he had no time to reject the contact, and the wolfwalker planted the antibodies as if sowing wild flowers, haphazardly but throughout the lymph glands, where they would grow and multiply themselves. She was still trying to concentrate on more when the shaking started and Hishn pulled her out, shocking her rudely into the present.

"Hurry," she said to Tyrel, shaking almost uncontrollably herself. "Help me tuck the blankets around him." Gamon's eyes changed as the convulsions grew, but they trapped his body in the bed between the sheets and blankets so that he could not fling himself against anything hard. "Now lean on him," the healer directed, giving in to her own weakness and collapsing on top of the old man's shaking body. The boy, his cousin, and the exhausted woman held him there till it was over and his eyes rolled back down and he looked at the room again with focus, though there was no coherence in those eyes—his age was sapping him as much as the virus was. Dion turned wordlessly to Aranur. She gestured for him to lie down, then started to put the sleeper hold on him.

"You won't need that," he said quietly.

Dion nodded again, too tired to argue and trusting that what Aranur had said would be true.

"Dion, wait," Rhom begged. "Let me help now. You need someone to do it."

"But not you, Rhom. You're too weak to put this strain on yourself."

"No more so than you."

She fought the urge to cry that she had no more strength to oppose him. "All right," she said finally.

Walk with me, Healer, the wolf said.

Her brother gripped her shoulders, but as he touched her, she jerked away as if shocked. Her mind was too open—his too closed. His strength—it was like a solid beam where Aranur's was like a river. She would fall off . . .

"Rhom—I can't—" she gasped. "No—don't touch me again."

"What is it? What did I do to you?"

He looked so injured, so weak, that she almost wept in her exhaustion. "I can't . . ."

"Just try again, Dion. You're just tired." He gritted his teeth and forced himself to stand taller in spite of the pain. "I'll do better this time."

"Rhom, you don't understand."

Aranur looked from one to the other. "What is it, Dion?"

She did not look at him. "What did you feel?" she asked her twin. "What was it like when you touched me?"

"Like a shock," he said slowly, his voice husky with the fire of the fever. "Little sparks that ran up my fingers. Like Gray Hishn was snapping at me even though I could hear her talking to you."

She nodded. "Rhom, it's no good. I can't do this with you." Her hands were shaking, and she pointed to a spot away from her. "Please, let me do this alone."

"Twin—"

"Please, Rhom." She took a breath and rested her hands on Aranur's chest. Abruptly, the wolf twisted her mind and flung it down. It was too sharp—too sudden. She lost the concentration and pulled out. Shaking, she tried to control her weakened body.

Walk with me, Healer.

They tried again, but she was too weak. She lost the focus and broke out again, shaking so badly that she could hardly sit up. Her physical weakness would not let her mind keep the contact.

"Too weak . . ." the woman said hoarsely. "It's okay, Rhom," she said quickly. "I just need to concentrate." How far could she push herself? Her face was already gaunt, as if she had gone without eating for two ninans, and her hands shook badly. "Relax, lie back, and breathe deeply," she said soothingly, calming herself as much as the man she was sitting beside. "Breathe in, breathe out," she said softly, gathering up her last ounce of strength. His will was so strong—if she was lost inside, she would never survive this last try at Ovousibas. "Let the beat of your own heart relax you."

Hishn? she asked. *I don't know if I'm strong enough for this.*

You are strong enough, the Gray One answered. *I am with you.* And in their melded minds, the tones swelled as other Gray Ones joined them, encouraging, coaching the healer with their strength till she felt the exhaustion slide from her like a heavy blanket dropping to the ground. *Walk with me, Healer. Walk with us. Run with us . . .*

"You can do it, Dion," Aranur whispered hoarsely.

Her vision melted into pain-wracked gray. There was an instant of absolute rejection that dissolved into the smooth feeling they had had the first time they had tried Ovousibas together. It was as if Aranur were walking with her in his own body. She could feel his strength, his own consciousness touch the places where the virus had settled, reach for the patches of sickness. Her knowledge guided her; his strength carried her. She built the antibody carefully, and Aranur deliberately sped his own blood to send the compounds to the lymph glands, but even so, she was weakening. She tried to pull out, but the force and strength of his consciousness dragged her back into his body even as she struggled away.

Down, down, and in. Past the consciousness like a whip of wind, and *there, the blood, the body, the virus, waiting, eating at the man. She needed elements—they were there, drawn from the blood as she barely directed the flow. Compounds bursting into life as the wolves backed her, pushed with their own exuberance of life. Blocks of the antibody growing, binding the virus, whirling it away aimlessly, crushing it in certain death. A weariness of death. The body indistinct, the focus fading in and out. Gray tones struggled to keep her in—in where? Consciousness intruding, shifting. So tired. Tired. Aranur? Rhom? No. No, it was just the wolves, snow and moss underfoot as the dome's floors melted into a softening ground and time burned away into the heat of a summer sun. The Gray Ones birthing, growing, changing, mating, singing, dying. Packs that shifted perspective as one view, then another became the focus of time, of the memories passed down the chain of gray minds. Time, time, to sleep through time till she woke. And the Gray Ones, floating her beside their legendary children while she dreamed of their lives and fell through their memories of time . . .*

Epilogue

Aranur's stomach was a pit. It had been that way for days, ever since Dion had gone into the coma, and he stared now at her pale form. They had been feeding her, but the hollowness of her cheeks and the gauntness of her face did not disappear. What else could they do? The woman's brother blamed him for her collapse, but Aranur knew, too, that if it had not been for what she had done, all of them would have died. He felt—admit it, he told himself—guilty. The fever that had held each of them in its grip was gone, thwarted by an antidote the woman had made with the last of her energy, but now she herself lay in a coma, and after four days Aranur was not sure she would ever come out of it.

He tried again, softly, to wake her. "Dion?" Rhom had already sat with his twin for three days, and Aranur had finally ordered the younger man outside with Shilia to get his mind off things. They were all better—all of them except Dion, he reminded himself bleakly. The healer had pushed too far past the limits of her body. Breathing but not moving, swallowing but not seeing, she lay as if already on the path to the moons. Even the Gray One who ran with her could not tell the man how to reach her. "Wolfwalker," he whispered. "Dion, forgive me."

The lean, hollow-eyed man stared at the pale, still form. And then he frowned. Had her eyes moved? The wolf whined suddenly against his leg and thrust her nose between his arms up onto the bed. Fluttering, the woman's eyes blinked twice, then she opened them to focus unseeing, squinted at the light, and frowned blankly.

Aranur stifled a shout. "Are you with us again?" he asked gently instead.

She met his gray eyes in confusion, then turned away, her violet eyes filling with tears.

"Dion, Healer." Aranur turned her back to face him limply. "What's wrong? It's been so long . . ."

"The dreams . . ." she whispered raggedly. Threads of gray songs that filled her unconsciousness, memories of hundreds of wolves that lived in her mind—the dreams had kept her alive as the Gray Ones supported her exhausted spirit while she healed from the strain of healing the others.

"You were asleep for a long time, that's all."

But he did not understand. The songs of the wolves—Dion had lived them. She was overwhelmed by loss as the beauty of ancient dreams faded and lost themselves as whispers in her mind.

"Go away." She trembled, turning from him again.

Hishn whined softly and nudged the cover by her hand. *Wolfwalker,* the wolf called softly.

Watcher, Dion returned, crying for real now. *You honor me.*

Feeling the echoes of their mindtalk, Aranur realized finally that it had been Hishn and the other Gray Ones that had kept Dion from the path to the moons when her own body was too weak. She had gone for too long without food and rest. That Ovousibas—it could have killed her. "Oh, Dion," he said softly, rocking her.

Swallowing hard, she managed to get control of herself. "I'm hungry," she said in a low voice.

"You should be," Aranur teased, though the shadow of concern was still heavy in his eyes. "You're pale, almost gaunt."

"You have such a way with compliments," she whispered dryly.

Aranur gave her a relieved grin. "Rhom just went to get some meat from Gamon's smoker," he told her, noting her glance around the empty room. "I was just sitting with you till he got back."

She was surprised. "The healing—" She hesitated and looked around again. That even Namina was gone finally hit her. "It worked that fast?" She still thought that she had just finished the healing and woken up; she was still remembering the struggle to plant the antibodies in her brother, Aranur, and the others.

"Fast?" He barked laughter. "No, and it was a near thing, too. We had tremors for two days after you did whatever it was you started in us, but we recovered. None of us have felt anything but slight chills since yesterday. Here,'' he said, propping her up with a pillow. ''Eat this.''

His words finally sank in. ''Two days?'' she asked blankly. ''Yesterday?''

''You were out for four days,'' he answered calmly. She clutched at him suddenly, and he held her. ''It's all right,'' he said, recognizing her fear at the realization of time and the empty room. ''Everyone is all right. We all made it. Even Namina's walking now since I made her a pair of crutches. You did a lot more for her than just stop the virus. Now, look at me,'' he commanded sternly, afraid to show the depth of his concern. ''And eat.''

She was too stunned to reply. Four days? And she was still alive. And Hishn, as well—the Gray One's thoughts were as clear as the vision of that panting mouth and too-long tongue hanging out. She shook her head, weakened again by the effort, and lay back, a faint smile on her face as she realized that she had survived. Ovousibas. And she had survived. Internal healing. She let the gray voices echo again in her head and relived the warmth of Aranur's touch on her face.

A ninan later the four men, the three women, and the wolf found themselves on a ridge overlooking the last row of foothills before they entered the county of Caflanin. Between two of the hills, where a deep V notched the greenery and split the range for their view, they could see a valley blotched only meagerly with farms. Dimly, in the distance, a thin road cut across the far end, leading south and east from behind the rounded humps of land where the drab, flat county of Bilocctar was hidden by a stumpy mountain.

''Two ninans,'' Aranur promised. ''Eighteen days and we'll see Ariye again.'' He squeezed Namina's shoulders. Odd, he thought, how different people are. Shilia had taken to the trail as if she had been born to it, but Namina had hated every meter they had hiked. He looked over the group, approving again of the way Tyrel had grown and his sister Shilia had proved her own strength. Namina was young, he told himself. But she would learn. Perhaps it was only the distance from home . . .

''This would be a good place to stop,'' Gamon suggested, glancing around.

Aranur nodded. "We have some unfinished business to take care of," he agreed, swinging his pack down to the ground and shoving Gray Hishn out of the way unceremoniously. The wolf gave him an injured glare, but Dion just tugged on her tail and then scratched her ears when the Gray One turned to the healer for sympathy.

Tyrel was already gathering tinder to start a small fire while Aranur dug the packet of letters from his bag. He sifted through the papers one more time, counting them to make sure none were missing, then threw them onto the tiny blaze, watching them curl at the edges and then flare up as the fire caught the paper and burned bright and brief.

"Are you sure about this?" Rhom asked. He was standing beside Shilia with his arm casually around her waist.

Aranur nodded. "I thought at first we could carry the letters in secret through to Ariye, but I've had more time to think. With the letters, any encounter with Zentsis's men could be death. Without them, we have a good chance of getting all the way across Ramaj Bilocctar without being suspected. Any search of our packs will bring only normal gear to light."

Tyrel bit his lip. "And you're sure we can convince the elders without the letters? Without proof?"

"It will be your first test, Tyrel. And one that, if you are to be Lloroi, you must pass."

Rhom smiled grimly. "What you sing in Ariye, we'll sing in Randonnen," he said softly. "Let this trouble burn in all nine hells."

Gamon chuckled. "For a blacksmith, you've a way with words."

Aranur agreed and slung his pack back over his shoulder. "Even a greedy raider would have given up by now." He gestured toward the notch that cut a pass through the hills. "There's the way home, Namina. And with the Gray Ones to guide us, you'll see Ariye before midsummer's eve." He looked at Dion and the wolf that stood beside her, and the gray mist of voices filtered through his mind. Nebulous, unclear—but a reminder of a dream they wove together. He looked back only once, then led them down the hill.

About the Author

Tara K. Harper lives in Northwest Oregon. She loves rock climbing, martial arts, and white water, and spends a lot of her time camping, fishing, hiking, and dragging her cameras through the wilderness. In the past, she scuba dived and played waterpolo; now she goes kayaking. And in her spare time, she plays violin and other stringed instruments. She loves to read. She has been hooked on astronomy since she was a child, and now works as a technical writer. Currently, she has long hair, blue eyes, three cats, two dogs, a brother and sister (with whom she shares many allergies), and a deep love of Nature.